M000033565

THE HARBOUR MASTER'S DAUGHTER

A compelling saga of love, loss and self-discovery

TANIA CROSSE

Devonshire Sagas Book 1

Originally published as
Morwellham's Child

JOFFE BOOKS

Revised edition 2021
Joffe Books, London
www.joffebooks.com

First published in Great Britain in 2004
as *Morwellham's Child*

Cover art by Jarmila Takač

ISBN: 978-1-78931-771-8

For my dearest dad, who loved ships and the sea.
And for my husband, who has kept me afloat.

CHAPTER ONE

Rebecca's heart was drumming with painful ferocity as she hurried up the steep track towards the farm, for heaven alone knew what might happen if she were caught. She kept in close to the hedge, holding the hood of her cloak tight about her face so that she wouldn't be recognized even if someone did see her. But the rutted lane was quiet now for it was fully dark and few people, if any, would have reason to tread the path at that late hour. She glanced back over her shoulder and strained her ears, but she could hear no hue and cry coming from her own home, and all seemed peaceful down in the little port.

She drew in a deep breath in an effort to subdue the quaking that reached down to her very toes. Opposite the entrance to the farmyard, the edge of the woodland joined the track at an angle. She hastened into the cover of the trees, only to be swallowed up into a shadowy world of eerie silhouettes and strange, startling noises. Her pulse accelerated wildly again, her wide eyes swivelling at the slightest sound. An owl hooted somewhere above her and flapped from its perch. A twig snapped not far away.

'Becky!'

The flood of panic drained from her body as she recognized Tom's voice. An instant later she was in his arms, laughing with relief and the joy of being with him. She lifted her face to his, eager and expectant, and his smiling mouth came down on hers, moist and sweet. It only lasted a moment, but for Rebecca it was the most beautiful experience in the world, and she turned her head, pressing her cheek against his chest.

'I'm so glad you came,' she murmured into his coat. 'I wasn't sure if you would.'

'Well, I knew you would, and I couldn't leave you to wander about in the woods alone at night, could I?' He stood back and held her at arms' length, his chastising words nonetheless light with teasing. 'We'd better go deeper in if we're not to be seen. I don't suppose we're the only ones to use these woods as a lovers' rendezvous.'

He held out his hand, and as she took it, a warm excitement tingled up her arm and into her whole body. She loved Tom, and she wasn't going to wait until her coming of age before she was even allowed to accept his courtship. For a few minutes she was lost in her own thoughts, instinctively ducking under the branches as Tom guided her through the trees.

''Tis quite secluded here,' he told her quietly, and gestured towards a fallen trunk where years of undergrowth had formed a natural arbour about it. She lowered herself into a sitting position, grateful that in her anxiety to get dressed without waking her younger sister Sarah, she hadn't bothered to pull on a petticoat beneath her full skirt. Tom sat down beside her, balancing his elbows on his spread knees. He shook his head slowly. 'I don't like this, Becky. 'Tis not in me to deceive.'

The affection glowed in Rebecca's veins and she reached out to touch his sleeve. 'Oh, my good, sweet Tom,' she breathed. ''Tis because you're so good that I love you so much, and I just can't wait to be your wife.'

She watched him turn towards her, and even in the darkness she could see his eyes travelling over her face. He cupped her chin in his hand and softly, gently, tilted her head upwards to receive his lingering kiss. Her arms went about his neck, and as he pulled her more tightly to him, she felt the passion tightening her stomach and her lips parted hungrily. She wanted it to last for ever, delighting in this strange sensation that was totally new to her, and when Tom finally drew away, she was quite breathless with surprise and longing.

'Oh, Tom,' she croaked, attempting to tamp down her sudden desire. 'I just wish there were a way to hasten my father's hand. I love him so much, but I do wish he'd understand that there'll never be anyone else for me but you. So we might as well marry now, and then we can, well, know what it is to love as man and wife.'

'Aye, I know.' Tom took her in his arms again. 'I want nothing more. 'Tis like a fire inside me! But on our wedding night, when 'tis right and proper. Even if it means we have to wait a while.'

Rebecca gazed at him, her feelings all topsy-turvy. 'But we can meet again like this?' she pleaded.

'I'll have to think about it,' Tom answered hesitantly. 'And you must go now, afore you're missed.'

'Yes,' she reluctantly agreed. 'You're so good to me, Tom. I don't know what I'd do without you.'

'You'd be tucked up safe in your bed, just where you should be.' But then he smiled softly. 'But I'm glad you're not.'

* * *

'Now don't you two be dallying along the way,' Anne Westbrook ordered, wagging her head at her daughters as they tied on their bonnets. 'And no going near the cooperage.'

Sarah tossed her bright curls and winked cheekily at her elder sister, knowing that their mother couldn't see her face. 'No, Mother, we won't,' she said solemnly, but her eyes were alive with mischief.

'I didn't mean you so much, young miss, as well you know.' Anne pushed her elbows forward as she placed her hands squarely on her hips. ''Tis that headstrong sister of yours I meant! So, did you hear me, Becky?'

Colour tingled in Rebecca's fine-featured face. 'Yes, Mother,' she agreed, but her voice wavered with a whispering sigh. 'Come on, Sarah.' And before another word could be uttered, they danced out through the front door, the hems of their full summer skirts flouncing about their ankles as they went.

Isaac Westbrook glanced up from the parlour table. 'Annie,' he called through the half-open door.

'Yes, my dear?'

'Do you really think 'tis wise letting those two young imps out alone?' Isaac questioned, his bushy grey eyebrows reaching up to his receding hairline.

But Anne answered cajolingly, 'Oh, Isaac, you can't expect them to stay indoors all the time, especially not on such a lovely day as this. And they're only going to Miss Martin's shop! They're really quite safe. No one will harm them. Everyone knows they're the daughters of the harbour master and chief assaying officer, the most important man in Morwellham!'

'Not everyone, Annie,' her husband frowned at her. 'The place is always full of strangers, you know that! There's nine ships in today, and only five of them regulars for the mines. I bet you there's more than one sailor out there who'd like to get his hands on our Rebecca. Sarah's little more than a child, but, well, it may have escaped your notice, but Rebecca is a very beautiful young woman.' He scratched his full, thick beard whimsically. 'Just like her mother.'

Anne's soft laugh tinkled about her like summer rain. 'You're an old flatterer, Isaac Westbrook. And you're not as observant as you think. Sarah's no longer a child either, you know. She's more . . . comely, shall we say, than Rebecca, and there's many a girl of seventeen that's married with a family on the way.'

'And not always in the happiest of circumstances, which is precisely why I don't like the idea of our daughters going out without a chaperone.'

'Oh, come now! They'll come to no harm.'

'Then why did you instruct them to keep away from the cooperage?'

Anne blinked her warm blue eyes. 'Because I know 'twould be your wish, although I really don't see what you have against young Tom. A qualified artisan and as respectable a lad as you could ask for. And Rebecca loves him.'

Isaac puffed out his cheeks. 'Thinks she does. She's grown up with him working not three doors away. She's never even looked at anyone else.' He let his breath out in a long, ponderous stream. ''Tis not that I've anything against Tom. But his apprenticeship were over less than a year ago. He's not yet on a full cooper's wage, and he's having to support his mother and the little ones since the father were killed.'

'You can't blame him for that.'

'You know I don't.' Isaac shook his head sadly. 'Terrible things, mining accidents. But how can he support Rebecca as well? No! I shall bide by my decision. If they still feel the same way about each other when she comes of age, and he can give her a decent home, rent one of the Bedford cottages, for instance, then they will have my permission to start courting. I'll not have a daughter of mine living in one of those tenements.'

'That's another eighteen months, Isaac. She won't want to wait that long. You know how high-spirited she is!'

'Stubborn as a mule, you mean!'

'And I wonder where she gets that from?' Anne came up behind Isaac's chair and linked her arms about his neck. 'Remember the tricks we used to get up to so as we could be alone together?'

'Hmm!' He rubbed his hairy cheek softly on the back of her hand. 'How could I forget! But I reckon as we had more sense than they do nowadays. However,' he stated emphatically, withdrawing the heavy watch from his waistcoat pocket, 'this'll not get my work done. I've the morning's report to write up, harbour dues to collect, some samples to assay, and then there's those two big schooners both wanting to sail on the tide, and another due in. Can't have them colliding into each other now, can I?'

Anne smiled knowingly to herself and saw him draw the great leather-bound ledger towards him as she left the room. His fingers paused momentarily on the flyleaf where the words, *Morwellham Quay, Devonshire — Harbour Master's Records 1867*, had been carefully penned in large, bold letters, and his chest lifted with not a little pride. Twelve years now he had been in charge of the busy little river port, the Tamar being an important waterway serving as the tortuous border between the counties of Devonshire and Cornwall, and every visiting vessel to Morwellham had been recorded in detail in Isaac's meticulous books. Trade had lessened, of course, since the railway had come to Tavistock in 1859 and many of the mines had begun to send their ore to Plymouth pulled by the smoke-belching steam engines. But there were still those that sent tons of the glinting rock along the canal and down to the river, and the Devon Great Consols mine had its own inclined plane railway that kept its own extensive quay and dock throbbing with activity. Oh, yes! As he approached his fiftieth year, Isaac Westbrook was content with his life. Not only was he the harbour master, but also the chief assaying officer, testing ore samples in his laboratory to ascertain the percentage of copper they contained. Four pounds a week he received and a rent-free cottage, so he considered he had done well for himself since the humble start of his career as a miner. If only he could see his two daughters settled, he would be satisfied.

He opened the heavy tome at the last entry, took up his quill pen, dipped it in the ink and wrote in his elegant hand, *16 June 1867*.

* * *

Rebecca paused at the side-gate of the courtyard in front of Copper Ore Cottage. Keep away from the cooperage indeed! But the familiar sight of the port, bustling in the bright morning sunshine, quelled her anger. It wasn't as if the immediate view was particularly beautiful, although the village itself nestled in one of south Devonshire's most picturesque valleys, but Rebecca couldn't remember living anywhere else, and the feverish activity of the quays flowed through her veins. Even the near outlook was partially obliterated by one of the branches of the massive overhead gantries of the mine railway, which swept across that end of the port. The three gantries amalgamated immediately to the side of the cottage and then disappeared into the tunnel behind, a dark, awesome hole in the hillside. As a child, Rebecca had always eyed the black, gaping cavern with terror, convinced that fiendish witches and evil spirits emerged from it at night to conduct their wicked deeds. But the days of childhood fear were long gone, and now the tunnel, the railway, the particular odour given off by the heaps of copper ore as they lay in the sun, especially if it had been raining earlier, were as much part of her life as waking up in the morning. Men scurried over the quays like ants around a jam jar, calling instructions to each other or busy shovelling the piles of gleaming rock. Seamen, released from duty for a few hours, strolled up to the village centre for a tankard of ale, their hungry eyes devouring any female they encountered, but knowing that any misconduct would be more than their jobs were worth! Isaac Westbrook's daughters were only supposed to be acquainted with the assayers, agents and ships' captains whom they met through their father and who stayed overnight at the Ship Inn when necessary. But they knew many a common sailor by sight, or even to exchange pleasantries with, for a certain number of ships were on regular contracts to take the ore to south Wales for smelting, and to return with the much-needed coal for the mines' engines. Sarah had never been over-interested in the goings-on of Morwellham's trade, although she was quite content to assume that she would live her entire life at the port. But Rebecca had always been fascinated by the beehive of workers and how each one had his place. The whole affair ran like a well-oiled machine, with her father as the main cog, at least as far as the assaying and shipping were concerned. She had always watched intently as Isaac heated the powdered rock samples in the furnace, and had learned at an early age to recognize a shallow-draught barge, and to distinguish between a sea-going ketch and a small schooner by their differing masts and rigging. She sometimes thought that had she been a boy, she might have become a master mariner, and she often had the feeling that her interest in both the ships and the copper trade, limited as it was, pleased Isaac and compensated a little for the loss of his two sons in infancy. But she was a girl, a young woman in fact, and her main objective in life at present was to secure her future with the man she loved.

The ground suddenly trembled, a deep grumbling like distant thunder quickly grew to a deafening roar, and two enormous trucks clattered out of the tunnel mouth and trundled past them high up on the groaning gantries, finally being halted at the desired spot. The sliding bases of the trucks were drawn open and tons of ore tumbled noisily on to the green-stained tiles of the quay. The two sisters looked at each other and laughed, for even though they lived next door to the railway, the unexpected arrival of the laden trucks could quite easily stop one's heart!

They linked arms, their young faces bright with merriment, and turning their backs on the Devon Great Consols quay, set off towards the centre of the village and Jane Martin's shop. But they had only gone a few yards when Rebecca's footsteps deliberately slowed and her lips pursed with determination. The usual display of half-assembled wheels, and broken spokes and cogs awaiting repair was strewn under the lean-to outside the cooperage, but it would be obvious to any stranger that this particular establishment made its money from barrel making. A mountain of carefully stacked casks stood ready for collection by the lads from the manganese mill just a stone's throw further on, and several half-made barrels, which Rebecca knew would have previously been soaked for some time in warm water, had been upturned each over its own crucible of smouldering ashes so that the wood might become flexible enough to bend to shape. As the two girls looked on, one of the six coopers who worked there came out to feel if his own piece of work was ready. He seemed satisfied and when he gave the familiar call of 'Truss Ho!', two other men came out to assist him. But the young artisan Rebecca sought was not among them, and her swift dark blue eyes searched avidly among the shadows of the workshop through the wide-open doors. But when she still couldn't see him, she stole a sly glance at the windows of the cottage they had just left and, disengaging herself from her sister, took a purposeful step across the path.

'Becky, no!' Sarah hissed through clenched teeth, her hand closing fiercely on Rebecca's arm. 'You promised Mother.'

'I didn't promise anything.' Rebecca was still craning her neck. 'I simply said I had heard.'

'But what if you get found out?'

'I won't! Not unless you tell on me.' She whipped round to meet Sarah's worried frown, her eyes brilliant with teasing. 'I'll keep quiet about your Russian sailor if you keep quiet about me still seeing Tom!'

Sarah's jaw gaped open as a scarlet blush travelled into her cheeks. 'He's not *my* Russian sailor,' she said, trying to shrug. 'And he's not just a sailor, either. He's the equivalent of a second mate, and soon to move up, too,' she protested.

'There you are!' Rebecca grinned with triumph. 'He *is* your sailor, sorry, officer!' she corrected herself. 'Anyway, 'tis far worse than me wanting to marry Tom! You hardly know him. You can't even pronounce his name.'

'Yes I can! 'Tis Misha K . . . K . . . something-or-oth-er-evich. And Misha's short for Mikhail. That's Russian for Michael,' she informed her sister knowledgeably. 'And he comes from quite a good family. Else how would he have learned such good English?'

'But you don't want Father to know about him.'

'No. Not yet.' Her face clouded and she looked at Rebecca, pleading now. 'Oh, please don't say anything, Becky!'

But Rebecca reared her head with that radiant smile. 'You know I won't! And I know you won't tell on me either.' And so saying, she set her jaw and marched boldly into the cooperage, with Sarah following timidly several paces behind and nervously checking to see who was present to witness this act of defiance. 'Good morning, Mr Gimlett,' her sister called boldly. 'Morning, Tom.'

Ned Gimlett, who owned the business but, of course, leased the site from the duke, raised his eyes warily. If he hadn't had both his hands occupied in the task of using the knocker-upper to fix the second head to a cask without taking off the fingers of the apprentice who was helping him, he would have scratched his head. Now here was a difficult situation! And, as he glanced about him, he noticed that his fellow workers had discreetly averted their eyes. They all knew that Isaac Westbrook didn't want his daughter to see young Tom, in the hopes, no doubt, that she would eventually find someone more distinguished to marry. Ned respected Mr Westbrook. He was an upstanding, fair and worthy man, and Ned didn't want to upset him. But by the same token, Tom Mason was an honest, upright lad, and a fine artisan, too, and Ned considered that Miss Rebecca would be hard put to find a better spouse. He apprehensively looked across at Tom, but the young man kept his curly, ebony head bowed over his work.

'Can I be helping you, Miss Rebecca?' Ned greeted her cautiously.

Rebecca flicked up her head, showing to perfection the fine line of her jaw. 'No, not really, thank you,' she beamed, her whole face, even her eyes, smiling warmly. 'I was just passing and thought I'd call in. 'Tis such a lovely day!'

'Aye, 'tis that.' Ned's gaze flickered in Tom's direction. This really would not do! But of course, if the couple met out of his sight, it would let him off the hook, wouldn't it? 'You've a barrel steaming, haven't you, Tom?' he suggested meaningfully.

Tom lifted his head, his deep brown eyes scarcely meeting Rebecca's. 'Aye, Mr Gimlett,' he murmured, and disappeared outside.

Rebecca chewed on her lip for an instant, then smiled perkily once more. 'Good day, then, Mr Gimlett.'

'Good day, Miss Rebecca, Miss Sarah. My regards to your parents.' And he ran his finger around the collar of his shirt as the two young ladies swept out of the open doors.

'Becky, how could you!' Sarah grimaced, her own face flushed a ruby red while her sister's skin retained its usual peachy hue. Well, she would not be a party to Rebecca's open disobedience! She tightened her fingers into frustrated fists and strode on to wait for her sister outside the farrier's where a patient horse was being shod.

Rebecca sucked in her cheeks. The other coopers were inside the workshop again now, and anyway, would it really matter if anyone saw her with Tom? She only wanted to talk to him for a few moments after all! And the sight of his pliant body, bent over as he felt the steaming wood with the palm of his hand, was simply irresistible.

'Tom!'

Her sharp whisper raised the young man's head and his eyes looked anxiously at her from his worried face. 'You shouldn't be here, Becky,' he admonished, his handsome brow creasing into a deep frown.

'Oh,' she pouted insolently. 'Are you not pleased to see me, then?'

'Aye! Of course I am! But your father'd be furious if he found out.'

Rebecca huffed up her shoulders, her chin jutting out obstinately. 'I don't care! 'Twould be his own fault for not letting us marry.'

'Oh, but you know what he said.' Tom's dark eyebrows almost met. 'We've only to wait till you're twenty-one—'

'I shall be an old maid by then!'

'No, you won't!' he chuckled with amusement. 'And I'm willing to wait a while if 'twill mean I can have the most beautiful girl in Devonshire as my bride! 'Tis not long, anyway. And besides,' his mouth twisted awkwardly, 'in some ways, I agree with him,' he muttered.

Rebecca staggered backwards as if she had received a physical blow. 'What!' she cried, her eyes wide.

But Tom stood firm. 'I want to provide decently for my wife,' he told her adamantly. 'Very soon, I'll be earning a pound a week, and by the time we're wed, I should be able to rent one of the Bedford cottages. But you know I've my mother and the little ones to support, and they must come first. God knows they all went without so as I could go through my apprenticeship!'

'But what about your mother's widow's pension from the mine fund?'

'Oh, that ran out long afore I started earning, and it scarcely paid the rent anyway. So I'm still paying off all we owe. And you know Hetty's always worked so hard so as I could go on learning how to make a barrel, so 'tis time I paid her back. And I've sworn not to let the boys go down the mine, not while there's breath in my body.'

Rebecca blinked hard at him and then lowered her eyes. The thought of Hetty, Tom's younger sister and her own best friend, hammering away at the larger lumps of rock all day long at the George and Charlotte mine, exposed to whatever the weather chose to throw at her, or sifting through the broken stones as they were washed with running water until her chapped hands bled, drained the colour from her burning cheeks. Of course Tom was right.

'But I can't wait that long,' she groaned desperately. 'Why can't I come and live in the tenement with your family? I'd live in a cave to be with you, Tom!'

She gazed earnestly into his eyes, the love she had for him welling up and almost choking her. But Tom shook his head, his eyebrows raised in sympathy.

'In a cave, aye, but not in that tenement,' he said, his voice cracked. 'All we have is two rooms. Mother and Hetty and the boys sleep in the back, and I sleep on a mattress on the floor in the front. 'Twould be no proper married life. We'd have . . .' he faltered slightly, 'we'd have no privacy. And you have to fetch the water from the tap out the back, and the closets are shared, and sometimes the smell's so bad it turns your stomach over. 'Tis hardly what you're used to. No, my lovely maid. We'll just have to be patient.'

'But I love you, Tom,' she murmured distractedly.

'Aye, I know,' he whispered. 'But 'twill be worth waiting for.'

'But I *can't* wait!' she moaned. 'If only Father would let us see each other openly, 'twouldn't be so bad.'

'Aye . . .' he soothed.

'Oh, Tom, I can't not see you! We'll have to meet in the woods again. What about tonight?' she demanded impulsively. 'Same time as before!'

Tom stared at her, and then shook his head. 'You're mad, Becky!' And he looked stealthily around to see if anyone could have heard his exclamation.

'Yes, mad with love for you, Tom! Oh, please say you'll come! I'll kill myself if I can't see you!'

Her voice was so broken, her eyes so full of despair, that Tom's heart softened. 'Well, all right, then,' he said uncertainly, cursing himself even as he spoke. 'But you be careful. I don't like—'

'I will, Tom, I will!' And planting a fleeting kiss on his cheek, she flitted away down the road.

She would not be satisfied, of course, until she was walking down the aisle on Tom's arm, but if the only way she could be with him in the meantime was at a secret tryst, then she would have to be content with that!

CHAPTER TWO

'You look tired, my dear,' Anne Westbrook commented as she cut into the crusty meat pie at dinner time later the following day.

Rebecca's heart almost stopped and she glanced furtively at her sister. Sarah had heard her come in after her meeting with Tom the previous night and was sworn to secrecy, but promises could so easily be broken.

'I didn't sleep well,' she answered truthfully, and her hair stood on end as Sarah turned away with a snigger.

'You'd better get to bed early tonight, then,' Anne suggested as she handed her husband a laden plate.

'Mmm, that looks good!' Isaac's eyebrows lifted appreciatively. 'I always look forward to Mrs Payne's day off, but don't you be telling her, will you? And I hope you two girls are learning your mother's skills in the kitchen, too. Which reminds me.' He scratched his cheek with his little finger. 'I wonder if you'd mind us having a dinner guest one day soon, Annie? I met the new owner of old Joshua Farthingay's little fleet today.'

'Oh, yes?' Anne replied. 'From Plymouth, too, is he?'

'No,' Isaac told her, cutting enthusiastically into his thick slice of pie. 'From London, surprisingly. Wants to settle here in Morwellham. 'Tis why I thought 'twould be neighbourly to ask him to dinner, being a stranger and all. Seems a pleasant enough fellow. Name of Captain Bradley.'

'Taking a bit of a risk, isn't he?' Anne enquired as she tucked into her own food.

'With so much less ore coming through the quays nowadays, you mean?'

'Perhaps he doesn't know how things are,' Anne wondered. 'And 'tis not just the copper trade that's declining. 'Tis everything.'

'Aye, 'tis true enough.' Isaac rubbed his hairy jaw wistfully. 'But I don't see Captain Bradley as a fool, even if he did put in the highest bid for the ships.'

'Got more money than sense, then,' Rebecca commented absently.

'Well, he certainly can't be short of a penny or two,' her father agreed. 'But a ship be a ship, when all's said and done. Just because he bought them in Plymouth, doesn't mean he has to keep them there. Mind you, if he plans on settling in Morwellham, I imagine he will, the barge and the ketch at least. That's still under contract to Devon Great Consols anyway, so he's obliged to honour that agreement. And even if the ore's slowly being exhausted, there's enough to keep their contracted carriers in business for some time yet.'

'And what about the barge? That's the *Sure*, isn't it?'

'Indeed it is, Becky.' Isaac smiled fondly at his elder daughter, feeling warmly gratified at her interest. 'And engaged in regular trade, too, up and down the river. She calls in here with limestone from the Plymouth quarries about every ten days or so. Doesn't need to wait for the tides, you see. She's so shallow draughted, she could sail on dry land, that one!'

'Oh, you old fool!' Anne chuckled.

'Well, 'tis true she only draws a few feet of water,' Isaac continued, 'so she's never held up by a low tide, and with a crew of only two to pay, I should say Captain Bradley's unlikely to change her trade. She must make a steady — if moderate — profit, and at the end of the day, he's got a good sturdy vessel to sell.'

'If anyone wanted to buy it,' Rebecca put in as she neatly fixed a stray cube of meat to her fork.

'Let's hope for all our sakes trade never gets that bad,' Isaac smiled. 'As for Captain Bradley, he's taken over from a man who very definitely believed in not putting all his eggs in one basket, and if he's any sense, he'll do the same. The third ship, the *Swallow*, now she's different again, you see. She's bigger, and being a schooner, she's faster once she gets out to sea, so she trades on longer routes around the coast. Keeps more or less the same crew, so I believe, but operates like most merchantmen, picking up cargoes where they're available, St Austell clay up to the Potteries, grain up to London, that sort of thing. She only comes up here occasionally, usually with pig iron for the foundries, or sometimes salt, and then picks up manganese for Liverpool or Cumbria. But there's no telling what plans Captain Bradley has for her, though he only owns forty of her sixty-four shares, so he'll have to consider the other shareholders' wishes.'

'Sounds as if he's taken on a deal of hard work,' Anne considered.

'I agree with you there. So . . .' He paused, a little enigmatically, Rebecca thought. 'You don't mind if he comes to dinner one evening soon, then?'

'Not at all.' Anne beamed at her husband, knowing how he felt he had to know every last detail of what went on in his port.

'And you two daughters of mine,' Isaac lifted his chin authoritatively, 'do you think you could behave at the dinner table like two young ladies, or ought I to banish you upstairs for the evening?'

Rebecca shrugged. It wouldn't be the first time her father had offered hospitality to some belligerent old sea captain, and she usually managed to find it in her to conduct herself politely enough. But at the moment, all she could think about were those delicious stolen minutes alone with Tom in the woods. That glorious yearning deep in her belly was almost too much to bear. She glanced across at Isaac now, at his strong, kind face. If only he'd let her marry Tom at once. Why couldn't he understand? He respected her. Not just as a daughter as he did Sarah. But as someone with intelligence and a strength of will. She had sensed the difference for some time as she'd grown from a child into a young woman. But . . . did she really want to ruin that special bond by challenging him again and again over Tom? Her thoughts were chasing each other round and round in her head until she felt giddy, and the last thing on her mind was some pompous stranger coming to dinner!

* * *

'Tom?' she called in an urgent whisper, her heart pounding hard in her chest.

'Aye, Becky, I'm here.'

Tom stepped across to her, and she all but swooned in his protective arms. It was so good, leaning against him as he led her to the same spot as before. When they sat down, she snuggled up to him, half as a child seeking comfort after the trauma of her walk alone in the dark, and half as a lover wanting to be soothed and caressed.

'I didn't think you were coming,' Tom said in a low voice as he fingered the loose strands of hair about her face. ''Tis so late, I were about to go home.'

'Father didn't come in till late,' she explained, relaxing now that she was safely with Tom. 'And after dinner he took ages writing up his report. I was lying in bed listening for him to come up, and then I had to wait some time to be sure he was asleep. I nearly dozed off myself.'

'Aye,' Tom smiled, lovingly stroking her cheek. 'We won't be able to do this every night. I'll be dead on my feet tomorrow.'

'When can we meet again, then?' Rebecca straightened up, bright and alert as a rabbit now.

'Well, not tomorrow,' he considered. 'We'll both need a decent night's sleep. And the next evening there's a cricket match over near Gunnislake, so I'll be late back anyway. So the night after that.'

'Oh, no, I can't!' she said, grimacing with annoyance. 'Father's invited someone to dinner and you never know how long those things can go on. Some Captain Bradley or other.'

'Aye! He were at the cooperage today. Discussing something with Mr Gimlett and some of the others. Looking at casks and so on. Didn't tell me what it were all about, mind.'

'Then I shall treat Captain Bradley with the contempt he deserves when he comes to dinner!' She tipped her head to one side with the same delightful, tinkling laugh as her mother. 'Oh, Tom! 'Tis so good to be with you again. To be able to talk to you freely, like when we were children. Remember the times we spent together?'

'Aye. And when I began my apprenticeship, you used to spend hours at the cooperage. I reckon you know as much about making a barrel as I do!'

She laughed again, her eyes dancing with mirth before coming to rest on his face. The dark curls were silhouetted like a halo around his head, his familiar features dimly visible in the glimmer of moonlight that filtered through the trees. She took his chin in her hand and gently pulled him towards her, lifting her own mouth until their lips brushed, lightly at first but then growing in strength as their passions mounted. The soft, moist contact aroused the same strangeness in her as she had felt on their previous meetings, the lingering kiss sending shock waves down her spine. Her hand slipped to the back of his neck, her fingers entwining in the thick hair about his collar, and when he finally tried to draw away, she dropped her mouth to his throat, planting playful kisses on his skin and then giggling as she deftly unfastened the top studs of his shirt.

She felt him stiffen, and then he laughed awkwardly. 'What on earth are you doing, Becky?' she heard him gulp, but she was enjoying the warm, smooth touch of his chest, enjoying teasing him, but not really knowing what she was doing. Not understanding the desire that cramped her stomach and set every nerve of her body on edge.

'I love you, Tom,' she whispered, looking up at him joyously, almost like a child at play.

But Tom's brow was furrowed, his heart thundering like a hammer. What in God's name was she trying to do to him! Enticing him until he had no more control over himself? He groaned and turned away, trying to blot the longing out of his mind, but all at once her lips were playing over the skin between the open V of his shirt. She smelled so sweet, so clean, and he buried his face in her hair and murmured softly to her. But the closeness made the ache even more unbearable, and the pulse at his temples seemed to throb in his skull. Surely . . . surely just to touch her would do no harm? After all, he meant to marry her! There was nothing dishonourable in his intentions! His fingers fumbled beneath her cloak to unhook the looped fastenings of her summer jacket, and quickly slid the pearl buttons of her blouse from their finely sewn holes. He sensed her small breasts swell beneath her camisole, her ragged breath trembling, and he carefully took the soft roundness in his hand as if it were a piece of precious porcelain.

For an instant Rebecca froze, fear almost choking her. But then she dropped back her head at Tom's gentle caresses as some force inside her, much stronger than herself, took over her entire being. She held on to his hair as he bent to explore her delicious body, praying he would stop, but yearning for him to go further, deeper. Her voice was powerless to utter the word of restraint that would halt him, her mind numbed to the frenzied torture that beat furiously in his breast. And when she allowed him to reach beneath her skirt and untie the string of her drawers, they were both totally lost. And suddenly she could have cried out with the searing pain and had to bite down hard on her lip. Dear God, was this what it led to? This screaming agony, as Tom did what all men did? She tried, but she could not stand this vile burning. But as she went to push him away, he was already withdrawing from her. But the tearing fire was still there, boring into her tender flesh, and her body convulsed with tears of pain and shock as Tom held her close.

'Oh, my sweet Becky,' he muttered into her neck. 'I do love you so much. I know it were wrong of me, but . . . I'll look after you if anything happens, you know that. I'm a grown man. I'll stand up to your father if I have to, and we'll be married just as soon as ever we can!'

Rebecca sniffed back her tears and buried her face against his chest. Well, that was what she wanted, wasn't it? And surely she would soon get used to this agony she had just endured. After all, it couldn't be that bad, or the human race would have died out, wouldn't it? But she hadn't expected it to hurt so much, even if she loved Tom and it was the natural thing to do. But, maybe . . . next time . . . it wouldn't be so painful. She set her mouth determinedly. If it turned out that because of what they had just done, she had to marry Tom as soon as possible, then at least she wouldn't have had to wait until she was a wrinkled old woman before she became his wife!

CHAPTER THREE

'Oh, do hurry up, Becky! You'll never be ready!' Sarah chided as she stood back to check her reflection in the long mirror. 'Oh, I wish I hadn't grown so much! This is the best outfit I can still get into, and it really isn't suitable!'

Rebecca rolled her eyes skywards. 'Huh! Anyone would think 'twere the queen herself coming to dinner instead of some pox-ridden seadog who smells of baccy and mothballs! Oh, bother these stays! I'm not wearing them!'

Sarah's lips pressed together in a grimace. 'You don't need to, you're so thin anyway,' she murmured enviously, and then perched on the edge of the bed, her eyes twinkling. 'He's quite a gentleman, Father says, and from London. He should have some interesting tales to tell!'

'He could come from the moon for all I care! Besides, he and Father will probably spend the entire evening talking business. You know how dull these affairs usually are!'

'You're determined to dislike Captain Bradley, aren't you, just because he's stopping you from meeting Tom tonight?'

'Ssh!' Rebecca rounded on her, blue eyes blazing. 'One word about it,' she hissed dangerously, 'and I'll tell all about your Misha!'

Sarah shrugged dismissively, but colour nonetheless flushed into her cheeks. 'They'd give you a bit more bosom, though, the stays,' she neatly changed the subject. 'You could do with it, especially in that dress.'

''Tis not that low cut,' Rebecca protested, crossly wriggling her arms into the sleeves. ''Tis not an off-the-shoulder ballgown like you see in those fancy magazines. You wouldn't catch me flaunting myself like that! I'd as soon wear a day dress tonight, but Mother would have us pretend 'tis some society dinner. Oh, do it up for me, would you?'

Sarah got to her feet and obligingly came round behind her sister, watching in the looking glass as the bodice of the light muslin dress came into place over Rebecca's slender figure. 'You look lovely, Becky,' she smiled. 'Now let's find something for you to wear around your neck. Hmm! If only Tom could see you now, he'd be knocked off his feet!'

Rebecca didn't answer and instead stared silently at her reflection. Yes, she supposed she did look nice, sophisticated almost, in the demurely appealing white muslin. But beneath the youthful facade beat the heart of a woman already initiated into the ways of the world. The soreness had worn off now, and she felt confused because it was as if it had never happened, like a dream only half remembered.

She sighed and turned back to Sarah's eager face. 'I suppose we must wear gloves, too,' she groaned sullenly.

* * *

'Captain Bradley, sir, ma'am,' Mrs Payne announced with a slight dip of her arthritic knees, since the stranger had inspired in her some sort of natural respect.

Rebecca rose to her feet, smothering a sigh of resignation. She was glad it wasn't considered polite for a young lady to make a show of greeting a stranger and kept her eyes trained on the floor. If it weren't for this . . . this intruder, they would have eaten some hours earlier and before too long, she could have been in Tom's arms again!

'May I present my wife Mrs Anne Westbrook,' her father was saying. 'Anne, Captain Bradley.'

'Delighted to make your acquaintance, Mrs Westbrook.' The lightly spoken tones of a cultured London accent reached Rebecca's ears, and her lips compressed in disappointment. She had wanted the fellow's voice to be pompous and self-righteous in order to confirm the disagreeable picture she had formed of him in her mind but, to her annoyance, it was neither. 'It is so very kind of you to invite me into your home.'

'Well, I hope you will be very happy, Captain, if you are to live here at Morwellham.'

'Indeed, I am sure I will, ma'am, but of course, much of the time I shall be away at sea.'

'Of course,' Anne agreed with a smile. 'Now, this is our younger daughter Sarah.'

Rebecca cringed as she felt the movement of Sarah's skirts beside her. 'Charmed to meet you, Miss Westbrook,' the sharply dictioned voice spoke softly again. 'I must say that I find the country air hereabouts seems to bring a pretty bloom to a young lady's cheeks.'

Rebecca shuddered. Sarah would doubtless be flattered by the captain's remark, but she would not be beguiled by such fancy words. Bringing his fine London manners down here, well, it wouldn't work with her!

'And our elder daughter Rebecca,' her father completed the introductions.

Rebecca pursed her lips and held out her hand which the captain took gently by the fingertips and bent over in the perfect implication of a bow. But as he lifted his head, Rebecca decided it might be satisfying to have a visual image for the focus of her contempt. She glanced up. And was stunned to meet the most beautiful pair of eyes she had ever seen; the colour of highly polished chestnuts, they gazed at her out of a strong, handsome face hardly lined at all except for a crease at the eyes from squinting into the sun. This man was certainly not what she had expected, and for a moment the surprise numbed her. Captain Bradley could scarcely be more than thirty, with a full head of light brown hair that was not plastered in macassar as might have been the case in a London gentleman, although he was dressed impeccably in the traditional sea captain's uniform. A faint fragrance of lemon and spices lingered about his closely shaven jaw which quite startled Rebecca, for she had heard about but never known anyone who used such lotions. She found it not unpleasant, and what was even more unsettling was that, in the fleeting moment when their eyes met, she caught the quickly concealed astonishment on the captain's own face.

'I . . . er . . . Delighted, Miss Westbrook.' He managed at once to disguise his enraptured stammer.

'Do you not think 'twould be better for the captain to address us as Miss Rebecca and Miss Sarah, Father?' Sarah enquired with a gay toss of her head. 'Or we won't know which of us he's talking to?'

Isaac nodded with a faint smile. ''Twould not seem inappropriate. Now, Captain Bradley, can I interest you in a glass of claret before we dine?'

'That would be most acceptable, thank you.'

But even as he spoke, he glanced swiftly in Rebecca's direction as if he simply couldn't keep his eyes from her. Rebecca drew a seething breath through her nostrils as she watched him cross the room to take the glass from her father's hand. So, he had an eye for the girls, did he? Well, if he thought he could work his charms on her, he would have to think again! He might be tall and attractive and a fine figure of a man, but she was already spoken for! As far as she was concerned, Captain Bradley could pack his fancy ways in his sea chest and take himself back to London on the next ship!

'I'm afraid you will find the choice of wines somewhat limited in these parts,' Isaac was telling him with a hint of apology in his voice.

'But this is of excellent quality.' The captain raised his glass appreciatively. 'A good wine and congenial company, what more can one ask for?'

That you hadn't come at all so that I could have gone to meet Tom, Rebecca inwardly scowled. For one reason or another, it would be several days before they could be together again. Would Tom repeat their lovemaking, she wondered? She knew it was wrong, but she was curious to see if it would be less painful a second time, if she would even take some pleasure from it.

'Rebecca!' Isaac's sharp tone brought her from her reverie. 'We're about to take our seats at the table. I assume you will join us?'

Rebecca blinked her thoughts back into focus, and her indignation flared as she saw Captain Bradley offer his arm. Well, if he thinks . . . But relief flowed through her as she realized that the gesture was politely directed towards her mother. She followed them to the table, noticing with disdain how the well-tailored jacket fitted perfectly over the captain's broad shoulders. Trying to impress us with his fine attire, is he? She scorned silently, forgetting that her father was dressed in his best frock coat and white silk cravat, and that she was wearing the nearest thing she possessed to an evening gown.

'Would you like to sit here, Captain?' Anne indicated with her gloved hand.

Rebecca quickly skirted around to the opposite side. If she was going to be obliged to sit at the same table as Captain Bradley, then she was determined it wouldn't be next to him! But she saw Isaac raise a disapproving eyebrow at the swiftness of her movement.

'Rebecca will say grace for us,' he announced as if to reprimand her.

She swallowed hard. If her father would force her into opening her mouth, then she would let Captain Bradley see that she was no little country idiot! She proceeded to recite in Latin the prayer of thanks her teacher, a rigorous Catholic, had always insisted upon during the two years she had spent away at school in Tavistock. Her gaze flashed boldly across at the stranger. But those richly coloured eyes twinkled back at her as he guessed her game, and she was sure he was trying not to laugh. Damn him! And she bowed her head as scarlet flooded into her cheeks.

As they all sat down, she was aware of Captain Bradley first drawing out the chair for her mother. Huh! Politeness itself! Had to be, didn't it? Well, she would let him get on with it. Empty gestures! It was what was in one's heart that counted. She'd like to see him cope with Tom's life, toiling twelve hours a day, or more if business was good. Hard, strenuous work that demanded unbelievable skill as well as physical strength. She could just picture the captain tucked away in his cosy cabin, eating and drinking the finest fare, and issuing impossible orders to a hungry and exhausted crew!

'You must forgive my curiosity, Captain,' Isaac began in a friendly tone, 'but we are all anxious to know why you should choose to come to Morwellham.'

The visitor glanced across at his host and then set his spoon carefully into the soup dish. He seemed to hesitate for an instant before taking a deep breath as if he were about to deliver a confession. 'I am sure there has been a great deal of speculation as to my background,' he began guardedly, 'so I might as well set the record straight from the beginning. My . . . my father,' and even Rebecca looked up at the unexpected crack in his voice, 'was a merchant, shall we say, of reasonable standing. In London, as I am sure you are aware. I . . . well, I did have quite a lot to do with the business, but, to my father's chagrin, I had always wanted to go to sea, and my father, being the sort of man he was, arranged for me to be properly trained. While I was still working for other shipping lines, I saved as much as I could from my earnings, and when I eventually gained my master's certificate, I borrowed the rest of the money from my father to buy my own ship, paying him back over what was to have been a twenty-year period, but . . .' He lifted his hand in a gesture of despair and then lowered his eyes. 'I built up a good trade for myself, although I admit it included a good deal of shipping for my father. But . . . I'm afraid I wasn't the dutiful son. I should have been where he needed me, at his side, to take some of the responsibilities from his shoulders as he got older. The strain of it all became too much for him. He had two strokes, but kept on working, even though . . . And then he died last year. If only I . . .'

He broke off, and as he looked up, gazed directly at Rebecca. The sadness in his eyes took her by surprise, but if he thought to gain her sympathy, he was mistaken. She would never abandon either of her parents in their hour of need! But their guest almost at once addressed her father again.

'I do not wish to bore you with my personal affairs, but those are my reasons for coming here. To get as far away from London as possible. It was never my spiritual home. That has always been the open sea. So I sold forty-nine per cent of the business, and my father's house. Too many memories, you see.'

'I assume your mother . . . ?' Anne prompted gently.

'I never knew her. She died two days after I was born.' He gave a wry smile. 'So I am guilty on two counts.'

'And with that money, you bought old Joshua Farthingay's ships?' Isaac concluded.

'That's right. I am often in Plymouth with the *Emily*, and when I heard that Captain Farthingay's ships were up for sale, it seemed an ideal opportunity. I am a sailor, not a businessman, you see.'

'You . . .' Isaac cleared his throat, 'you do realize that though this has been an excellent year so far, there is every reason to predict that the amount of copper passing through Morwellham could soon start dwindling fast? And that trade in just about everything else is also declining?'

'I do indeed, Mr Westbrook. But I wish to make a living, not a fortune. The *Swift* at least is contracted to Devon Great Consols, so her future is secure for a little while yet. And there is another commodity . . .' His eyes swept about the table. 'I . . . I can speak before you in absolute confidence, I assume?'

Rebecca felt heat rising at her throat. How dare he question the integrity of the ladies present! Her eyes darted across to Isaac, but her father's expression was inscrutable.

'You may rely upon our silence,' he replied gravely to his guest. 'My family is used to being in a position of trust.'

Captain Bradley wet his lips. 'Thank you, sir. And thank you, too, ladies. And please forgive my enquiry, but in London, you see, you cannot trust anyone.' He turned his head towards Isaac again. 'As you know, Mr Westbrook, the Devon Great Consols mine exports certain quantities of arsenic. And now that it seems the lodes of copper are approaching exhaustion, and copper prices are falling anyway now that cheaper, lower quality ore from abroad can be processed so much better, they're planning on making arsenic their main concern. I am sure you are aware that work is about to start on an arsenic refinery at Wheal Anna Maria. And therein lies my own interest, as I wish to be one of the first to have a regular contract to transport that commodity.'

'But arsenic is a poison.' Rebecca blinked her eyes meaningfully, as if she was telling him something he didn't already know.

But her cheeks flushed crimson when she heard him chuckle with amusement. 'My dear young lady, I can assure you I have no intention of doing away with anyone! Like the manganese produced here, arsenic has many uses. In paint and glassware, for instance, but most of it will be destined for the southern states of America as an insecticide for the cotton crop.'

'I am quite well aware of the uses of arsenic, thank you, Captain Bradley,' she retorted coldly. 'But I am surprised that you would help those monsters who fought a war so that they could try and keep their slaves.'

The satisfaction glowed within her as she saw the captain's jaw drop in astonishment, but then he nodded slowly. 'That is a fair comment, Miss Rebecca. But I saw the poverty the cotton famine caused in Lancashire, with millworkers thrown out of work by the thousands, and then the bargees, the sailors, the shopkeepers, everyone! It wasn't just the mill owners who suffered, you know. I would not want to witness that again. As far as slavery is concerned, I am delighted it has been abolished. But the fact is that the world still wants cotton in vast quantities.'

Rebecca puffed up her small chest, but her mouth remained tightly clamped, for she couldn't find the words to express her contempt. Captain Bradley was looking at her challengingly, but with a sparkling glint in his eyes. His gaze lingered on her longer than was necessary, and she was grateful when Isaac addressed him further, even if he threw her a warning glare as he did so.

'So you would be among the first to secure a contract to carry the arsenic? Hmm! You'd be more of a businessman than you think, sir! But 'tis a dangerous cargo to carry.'

'Indeed it is, which is why I have spent some time at your cooperage discussing the casks with Mr Gimlett. I don't want my crew being poisoned, or for the hold to become contaminated. The mine is to have its own cooperage eventually, but in the meantime, they will be buying mostly from here in Morwellham, and even when they're making their own casks, they won't be able to keep up with their own needs if all goes as well as is predicted.'

Rebecca lifted her head sharply. So that was what it was all about! Well, it would certainly mean good business for the cooperage, and better wages for Tom, which would mean . . . Perhaps there was some good in what Captain Bradley had said, after all.

'So you would have the *Swallow* engaged in transatlantic trade?' Isaac continued.

'And force men only used to river and coastal trade to leave their families for long periods and risk their lives upon the high seas just to line your pocket?' Rebecca could not restrain her angered outburst.

She heard Sarah's stifled gasp beside her, and then a stony silence settled ominously about the dining table. Rebecca's heart jerked and she pulled back her shoulders, making herself look a great deal more confident than she felt.

'Rebecca, you will apologize to our guest at once!' Isaac exploded. 'You have shown him nothing but rudeness all evening!'

She felt her chin quiver, humiliation scorching her cheeks as she lowered her eyes. Oh, how she hated Captain Bradley! But to her astonishment, it was his clear-cut voice that spoke before she had a chance to utter a word herself.

'Come now, Mr Westbrook, your daughter is merely expressing a reasonable opinion. But let me explain, Miss Rebecca.' And when she dared to glance up, he was smiling gently at her. 'When a man becomes a sailor, he has to accept that sometimes he may have to sign on for voyages that may take him away for long periods. Many of them prefer it. And I can assure you that it would be no more dangerous for the *Swallow* to cross the Atlantic than to navigate the treacherous Cornish coast as she does all the time. But as it happens, it is only the barge I am thinking of. Most of the arsenic is to be taken down river by barge and then transferred on to vessels far larger than the *Swallow* in order to be transported to America more cheaply. Now the *Sure* comes upriver with Plymouth limestone for the kilns here. I'd prefer her to bring culm as it pays higher rates, but as you know, most of that comes direct from south Wales, so it isn't really viable. However, once here, the *Sure* is generally delayed by having to wait for whatever is available for the return trip, which all wastes time. But, if she had a cargo of arsenic ready and waiting, she could regularly make the return journey within a week. And of course arsenic will carry a high freight charge, so I can't think of a better way to secure her future and to increase her profits as well.'

'And your own future is to be here in Morwellham?' Anne put in, grateful to the captain for having defused the tension so adeptly.

'Oh, indeed. I'm staying at the Ship Inn at the moment, but I take up the lease of Lavender Cottage opposite the chapel next week. I was wondering, actually, if you might be able to recommend someone as a housekeeper, Mrs Westbrook?'

'Well, I'm sure I can think of more than one woman who'd be interested in such a position,' Anne nodded thoughtfully. 'I'll make some enquiries for you. And will your wife be joining you soon?'

Captain Bradley lifted his eyebrows wistfully. 'I regret I am a widower, Mrs Westbrook.'

'Oh, I'm so sorry.' Anne blanched with embarrassment.

But the captain shook his head. 'It was some time ago now, and it was never a love match anyway. My wife was my father's choice, and it was the one thing in which I did obey his wishes. But I grew very fond of Felicity. She was a good woman, and I missed her more than I expected when she died.'

'You had no children?' Anne suggested.

'No. My wife never . . .' And to Rebecca's surprise, their guest looked strangely perturbed and caught his lip between his teeth for a moment before beginning afresh. 'She cared more for looking after the destitute of London. That was how she died. Of typhus.'

'Typhus!' Sarah gasped with childlike shock.

'Yes. Spread by lice in overcrowded backstreet slums. So you can see why the open countryside has such appeal for me. Besides, I have fallen in love.'

'In love?' Isaac muttered with disappointment. 'And may I enquire who the lucky lady might be?'

But Captain Bradley replied with a soft, nervous laugh. 'With Morwellham! The place is quite enchanting!'

'Well, if you are to live here, you had better learn to pronounce it properly. 'Tis Morwell*ham*, not Morwell'am.'

Rebecca stared at the captain, pleased with the hint of chastisement she had skilfully lent to her voice, but he met her gaze with one eyebrow cocked roguishly. 'Ah, I thank you for that information, Miss Rebecca. I must admit, I had noticed people say it like that, but thought it to be some local pronunciation. Now I shall know better.'

Rebecca's mouth knotted with irritation. The insolent fellow was laughing at her! He was treating her like some idiotic child, when . . . when she was a woman who knew what it was to be loved by a kind, stalwart man, and not some self-satisfied, complacent hypocrite who used other human beings to further his own fortune. And to think her parents had been deceived into inviting him into their own home!

'Tell me about your own ship,' Isaac was asking amicably.

The captain's brown eyes visibly glowed. 'The *Emily*? She's a beauty. A brig of a hundred and forty-five tons. Cuts through the water like a dream.'

'And you say you mainly carry merchandise for your own company in London?'

'On the importing side, yes. My father is . . . was a wine and spirits merchant. He was an expert on the subject, and I must say that the loss of his knowledge has dealt quite a considerable blow to the company.'

'But you must be reasonably familiar with the subject to carry on the business?'

'But not as I would wish. And my father would travel abroad to the vineyards and deal with them direct. It had been a tremendous asset in his last years, for as you may know, most European vines were destroyed by the phylloxera aphid and had to be replaced by vines grafted on to resistant, American root stocks. Fortunately, that appears to be in the past now, for I have neither the time nor the expertise for such situations. But overall, our trade has been affected, and we have to rely mainly on exporting merchants instead.' He paused, and looking across at him, Rebecca noted the regretful lift of his eyebrows. 'I could sell out, of course, to one of the big companies, but that was always something my father fiercely opposed. So, I do what I know best to keep the business a going concern, which is to ship as much of the merchandise as I can myself, and so reduce our shipping costs.'

'And has the acquisition of the *Swallow* anything to do with it?' Isaac pressed him.

The captain gave a furtive smile. 'You have read my thoughts, sir. So you see, Miss Rebecca, the *Swallow* will be sailing European waters, not the Atlantic. Besides, her present master is not so qualified, and although I am, I cannot sail two ships at once. I have taken the *Emily* to Jamaica twice to collect rum, but it makes more sense to leave that to the larger merchantmen.'

'And what do you take out to the European ports?'

'Mainly what their own colonies don't produce in such quantities as our own do. And, I trust Miss Rebecca will forgive me . . .' He hesitated, and as Rebecca felt her gaze drawn towards him, she saw the corners of his mouth twitch slightly. 'There is a strong market in southern Europe for cotton goods. Not quite the same as the amount that we export to India or Australia, for instance, but a demand nonetheless.'

Rebecca felt the hairs bristling down the back of her neck. 'And what does everyone else involved think of your plans for the *Swallow*?' she asked curtly.

'Everyone seems quite happy, actually. The shareholders and the crew. They all want to keep signing on. Looking forward to seeing a little more sunshine in their lives. And they'll be calling at Plymouth on each return trip, so they'll still be able to see their families. I usually have some wine to unload at Sutton Harbour for a small concern my father always supplied. That's how I got to hear of Joshua Farthingay's ships being up for sale. And of Morwell*ham*,' he added with extra emphasis on the final syllable.

'It sounds as if you will have little enough time to come here, though,' Rebecca commented with satisfaction.

'Unfortunately you are indeed correct. But I know of an old and trusted sea captain in Plymouth. He is quite willing to take the *Emily* on to London for me on occasion. He is recently retired and would be glad of a little extra cash once in a while.'

'You do not intend to bring the *Emily* up here then?'

'Not as a rule. She is quite small as brigs go, but she's still a deal bigger than most of the ships I see up and down the Tamar, and it's obviously not an easy river to negotiate. So I intend to learn to navigate it from the masters of my new vessels before I attempt it myself.'

'Very wise, Captain.' Isaac nodded his approval. 'Many of our visiting ships use pilots or have themselves towed, 'tis so tricky. But I fear we will bore the ladies with our talk of business. Would you care to retire with the girls, Anne? And perhaps you would like a cigar, Captain Bradley?'

Rebecca noticed that their guest was on his feet in a trice, and as she escaped his company as swiftly as she possibly could, she heard him reply, 'Thank you, sir, but no. I smoke but rarely, and then only my trusty pipe which, alas, I do not have with me.'

And I hope next time you light it, it burns your tongue! Rebecca thought bitterly.

* * *

Captain Adam Bradley walked away from Isaac Westbrook's cottage with a spring in his step, and it was all he could do to stop himself throwing his cap in the air and whooping for joy. It was pitch black and he could hardly see where he was going, and it was only when he twisted his ankle in a pothole in the unfamiliar path that he checked his gait. But he didn't care. His heart felt as if he were soaring high above this lovely little port and gazing down on the most beautiful girl he had ever seen. Oh, Rebecca! She was exquisite! So young and passionate! Slight as a fairy, and possessed of the intelligence and sharp wit of any society dame, and yet, oh, what innocence! He wanted to take her in his arms, love her, protect her. They would fight, of that he was certain, as her blue eyes snapped at him with anger, but knowing all the time that deep down there was a rock-hard trust between them. Oh, God! He had never felt like this before! Ever! He wanted Rebecca Westbrook as his wife, and he'd never been so sure of anything before in his life.

He couldn't bear to return to the confines of the inn, and as always when his mind was unnerved, he made for the water's edge.

CHAPTER FOUR

'Look at this one, Sarah. 'Tis only a cotton print, but 'tis so pretty.'

'I'm the one who needs some new clothes, not you, and I look my best in green. Oh, I just can't make up my mind.'

'We'll have to come back another day, Miss Martin,' Rebecca smiled sweetly at the owner of Morwellham's general store.

'That's all right, maid. You take your time.'

Rebecca tugged on her sister's sleeve and was close to dragging her outside. She turned on her as she shut the door behind them, her eyes a dark, fiery blue. 'You can't waste Miss Martin's time like that, Sarah. She must be so busy, running the shop on her own.'

'You're just jealous because Father won't give you any money for a new dress,' Sarah retorted. 'I really need one, I've grown so much, but what do you need one for? We never go anywhere as 'tis!'

'I do like to look my best, even so.'

'What? For Tom?' Sarah scoffed. 'But you only ever see each other in the dark.'

'Ssh!' Rebecca's eyes flashed at her. 'Someone might hear!'

'Well, you're going to get caught out sooner or later, carrying on the way you are! 'Tis over a month now you've been creeping out at night and up to the woods! I've heard you, and 'tis only a matter of time before Father does, too, and then he'll never let you marry Tom.'

Rebecca glared sideways at her sister and then her chest lifted as she filled her lungs with air and she let it out in a long, heavy stream. 'Oh, maybe you're right. But all I can think about is Tom! I want to have my own home, however humble. I want to wash and mend Tom's clothes, cook his meals, choose what we're going to eat, instead of just playing at being a housewife in Mother's kitchen. I feel so . . . so empty. I need more in my life than just waiting for each day to pass!'

Sarah blinked at her, her own paler, grey eyes opened wide. 'What you need is something to occupy your mind. Why don't we go along to the school and help Agnes with the children? 'Twould take your mind off things.'

'Oh, no,' Rebecca groaned. 'Try and teach little toads with nothing but sawdust between their ears! I need to stimulate my brain, not kill it off completely! Besides, there are so few children there anyway. Those that aren't dressing ore are working in the fields this time of year.'

'Oh, well, suit yourself.' Sarah shrugged, and then quickly placed a restraining hand on her sister's arm as a waggon, laden with copper ore, rumbled out on the iron rails between the shop and the Ship Inn. The two girls waited for it to pass as it trundled its way towards the quays. That area of the port wasn't as bustling as the Devon Great Consols dock, but it was nevertheless lively enough to arouse Rebecca's interest.

'I know,' she suggested half-heartedly. 'Let's cross over to Canal Dock and see if there's anything interesting come in.'

'All right, if you want. Though I'm sure one ship looks the same as another to me!'

Rebecca wrinkled her nose with feigned disdain. 'Nautical philistine!' she scorned, and then broke into a soft laugh as she linked her arm through Sarah's and they made their way across the cobbles towards the small, general dock. Unlike the open vastness of the Devon Great Consols quay, Canal Dock had a more enclosed feel to it, with the high wall on one side, the result of a dispute many years earlier between the duke and his lessees, and the schoolyard wall on the other. Yet the narrow dockside held much more fascination for Sarah in particular, as it was here that all manner of items for Morwellham's day-to-day life were delivered into waiting carts, from brass candlesticks for sale in the chandlery to lace tablecloths and wine for the inn.

Rebecca let her eyes wander pleasurably over the busy scene, refusing to admit to her disappointment that the one barge in the dock was simply being loaded with farm produce and hadn't delivered any interesting merchandise. But then she caught Sarah's arm excitedly. 'Look!' she breathed and pointed at the flag flapping merrily from the bare mast of the first ship moored against the riverbank.

Sarah followed the direction of her gaze and gasped aloud. 'Do . . . do you think it might be . . . ?' she whispered nervously.

'Well, we don't have that many Russian ships come here!'

'Oh, Becky! How do I look?' Sarah flustered, her hands fluttering suddenly about her bonnet.

'Oh, stop fussing. You look lovely. Now, come *on*!' And she fairly dragged Sarah along the cobbles. 'Yes! 'Tis his ship! I wonder . . . Yes, look!' she announced as they rounded the high wall. 'There he is!'

Beside her, Sarah was trembling, her face as white as almond blossom. Rebecca grinned, and when Sarah seemed unable to move an inch, she strode boldly up to the young man anxiously checking each enormous wooden crate against a list of what were to Rebecca strange hieroglyphics on a sheet of paper.

'Good morning, Misha.' She turned her head to look up at him and saw the shock on his bronzed face.

'Oh! Oh, Miss Rebecca!' A shy smile stretched his generous mouth and his startling blue eyes crinkled at the corners. 'I am very happy! I hope you is . . . no . . . I hope you are well. And . . . and Miss Sarah?'

'Yes, yes! She's well!' Rebecca bubbled with enthusiasm. 'Look! You see!' she laughed, pointing at the hesitant figure some ten yards behind her. 'You are the only person who can make her lose her tongue!'

His young, fresh-skinned forehead puckered with perplexity. 'Please excuse. I do not understand.'

Rebecca laughed again. 'She has been longing to see you, Misha. She waits only for you!' she expounded until she saw the happy comprehension on his face. 'Come on, Sarah! Can't you see Misha's busy! He can't wait all day!'

She watched as Sarah straightened her shoulders and then came quickly towards them, her cheeks flushed a beautiful rose and her eyes wide with expectation. The slender Russian at once stood to attention and, clicking his heels in semi-military fashion, dipped his head sharply.

'Oh, 'tis good to see you!' Sarah finally cried with elation.

'For me, it is very good, too. It is a long time we do not see each other, but this is good, too, because . . .' He broke off, biting his lip as he searched for the words. 'I work . . . I study . . . I write . . . so that now I am like, how you say in England, I think, first mate on the ship!' he concluded triumphantly.

'Oh, that's wonderful!' Sarah exclaimed with glee as Misha blushed proudly. 'So one day, you could become a captain!'

'*Da*, one day, perhaps.' He suddenly seemed embarrassed. 'But a long time yet, I think. And now I am here, and I do not want to go away again. So, instead to bring these woods from Memel only two or three times a year, I will try to be on a ship with . . . with the copper from here to . . . to . . .'

'South Wales, and back with coal?' Rebecca suggested.

Misha's eyes lit up with relief. '*Da*! Yes, that is it. So that I see you many times, Miss Sarah, that . . . that is . . . if it pleases you?'

'Oh, yes!' Sarah tossed her head, joy quivering in her voice. 'That pleases me very much!'

'And these are all staves for the cooperage?' Rebecca enquired.

'*Da*. Many staves,' Misha nodded vigorously. 'They are to be very busy, I think.'

'Yes, they are,' Rebecca agreed, her thoughts coming in rapid succession. 'Well, I'll leave you two to talk for a moment, and I'll go to the cooperage and tell them their staves are here.'

She moved quickly away, feeling very pleased with herself. It was turning out to be a better day than she'd expected. She now had a good excuse to go and talk to Tom, and she had been instrumental in bringing Sarah and Misha a little closer together. The young Russian's career was progressing well, and if he eventually qualified as master, it would be no disgrace for Sarah to marry him. If only her own plans could run as smoothly, she sighed to herself as she hurried back up the dockside, neatly avoiding ropes and bollards and crates, and even a makeshift stall where a fisherman was selling pilchards caught at sea the previous day. She wrinkled up her nose at the powerful odour, thankful that Morwellham was not a fishing port. But people had to eat, she supposed, and pilchards formed the staple diet of many a poor Devon or Cornish family.

'Miss Rebecca!'

She started in surprise and glanced round as the calling of her own name interrupted her thoughts. At first she wasn't sure who had hailed her, but then her memory connected the clear voice with the tall figure hastily approaching her, and she knew at once that it was Captain Bradley. Her heart sank, but at the same time, she was aware of her wits rising defensively as she recalled the humiliation he'd caused her to suffer over the dinner table a few weeks earlier. She felt her tongue sharpen, her natural animosity towards him soaring into hostility. Her eyes narrowed as he came up to her, smiling broadly as if they were long-standing acquaintances. She noticed he wasn't wearing the immaculate captain's blazer of the night of the supper, but was dressed in a knitted woollen tunic of the style that had originated among the Guernsey seamen. It was unquestionably smart, sitting well over his shoulders and falling loosely about his trim waist. But added to the fact that he was bare-headed and his hair blew about his forehead in the keen breeze, it seemed to rob him somewhat of his sophistication, and made him appear less formidable.

'Good morning, Captain Bradley,' she replied abrasively, and saw the mild astonishment in his eyes at her tone of voice.

'Good afternoon, I believe.'

'Is it?' she snapped.

But he turned his head with irritating calm and squinted up at the sun. 'I should say so, but only just. But it is of no importance now that the *Emily* is safely berthed.'

He gestured vaguely towards the river. Rebecca's eyes followed his direction, and she saw that beyond the Russian vessel was moored a brig, not so large for its class, but certainly of a greater tonnage than usually sailed up the Tamar and only just able to be accommodated at the quayside. She wondered why she hadn't noticed it before, as the square-rigging of its bare masts towered distinctively over those of the fore-and-aft schooners and ketches. She was impressed, but she was damned if she was going to let him see!

'Was it not a trifle foolish to bring such a sizeable ship up the Tamar when you are so ignorant of its waters?' she enquired, unable to prevent the scathing edge in her voice. 'And should you not have arranged a berth in the Devon Great Consols dock? 'Tis much more suited to a larger vessel.'

Adam Bradley's rich brown eyes blinked at her, but his mouth instantly stretched with amusement at her rebuke. 'Ah, but I considered it a challenge,' he replied in a devilish tone. 'And, as you see, it was one in which I succeeded, although I do admit to having engaged a pilot. As for my choice of berth, I am actually waiting for space to become available in your large dock, as I have some heavy machinery for the mine on board. But in the meantime, I have some crates of wine I had promised to Mrs Richards when I was lodging at the inn, so I thought I might unload them here while I was waiting.' He paused and drew in a deep breath, for a moment seeming unsure of himself, but nonetheless unable to conceal his proud enthusiasm. 'Do you not think the *Emily* a beautiful ship, Miss Rebecca? The men that built her must have been fine craftsmen. But perhaps you would care to come aboard and see for yourself?'

Rebecca had to stop her jaw from falling open at his forwardness. Did he really think she wanted to suffer him showing off to her what was obviously his prized possession in life? She lifted her chin with deliberate disdain and cast her eyes swiftly over the brig.

'I daresay she is a good vessel,' she answered coldly, and remembering Sarah's words not twenty minutes earlier, she went on, 'but one boat,' and she pronounced the belittling word with a touch of scorn, 'looks much the same as another to me, and no, I should not care to look over it, thank you.'

She looked the captain straight in the eye with a mocking smile on her lips, but to her intense annoyance, the muscles of his handsome face seemed to be struggling not to break into a laugh.

'Oh, please, Miss Westbrook, forgive my rash boldness!' he exclaimed. 'When I speak of the *Emily* I am inclined to forget my manners, you see. Of course I did not wish to compromise the reputation of such an elegant young lady!'

Rebecca stared at him, infuriated by the hint of sarcasm in his tone. So, he considered her some ignorant country bumpkin, did he? Well, she wasn't going to stand on the quayside and be insulted in front of the whole of Morwellham, she, the daughter of the most important and respected man in the port after the duke himself! Without answering, she spun on her heel, leaving Captain High and Mighty Bradley where he stood, and strode away. She trusted such a rebuff would put him in his place once and for all!

'Becky!'

It wasn't until she all but collided with Tom that she was shaken from her rage, and at the sudden closeness of the young man who meant so much to her, she wanted to surrender herself to the comfort of his arms and weep. But she could hardly do so where she was, for everyone to see, and besides, Captain Bradley would know he had upset her, and that wouldn't do at all! She wanted him to be the one to feel humiliated! And her fury flared again as she remembered that he had prevented her from having a long talk with Tom at the cooperage. Now, in public, they could only exchange a few words for fear it might reach her father's ears.

'Oh, Tom!' she smiled at his anxious face. 'I was just coming to see you. There's a shipment of Russian staves arrived.'

'Aye, I know.' Tom tossed the jet-black curls out of his eyes. 'I were coming down to organize the carts. Oh, Becky.' His expression suddenly darkened as he lowered his voice. 'Would you . . . would you be free tomorrow night? I can't wait to see you again.'

'Why, yes,' she answered eagerly. 'Tomorrow night. Same place?'

'Aye,' he nodded, his eyes serious. 'I wish it didn't have to be like this, you know. I want to be able to court you openly.'

'I know, Tom.' She raised her eyebrows wistfully. 'But you'd better go now. Till tomorrow, then.'

'Aye,' he agreed, and warmth surged through her body as he fleetingly brought his lips forward as if he were blowing her a gentle kiss.

* * *

'Oh, there you are,' Anne Westbrook greeted her daughters fondly as they entered the kitchen early the following evening. 'I'm glad you're back now. We've had an invitation. Captain Bradley has asked us all to dine with him at the Ship tonight.'

'What!'

'Becky?'

'Oh! Oh, 'tis just that I have a headache, and . . . and I feel a bit sick,' she added with conviction. 'I don't think I'd be very good company.'

'Oh, 'tis being too long out in the sun.' Anne shook her head. 'You should stay in the parlour when 'tis bright like this. Perhaps you'd better go to bed. What a pity!'

'Yes, I think I will,' she replied with feigned weakness. 'Give my apologies to Captain Bradley, won't you?'

She climbed the stairs, her mouth set with anger. The previous day Captain Bradley had prevented her from talking at length with Tom, and now his invitation had upset her plans once again! But when she undressed, she was careful to leave her underwear on beneath her nightgown, and her day dress and cloak she lay at the ready over the chair. She slid into the double bed she shared with Sarah, and waited. Perhaps she would doze for a while, but all she could see in her mind was Captain Bradley smiling at her with a mocking grin, his pearly teeth gleaming at her in perfect symmetry. And she had the most overwhelming urge to knock them out for him!

Sarah came into the room to change, and when she saw her sister was not asleep, proceeded to chatter on endlessly about her adored Misha. Rebecca listened indulgently. There was hope for Sarah, and she prayed that all went well for her. At least she wasn't being forced to take such underhand action as she was!

The party left for the inn, and the cottage went quiet. Mrs Payne brought her up a cup of chocolate when she came to bed herself at ten o'clock, and Rebecca heard her moving about in the room on the other side of the stairs until that, too, fell silent. The clock in the parlour struck eleven, and then midnight. Rebecca turned over and angrily thumped her pillow. It was too late now! Tom would have given up and gone home, believing she had let him down. Oh, damn Captain Bradley! She hoped he would rot in hell!

CHAPTER FIVE

'Oh, Becky!' Sarah whispered excitedly and linked her arm through her sister's elbow as they followed their parents' sedate pace past the manganese mill, its grindstones silent for the Saturday evening and Sunday's rest.

Rebecca smiled indulgently at Sarah's bursting eagerness to arrive at the village dance to be held in the small hall behind the Ship Inn. Usually it housed the elaborate formal dinners between the mine agents and the ore-buyers, but tonight it was to be the scene of a very different affair.

'Misha will be there,' Sarah confided in a low chatter for the umpteenth time. 'If Father seems in a good mood, do you think I should introduce him? Oh, Becky, my stomach's turning over like a waterwheel! Of course, if 'tweren't for Captain Bradley's kindness in giving him a job on the *Swallow*, he wouldn't be here at all! Still, 'tis a pity 'tweren't on the *Swift*. He could've been in port even more often then.'

'Oh, don't *you* start!' Rebecca groaned.

Sarah glanced at her with eyes stretched wide. 'Start? Start what?'

'Ssh! Keep your voice down!' Rebecca hissed back.

'But start what? I don't understand you sometimes, Becky!'

'Start singing Captain Bradley's praises,' Rebecca spat as if it burned her tongue to pronounce his name.

'But 'tis true! No one else would trust Misha, him being a foreigner. Captain Bradley were the only one willing to give him a chance.'

'Next thing you'll be telling me what a fine, hardworking man he is!'

'So?' Sarah frowned at her in confusion.

'Oh, Sarah, don't you see?' Rebecca caught her sister's arm now, bringing her to a halt. 'Father's always dropping hints about him and then looking over at me. He sees Captain Bradley as a prospective suitor for me!'

This time Sarah gazed at her unblinking as her mind recalled various moments since Captain Bradley had first come to Morwellham. 'But . . . but what about Tom?' she stammered in disbelief.

'Precisely! So now you know why I despise the captain so much!'

'But there's no need to dislike the man himself surely? He's never done you any harm.'

'Oh, hasn't he?' Rebecca rounded on her. 'Look at the way he humiliated me when he came to dinner!'

'You brought that on yourself!' Sarah dared to tell her. 'And I thought the way he rescued you was quite clever.'

'That's as maybe,' Rebecca snorted, 'but there's no way he's ever going to be a rival to Tom!'

She spun on her heel and hurried to catch up with their parents, Sarah trotting along behind her. Oh, how she wished Captain Farthingay was still alive so that Adam Bradley had never set foot in Morwellham. He might not be aware of it, but all he had ever done was to prove an exasperating obstacle to her clandestine meetings with Tom. And if her father saw him as a prospective husband for her, that was even worse!

As they ambled towards the inn, her eyes lifted to the gaunt, stone facade of the malthouse that over a decade earlier had been hastily converted into the crowded tenements where Tom and his family lived in two small rooms. Her father was worried she would end up somewhere no better than that, and she appreciated his concerns. But as for hoping that she might turn her affections towards Captain Bradley, well! She clenched her teeth resolutely. She would take the opportunity of the dance to show her parents that there really was no one else for her but Tom. She would accept no other partner, and Tom would behave so impeccably that her father would feel obliged to reconsider!

The lively strains of fiddle and accordion carried across to them on the August evening air as they turned the corner of the inn. People were coming from all directions, young girls done up in their best frocks in the hope of catching the eye of their favoured lad, and older folk, demure now, but likely to show their knees in the general frivolity of a jig once they had a few glasses of ale inside them. Several men doffed their caps at Isaac and his family, and wives nodded their heads in salutation. Bargemen, quay labourers, miners and farmworkers from Morwellham and further afield were all aiming for the hall, as well as sailors from the ships that happened to be in port that night. How they all expected to squeeze into the cramped building, Rebecca couldn't imagine, but that was half the fun, wasn't it? And when she glanced at her sister, she could see her eyes dancing with anticipation. It made her feel old, for her own heart was heavy. She didn't like deceiving her parents, but she would marry Tom Mason, or no one!

The music greeted them more noisily as they reached the open door of the hall, but the raucous babble of voices raised in enjoyment, and the cries and whoops of those who were joined on the packed dance floor, prevented the actual melody from being recognized. But it didn't stop the merrymakers who couldn't manage to fit inside from prancing up and down on the grass outside instead. But at the arrival of the respected Westbrook family, a semblance of a path opened up as if by magic, and they made their way to the table in the corner of the hall which had been reserved for them. Rebecca sat down and arranged her full skirt. The tune being played was quite clear now, wrong notes jarring on the ears, but no one seemed to mind. The dancers were enjoying themselves cavorting up and down, making wheels of eight or scudding beneath an archway of arms, laughing as they turned the wrong way or reached for the wrong hand, faces bright and flushed with exertion. Other revellers stood about the edges of the hall or lounged against the walls, tankards of ale or glasses of sparkling cider held precariously in a waving hand. The music vied with braying guffaws, and alcohol spilled from jostled receptacles, but nothing mattered except the pure pursuit of jollification and a few carefree hours.

Rebecca eyed the scene with envy. Everyone was so happy, young girls giggling behind their fingers or tripping about the dance floor with their desired partner, cheeks aglow with elation. They could all marry the boy they loved, but she . . . ! Just because her father held a position, she was forced to . . . Oh, it wasn't fair!

But her pursed lips stretched into a broad grin as her eyes travelled towards the door.

'Hetty!' she cried with relief, standing up and waving furiously, despite Isaac's obvious disapproval. She sat down again abruptly, but Tom's sister had noticed her and was already threading her way through the milling throng. She was a tall, willowy girl who moved with loose-limbed grace, and with her mass of dark curls tied back only with a bright-red ribbon, she looked so like her gipsy ancestors.

'Good evening, Mr and Mrs Westbrook.' She smiled with her easy charm as she came up to them. 'Sarah, Becky. Come to enjoy yourselves? Oh, you know Robin, don't you?'

Isaac inclined his head towards the young man standing quietly behind her. He was slightly shorter than Hetty, at least he appeared so with his shoulders stooped forward. You could always tell a miner, Rebecca considered grimly. Their faces were so pale and their thin, emaciated bodies belied the strength of their wiry limbs. As if to confirm her thoughts, Robin turned his head away and put his hand to his mouth as he was overtaken by a deep, rumbling cough.

Rebecca saw her father wince, and her heart swelled with courage. Isaac was a sympathetic man. If only she could convince him of how desperate she was to marry Tom, even if it meant living humbly for some time, she was sure he'd look upon her favourably. And perhaps this evening would be her chance.

'Good evening, Hetty!' she beamed, and tilted her head gaily to give the impression she was totally at her ease. But inside her ribcage, her heart was thumping painfully as she stole a glance at her father. 'Is Tom coming tonight?' she asked innocently.

'Why, of course. He be just behind us, see?'

Rebecca's gaze moved towards the door, and at the sight of Tom, her pulse raced even faster. He was wearing his Sunday best, hardly the quality of attire her father wore for his everyday business, but neat and clean nonetheless. He had stopped to speak briefly with some friends, but when he glimpsed Rebecca and after only a second's hesitation, came directly towards her, she had to take a deep breath to quell her trembling. She watched as Tom politely greeted her parents. Isaac's face was expressionless, but her mother . . . yes, her mother was smiling warmly.

'Good evening, Miss Rebecca, Miss Sarah.' He scarcely looked at her, but she recognized his nervousness in an instant. He was as anxious as she was, but just as determined to prove himself to her father. 'Have you been here long, sir? Let me get you all a drink. No, no, sir.' He waved his hand as Isaac went to get up. 'You stay there. I'll get them.'

Rebecca heard her father catch his breath and his pondering gaze rested on her as he sat down again. She smiled wanly and was grateful when she was distracted by Sarah digging her in the ribs. Across the hall, his light hair shining out among the crowd, was Misha Kastryulyevich, resplendent in his smart officer's uniform. Sarah's eyes were as brilliant as stars as she sought her sister's reassurance, and Rebecca nodded in response. There was no doubt in her mind that Isaac would find Misha an acceptable suitor.

'There we are, sir, lemonade for the ladies and a glass of ale for yourself.' Rebecca blinked hard at the sound of Tom's familiar voice. She'd been so deep in thought that she hadn't noticed him weaving his hazardous way towards them with the tray of drinks, and now her heart stopped beating altogether for a few seconds as Tom said, 'I know you disapprove of me, sir, but may I dance with your daughter tonight?'

Rebecca was sure she was about to faint as her father's chest inflated with agonizing slowness and his eyes did not move from Tom's face. But then he raised his voice slightly to make himself heard above the general clamour. ''Tis not you personally I disapprove of, Tom, but your present financial circumstances. You know what I've said. Wait a few years until you can provide decently for her, and then if she still feels the same way . . .'

'But for tonight, Father?' Rebecca pleaded, her fine eyebrows knitted.

She watched as Isaac puffed out his cheeks and then sighed weightily. 'All right. But just for tonight, mind.'

Rebecca was on her feet in a trice, like a young bird about to relish the freedom of its first flight. 'Oh, thank you, Father!'

'Thank you, sir.'

'And me, too?' Sarah chirped eagerly.

'Well, yes, I suppose so, child, if someone . . .'

Before she knew it, Rebecca had been whisked on to the dance floor and in a moment she was galloping up and down the hall in time to the jocund music, passing hands, clapping as the top couple romped down the line of dancers, being twirled and swung by Tom while laughing faces and brightly coloured scarves and hair ribbons flashed across her vision, her ears deafened by the lively rhythms of the reels and jigs and the joyous cries of the revellers. Out of the corner of her eye she saw Sarah approach their parents with Misha by her side. He gave a sharp half bow and after a few minutes' conversation they were swirling about the hall, Misha looking a little bewildered, but obviously enjoying himself as he managed quite successfully to follow the paces of the others.

When she was quite out of breath and felt she couldn't possibly dance another step, Tom led Rebecca back to her seat. She was still laughing, looking up at his face and brimming over with happiness, so that it wasn't until they came right up to the table that she noticed the tall, smart figure deep in conversation with her parents. She felt her heart give a bound of anger, and she would have quickly drawn Tom away, but at that moment, Isaac lifted his eyes and met her dark gaze with a satisfied smile.

'Miss Rebecca, how delightful to see you again.' Adam Bradley was already on his feet.

Damn him! How dare he come to ruin her evening, as she was sure he would! 'What an un . . .' she began tersely. But why should she say something that wasn't true, just because it was an accepted expression! 'How unexpected to see you, Captain Bradley,' she rephrased her greeting. 'I hadn't noticed the *Emily* in port.'

'She isn't,' Adam agreed amiably. 'She's in Plymouth awaiting her cargo, so I thought I would take the opportunity to come to Morwellham for a few days. I shall return to Plymouth on the *Swallow* when she sails on Monday.'

'Oh,' was all Rebecca could reply. It was of no interest to her what Captain Bradley was doing there, except that he should not spoil her evening with Tom.

'Ah, the young man from the cooperage, I believe,' Adam proclaimed, and as he cordially held out his hand, Tom, in his surprise, felt obliged to shake it. 'I hope you will allow me to take your place for a short while, that is, if Mr Westbrook will permit me and if the young lady will do me the honour?'

'Of course, Captain Bradley. You will find my daughter dances quite prettily.'

Rebecca's sapphire eyes glared furiously at Adam Bradley as he took her gently by the elbow and propelled her into the fray. She wished she could slap that smug, handsome face, but as that was hardly practicable, she instead commented icily, 'I'm surprised to see a man of your standing

50

here, Captain. I should have thought this was all somewhat provincial for you, and that a society ball would have been more to your liking.'

She'd expected him to cower under her sarcastic rebuke, but instead he gave a soft laugh which, she noticed with displeasure, made him look more attractive than ever. 'Miss Westbrook, I have yet to attend a society ball that I actually enjoy, and I have to admit that I avoid them like the plague. This is far more pleasurable, especially as I am to dance with the most beautiful young lady here. That pretty gown quite becomes you. It is made of a fine quality cotton, if I am not mistaken.'

His eyes were glinting with mischief at the oblique reference to their argument on the evening they'd met, and Rebecca clamped her jaw with indignation. He had to remind her of it, didn't he? And as for calling her simple dress a gown, well . . . ! But she wouldn't let him think he could humiliate her so easily and stared back at him with challenging defiance.

But as it was a circle dance and they were able to join in immediately, there was no longer any opportunity for conversation and Rebecca kept her lips compressed. And when the dancers had to break the circle and spin around with their partner, she simply scowled when her eyes met Adam's. She could feel his grip on her, strong and firm, and she wanted to shrug off his hand. The instant the music came to a cacophonous halt, she didn't wait to clap, but turned at once towards her seat, leaving him to follow unceremoniously behind.

'I was sorry you were unwell and couldn't join us for dinner at the Ship,' she heard him say hurriedly from behind.

'What?' She turned her head and gazed directly at him, forgetting her manners entirely as she wondered what on earth he was talking about. And then, as she remembered the lie she'd told and the way he'd ruined her meeting with Tom, she could barely contain her loathing for him.

'Perhaps another time,' Adam suggested, but she noted with triumph the uncertainty in his voice as she glowered at him in silence. 'And now I must take my leave,' he announced with sudden awkwardness as they reached the table.

'But you've only been here five minutes,' Anne declared in surprise.

'Ah, but I have much to do, Mrs Westbrook, and as your daughter has made me realize,' and he glanced swiftly in Rebecca's direction, 'this is no place for a stranger.'

He bowed sharply and a moment later was disappearing out through the door. Rebecca stared after him, the anger seething in her throat.

'Rebecca?' Isaac frowned.

She felt colour rise in her cheeks. Captain Bradley would have known his words would get her into trouble. Oh . . . oh, how she hated him!

'I've no idea what he meant, I'm sure!' she protested, and then quickly changed the subject, praying fervently that Isaac wouldn't press her. 'Where's Tom?'

'Tom? Oh, he's dancing with Hetty,' Anne told her with a sympathetic smile. 'That poor lad of hers were puffing like a steam engine in no time.'

Yes, and he'll be down the mine again come Monday, Rebecca thought bitterly. With a chest like that, Robin would never make it to the altar. It was no wonder Hetty liked to enjoy herself as much as possible while she could, when her own laborious job of picking out the copper ore from the wet stones allowed. And that's what she herself would do tonight, enjoy herself, now that wretched Captain Bradley had left. And enjoy herself she did, particularly since by the end of the evening, her father was talking quite civilly, even joking, with Tom, and she had arranged to meet him secretly in the woods again the following night.

* * *

Isaac Westbrook was making his Monday morning inspection of the port, but for once in his life his mind was not entirely upon his work. It seemed that both his daughters had found a match for themselves without his having to interfere. The young Russian appeared respectable enough, although he would try to make enquiries into his background if at all possible. As for Rebecca, well, she had her heart set on Tom and he was a good lad, when all was said and done. Not that Isaac would go back on his decision to forbid their marriage until they could properly afford it, but perhaps he would allow them to court openly now. He would discuss the matter with Anne tonight.

'Ah, Mr Westbrook! I . . . er . . . I was wondering if I might have a word with you. On a private matter.'

Isaac looked up sharply. 'Captain Bradley! You sail this morning, do you not?'

'We do, sir. The tide's on the turn, so we'll be away before too long. But there's no need to tell you that.'

'Of course,' Isaac smiled. 'But this private word?'

'Er, yes.' Isaac watched, a little perplexed, as the captain joined his hands and quite unconsciously entwined his fingers in agitation. He had always seemed so confident, never brash but certainly firm, in his business dealings, that this sudden nervousness took Isaac by surprise. 'I . . . er . . . I know this might seem, well . . . I mean, I've only known the young lady for so short a time, but . . . er . . . well, sir . . . I should like your permission to court your elder daughter.'

Isaac's eyes grew wide as he saw Adam Bradley bite his bottom lip apprehensively. Good Lord! This attractive, generous and well set-up man was almost begging him to permit his attentions towards Rebecca. Up until a few days ago, it had been exactly what Isaac had hoped for, but now he was so taken aback that for a moment he could find no words with which to reply, and taking his silence as a refusal, Adam's anguish visibly increased.

'I . . . I do hope you would not consider the age difference between us too great, sir,' he stammered desperately. 'Miss Rebecca is . . .'

'Twenty in December,' Isaac replied guardedly. 'And yourself?'

'I am just turned thirty, sir. But it means I am well established and could provide well for her. And, I mean, I wouldn't wish to rush the young lady. She . . . she may not find she cares for me at once, but . . . but I knew the moment I saw her that I wanted to marry her. And I shall be away about ten weeks and I simply could not wait that long to seek your permission.'

Isaac pursed his lips as he contemplated Adam's earnest expression. In his eyes the young captain would make a perfect match, steady, amicable, and handsome enough to sweep any girl off her feet. Except Rebecca. Isaac sighed with resignation.

'For myself, Captain, I could not imagine a better suitor for Rebecca,' he said slowly. 'But I'm afraid she is already spoken for.'

'What!' Isaac saw Adam's face blanch like snow. There was no mistaking genuine shock, and several seconds passed before he recovered himself. 'Oh . . . er . . . I had no idea,' he stuttered.

'You weren't to know,' Isaac sympathized. 'But I do thank you for such an honour, and I shall convey your compliments to my daughter.'

'No!' Adam protested, and a bright spot of scarlet appeared on each of his pale cheeks. 'I should not wish her to be embarrassed by the knowledge of my . . . my affection for her. In fact, I should be grateful if you could forget this conversation altogether. I have rented Lavender Cottage for six months, but although I now have business interests in Morwellham, there is no need for me to take up residence here. So I shall not renew the lease, for it would be unfair of me to inconvenience you by my presence now that I have made my feelings known.'

'There's no need for that . . .'

'I believe there is. Not least from my own point of view. And now I have things to do, so you must excuse me, Mr Westbrook. And I apologize for wasting your time.'

He spun on his heel and, springing across the gangway, disappeared below deck and into his cabin. He lowered himself on to the bunk and dropped his head into his hands.

All he could see behind his tightly shut eyes was the ethe-real vision of the beautiful girl in the pure, simple dress, her brown hair floating in cascades about her shoulders, and her deep blue eyes and pretty mouth smiling up at him as his hands closed about her tiny waist. The pain that burned into his throat was unbearable. He had come to Morwellham to escape the torment that had gripped him since his father's death, only to find himself racked by a torture far greater than anything he could ever have imagined . . .

* * *

'He did what!'

'Well, as soon as I told him your feelings lay elsewhere, he asked me not to tell you of his request so as not to upset you, but I really thought you should know. Think on it, Becky. Men like Adam Bradley don't come along every day. At least agree to get to know him better.'

'Know him!' Rebecca's eyes were almost on fire with anger.

'Aye.' Isaac spoke with authority now. 'He's a shrewd businessman, but 'tis not only that he could offer you secu-rity. He's most considerate to the men he employs, he's cour-teous, good-looking—'

'Conceited, arrogant, always mocking . . .'

'Becky, he's none of those things!' Isaac reprimanded, his own temper beginning to flare. 'He simply has the man-ners of someone brought up, I hate to admit it, but in a class far above ourselves. Becky, he's doing you quite some honour, you know.'

But Rebecca's face was enraged with fury. 'He has an answer for everything, you mean!'

'That shows he has a quick wit.'

'And he's old!'

'Old! He's just thirty! I don't consider myself old, and I'm twenty years his senior. Oh, Becky, think about it,' Isaac begged.

'I don't need to think about it! I shall marry Tom or no one!'

Isaac stared at his daughter. She was beautiful enough to capture any poor man's heart, and yet she had a will of iron. Was that what Adam Bradley had recognized and been enraptured by? For she had certainly not shown herself meek and submissive in his presence! What a terrible shame. They would have made such a handsome pair.

Isaac sighed deeply. 'Well, since you seem so set on young Tom, he may begin to court you. But, although I'll give you a generous dowry, there'll be no wedding until I'm satisfied he can provide a fitting home for you.'

Rebecca caught her breath as her heart stood still with joy.

CHAPTER SIX

The two girls looked up at the timid rap on the front door. Both their parents were out, and they knew that Mrs Payne was up to her elbows in flour in the kitchen. So Rebecca rose to her feet, placing the book she'd been reading on the parlour table.

'I'll go,' she said disinterestedly. ''Twill probably be someone with a message for Father.'

She walked out of the room which had been dark and depressing that afternoon because of the low, grey clouds outside and the summer rain that had fallen in heavy bursts all day long. But as she opened the front door, a gasp of delight escaped her lips.

'Hetty! What are you doing here? Shouldn't you be at work at the mine? Oh, do come in out of the rain!'

She stood aside as the tall, dark girl stepped across the threshold and slid the wet shawl from about her head. 'Your father's not here, is he?' she asked cautiously.

'No,' Rebecca assured her with a smile. 'But he wouldn't bite if he were, you know.'

'Aye, I knows.' Hetty's red mouth twisted. 'But he always makes me feel nervous.'

'I don't know why, especially now he's let Tom and I start courting!' Rebecca reminded her as her heart gave a little bound.

'Aye, that be good news,' Hetty grinned. 'And I've some good news, too, which is why I came straight here. I wants you and Sarah to be the first to know.'

'Well, you'd better come into the parlour, then.' She opened the door and watched as Hetty's eyes moved swiftly over the well-furnished room she had never seen before. It was certainly nothing like the spartan tenement she shared with her family!

'Hetty!' Sarah stood up as soon as she saw her sister's friend.

'Hetty has some news for us,' Rebecca announced mysteriously, 'but I can't think what it can be.'

'Well, I'll tell you then!' Hetty's eyes radiated with happiness. 'You knows the duke arrives at the weekend with a shooting party?'

'Yes, we do!' Rebecca groaned. 'Father has to arrange everything for the docking, and it makes so much extra work for him. A lot of pretentious nonsense, all this ceremony, if you ask me!'

'But the duke do own Morwellham! Heaven knows where we'd all be without him! I knows I'd still be hammering stones at the mine . . .'

'Hetty?'

'Aye!' she suddenly burst out. 'I hears they wants more staff at the House, so I goes along this afternoon and they takes me on! Only as a laundry maid, but at least I'll be indoors and the water'll be hot instead of cold like on the dressing floor!'

'Oh, that's wonderful, Hetty!' Rebecca cried. 'But won't you lose your job at the mine? I mean, when the season's over . . .'

'No, 'tis to be permanent. You knows they keep the House open all year with a skeleton staff, well, I'll be one of them. Of course, the wages are even lower,' she grimaced slightly, 'so I won't be able to give my mother so much as now, but then as it's live-in, she won't have to feed me no more. And as I gets promoted, I'll be able to bring more money home. I wants the boys to do an apprenticeship, see, just like Tom did. I don't wants them ending up down the mine. Like our father, and poor Robin.'

Rebecca bit her lip as a shadow darkened her thoughts. Tom had vowed to keep his younger brothers from working down the mine, but how could he if he was trying to save for his future life with her? As it was, the boys often went to work on the dressing floor instead of going to school. Oh, they would never be married, not while her father insisted on Tom providing a fancy home for her first!

'How is Robin?' she asked quietly.

Hetty shrugged. 'Not good. The mine's slowly killing him. Like so many others.'

'Can't he get a job on a farm, then?' Sarah suggested innocently.

Hetty blew out sharply through her nostrils. 'Only in the summer, and only if he don't mind earning half what he gets now. He be a skilled miner, you see. Working the lodes since he were fourteen. Still, maybe if I gets on well at Endsleigh, I'll be able to get him a job there, and all. Anyway,' her face brightened, 'I must go and gather my things together for my new life! Six o'clock tomorrow morning I've to be there.'

'Oh, let me come and help you!' Rebecca offered eagerly.

'I hardly needs help to pack the few bits I do have!' Hetty chuckled. 'Besides, 'tis pouring, and I thought your parents had forbidden you to enter the tenements, and rightly so! 'Tis no place for people like you. I knows my mother do keep our rooms spotless, but others be not fit for pigs. And there's a sickness been brought in by a sailor who lodges there on occasion. Right ill, he's been, and passed it on to a couple of children.'

'I'm certainly glad Misha will never have to stay there,' Sarah agreed. 'Or in a lodging house anywhere, for that matter. Captain Bradley's asked him to stay on board whenever the *Swallow*'s in port, like he were master.'

'Only because he wants someone to keep an eye on his ship!' Rebecca scoffed as a flush of anger bubbled up inside her at his name.

'Oh, Captain Bradley's a good man, I've heard tell,' Hetty replied. 'He really seems to care for his men. Better to work for than Joshua Farthingay, they say.'

'And I wonder how long that'll last! Just trying to make a good impression, like he did with Father! Do you know, Hetty, he had the audacity to ask permission to court me?'

'What!' Hetty's jaw fell open but, almost instantly, she threw up her head with a throaty laugh. 'After you'd been giving him the cold shoulder? My, he must be smitten with you, maid!'

'Well, all I can say is, thank goodness he's gone away on a long voyage and won't be back for some considerable time!'

* * *

They strolled leisurely back down the hill from the canal, Tom in the middle and Rebecca and Sarah on either side. Anne and Isaac walked some yards ahead, arm in arm, talking in low voices and Anne's sparkling laugh mingling occasionally with her husband's deeper chuckle.

'Quite the lovebirds, your parents,' Tom observed in a kindly whisper.

'Hmm, they are, aren't they?' Rebecca smiled affectionately, her eyes twinkling as she looked up at him. 'Do you think we'll be like that when we're their age?'

'I sincerely hope so,' Tom grinned at her, his strong white teeth gleaming like a crescent moon in his dark face.

Rebecca sighed with contentment. She was happy, for the moment anyway. It was Sunday. Her father had been bustling to and fro all morning with a worried frown on his face and an uncharacteristic short temper, making sure everything was perfect for the Duke of Bedford's arrival on the noon tide, which of course, being Isaac, it was. No ship was allowed to mar the progress of the duke's vessel, the quayside had been swept and was completely clear for the splendid carriage, and the dockworkers who were to see the visitors safely berthed had been inspected for cleanliness and neatness of attire. Anne had arranged for streamers of fluttering ribbons to decorate the dockside, and the inhabitants of the entire port had turned out to greet their benefactor. It wasn't quite as it had been for Queen Victoria's visit in 1856, but Isaac was well satisfied as he stood among those who officially welcomed the old duke to his country residence.

But now it was all over, and after Sunday dinner, to which Tom had been cordially invited, the family had decided to take an excursion up to the Tavistock canal. Even though the waterway was as familiar to Rebecca as the back of her hand, she always found it impressive, and she always felt compelled to spare a thought for the labourers who'd constructed it at the beginning of the century. Since its completion, it had been the principal route for conveying the thousands of tons of copper ore from the Dartmoor mines to Morwellham's busy quays, but since the coming of the railway, it had been used less and less. Now, being a Sunday afternoon, it made a pleasant spot to take a stroll.

'I wonder how Hetty's getting on,' Rebecca mused aloud.

'Well, we'll hear all about it afore too long,' Tom told her. 'She's to have one afternoon off a fortnight while the duke's there, but when there's no visitors, 'tis all a deal more lenient, they said.'

'She won't see much of Robin, then.'

'More than I'll see of Misha,' Sarah moaned. 'Three or four weeks 'twill be before he's back.'

'Oh, poor Sarah!' Rebecca reached across Tom and squeezed her sister's arm. 'Still, if Captain Bradley had taken him on his precious *Emily*, 'twould have been at least ten weeks this time, and sometimes even longer. Mind you, he'd have been on a wonderful ship!' she grinned with mockery. '"Do you not think the *Emily* a fine vessel, Miss Rebecca?"' she mimicked in as near to an upper-class London accent as she could manage.

At once, all three fell about laughing, and Isaac and Anne turned and waited patiently for the youthful trio to catch them up.

'You three look happy,' Anne beamed.

'Aye, it's been a nice afternoon.' Isaac smiled with relaxed abandon. 'If I can leave the port long enough next Sunday and the weather's good, shall we take the pleasure steamer down the river? Take a picnic? Would you be free, Tom?'

Rebecca felt she would explode with jubilation. Her father seemed to have accepted Tom at long last, and she could see their future stretching ahead in peaceful bliss. But how long would it be before they could marry? Should they continue with their midnight trysts, or should she be content to enjoy Tom's company at every available moment in public? They hadn't made love in the woods since the night before Isaac had told her of Captain Bradley's bold approach. But now they had tasted that secret intimacy that was giving Rebecca increased pleasure with each occasion, could they live without it? But what if they were discovered? She would have to think long and hard about it, for one thing was certain — she didn't want to lose the love and respect of her family at any cost.

* * *

'Tom's late,' Anne observed as she put the last of the food into the wicker basket.

'Oh, I expect he'll be along any minute,' Rebecca called over her shoulder as she adjusted her bonnet in the mirror. 'He'll have had some chores to do for his mother, and they don't possess a clock. Father's not back yet anyway.'

She hummed to herself as she sauntered across the kitchen. The cheese was still on the table and she cut herself a small cube and popped it into her mouth beneath Mrs Payne's admonishing chuckle. And when there was a loud knock on the front door, she ran to it quickly with her hand over her mouth as she tried desperately to swallow the now offending morsel.

She opened the door, and her eyes dropped in disappointed surprise to see not Tom, but one of his small brothers standing there.

'Good day, Matt,' she frowned. 'What are you doing here?'

'Tom's not coming,' the child said bluntly.

'What?' Rebecca felt her heart sink. 'What do you mean?'

'He's not been feeling well the last few days and he's gone to bed.'

'Oh, dear, poor Tom,' Anne sympathized, coming up behind her daughter. 'Well, I expect he'll feel better in a day or two.'

'What's that?' Isaac demanded as he entered the front courtyard.

'Tom's not well,' Anne answered.

'Oh.' Isaac glanced at his wife and then at his daughter whose cheeks had been glowing ever since he'd given his approval to Tom's courting her. 'I'd heard there'd been some sickness in the tenements,' he said, 'brought in by a seaman, I believe.'

Rebecca's chest had tightened and her limbs felt peculiar, as if they were made of lead. 'What . . . what sort of sickness?' she croaked.

'Oh, some sort of stomach upset,' Isaac shrugged. 'Fellow's gone back to sea now. But that sort of thing spreads like wildfire in the conditions people live in in those kinds of places. So perhaps you can understand now why I won't let you marry Tom until he can afford a decent home for you. Now, come along, child.' He fondly rubbed his hand on her shoulder, his tone changing completely. 'We've a nice picnic to go on! I must say I'm enjoying these outings. It's making me feel quite young again!' And he looked at his wife with a mischievous gleam in his eye.

He didn't hear Rebecca's whimpering sigh. She supposed Tom would be better in a few days, but how could her father expect her to enjoy herself knowing her lover was lying sick in his bed?

CHAPTER SEVEN

There was such a spring in Rebecca's step that she almost skipped the few yards to the cooperage. It was Wednesday morning, and a dull, overcast sky and a faint sharpness in the air served as a reminder that August was nearly over with autumn soon on its tail. Anxious to please her parents, she had dutifully kept away from the tenements, but she was sure Tom would be better today and back at his work.

She entered the cooperage with a light heart and her nostrils flared pleasantly at the strong scent of sawn wood, but her expectant eyes counted only four workers, and Tom was not among them. Ned Gimlett was busily hammering the trussing hoop over the staves of a cask in the early stages of its construction, and he straightened up when he saw her.

'Good day, Miss Rebecca,' he greeted her. 'I'm afraid if you're looking for Tom, he's not here. Still sick, I suppose.'

'What?' Rebecca's young brow creased into a frown and a tremor shivered through her body. The workshop suddenly seemed cold and echoing, like an empty house. 'Thank you, Mr Gimlett,' she murmured distractedly as she turned away, and the older man nodded gravely.

Still sick? Oh, he couldn't be. She stood outside the cooperage with her bottom lip drawn in tightly under her teeth. She could walk up to the mine to ask Hetty, but Hetty wasn't there anymore, was she? But what of the little boys? Would they be working on the dressing floor, and would she get any sense out of them anyway?

Her feet took her past the manganese mill, and then they came to a halt as she gazed across at the unfriendly walls of the tenements. A sense of dread set her stomach churning. The extensive building, once the port's malthouse, had been hastily converted to accommodate those who had flocked to the quays for work when the copper trade had been at its height. But little thought had gone into the conditions or sanitation for those who would actually have to live there, and the one official who had wanted to create less crowded dwellings had apparently been overruled. And now the malting seemed to eye Rebecca with the same hostility as a workhouse.

She shuddered, and her pulse began to race. She had been forbidden, but within those heartless walls, Tom lay ill. She only wanted to satisfy herself, and then she would come away. But she couldn't rest until she knew he was at least on the mend.

The main door to the building hung wide open, tied back permanently with a length of now fraying string because one of the rusty hinges had broken. Tom had offered to mend it if the landlords provided a new hinge, but so far it had not been forthcoming. But if they were not concerned over the few earth closets shared by innumerable families, and the fact that there was one standpipe between them — and that right next to the foul privies — they were hardly likely to bother about a door that didn't shut.

Rebecca cautiously crossed the threshold, her eyes sweeping nervously over the interior walls of the building. The stones had once been coated with limewash, but now it was a dirty grey and peeling away in tiny flakes, and dampness was visibly seeping up from the ground. The whole place reeked of the acrid mustiness of decay, and Rebecca was sure she could make out the smell of stale urine. Surely Tom and Hetty didn't live among such squalor? A squeal escaped her lips as something scurried along the wall right next to her and a long brown tail disappeared down into some hidey-hole. A battered door creaked open and two small children, one of them barely able to totter on its bandy legs, sidled past her, struggling with an empty bucket. She was used to seeing children coming home understandably dirty from working at the mine, but these little creatures were no more than babies, and they were filthy. The rags they wore looked as if they had never been off their backs, and the younger one's lower garments were stained dark yellow.

Rebecca held her breath, her body taut, as her eyes moved with morbid curiosity towards the open door. The room beyond was such a jumble that she could hardly make it out — a broken shoe, a ripped rag doll, a tattered shawl, two mangy kittens and a blackened kettle on its side littered the muddy floor. The remains of several meals were providing a tasty morsel for two house-mice on the table, and washing, still grey and pungent, was hanging from a rope tied between two chairbacks.

'What do 'ee be gawping at?' Rebecca nearly jumped sky-high at the voice of the woman peering at her from a chair in the corner. ''Ee be Isaac Westbrook's cheel, bain't 'ee? Well, 'ave 'ee seen enough yet?' And she glanced down with irritation at the tiny infant, wrapped in a dirty shawl, that was suckling from her voluminous, blue-veined breast.

Rebecca gulped down her shock, backing away until her spine came up against the cold, damp wall. She gasped, and then fled up the creaking, wooden stairs. She knew that Tom and his family occupied a tenement on the first floor. She stopped on the small landing, taking in several shaky breaths and straightening the front of her jacket. Was this really where Tom lived? It couldn't be! Perhaps her father was . . . No! She threw the hateful thought out of her head, refusing to allow the slightest doubt . . .

She was faced with three doors. Hetty had waved to her often enough from the window, so it only took a moment to work out which one she should knock at.

'Aye, 'tis open.'

Mrs Mason's familiar voice, but sounding oddly feeble, reached her ears in a thin trail. She pushed open the door, and her hand went over her mouth at the rancid air that stung her nostrils and made her stomach want to heave. She swallowed down the nausea and stepped inside, her quick eye taking in every detail. Unlike the tenement below, the room was quite tidy and looked as if it were regularly cleaned, but at that moment the fetid stench of vomit made it seem like a filthy, stinking slum. On the floor in the corner was a mattress with what appeared to be a heap of blankets piled upon it, and Mrs Mason, thinner and more haggard than ever, and with her jet-black hair falling about her face in greasy curls, was rocking herself in the one easy chair they possessed.

'Oh, Miss Westbrook! 'Ee shouldn't be yere!' she grated, and when a faint moan turned Rebecca's head, she added, 'I thinks the poor lad's been sick again, but I cas'n clear it up! My head's fit to burst, and every bone in my body aches.'

Rebecca stared at her, numbed, and then her eyes moved slowly and unbelieving towards the mattress. Her limbs froze rigid, and she had to force them to take her across the wooden floor where they finally buckled. She sank to her knees, for half-hidden among the tousled blankets was Tom's dark, beloved head.

She didn't know how many moments passed before she found the courage to reach out her hand, and then it seemed to move with a will all of its own. There was a strangeness about her, as if in a dream. So unreal. Not true. But it was Tom, with vomit on the blankets all around him, and a green liquid drying where it had trickled down from his mouth. Those tender lips that had kissed her so rapturously . . .

She carefully drew back the soiled blankets that smothered his face, her distaste fleeing before the terror of what she had found. She instinctively laid her hand across his forehead and her fingers met with a dry, searing heat. She drew away in fright as Tom groaned pitifully and half opened his eyes.

'Becky! Get away!' he muttered in a scarcely audible whisper. 'Get out of here!'

But the effort of speech was exhausting, and his head rolled to the side again. Rebecca stared at him, a chilling ache gripping her stomach. And then Tom's low mutterings penetrated her shock.

'Water?' she mumbled. 'Yes. Yes, of course.'

She looked quickly about the room and her eyes spied an enamel jug and mugs on the table. She poured out some of the liquid. It wasn't fresh and cool, but she was at a loss as to what to do, her brain still not functioning. So she knelt at Tom's side and lifted his head so that he could drink, but although he drew voraciously on the water, he had difficulty in swallowing it, and a little rivulet dribbled down his chin.

'My mouth be so sore,' he struggled to apologize, and then broke out in a terrible, rattling cough that set fear running down Rebecca's back.

''Twill be all right, my love,' she crooned, stroking the hair from his scorching brow. 'I'll take care of you.'

'Becky, no!' he breathed, and then let out a stifled cry and drew up his knees, his face twisting in pain.

Rebecca felt as if her heart had been wrenched from her chest, and she fought to draw a breath. She patted his shoulder. Unsure. Petrified.

'I'll have to leave you for a few minutes, Tom,' she told him, 'but I'll be back.' She rose unsteadily and turned to his mother, herself collapsed in the chair. 'He needs a doctor,' her voice trembled. 'And so will you if you're going the same way.'

'We don't have no money for a doctor,' Mrs Mason replied, and it struck Rebecca that the woman was totally bereft of her usual admirable spirit.

'Don't you concern yourself with that. I'll be back soon.'

And suddenly she found her feet. She flew down the stairs and out into the fresh air, then fled through the village so that those who saw her stopped to stare. Isaac Westbrook's daughter racing along as if the devil himself were after her. When she reached Copper Ore Cottage, she flung open the door so that her mother hardly had time to glance up in surprise.

''Tis Tom!' she squealed in panting gasps, unshed tears clawing at the back of her eyes. 'He's really sick, Mother! He needs a doctor, but they can't afford it! I think . . . I think 'tis cholera!'

Anne Westbrook's chin dropped open and her face turned grey as she remembered the outbreak of the terrible disease the previous year. It had engulfed London and other parts of the country but had mercifully bypassed the little port. But it wouldn't be the first time the pestilence had been introduced somewhere by a visiting seaman.

'Are you sure 'tis . . . 'tis . . .' she stammered.

'No! I'm not a physician, am I?' Rebecca snapped. 'But he's really bad, in a fever and vomiting with awful pains . . .'

'I'll send for Dr Seaton. One of Ann Richards's stable boys'll go.' She came forward, grasping her bonnet from the hook. 'Now you stay here and scrub your hands with carbolic soap.'

Rebecca stared at her, desperation strangling her throat. 'No! I can't just sit here and do nothing! Mrs Mason's ill, too, and can't look after him.'

Anne gazed at her daughter's agonized expression, and realized that in those last few minutes, the child had become a woman. And besides, she knew Rebecca well enough to realize there would be no restraining her. 'All right,' she nodded emphatically. 'But don't eat or drink anything there, and keep your hands away from your face. Boil all the water for them to drink, and keep scrubbing your hands with carbolic. I think they say 'tis spread by infected water and not washing your hands properly after touching . . . well, after caring for someone who has it. So!' Her eyes bore into her daughter's. 'Promise me you'll do all that. If 'tis cholera, then 'tis your own life you'll be risking.'

Rebecca met her gaze. She didn't need to be told how serious it was. She suddenly felt sober — the panic fled, and in its place, a stone-cold heaviness. There was no need to answer, and mother and daughter ran in silence, sharing the dark secret, up through the port, Rebecca veering off into the maltings again, while Anne hurried on up to the Ship Inn from where she knew one of Ann Richards's stable lads would ride like the wind over the hill to Tavistock.

This time the dilapidated building held no fear for Rebecca, just a deep and hostile reality. She found Tom and his mother just as she'd left them, and the first thing she did was to throw open the window to freshen the putrid air. Then she dropped on her knees by Tom's side again. His eyes were closed, his limbs thrashing weakly as he sank deeper into the fever. Rebecca bit down hard on her lip. Tom was moaning, his head back and his breathing laboured in his suffering. But she mustn't succumb to the numbing despair that threatened to paralyze her. Tom needed her help.

She pulled off her jacket and rolled up her sleeves. The tenement was one of the better ones and had a small range. The fire was out, but there were two full scuttles of coal, and Mrs Mason told her where she could find all she needed. She soon had a blaze crackling away in the fire box, and she thanked God for the domestic skills she had learned under her mother's eye. The water bucket was empty so she went down to refill it, retching at the stench from the adjacent closets. Back in the room, she poured some water into the kettle and after it had boiled, put some aside to cool for Tom, and made Mrs Mason a cup of tea. Then she braced herself to strip Tom's bed. She piled the bedding in a corner, turning the soiled sides inwards. But if she washed them, where should she pour the foul water? Even in her own home, the water-sluice in the wash house joined a leat that ran out into the dock. Sanitary enough under normal circumstances, but with this . . .

She managed to put clean sheets on the mattress, for Tom was still semi-conscious and able to move a little for her. But his stomach was causing excruciating pain and every limb was throbbing. His harrowing groans seemed to pierce Rebecca's breast. She peeled off his nightshirt, moving him as gently as she could. She scarcely noticed the odour from his unwashed flesh as she set about the task of bathing the adored body she'd never seen unclothed before. But this was no time for thoughts of what they'd been up to during their illicit meetings in the woods. This was Tom, and he was seriously ill, and when she found two outcrops of rose-coloured rash among the dark, swirling hairs on his chest, her pulse began to race even faster. Forcing back her own terror, she made him as comfortable as she knew how, and then helped him to take down some sips of water. His bloodshot eyes opened fully and his gaze riveted on her anguished face.

'I love you, Becky,' he croaked in an agonized whisper, and as his eyes closed again and his head sank back into the crook of her arm, a single tear slipped over her lower eyelid and meandered, slowly and despairingly, down her cheek.

'Becky?'

She turned her head at the low, tentative voice. Anne Westbrook was standing nervously by the door. Rebecca slid her arm from beneath Tom's head and went to get up, but her mother was already by her side.

'Oh, poor lamb!' she breathed, gazing down at Tom's restless, prostrate figure.

Rebecca sniffed hard and swallowed. 'I've cleaned him up a bit,' she said limply. 'And there's Mrs Mason,' she nodded over her shoulder. 'She's going down fast.'

'I'll get her into bed. You stay with Tom. I've sent for the doctor. He should be here before too long.'

Rebecca looked up and their eyes met. 'Thank you, Mother.' But the expression on her face said more than any words.

A grim, fleeting smile crossed Anne's lips, and then she winced as Tom coughed horrendously. 'I sent someone to find your father. He had to know.'

Rebecca nodded. This was no trivial stomach upset. It could involve the public health authorities. It could be the start of something terrible. If it was cholera . . .

She shook her head as a shiver of dread turned her blood to ice, but it was a relief to have her mother there to share the awesome fear, even if they both somehow felt too afraid to speak.

By the time the physician arrived, Tom had been sick again, but this time Rebecca had a bowl at the ready. But the retching had caused him so much pain, he was almost crying like a child.

'Hmm.' Dr Seaton rubbed his chin as he glanced into the bowl. 'Now, let me have a good look at you, young man.'

Rebecca stood back, hardly daring to breathe, as he gave Tom a thorough examination. He frowned at the pink rash, touched it gently and watched as it reappeared. And when Tom cried out as the doctor felt over his stomach, a knot of anguish twisted in Rebecca's gullet.

'How long has he been like this?' Dr Seaton questioned her.

'I . . . I don't really know,' Rebecca forced the sounds from her dry mouth. 'He felt unwell last week, and took to his bed on Sunday, but 'tis all I know.'

'Well, it isn't cholera,' the doctor pronounced gravely. 'But it is a classic case of enteric fever. Or typhoid some people call it. Not necessarily fatal.'

'And . . . and Tom?' Rebecca choked.

The doctor rose to his feet and quietly took her by the elbow. 'He has complications. Lung congestion, and it looks like peritonitis. Does he have diarrhoea?'

She nodded and glanced at her mother. She felt cold and numbed, as if someone else had answered the question. 'But . . . but he's young and strong . . .'

'I'll leave some of this. Shake it well and give him an ounce every three hours. It'll ease the pain and help prevent the vomiting and diarrhoea, and generally make him feel more comfortable. Expect delirium at night. Bathe him to keep down the fever, and when he is lucid, feed him boiled milk with a little brandy, egg custards, beef tea, that sort of thing, to keep up his strength. But I can't promise . . .'

'Becky! Anne! What in the name of God are you doing here?'

Rebecca jerked up her bowed head as Isaac burst into the room, his face suffused with agitation. But Dr Seaton went calmly forward to meet him.

'There's no need to be alarmed, Mr Westbrook. Your wife and daughter are as safe here as anywhere, provided they follow a few simple rules. Boil all the water for about five minutes, particularly for drinking, and scrub your hands with carbolic every time you touch him. But this is indeed a serious matter. Are there any others sick in the family?'

'The mother's in bed in the other room,' Anne replied, 'but she's not so bad. And there's three young boys, at work at the mine, I expect. And an elder daughter who works at Endsleigh.'

'Then I must see them also. This could turn into an epidemic if the proper precautions aren't taken. And it would be useful to know how the disease was introduced here.'

'They said there were a sailor quite sick in the building for a few weeks.' Rebecca was surprised to hear her own voice. 'Only he got better. And some children, too.'

'That's probably the answer. We can't be absolutely sure, but it's commonly believed the disease is passed on through the excretions of an infected person, and unfortunately it isn't always enough to wash one's hands properly after using the lavatory, particularly communal ones, as I imagine they are here. If leaking effluent from an insanitary privy seeps in through a cracked underground pipe, it can contaminate the entire water supply.'

'Good God!'

'Quite so. Which is why all the water must be boiled properly, even for washing the hands. Now tell me, who owns this building?'

'The duke,' Isaac answered. 'But 'tis leased out and then sublet.'

'No use talking to the lessees,' the doctor snorted. 'I'll go and speak to his Grace. I believe he is in residence at the moment. The exact source must be traced before we have a major outbreak on our hands. Hopefully, it's only the water supply to this building that's affected, but in the meantime, we need to alert the whole port. I'll take a look at the mother first, and I'll come back after I've seen the duke. This could be a very sorry business indeed.'

He went through into the other room, and Rebecca took up her post kneeling beside Tom. His eyes were closed, his skin flushed and his mouth compressed in a grimace. Rebecca felt a heaviness dragging down inside her, and tears stung her eyes again.

Anne's hand on her shoulder startled her. 'Let's give him this medicine,' she said softly. 'And don't worry. Dr Seaton's good at his job. He's forgotten more than most doctors ever know.' But as she glanced down at the already emaciated figure, she wished she felt as confident as she sounded.

* * *

Anne looked up from straining yet another egg custard. Rebecca was fast asleep just where she'd sat down, her head resting on her arms which were folded on the kitchen table. For nearly two weeks she'd scarcely left Tom's side, her heart growing ever more weary as he seemed to make no progress, despite her constant care. That afternoon he'd become quieter, and Hetty, given leave from the House, had sent her back to Copper Ore Cottage to rest. Anne hoped that the sharp knock on the door wouldn't wake her and crossed the room to answer it.

She stepped back with a little gasp as cold horror trickled down her spine. Hetty was half supporting herself on the doorpost, her chest quivering as she tried to draw breath between her trembling sobs. And Anne knew at once. And shuddered as she sensed Rebecca come up behind her.

''Tis Tom,' Hetty gulped, and her face crumpled so that she could say no more.

Rebecca's stomach cramped like a vice. She couldn't breathe. The world about her turned silent. Motionless. As if in a dream. A hot, burning sweat flushed through her veins, followed by the icy wave of ultimate terror. Her feet took her forward, went to break into a run. But Hetty's grip on her arm swung her round, and the raven-haired girl shook her head meaningfully, her own tear-ravaged face contorted with agony.

Rebecca stopped then, and stared. Transfixed. Suffocating as her chest refused to move. Then her lungs suddenly heaved, and such a savage wail of anguish screamed from her throat that the workers on the quayside stopped in their tracks . . .

CHAPTER EIGHT

Anne's eyes shifted anxiously across the table as Rebecca aimlessly turned over the food on her plate without a morsel of it ever reaching her mouth. It was six weeks now since Tom's tragic death and the girl hadn't eaten a decent meal yet. The skin had become taut over her cheekbones and her eyes had sunk into their darkened sockets. She'd grown so thin that Anne was beginning to fear for her daughter's health. The duke had paid out at once for repairs to the water supply at the malthouse tenements which had indeed been discovered to be at fault, and the outbreak had been quickly contained. But it would not bring Tom back, and Rebecca was inconsolable.

She rose from the table with a bound and disappeared out through the back door. Anne went to go after her, but Isaac placed a restraining hand on his wife's arm.

'Leave her be,' he said grimly, his thick grey eyebrows meeting. 'She needs to grieve alone. She knows we're here if she needs us.'

'But she's making herself ill,' Anne moaned in dismay. 'I've heard her being sick.'

'She'll get over it,' Isaac assured her, but in his heart, he wasn't so certain.

'I doubt it,' Anne sighed despairingly as she sat down again. 'She loved Tom so much. More than any of us knew.'

* * *

Rebecca ran up the steps from the sunken backyard and into the privy, her pulse racing sickeningly. She leaned over the hole in the wooden bench and retched, the strength of the spasms bringing tears to her eyes. But as had happened time and again over the last few weeks, she brought up nothing but a little bile.

When the painful heaving at last was over, she leaned her back against the wall and slithered, exhausted, to the ground, heedless of the state of her skirts. She dropped her head on her knees and let the silent tears wash down her weary cheeks. There were no sobs. Her body was too drained, too empty, for that. She sat without motion, without feeling almost. For all she knew now was a deep, bottomless void.

Dear God, she wished she were dead.

She saw him lying there again, his face like grey marble, lined but strangely peaceful after the long, horrific struggle. She had wanted to hold him one last time. To cradle the lifeless body against her breast, to stroke the jet-black curls she adored. Just one more time. But they had held her back from the contamination, and he had been quickly spirited away. No longer Tom. Just a carcass of rotting flesh. Man that is born of woman hath but a short time to live . . . But it wasn't his time. He was only twenty-two. Earth to earth, dust to dust. She had thrown the first handful of soil on to the coffin, together with a single red rose. The clods of dirt had landed with a dull thud.

But she hadn't been able to say goodbye.

In sure and certain hope of the Resurrection to eternal life. If only she could die. He would be waiting for her on the other side. But some cruel force was holding her back. The endless nights when she couldn't sleep, watching Sarah slumbering beside her, sometimes muttering Misha's name, for she never mentioned him to Rebecca during the day. But Rebecca would not have minded. Be happy for both of us, little sister. Never suffer what I am having to endure. So tired, and yet the blessed relief of sleep would not come. And the sight of food sickened her stomach. Surely she must die soon. Life had no more meaning for her. She wanted to leave her beloved Morwellham, her family, before anything else changed. She didn't want to remember her life as it was now, broken and wretched, with no Tom at the cooperage. There was nothing for her anymore, no hope, no existence. Just emptiness.

And yet . . . She had a duty now, didn't she? Something she had to do for Tom. In his memory. He would have wanted her to, wouldn't he? But for the moment she didn't really care very much for what she was sure was growing inside her. It was the second time she had missed. She had wanted to put it down to her grief, but there were other signs, too. Her breasts were swollen and sore, and this dreadful sickness. No. She must face up to it. She was carrying Tom's child.

It was all she had of him. She should love it, but she was too exhausted to feel anything at all. And what about the disgrace it would bring on her family? They'd been so good to her, always there, but never crowding in on her. Could she really do this to them, let them know how she'd been deceiving them? She had to do something, but she had no idea what.

She hauled herself to her feet and went back down to the wash house to rinse her hands. But she couldn't bear to go back inside and join her parents and Sarah at the dinner table. So she walked down the side of the cottage and towards the quayside, not choosing which way she went, but letting her feet take her wherever they pleased, as if in a trance. It didn't matter anyway. It was just one foot in front of the other. Another second of her life less to endure.

It was mid-October, but a pleasant sun-filled day, so she wasn't aware of being clad only in a lightweight day dress.

Labourers on the quayside looked up and shook their heads. They were used now to seeing Isaac Westbrook's poor daughter wandering up and down the port like a little ghost, bareheaded and her brown hair, once shining and glossy, hanging loose and lack-lustre down her back. A forlorn, desolate figure growing more wizened by the day, and surely heading for an asylum.

The sun was warm on her face, low in the sky and blinding her, reflecting on the water in dazzling spangles. The brilliant diamonds of light beckoned her, entrancing, magical, calling her to the tranquil days of her future life with Tom, stretching ahead like an endless plain. She could see his face, glowing with love, and showered with golden shafts of light. All she had to do was to keep walking towards him, the water would swallow her up, close over her head, and she would be reunited with him for ever . . .

'God Almighty, child! What the hell are you doing!'

The strong, shocked voice cut through her reverie like an executioner's axe, and a grip of steel on her arm jerked her to a standstill. She blinked slowly, as if waking from a deep sleep and, glancing down, noticed with curiosity that her feet were on the very edge of the wharf. One more step and she would have been in the river, dragged under by the turbulent water as the tide swept inwards against the strong downward current. In a few moments, it would have been over and better for everyone.

The hand on her arm drew her firmly away from the danger. She raised her eyes to see who had held her back from the fate she craved. She recognized the tall, broad-shouldered man at once, but she couldn't place him in her mind. For his mouth was not mocking her in the way she had expected. Rather, the handsome face was quite still, the fine brow gently furrowed, and something inside her lurched as she saw in his tired brown eyes an anguish as deep as her own.

It was those eyes that made her remember who he was, and her spine stiffened. And yet what did she care? What did she care about anything? She didn't even care that he had prevented her from drowning. It was all the same to her. She stared up at him, waiting for the tirade of humiliation, but he said nothing. And when she turned and walked away, he did not restrain her. He took a few worried steps after her, but reluctantly checked himself. And as she dragged her feet back towards the centre of the port, she felt his eyes upon her until she disappeared from view.

She didn't go straight home, however, but took the lane up towards the farm. It wasn't so quiet now, for near it ran the railway from Devon Great Consols powered by the steam engine at the top of the hill, and almost parallel to it the original inclined plane tracks stretched up to the canal. It was a relatively busy afternoon, but Rebecca scarcely noticed the activity. She weaved her way between the trees until she came to the natural arbour where she and Tom . . . Oh, Tom, Tom! Oh, my love, why aren't you here? I can feel you beside me. Oh, my sweet love . . . And she cried the tears she had not shed for some weeks, her head thrown back and her mouth wide in a hideous grimace of agony.

And as she wept, the sterility of her mind was washed away. And she knew what she must do.

* * *

'I wish to speak to you about my daughter,' Isaac announced gravely as Adam Bradley quietly closed the cabin door behind them.

'Miss Rebecca?' Isaac noticed the young captain's sudden agitation. 'Did she tell you what happened this afternoon? She nearly walked straight into the river, as if . . . as if she were sleep walking! And she looks dreadful. Has . . . has she been ill?'

Isaac looked at the genuine concern on Adam's face and took courage from it. He wasn't sure he liked what he was about to do, but he was sure that what everyone said about the newcomer was true, that he was a good, trustworthy man.

'You have only docked today, so you probably won't have heard,' Isaac began slowly. 'Soon after you sailed there were an outbreak of typhoid fever. 'Twere quickly contained, but Rebecca's young man . . . her betrothed . . . lost his life.'

Adam's jaw fell open with a gasp of horror. He met Isaac's gaze and then lowered his eyes, little by little. He turned his head away and muttered something terrible under his breath. Isaac didn't care for the oath, but it was breathed with such feeling that he realized Adam was deeply shocked.

'The child grieves terribly,' Isaac said miserably, becoming hot under the collar. 'But she knows that her own life must go on. She came to me this evening and said she had seen you. I'm afraid I had told her about your affection for her. I thought it only right she should know. But now she asks that, if your offer of marriage still stands, she would be pleased to accept.'

He had blurted out the words in a rush, and now he held his breath as he awaited Adam's reaction. The younger man's wide eyes opened even further, his tanned cheeks blanched and Isaac saw that although he tried to disguise it, he had started to tremble. He swung his head from side to side, opened his mouth several times, but couldn't find any words, and finally stammered, 'I . . . I don't understand.'

Isaac cleared his throat. 'Rebecca wishes to marry you. But straight away. Before she changes her mind. Of course,' he hesitated, 'if the offer no longer stands . . .'

'No . . . forgive me . . .' Adam ran his hand across his forehead and down over his mouth and chin. 'I'm just . . . It must be her grief speaking.' He shook his head, lifted his hands in a gesture of bewilderment. 'So soon after her bereavement . . . She hardly knows me. And I always gained the impression that she held me in contempt. The trauma must have . . .' He broke off and suddenly drew himself up to his full height as he met Isaac with a challenging gaze. 'I trust she is not being pressurized into this?'

Isaac blinked hard. He could have taken it as an insult, but he could see further than that. Adam Bradley wanted to protect Rebecca even if it meant accusing her own father. It was evidence enough for Isaac.

'You would be doing me a great honour, 'tis true,' he admitted. 'But when Rebecca came to me, she were more lucid than at any time since Tom's death. We were beginning to fear for her mind, but . . . She has suddenly come to life again. Her old fighting spirit seems to have returned. I believe she realizes a new future to look forward to is the only way she will recover.'

Adam swallowed hard and bit on his bottom lip, a not unattractive habit Isaac was beginning to recognize. 'My feelings for your daughter, sir, have not changed, and I would gladly marry her. But . . . I cannot believe she knows what she is doing.'

'Her proposal came as a surprise to me, too, Captain Bradley, but one thing you will learn about Rebecca is that she very definitely knows her own mind, and has done since the very day she were born.'

The hint of a wry smile flickered across Adam's features. 'I can imagine that. But do you think she may one day come to love me? I don't want her going from one disaster to another.'

'That I cannot answer,' Isaac told him honestly. 'She is a wilful child and needs careful handling. But she is not blind to virtue, and 'twill give her something to live for. Even if it means you will have a fight on your hands.'

'Then . . .' Adam shook his head with a soft, ironic laugh. 'God, I must be insane! But, yes! I will speak to her, and if it's really what she wants, I will marry her.'

* * *

Everyone thought what a strange wedding it was. Particularly the vicar of St Peter's at Gulworthy, the nearest Church of England to the busy port. He knew Isaac Westbrook and his family well. They regularly made the three-or-more-mile haul up the hill for Sunday worship, and wasn't that the only reason he had allowed the hurried marriage? He couldn't make it out. It couldn't be that the bride was carrying the groom's child. He had it on good authority that Captain Bradley had been away at sea for some time, and besides it was common knowledge that Rebecca Westbrook was crazily in love with the young man they had buried scarcely two months since, and at whose funeral the girl had been distraught. And hadn't he spied her almost every day setting fresh flowers, or ornamental foliage as autumn came upon them, on his grave? As she had come out of the church on her new husband's arm, she had glanced longingly across to her lover's final resting place. Then bride and groom had climbed up into the waiting trap. The driver remarked to his wife that evening that scarcely a word had passed between them as they descended the steep, winding lane between the high banks.

There was a dinner for the Westbrook family at the Ship Inn. As it was understood the captain had no kin, the only outsiders to join the table were Miss Sarah's Russian seaman, the sister of the bride's former betrothed, and the miner to whom she was promised. It was a sombre affair, and Ann Richards had the distinct impression that everyone was relieved when it was over.

The groom led his wife up the hill away from the village to the substantial cottage that was to be her future home. Mrs Blatchford, the housekeeper that Adam employed, greeted them with blazing fires in all the rooms, a pot of hot tea, and a cold spread arranged on the dining-room table, and then scurried home from the tense atmosphere. Adam tried to coax Rebecca into conversation, but she hardly looked at him, her gaze trained on the brilliant, vacillating flames in the grate. He eventually left her and went into the study to check over some new charts, and when he returned more than an hour later with a good measure of brandy and a mug of hot chocolate each, she drank hers down at once and announced she was going to bed.

Like all the rooms in the cottage, the main bedchamber was sparsely furnished, but there was a little posy of dried flowers on the bedside table, and Rebecca wondered vaguely who had put it there. Mrs Blatchford had arranged neatly on the dressing table the few personal effects she had sent up the previous day, a change of clothes hung in the wardrobe, and her nightdress lay folded on the pillow.

Captain Bradley must have been up to the room, for the fire showed evidence of having been recently tended and the coals glowed brightly. Oh, yes! He'd want it nice and warm, wouldn't he! she scoffed bitterly. Suddenly all the seething rancour returned to her heart. She'd tried to put it out of her mind, the wedding night. And all the other nights to follow. But now it was here, and as she undressed and let down her hair, her whole being began to quake with terror. She buttoned the nightdress up to her neck and got into bed, sitting with the pillows behind her back and her knees drawn up to her chin.

And waited.

In five, ten minutes, the man she loathed would have his hands all over her, taking her body and using her flesh just as he pleased. Her lips screwed into a knot. She would have to alienate herself from her suffering, close her eyes and transport herself to some faraway place. It would not be her body. It would not be her.

But she knew it would.

Her heart was thumping sickeningly, her stomach clenched into a painful block of stone. She heard him climb the stairs and go into one of the other bedrooms. Her brow puckered. Listening. Alert as a fox. And when she heard him come back out and pace up and down the landing like a caged animal, her pulse beat even harder and she could hear the blood rushing frenziedly inside her skull.

The door finally opened.

She was transfixed as he came towards her. He was still dressed but had removed his coat and waistcoat. His shirt was open at the neck, showing the tanned skin at the top of his chest as he clearly wore no undervest beneath, and the sleeves were rolled up to the elbows. He looked altogether less formidable, but Rebecca heard the tiny whimper inside her as he sat down on the edge of the bed. His eyes travelled lingeringly over her face and when he reached out his hand, she went to swallow her fear, but her mouth was so dry she nearly gagged. Her gaze was riveted on his bare forearm, since she couldn't bring herself to look at what he was about to do to her. His arm wasn't thick and swarthy like many of the seamen she knew, but was lean with a hard, wiry strength. There would be no fighting him off. She shuddered as she felt him touch her throat, unfastening the top button. And then the next. And then . . .

He lowered his hand. And his eyes narrowed in a slight smile. 'There,' he said softly. 'You won't choke now.' He drew in a sharp breath and, letting it out in a long sigh, took her hand in his and gently caressed it. 'I don't know why you wanted to marry me,' he almost whispered. 'You have no feelings for me, and you've made it perfectly clear that you still love your Tom. I . . . I agreed to marry you to . . . to save you from whatever it was you need saving from. And because, heaven help me, I do love you. But I won't force myself on you. Maybe, one day, you will come to love me, and that will be the time. So,' he looked up and tenderly stroked a strand of hair from her face, 'sleep well, Rebecca.' And dropping a swift kiss on her forehead, he got to his feet.

Rebecca stared after him, utterly stunned.

'Goodnight, Captain Bradley,' she heard her voice croak.

He stopped. And with his hand still on the half-open door, he glanced at her over his shoulder. 'Seeing as we would appear to be married,' he said with a wistful grimace, 'you might see fit to call me Adam.'

And then he was gone.

Rebecca sat motionless, hardly daring to breathe. She couldn't believe that she'd been saved from the humiliating ordeal. Captain Bradley — Adam — her husband, had behaved like a gentleman. Huh! But for how long? Words were all very well! He sailed in just three days. The *Emily* had already been delayed in Plymouth for a week because of the wedding, and it was to be a long voyage through the Mediterranean and across to Italy, and calling at Gibraltar and Lisbon on the return. Rebecca would be safe for perhaps a few months. Oh, dear God! An awful tremor shivered down her spine. Vile as it would be, she *needed* him to make love to her, or how else could she make him believe it was his child? But . . . but would she have the courage to entice him to her bed before he sailed? Had she betrayed her love for Tom for nothing?

She buried her head in the pillow, and listened to the silent house.

CHAPTER NINE

'I should like to propose a toast to the cook,' Isaac beamed across the table, his cheeks somewhat flushed. 'That were the finest Christmas dinner I've ever eaten!'

'Oh, you say that every year, Isaac Westbrook!' Anne chuckled. 'And there were three cooks anyway,' she smiled warmly at her daughters. 'And I hope you're enjoying your English Christmas, Misha?'

'Yes, I like very much! It is good the *Swallow* is here.'

'And this wine Captain Bradley had sent on to us is very good, too.' Isaac smacked his lips after another sip. ''Tis a pity he couldn't be back for Christmas.'

At Isaac's remark, Anne glanced across at Rebecca. The girl hardly flinched at the mention of her husband and made no reply. A frown darkened Anne's features. It was strange. Rebecca never spoke of the captain, and yet something good must have happened between them during those three days before he sailed. Rebecca seemed altogether happier, and although Anne knew she visited Tom's grave almost daily, she was no longer enshrouded in misery. Could it be that she was beginning to recover from her grief, and that her new life really had revived her indomitable spirit? Her husband had made her over a generous allowance to keep herself and

Mrs Blatchford, who'd moved into Lavender Cottage to keep Rebecca company after the brief honeymoon. Adam had told her to add to the furnishings of the cottage as she pleased, with instructions to the bank to forward any other monies she required. Rebecca had enjoyed the sudden wealth, but had bought thriftily nonetheless. She was obviously delighting in playing the housewife, and for that Anne was thankful, but it seemed that Rebecca was quite content to put the man responsible for it all completely out of her mind.

'I know I shouldn't like my husband to be away on our first Christmas!' Sarah announced innocently, and her sparkling gaze darted across at Misha.

'Oh, he'll be home soon enough,' Rebecca murmured as she began clearing away the dishes.

'And is that why there's a good colour to your cheeks,' Sarah went on jauntily, 'thinking of what goes on between a man and a woman once they're wed?'

'Sarah!'

'Well, 'tis right and true, so why pretend it doesn't happen?'

'But we don't talk about it in public!'

'This isn't public, 'tis family!'

'All the same, 'tis not a fit topic of conversation.'

Sarah shrugged, and the corners of Rebecca's mouth lifted. She didn't know how she would have got through the past months without Sarah to lighten her spirits. As for Hetty, she had been so deeply steeped in grief herself that she had been of little comfort, and since Rebecca's sudden marriage to Captain Bradley, a coldness had come between them that had yet to be resolved. Hetty couldn't understand how she could be so disloyal to Tom's memory. In a year, possibly two, she could perhaps seek solace in another man's arms, but not so soon, and certainly not with the subject of their former derision! Rebecca knew exactly what her friend was thinking, but she hadn't found the courage to explain, even though Hetty was probably the only person in the world she could confide in. But somehow she wanted to hug the secret to herself a little longer, lacing her stays a little tighter every day. Since the wedding, she had begun to love the tiny embryo inside her and felt that the home she was preparing was for herself and the child alone. Adam Bradley had nothing to do with it. After all, he would be away at sea most of the time. All she had to do was tolerate his short visits.

There was just one matter she had driven from her mind, too horrendous even to contemplate . . .

Tom had gone. Gone from her in body, no longer by her side. But he was always with her, inside her head, in her heart. She talked to him aloud when she was alone, telling him what she was doing, of her plans. Sometimes she would lie on the bed and conjure up an image of him stretched out beside her, his dark head on the pillow. And when the child was born, particularly if it was a boy, she would have Tom back again in miniature, and she would be content.

'But you must agree Becky looks very well on married life!' Sarah chirped on with a sly grin.

Rebecca paused just for an instant as she gathered up the dinner plates. She went cold, and pretended to search the table for more dirty crockery.

'Blooming, in fact,' Isaac chuckled knowingly.

'What!' Anne looked up with a shiver and took in Rebecca's suddenly drained face. 'Becky?' she stumbled, and was met with a blank gaze that confirmed her husband's suspicions. 'How . . . how did you know?' she stammered at Isaac.

'I've seen that same bloom on your own cheeks, my dear,' Isaac answered fondly.

'Oh . . . oh, put down those heavy plates, Becky!' Anne flustered. 'You mustn't strain yourself! Oh, oh, Becky, why didn't you tell us before!'

Rebecca's brain was whirling, a cold sweat dampening her back. They had guessed. She wanted to flee the room, but managed to force a serene smile to her lips. 'I'm only just sure of it,' she lied. 'And . . . and I thought Adam should be the first to know.'

It was odd, that she had begun to think of him as Adam. He had been so courteous to her those three days of their marriage. She was no longer half afraid of him, yet the courage to entice him to her bed had failed her. And God alone knew what he would do to her when he found out! He wouldn't be so polite and refined then!

'Oh, of course!' Anne's face shone. 'Well, we won't let on! Oh, congratulations!'

'Yes, congratulations!'

There were embraces and kisses all round. Such a happy, natural occasion. Rebecca suddenly felt at ease, the fear fled. She had to keep the truth inside, tucked up safe with the child. But it was one hurdle over.

The news made the Yuletide celebrations even brighter. They sat around a blazing fire in the parlour, pulling crackers and laughing at the tiny explosions. They exchanged presents, marvelling at the gifts Rebecca had bought them with Adam's money. They played Hunt the Slipper, Simon Says and Shadow Buff, Misha curled up almost hysterically at the false noses and other ruses they employed to disguise their silhouettes, Isaac in a bonnet being voted by far the most amusing. The room rang with high spirits and Isaac, usually so solemn, became quite merry. Rebecca felt warm and relaxed, cradled in the loving support of her family. It was as if there was nothing amiss in the situation, and all was well with the world.

Her mother observed her with a scrutinizing eye. The girl had certainly put back all the flesh she had lost, both on her face and on her body. In fact she was already beginning to show, if Anne thought about it. And her breasts, normally small and pert, were full and rounded. A shiver of horror shook Anne rigid. Rebecca was more than two months gone — she was sure of it! And when she thought about the way Rebecca had been sick . . . Oh, good God! It was Tom's child! So . . . so no wonder she had wanted to marry Captain Bradley in such a hurry!

Anne knew she went quiet, for she couldn't think of any words, her mind numbed by the realization. It wasn't until much later, when Rebecca flitted out, laughing, to fetch something from the kitchen, that Anne could speak to her alone.

She felt her spine stiffen. 'What have you done, child?' she forced the words from her dry throat.

Rebecca's bright face became still. 'What do you mean?' she tried to shrug.

'You're more advanced than two months. 'Tis not your husband's child. 'Tis Tom's.'

Rebecca blinked hard at her mother, and her expression twisted with such torment that Anne's anger instantly evaporated. ''Tis all I have left of him,' the girl croaked in a tearing whisper. 'Be happy for me, Mother.'

Anne held her breath, her heart clenched in her chest. 'But . . . but why did you deceive us like this? And why deceive poor Captain Bradley? Why didn't you come to us? We . . . we could have come to some arrangement!'

Rebecca's blue eyes filled with tears, her chin quivering. Oh, dear God! How had her life come to this? But she knew that only the truth would suffice. 'Because . . . because I was ashamed,' she stammered. 'And because I didn't want Father to think ill of Tom now that he's in his grave.' She looked up and gazed openly at her mother. 'What do you think will have happened to his body by now? Will his flesh be crawling with maggots, or will the worms have done their job? And . . . and what about his eyes? Will they have eaten them, too?'

Anne stared, aghast with horror. The sorrow that she had thought was beginning to subside was just as alive in her daughter as the day Tom had died. 'Don't think about him like that,' she said slowly and deliberately as she searched for the right words. 'Just remember what he was to you. In your heart.'

''Tis all I do think about. You . . . you won't tell Father?' she begged.

Anne drew in her lips. She had never lied to Isaac in her life. 'No,' she promised. 'But that doesn't mean he won't realize for himself. But 'tis not your father you should worry about. 'Tis your husband. I should pray he's not versed enough in the subject to guess the truth!'

Rebecca's heart quite definitely missed a beat. For she didn't have the courage to tell her mother their marriage had not been consummated.

* * *

She was dozing in a chair by the moribund embers of the fire in the parlour grate. Mrs Blatchford had already retired to bed and Rebecca was alone, sipping at her cup of hot chocolate and already in her nightdress with a shawl about her shoulders. They'd celebrated the New Year the previous evening, and she was dreaming contentedly of the jolly antics of her family and friends.

She didn't hear the key in the lock or the light footsteps in the hallway, and it wasn't until Adam leaned over the back of the chair and kissed the top of her head that she realized she wasn't alone. The shock made her jump to her feet, her pulse racing, and she was so taken aback when Adam hugged her to him that she didn't have a chance to put her thoughts in order.

'I . . . I didn't know the *Emily* had come in,' she stammered.

'She hasn't,' Adam grinned, stepping back. 'I've left her in Plymouth for a few minor repairs, and the *Sure* just happened to be sailing. Docking in the dark isn't too desirable, mind, but I wasn't waiting for the next tide when I wanted to see my wife!' He sighed with profound pleasure, and then his eyes lit up again. 'I've got something for you,' he said, and went to rummage in the bag he had left by the door.

Rebecca crossed to the fire and, after poking the glowing coals into fresh life, added some more fuel. Coming in from the cold winter's night, Adam's coat against her had made her shiver. She straightened up and stretched her back.

'Here.'

She looked across the room to Adam's smiling face, but then the muscles around his mouth slackened and his broad forehead corrugated in disbelief. Rebecca shuddered as she saw his eyes rest on her thickening stomach. Without her stays and dressed only in her nightdress, the change in her figure was quite discernible, and she knew he had guessed.

A tremor quaked through her body, her heart ramming agonizingly against her ribcage as she waited for Adam's reaction. Would he stride across the room and strike her to the floor, for surely he had the right to do so? Or would his fury enflame the fires of jealousy and enrage him to take her by force? There was no law against it, and surely she deserved anything he did to her? In one terrible moment, she almost wished he would commit some act of violence, for it would help to confirm her loathing for him.

But he didn't move except to allow his outstretched arm to fall to his side.

'My God!' She heard the vehemence crackle in his voice. Several seconds passed and still he stood there motionless, giving her time to rally from her fear. She met his gaze, her chin set in defiance and her lips compressed into a line. She was ready to fight him. For the sake of Tom's child.

But a vicious, bitter laugh suddenly erupted from his throat. 'Oh, what a bloody fool I've been, haven't I? And there I was, thinking that you actually felt something for me, however small! That I could find some peace at last.'

His mouth curved upwards in an ironic grimace, and he walked straight past her to rest his forearms on the mantelshelf and drop his forehead on to them. And there he remained, stock-still and staring into the burning coals. Rebecca swallowed hard, scarcely daring to breathe, and waiting for him to move.

'Go to bed, Rebecca,' he muttered at length, without even lifting his head.

His reaction had triggered a sense of guilt and she wanted to say something, but her courage failed her. Instead, she crept out of the room as silently as she could and fled up the stairs, her heart still pounding.

She slid into bed and pulled the covers up to her chin. But her eyes remained open, darting about the darkened room. Listening. Not daring to move.

At long last, she heard him go out to the privy and then return to the parlour. But then there was silence again. Deafening silence. Until eventually her eyes grew heavy, and she drifted into a fitful sleep.

She wasn't sure how much later it was when she awoke with a start and her stomach cramped into a knot as she remembered what had happened that evening. The house was still as quiet as a graveyard, and almost sick with dread, she tiptoed down the stairs.

The door to the parlour was slightly ajar. Through the narrow gap she could see the figure of a man, the stranger who was her husband, slumped in a chair. Something akin to curiosity led her forward. He was fast asleep, one hand dangling near the floor next to a half empty bottle of rum. His brow was creased into a frown, his handsome face twitching restlessly. She jumped when he turned his head and moaned her name, and a pang of shame twinged in her breast. She noticed him shiver, and it dawned on her that the air in the room was now quite chill. The fire was almost out, and Adam had undressed to his shirt sleeves. Frightened lest it woke him, she nevertheless draped his coat over his sleeping form, then went to coax the ashes back into a blaze. Hurrying back upstairs, she snuggled down in her own bed again, satisfied that she'd made a small gesture towards assuaging her guilt, and slept like a log.

It was brilliant daylight when she awoke, the cool air nipping at her nose and condensation running down the windowpanes from the biting frost outside. Her mind sprang into action at once. Adam. She must talk to him. Explain. Try to tell him she was sorry. Much as she disliked him, she owed him that, at least.

She pulled on her thick dressing gown and slippers, and hurried downstairs. She was ready to face Adam now, her fear controlled, and with Mrs Blatchford up and about, he was unlikely to display his temper.

'Good morning, ma'am,' Mrs Blatchford's thin face smiled at her as she entered the warm, cheerful kitchen. ''Tis a cold one, but clear.'

Rebecca agreed with a nod of her head and then gritted her teeth. 'Where's the captain?' she asked quickly.

'The captain?' The little woman's eyebrows reached towards her lace cap. 'Why, has he been here?'

'Oh, oh, yes,' Rebecca stuttered. 'Late last night. It . . . er . . . it was just a flying visit. I . . . I was just hoping to . . .'

She turned and hurried into the parlour. It was just as it always was, not a thing out of place, nothing to show that Adam had ever been there. Perhaps . . . perhaps she had imagined it.

But then something on the table caught her eye. She picked up the small package and twisted round the label. In a neat, regular hand were written the words, *A Happy Christmas to my dearest wife. With all my love, Adam.*

Rebecca bit her lip and fumbled to open the little parcel. Inside a tiny box glittered a filigree and diamond brooch in the shape of a heart. She gasped at its beauty, but then snapped the box shut and ran upstairs to hide it at the bottom of her deepest drawer.

CHAPTER TEN

'Thank you, Mrs Blatchford. Leave it on the table, would you?'

'Yes, ma'am. But mind you eat they scones while they'm still warm.'

Rebecca nodded gratefully as her housekeeper left the room, and then she turned to her guest. 'I'm so pleased you've come, Hetty,' she began cautiously. 'I've missed you so much.'

'Aye. I knows. 'Tis stupid I've been. I's sure you had your reasons for marrying so soon.'

Rebecca bit on her lip and busied herself with pouring the tea. Perhaps it wasn't going to be as easy as she'd thought. 'Yes, I did,' she said unsurely, and handed Hetty the cup of tea. 'Do have a scone.'

'I don't mind if I does,' Hetty smiled, making her look so much like Tom that Rebecca's heart turned a somersault. 'They looks really good.'

'Yes,' Rebecca agreed. 'Mrs Blatchford may not be good at everything, but she is a wonderful cook.' And to prove it, she bit lustily into one of the delicious scones, dripping with melted butter. 'And what about you, Hetty? Are you still enjoying your life at Endsleigh?'

'Aye!' Hetty replied with marked enthusiasm. ''Tis ironing I does now. Only sheets and pillowcases, but 'tis a step in the right direction.'

'Well done!' Rebecca congratulated her. 'And Robin, how is he?'

Hetty's smile faded. 'Oh, he goes from bad to worse. He be coughing black phlegm now, poor soul, and he be working down the deepest adits off Ley's shaft which do make the air even worse. But they never did find that extension to the Devil's Kitchen, and they do say the mine's working at huge losses. There's talk of it closing down . . .'

'Yes, I know,' Rebecca answered anxiously. 'And what will Robin do then? Traipse up to Devon Great Consols?'

'I don't know.' Hetty gave a sigh of despair. 'I don't wants him going down the mines no more, and 'tis very likely he won't get set on. If the George and Charlotte do close, there'll be so many looking for work, and with his cough . . . Still, it could save his life. And then he can starve to death instead,' she snorted wryly. 'But it could affect nearly everyone in the long run. Not just those who work at the mine, but the waggoners, quay workers, bargemen . . . And if a lot of them move away, 'twill mean less general trade for everyone, including Jane Martin's shop and the Ship Inn. Mrs Richards has so few ore-buyers staying there as 'tis. To say nort of the ships and the sailors.'

'Yes, I'm glad none of Adam's ships have anything to do with the George and Charlotte,' Rebecca admitted as she poured more tea. 'With arsenic production getting underway at long last, the barge'll be in non-stop work, so I don't think we're in any danger of becoming destitute. And Adam always has the three other ships and half his business in London, as well.'

'Aye,' Hetty nodded. 'You be well set-up, and I can't be the one to blame you for that. And you must be very happy, with a good husband and a baby on the way.'

Rebecca caught her breath and lowered her eyes to her mountainous stomach. She had to tell Hetty, but she really didn't know how. 'I . . . I don't know if I'm happy or sad,' she began, her voice dropping to a tremulous whisper. 'I'm married to a man I scarcely know. He's never here, and . . .' She wrung her hands in her lap, not daring to look up and meet Hetty's inquisitive gaze. 'I . . . I said just now I had my reasons for marrying him in such haste. And love certainly wasn't one of them.'

She heard Hetty suck the air in through her teeth, and when she instinctively glanced up, her friend's brow was wrinkled with consternation. 'It . . . it must've been dreadful, then . . . the wedding night . . .' she stumbled.

But Rebecca shook her head and leaned forward as far as her bulge would allow. 'No. You don't understand. I . . . I married Adam because . . . I was already with child.' She clenched her jaw, the sweat running down her back. 'Tom's child,' she barely croaked.

She watched the shock drain the colour from Hetty's face, and the girl's dark eyes narrowed in disbelief. 'My God!' she almost choked. 'And your . . . your husband? Does he know?'

'Yes,' Rebecca gulped, and turned her head away. 'You see . . . Adam wouldn't come to my bed on our honeymoon. So I never had to . . . well, you know . . .'

'What!'

She lowered her eyes, ashamed, confused. But she had to tell Hetty everything now, and somehow it was a blessed relief. 'He knew about Tom, you see, and how I loved him. He said . . . it was too soon after my bereavement . . . that he would wait . . . He didn't know about the baby then, though. It was when he came home on New Year's Day . . . 'Twas late in the evening, and I was only in my nightdress and he guessed at once. And when I woke in the morning, he was gone.'

'My God,' Hetty repeated, hardly able to take in what she had just been told. 'So . . . so you only married him because of the child?'

'Of course!' Rebecca groaned. 'You don't think I'd have done it for any other reason, do you? 'Tis Tom I love and always will. I think about him still at every moment. But I had to do it. For his sake. For the sake of his child. You do understand, don't you, Hetty?'

Her eyes were as deep as cobalt and glistening with unshed tears. Hetty nodded slowly and reached across to squeeze her hand. 'Aye. It must be hard, wed to a man you don't love. And . . . and who must despise you in return now. What . . . what did he do when he found out? He . . . he didn't hurt you?'

'Oh, no,' Rebecca assured her. 'He was very . . . controlled. He just told me to go to bed. And later I found he'd drunk half a bottle of rum, and that was it. He didn't lay a finger on me. Didn't even shout at me . . . nothing.'

Hetty's lips compressed into a line. 'There's plenty of husbands would've near murdered you. And have you . . . have you really thought how he must be feeling?'

'Adam?' Rebecca raised her eyebrows at her friend's words. 'Well, I suppose he must feel cheated, but he hasn't given me the chance to talk to him about it. All I know is that I've felt so alone all this time, keeping it to myself. Oh, Hetty! I'm so glad you came! I feel so much better now I've told you. You're the only person in the world who knows the whole truth.'

'Apart from your husband,' Hetty reminded her quietly.

* * *

'What do 'ee be doing here?' Mrs Mason's small face tightened when she found the heavily pregnant girl waiting by the tenements.

Rebecca swallowed hard at the hostile reception. 'I . . . I have something for you. For you and the boys.' She held out her hand and opened her fingers.

'What be that?'

'The key to the empty Bedford cottage. 'Tis yours. You can move in today if you like. The rent'll be paid for you. For as long as you like.'

'I don't wants no charity.'

''Tisn't charity.' Rebecca was ready with her reply. 'I know 'twas Tom's wish, and I've carried it out. 'Tis all.'

'Tom!' his mother snarled. 'What do 'ee knows of Tom's wishes? 'Ee who went and married your fancy man afore the lad were cold in his grave!'

Rebecca drew in a gasping breath. She was reeling with humiliation, but also with surprise. 'Didn't Hetty tell you?' she managed to croak. And as the woman looked at her blankly, she went on, 'Well . . . this really is not the place, but . . . but since you refuse to speak to me in private . . .' She paused, felt her heartbeat quicken, but there was nothing else for it. She lowered her eyes to the great mound of her stomach. ''Tis Tom's child I'm carrying,' she confessed in a whisper. 'I married the captain for the baby's sake, not mine. I don't love my husband. Quite the opposite in fact. 'Tis Tom I still love, and 'tis because of him that I want to do this for you.'

Mrs Mason's face had become quite still. 'With your husband's money? 'Tis nearly two shilling a week the rent on one o' they cottages.'

The woman's return to the practical personage she had always admired filled Rebecca with hope. 'My husband will know nothing of this. The money will come from my own allowance. And I should be obliged if you would make arrangements for each of the boys to be apprenticed when the time comes. I will pay the premium.'

'But . . .'

'Please don't argue with me, Mrs Mason. I'm as determined as Tom was that they'll not go down the mine. Besides, you must know there's talk of the George and Charlotte closing. And as blacksmiths or carpenters, or . . . or coopers . . . they'll earn a much better wage than even a skilled miner.' She tilted her head with the hint of a smile as she saw temptation registering on the older woman's face. 'They can pay me back when they're established if they want, though there'll be no need.'

Mrs Mason at last returned her smile. 'God bless 'ee, then. And your child. My grandchild,' she mused with a shake of her head as she took the key from Rebecca's hand.

'Just one thing,' Rebecca said urgently, realizing with horror that she'd been forced to entrust her secret to yet someone else. 'You won't breathe a word of this to anyone? For Tom's sake? To keep his memory untainted? 'Tis only you, Hetty and my mother that know.'

Tom's mother tapped the side of her nose. 'And you doesn't want your husband finding out,' she suggested knowingly.

Rebecca's blood ran cold. She couldn't tell her that he already had.

* * *

She was taking an afternoon nap with her feet up on the sofa in front of the parlour fire, not really asleep but dozing lightly while her brain tried unsuccessfully to settle on a name for the child. She'd felt the need to rest more and more over the last weeks, her back aching as she waddled awkwardly about the cottage. The infant kicked painfully under her ribs, but it meant that it was alive and strong, and she thanked God for it.

A gentle hand tapped on the door, and Mrs Blatchford sidled into the room, glancing nervously over her shoulder. ''Tis the captain, ma'am.'

But before the words were out, Adam strode in behind her. 'Make us some strong, hot tea, would you, Mrs Blatchford?' he commanded, and the woman scurried out to the kitchen.

Adam stood and watched while Rebecca blinked away her somnolent daze and hauled herself to her feet. He wanted to step forward and help her, but the fear of rejection held him rooted to the spot. The passing months had given him time to calm down, to think rationally about the situation. He no longer minded that the child wasn't his. He had no right to. It had all happened before he had become part of Rebecca's life, and God alone knew what she had suffered. He just wanted to take care of her. But, no! She wanted none of him! What she had done to him, she would have done to no other man. She had only deceived him like that because she felt nothing for him, more than that, she despised him! And the knife cut so deep, he could have cried out with the pain of it.

'I see you haven't given birth yet,' he said curtly. 'But then you wouldn't have, would you? You're not due for another two months!'

Oh, God! Why had he said that? He hadn't meant to. It was just so hard, keeping the hurt to himself all the time.

Tears of humiliation pricked at the back of Rebecca's eyes. She'd seen the way his gaze had moved over her vastly swollen figure. With contempt, she had decided. But she wouldn't let him get the better of her emotions, and she glared back with open hostility.

'I trust you have engaged the services of a physician?' he demanded.

Her eyes stretched with mild surprise. 'Oh, well, no,' she stammered. 'I have been well enough. I thought the midwife would suffice.'

'Who is the best physician in these parts?'

'Oh, why, Dr Seaton from Tavistock. He saved Tom's mother from the enteric, and the others who caught it. He . . .' She hesitated at the horrific memory, but then went on deliberately, knowing it would rub salt in the wound. 'He would probably have saved Tom if he'd been called earlier.'

Adam bit on his bottom lip and Rebecca felt a dart of remorse as she realized her arrow had found its mark. 'Then engage him,' he said quietly. 'I don't want some ignorant peasant looking after my wife. At least . . . It may not be my child, but it must look as if it is. As if I care about it.'

Rebecca felt the bile rise in her gullet. 'I take it that means you don't.'

'Give me one good reason why I should!'

Her spine stiffened, and had she been standing near enough, she might well have hit him. She didn't notice him shut his eyes tightly and shy away from the cruel words he instantly regretted. He drew in a breath, summoning the courage to apologize, but at that moment, the door opened and Mrs Blatchford came in with the tea tray and, sensing the antagonism between her master and mistress, instantly retreated.

They sat down cautiously, one on either side of the low table. Rebecca poured the tea, avoiding his eyes until the last moment as she handed him the cup.

'Thank you,' he said instinctively, at once the impeccable gentleman again. 'I . . er . . . Rebecca?'

'Yes?'

'Oh . . . nothing,' he muttered, and sipped gratefully at the scalding liquid. Somewhere at the back of Rebecca's mind, it registered that he looked tired, but it was his problem, not hers. 'You've made this room look nice,' he remarked politely.

But she ignored his comment, doubting his sincerity. 'I didn't know you were coming home,' she answered tersely. 'You never wrote.'

'I didn't think you cared.'

'I don't, but 'tis embarrassing if anyone asks.'

'Ah,' he nodded with a grunt. 'Well, I'll try and send word next time.'

''Twould be appreciated.' Cold. Like strangers. 'Did you sail the *Emily* upriver?' she asked mechanically.

'No. We stopped at Plymouth to drop off some cargo, and I engaged old Captain Harvey to take her on to London for me. I wanted to come to Morwellham to make sure all's running smoothly for shipping the arsenic,' he lied, for how could he tell her the main reason for his visit was to see her?

'And how long will you stay?'

She'll have me out of the house before I've even arrived, he thought grimly to himself. 'Two or three days. And then I'll go up to London by train to sort out the mess up there.'

'Mess?'

'Oh, they've managed to bugger up . . . I mean, mess up one of my major wine contracts. When we got to Bordeaux, there was no cargo waiting. They'd had no contract renewal through, so they'd given it to someone else. It took me three days to arrange another shipment, and that at a lower rate, and every day's delay costs money. And then we hit a calm, so that delayed us even longer.'

Rebecca smiled with satisfaction. The slip of his tongue showed he was not as refined as he thought he was! But then, a sea captain was dealing with rough sailors all the time. It wasn't an occupation for a true gentleman, was it? Not like being a member of parliament or a doctor . . .

'And what news is there in Morwellham?' he was asking.

'Oh, more mines using the railways, as ever,' she answered, relieved the conversation had taken a different direction. 'And more rumours about the George and Charlotte. Copper prices still falling . . .'

'So I've seen. Which is why I'm glad our interests are spread. And why I must get up to London to see what's been going on. My father would think poorly of me if I let the company go under after his lifetime of hard work.'

'When will you go, then?'

Like it to be tomorrow, wouldn't you? he thought. 'As I said, in a couple of days. But don't worry. I'll not trouble you. You just carry on as if I'm not here. And don't worry about the future for yourself and your child. There'll always be enough for the pair of you to live comfortably. I'll make sure of that.'

But he couldn't keep the biting rancour from his voice, and Rebecca sat bolt upright at the intimation. ''Twas not your money I married you for, Adam, but for respectability and a name for my child, although God knows I'd rather it bore Tom's name than yours! But there's one thing you must know. My parents had nothing to do with this arrangement. 'Twas only at Christmas they learned I was with child. My mother guessed the truth, though. Not that I told her you and I . . . never . . . But my father and everyone else believes it to be your . . . our child.'

His liquid brown eyes were staring at her unblinking, and then he rubbed his hand hard over his forehead and down to his chin. She gritted her teeth, not knowing what he could be thinking, angry and frustrated at his silence. She leaned across and almost shook his arm. 'You do believe me?' she questioned him urgently. ''Twas none of their doing. Only mine.'

He raised his eyes to hers and nodded slowly. 'Oh, yes,' he grated. 'I believe you. Your father's a good man. He'd never have had the bloody gall to do what you did!'

The words stung on his tongue like venom, for wasn't the spirit that had led her to the deceit the very same he had recognized in her the first time they'd met, that had captured his heart, made him admire, love her? And now it had turned against him, and she was glaring at him with eyes narrowed into feline slits.

'And were your motives any better?' she demanded bitterly. 'You only married me because you wanted a toy, a . . . a plaything for your own amusement! To tease and make fun of whenever it took your fancy!'

Adam snatched in his breath. He wanted to protest, but his brain was too numbed to think of the words. Good God! Was that how she really saw him? Did she despise him so much? But he knew it was true, for if looks could kill, the disdainful way in which she was glowering at him now would have had him dead where he sat.

CHAPTER ELEVEN

Oh, dear God, no! Not again! Not so soon! I can't stand the pain! Oh, sweet Jesus, give me some respite! The crushing vice, my own body killing me! Oh, save me, someone! The tunnel is dark, and so . . . so deep . . . They are hammering, hammering at the hoop, but the barrel won't bend . . . 'Tis destined for a ship, a tall, fine ship, but the mast is broken, the sails in shreds . . .

'Why wasn't I called before?'

'I sent for you as soon as Mrs Blatchford came to me, Dr Seaton. But 'tis a long way to fetch you from Tavistock.'

Oh, Mother, that's right! Hold my hand! Don't let it go!

'I should have been called when labour started. Presumably you knew it was breech?' he said, addressing the midwife.

'Aye, but I've dealt with breech often enough. 'Twere going all right at first. But I sent for you the moment I realized summat were amiss.'

'Well, let's hope I've got here in time. She's so weak, she's becoming delirious.'

'She . . . she will be all right?'

All right? Tom's child. They must . . . One suffocating effort to raise my head . . . 'Save my baby!'

'The child means everything to her.' Far, far away . . .

'Well, I'll do my damnedest to save them both. I'm going to have to push the baby back inside and turn it between contractions if I can. But first I want the poor girl to have some chloroform, and once she's asleep, I'll need you to sprinkle a few more drops on the mask whenever I tell you, Mrs Westbrook. You can do that, can't you? Now, Mrs Bradley, it's Dr Seaton here, and I'm going to help you. I'm just going to hold this over your face, and I want you to breathe nice and deeply for me . . .'

Strange, intriguing odour . . . oh, the pain . . . the agony is . . . sinking . . . floating. Tom, oh, Tom, be with me now . . . But Tom is gone . . . Mother, she is here, I feel her . . . But I need a man . . . a strong man to hold me up, keep me afloat . . . Tom is gone . . . far away . . . help me . . . Adam . . . anyone . . .

* * *

Adam Bradley had to check his gait as he hurried down the steep descent into Morwellham from the canal. He'd been delayed in London for ten days and still wasn't satisfied with his business affairs, but his mind had been so unsettled that he could stay away no longer. He'd travelled back to Tavistock by train and then cadged a lift on the first barge coming along the canal. Its progress had seemed painfully slow, though as he didn't ride and indeed had his travelling bag to carry, it was probably quicker than hiring a cab. Now he ran through the village and up the steep hill to his home nestling in the sloping garden opposite the chapel. A terrible sense of foreboding churned in his stomach, his dry throat almost making him gag.

Surely Rebecca must have given birth by now, but although she had the address of his offices in London, he'd received no word. But then, it wasn't his child, was it, and she probably considered it was no business of his. But . . . but what if . . . oh, no! It was unthinkable. But his mother had died giving birth to him, hadn't she? And Rebecca was so slight, it was one of the many attributes that had made him fall in love with her so instantly, the desire to protect her, keep her safe. But she had never let him close to her, and now . . . Oh, dear God, what if . . . if she were dead? How often in those past days the terror had suddenly ripped through his brain when he least expected it, in the middle of an important business meeting, or waking him with a start in the dark hours of night. God knew it was hardly a proper marriage, but he didn't think he could live without her. But that . . . that was just how she must have felt when Tom Mason had died. He couldn't blame her for that, but couldn't she just try to see him for what he was, and stop hating him for not being Tom? He was as much at fault, he knew, for he had been helpless to control the sharpness of his own tongue, but . . . Perhaps when the baby came . . . But if she had died . . . or the baby. Oh, if only the thoughts would stop tumbling around in his head making him want to scream.

He stopped dead in his tracks. In the lane outside the cottage, a small boy was holding a magnificent horse that looked as if it would eat up the miles from Tavistock.

The doctor. It could only mean one thing, and Adam's heart thundered against his ribs as if it would explode.

He dragged his feet towards the gate and down the garden path. And gave a startled gasp when the door opened just as he reached it.

Dr Seaton raised his eyes at the tall, well-dressed man who, with his tanned face, had the unmistakable look of a seafarer. 'You are Captain Bradley, I take it?' he asked, never one to waste time beating about the bush.

The younger man seemed unable to speak and nodded instead. So this was the enigmatic captain who came and went like a spirit of the night and whom everyone seemed to hold in awe, the doctor thought to himself.

'My . . . my wife?' Adam managed at last to stammer, his eyes stretched with dread.

Warm, expressive eyes, Dr Seaton considered. You could tell a lot from people's eyes. 'I delivered your wife of a son three days ago,' he smiled reassuringly. 'All is well, but I should like a word with you.'

'Yes, of course,' Adam murmured, the crippling anxiety making him feel weak. He gestured to the physician to go back inside and into the parlour. 'I was detained on business,' he explained limply as he dropped his travelling bag on the floor as they passed through the hallway.

'Nature doesn't always have the best sense of timing,' Dr Seaton replied good-naturedly. 'Now, there's nothing to worry about,' he said as Adam closed the door behind them. 'But your wife had a very bad time of it and it's left her quite debilitated. If I'd been called earlier . . .'

'Earlier?' Adam gave a bewildered shake of his head. 'But I thought . . . I told her to engage your services beforehand.'

'Unfortunately she didn't, Captain Bradley. I wasn't summoned until she really needed help.' He saw Adam's face drain to such a deathly pallor that for a moment he feared he was about to have another patient on his hands. 'Perhaps you should sit down, sir.'

'Er . . . yes.' Adam sank gratefully on to one of the upholstered chairs and indicated absently for the doctor to do likewise. 'Forgive me,' he murmured apologetically. 'I should have asked you to take a seat earlier.'

'No matter. I'm sure the news has come as a shock, but I see no reason why your wife should not make a full recovery. It was an exhausting and difficult birth. She lost a great deal of blood and I have to tell you that her life was in danger for some time. It has left her very poorly and I don't want her moving from that bed for some weeks.'

Adam nodded and ran his hand over his forehead. 'You just tell me what she needs and she shall have it.'

He looked up beseechingly, his eyes shining with moisture. Dr Seaton considered him for a moment. He had seen men visibly shaken before, but few appeared as shattered as

Captain Bradley seemed now, and he was a man who had to deal with danger and hardship each day of his working life.

'Everything is in hand. It is a long way, but I shall call daily. But should you be at all worried, please don't hesitate to fetch me at once.'

Adam rose to his feet, drawing in a deep breath and letting it out shakily. 'And . . . and will she . . . will it be safe for her to have other children?'

Good God, whatever possessed him to ask that? She was hardly ever likely to bear him a child, was she?

Dr Seaton pursed his lips. 'I shall need to examine her thoroughly when she is recovered, but I don't believe any permanent damage was done. However, it would be wise to wait a year or so before . . . Well, I think you understand my meaning. Not easy for a young man, I know.'

Adam threw back his head with an ironic snort that the doctor did not comprehend. 'If only . . . !' he muttered, and bit down on his bottom lip.

Dr Seaton wasn't sure what to make of it. 'Your wife is awake at the moment,' he said, relieved at the opportunity to change the subject. 'She must be longing to see you. And I expect you are anxious to meet your son.'

'What?' Adam frowned at him, still looking dazed. 'No, no. I don't want to disturb her. Not while she's so unwell. Er . . . tell her I've been, will you? I'll stay at the Ship Inn so as not to be a bother. I sail in a few days anyway.'

The doctor stared at him from under raised eyebrows. How odd that this clearly distraught fellow did not want to see his wife and new son. 'As you wish.'

'And . . . and, Doctor.' Adam seemed to regain his composure. 'On one point we must be quite clear, and I should be obliged if you would remember it. For my wife's sake,' he added as if to add force to his words. 'The child was born prematurely.'

He spoke with slow deliberation and held Dr Seaton's gaze steadily. Of course, the doctor realized at once. That explained it all. There was no way the fully developed infant had arrived early. But Captain Bradley wanted it to be known that his wife had been delivered well before term, and who was the doctor to argue with him? After all, quite what had happened between the stranger and Rebecca Westbrook was anyone's guess. For hadn't the girl been devastated at the tragic death of young Tom Mason last August, only to marry the captain in a mighty hurry two months later? Strange what bereavement could do to a person's mind. Had she sought solace so soon, clinging to the newcomer and taking from him the physical closeness that had been denied her from her dead betrothed? And it must be admitted that Captain Bradley was strikingly handsome and had a most engaging manner. The doctor's esteem of him immediately plummeted as he imagined him taking advantage of the grief-stricken girl. But then . . . the man quite obviously cared deeply for his wife, whereas she had never asked for him once. Oh, dear. Still, it was really none of his business.

'You can rely on my integrity,' he answered gravely.

* * *

'Why, ma'am, you shouldn't be trying to feed the little one yourself,' the housekeeper gently reprimanded her mistress as she busily tidied the room. 'Not after all you've been through.'

'I don't want a wet nurse.' Rebecca screwed up her face petulantly. 'Dr Seaton says 'twill not harm Toby if I have enough milk for him, and I do seem to. And I'm eating every morsel you put in front of me!' she added with a grin.

''Tis as well your husband can afford all this expensive food,' Mrs Blatchford agreed. 'And 'tis kind of you to have me share it. I'd be as happy with a bit of bacon, you knows.'

'Oh, 'tis silly for you to cook twice. Besides,' she glanced up affectionately, 'you've looked after me so well since I was so poorly bringing Toby into the world.'

'Well, you know I wanted you to have the doctor in the first place.'

Rebecca pulled a guilty grimace. But she would not explain that the only reason that she hadn't arranged for Dr Seaton to oversee her pregnancy was because Adam had told her to. His instructions had made her feel like a small child, when she was sure now she was a grown woman, and she resented anything Adam said to her with bitter intensity. As it happened, he had been quite right, but she wasn't going to admit it. 'But all's well now. And isn't Toby the most beautiful baby you've ever seen? I mean, apart from your own children, of course.'

A broad smile split Mrs Blatchford's face as she came over to the bed. The infant's pink lips were firmly latched over his mother's nipple, his eyes shut and his little gullet working furiously. His tiny hand rested lightly against Rebecca's swollen breast, and when she reverently stroked his palm with a fairy touch, he responded at once to the stimulus and his minute fist closed around her little finger. She smiled serenely, her face softly radiant, and bent to brush a kiss on to his dark, downy head.

'Aye, he be a little treasure,' Mrs Blatchford breathed.

'Worth all the effort,' Rebecca sighed contentedly. If only . . . She didn't want to think it, but she couldn't stop herself. If only Tom were there to see his son. To share her joy. The lump which had been lurking in her throat ever since she'd regained consciousness from the chloroform welled up again and she had to force back her tears. Oh, why, *why* did Tom have to die! It just wasn't right, when he had given her the gift of the precious life she now cradled in her arms and which he would never see. Toby had stopped sucking as her breast emptied, and as she leaned his helpless form against her shoulder and soothingly rubbed his back, she brushed her cheek against his head to draw comfort for her grief.

'Oh, I nearly forgot. The captain called again this morning. I told him you was feeling a little stronger each day and that the baby be doing well. I tries to persuade him to come up, but he'd not hear of it. He just gave us more money and tells me to make sure you have all you needs. But don't you fret none. It takes some men that way. They takes their pleasure, and then seem surprised by the consequences,' she declared merrily. 'Aye, he's a lovely little fellow! Oh, oops!' she laughed as Toby gurgled and wrinkled up his rosebud mouth in distaste at the deposit of white, curdled milk that dribbled down his chin. And before Rebecca could wipe it away, a long spluttering noise issued from the direction of his napkin.

'Oh, no!' she grimaced. 'I've only just changed him!'

'Well, you let me see to him for you,' Mrs Blatchford beamed benevolently, whisking the child away before Rebecca had a chance to argue. ''Tis time you had a sleep. Oh, and the captain says to tell you he'll be sailing with his barge on the afternoon tide to join his own ship, which'll be back in Plymouth by the time he is.'

'Oh,' Rebecca uttered flatly. And then with more expression, a more audible, 'Oh!' But what was it in her voice? She hardly knew herself. Relief that she hadn't had to face him, or disappointment that she hadn't been able to show him the blessed miracle that had at long last put some meaning back into her life? Toby might not be his son, but it might have been pleasant to share her joy with him. But . . . Damn him! He might have had the common decency to visit her. Just once. But that was typical, wasn't it? Everything always had to go the great captain's way, and if it didn't, he simply turned his back on the situation and took himself off!

'He works very hard, does the captain,' Mrs Blatchford remarked with her usual subtlety. 'Not just the business side of things, but they say he'll roll up his sleeves and get on with the manual work on board alongside his men, up aloft and all. 'Tis a good man you have there.'

Huh! Good man, indeed! Who couldn't even be bothered to see her when she nearly lost her life giving birth! 'Oh, yes, he does work hard,' Rebecca agreed uninterestedly. 'I expect that's why he stayed at the Ship. Came home for a rest and didn't fancy all the disturbed nights with Toby!'

She'd tried to make a joke of it and the housekeeper chuckled in response. 'Aye, I expect so. Now you have a rest, ma'am, and I'll look after our little man here.'

'Thank you, Mrs Blatchford. I do feel tired.' Yes, tired and hurt. Angry that Adam should sail again without seeing her. How could he be a father to Toby when he was never there? But was that what she really wanted, for him to take Tom's place? No! Of course not! She had married Adam for security and to prevent Tom's child being labelled a bastard. As far as she was concerned, the more he kept away the better. Oh, Tom! If only he were still alive! He'd have been such a good husband to her.

Not like Adam!

And alone in the room at last, she buried her face in the pillow and cried herself to sleep.

CHAPTER TWELVE

'Thank you for the tea, Mother. And you'll come to me on Friday?'

'Of course! Oh, but let me give my grandson another kiss!' Anne Westbrook took the infant from her daughter's arms. 'My, he's getting heavy! There! Now, don't you dawdle along the way. 'Tis getting chilly.'

'Yes, Mother,' Rebecca chuckled, taking Toby back in her arms. 'And you'll come, too, Sarah? Hmm! Engaged to Misha!' she grinned. 'And about time, too!'

'But 'twill still be some time before we can be wed,' Sarah told her in a most practical tone. 'But I am only eighteen, so I don't mind waiting. It just feels so . . . well, so nice to know that we're officially promised.'

Rebecca turned and went out through the gate, waving with her free hand. Sarah had instantly matured with her betrothal to Misha Kastryulyevich and seemed so calm and content. Rebecca prayed that nothing would destroy her sister's happiness and force her to suffer the draining grief that never seemed to release her own heart from its clutches for more than a moment.

She pushed the thought aside and stepped out briskly. But she had hardly gone a few yards when she came to a standstill. The doors to the cooperage stood wide open, for even on a cool, late September day, the heat from the physical exertions of six men and several boys all working in a confined space could be overpowering. But there weren't six, were there? Ned Gimlett still hadn't found a skilled cooper to take Tom's place, and secretly Rebecca was glad. For Tom was still there, really, wasn't he? She could feel him, see him so clearly, hammering down the hoops with his wiry strength, his raven locks hanging about his forehead in tight, unruly curls.

She shook her head and bent to kiss Toby's soft, downy hair as moisture misted her eyes. ''Tis where your father worked,' she whispered hoarsely. 'You don't understand what I'm saying now, but I'll tell you all about him one day.' Yes, she thought to herself as she walked on. She would not hide the truth from her son. One day, when he was old enough, she would explain to him who his real father was. That was if the child ever believed he had a father at all, seeing as Adam was never there! One letter he'd written since he'd sailed a few days after Toby's birth, and that so short and curt it might have been meant for the man on the moon! And now the boy was almost five months old, and all she knew was that Adam was somewhere on a ship between London and the Atlantic coasts of Europe, or possibly the Mediterranean. She might as well take a pin and stick it, blindfolded, into a map as guess where he might be.

'Rebecca?'

Her gasp was clearly audible as she recognized the strong, level voice, the shock of seeing Adam suddenly materialize beside her sending a wave of unease down her spine.

'Oh, so you've deigned to come home, have you?' she greeted him.

Adam drew in a sharp breath. 'You could at least pretend to be pleased to see me,' he said flatly.

'Well, I'm not. Not after the way you treated me.'

'What?'

'Not once did you come to see me when Toby was born.'

She glared at him, eyes flashing, as she watched his reaction. His prominent Adam's apple moved up and down his throat as he swallowed hard.

'I thought I was the last person you'd want to see.'

'Well, you were right there! But 'twould have been common courtesy when your wife had just given birth.'

Adam's brow puckered earnestly. 'I called every day, twice sometimes. I was worried sick about you.'

'Well, you had a mighty queer way of showing it!'

She held his gaze, her whole countenance ready to do battle, but Adam did not respond and instead released a heavy sigh. 'Let's not turn everything into an argument,' he pleaded with her. 'I'm sorry to have to intrude on your cosy life, but it really is time I checked on my business here. I can't very well stay at the Ship this time. I gave the excuse before that I didn't want to be a burden with you just having had the baby, but I can't say that now. So I'm afraid you'll have to put up with my company — in my own home — for at least a few days.'

She wanted to rear away from the hint of sarcasm in his final words, but his eyes darted swiftly to the side as he heard someone approach from behind, and she suddenly found herself enveloped in his arms. Her instinct was to fight against him, but then she saw the wisdom of his forced show of affection and suffered his attentions with resignation. After less than a few seconds, he released her and instead deftly drew back the shawl from Toby's face.

'So this is my son,' he said gently.

She clutched the child fiercely to her, totally ignoring the curious softness that had come into Adam's eyes. His son? Not over her dead body! Toby was *her* son! Hers and Tom's! And there was no way she would ever let Adam forget it!

* * *

They sat at opposite sides of the dinner table, Rebecca's back remaining as stiff as a ramrod as she ate her meal, replying to any conversation Adam tried to open with a monosyllabic grunt. He finally put down his knife and fork with an exasperated sigh.

'For God's sake, Rebecca,' he said with fraying self-control, 'I've been at sea for five months with only a few days' rest in port, if you can call negotiating cargoes a rest. I'm tired, and I really could do without this stony atmosphere.'

She looked up sharply from her plate. 'Don't expect any sympathy when you showed little enough to me.'

He gazed at her with wide eyes and then ran his hand over his forehead. 'All right, I apologize if I made a wrong decision. At the time, I thought you'd want me to keep away. And by your attitude now, it would appear I was right.'

Rebecca chewed lengthily on her mouthful of food. Perhaps she was being a little hard on him, and she wasn't enjoying the tension any more than he was. 'I didn't know you were coming,' she answered hesitantly. 'And there's been no ships come in today.'

'Oh, I caught the paddle steamer to Calstock, then walked across the parish and got the ferry across the river.' He waited for some tart reply, but when she simply nodded, he at once felt more relaxed and the ravenous hunger that had gnawed at his empty stomach all day returned with a vengeance. 'Old Captain Harvey's taken the *Emily* on up to London for me,' he went on between mouthfuls. 'I'll only inconvenience you a few days, and then I'll go up by train to join her. And I must have a meeting with the bank and my accountant. It's so damned difficult trying to keep track of everything when I'm away so long. That's why I must secure regular contracts for all three ships rather than have them pick up whatever cargo's available. I particularly don't want the *Swallow* going back to doing that. It's too easy to lose money that way.'

Rebecca dropped her head to one side. She supposed it must be quite a worry for him, but he was the one who'd taken it all on in the first place. 'The George and Charlotte's being put up for sale next month,' she offered.

'Is it?' Adam raised his eyebrows.

'Had you not heard?'

'Oh, the paddle steamer was full of gossiping women returning from market, and then the ferryman wasn't exactly talkative. I've spoken to no one but you, Rebecca. Still, I suppose it's no surprise. The mine, I mean. It's amalgamated with the William and Mary, isn't it?'

'Yes,' she answered, grateful for the opportunity to discuss a less emotive subject. 'I imagine the whole company's up for sale.'

'And will anyone buy it?'

'I doubt it. The two mines work opposite ends of the same vein. What they can get at, they've exhausted, and they never did find the new lode they thought must be there. They've some stockpiled ore waiting to sell, but 'tis commonly held there'll be no more mining this time next month.'

'It'll throw many a man and boy out of work.'

'And women!' Rebecca cut in. 'Trust you not to think of the women.'

Adam closed his eyes for a moment. 'Yes, and women,' he murmured.

'They'll all be looking for work. I'm just so glad Hetty got out when she did.'

'And what about her young man, Robin?'

'Working till the last moment he can, though 'tis killing him,' she answered with bitterness trembling in her voice. 'Then I expect he'll drag himself miles in all weathers to another mine. Then 'twill be an eight- or ten-hour shift soaking wet and in temperatures over a hundred degrees, and then climbing back up several hundred fathoms of rickety ladders to the cold outside air. He'll be lucky to see Christmas with his chest, I reckon.' Her lips pursed angrily as she saw Adam nod and then cut enthusiastically into his meal. She couldn't understand how he could eat with such relish when she was envisaging what Robin and so many others like him had to endure. 'You can have no idea!' she accused him crossly.

Adam lifted his chin with a forceful, commanding expression she had never seen before, and she almost recoiled in her chair.

'I think I can use my imagination. After all, it's not always a picnic on board ship, you know,' he informed her tersely, and then poured himself some water with deliberate slowness as if to close the matter. 'I expect some people will move away from here altogether, even emigrate. There's many a west country miner to be found in the mines of America, and even Africa and Australia. I read in the *West Briton* a while back they reckon over nine thousand miners emigrated from Cornwall in one year. And they're always advertising for agricultural labourers and craftsmen of one sort or another to go to Australia.'

'Yes, I know.' Rebecca let out her breath in a long sigh as she realized that he was trying to return the conversation to a civil level. 'But 'twill be a pity if too many leave Morwellham. But not everyone who works at the George and Charlotte actually lives here. Far from it. But 'twon't affect your trade at all, will it?'

'Not if I can keep on with the contract work,' Adam replied. 'But it will all mean increased competition when it comes to renewing them. And if Devon Great Consols exhausts its copper completely, then the *Swift* will lose that part of her trade at least. And they are running out of copper, which is why they're developing the arsenic production. But I'm not worried about it as yet,' he assured her. 'She could carry arsenic instead, or I could use her for my London trade as well as the *Swallow*. It's certainly saving the company money, but now the *Swallow*'s other shareholders think they should be taking more profit from her. That's another reason why I need to go to London, to negotiate a new rate to keep everyone happy. And I must secure various exports for both her and the *Emily*. Trouble is, these damnable steam ships are trying to take over. They don't need to rely on a good wind, and their engines are so much more reliable nowadays.'

Rebecca had been listening intently, just as she always had to her father. She pensively tipped her head to one side. 'But surely their freight charges are much higher to pay for the coal?' she asked.

She was somewhat taken aback to see him smile warmly at her, and even more surprised at the glow of pleasure it aroused inside her. But surely . . . surely she detected that sardonic lift of his eyebrows?

'What it is to have an intelligent wife,' he commented so enigmatically she was sure that behind the apparent compliment, he was mocking her for stating the obvious. She was quietly seething, her pride seeking a cutting rebuff, when he added, 'Of course, you're right, although the engines they have now use far less fuel. But it still pays some merchants to have a faster turnover even if it costs more in freight charges, and some of them insist on such high penalty clauses that they cover themselves either way. And if you're trading in fresh produce, it pays to have your merchandise arrive more quickly and in better condition.' He stopped to rub his hand over his eyes and Rebecca watched him struggle to stifle a yawn. 'Anyway, I'm sure you don't want to tax your brain with such tedious matters.'

She glared at him across the table. 'I'm quite capable of following your business affairs,' she informed him stiffly. 'I'm not an idiot, you know!'

'No. I know you're not,' he answered, his voice like gravel. 'That's one of the reasons I wanted to marry you. And why I should like you to accompany me to London.'

'What!' The exclamation was out before she could stop it, and she bit her lip in remorse. But Adam had latched on to her reaction at the unexpected invitation, and his eyes glinted with mischief.

'We could stay in a decent hotel, with a fixed bath with running hot and cold water. And proper lavatories that flush away when you pull the chain. I don't suppose you've ever seen one of those.'

His face was quite still, but his gaze was riveted on her and she was convinced he was laughing to himself. Making fun of her, just as he had on that dreadful evening they had first met. She felt hurt, humiliated, but she wouldn't let him see that he had upset her.

'I'm surprised you would risk displaying your country bumpkin wife to all your associates,' she said curtly, her chin lifted high.

'Oh, come now, Rebecca!' And she felt the satisfaction as his expression twisted in earnest. 'That isn't what I meant!'

'Isn't it?' she snapped.

'No, it isn't! I thought you might enjoy a short trip. It wouldn't be all business. I'd like to take you to the theatre. To a concert. With a full orchestra.'

'And have everyone stare at my country clothes?' she enquired, lacing her voice with sarcasm.

'No!' Adam rolled his eyes. 'But you could wear a farm labourer's smock and a straw hat for all I care, and you'd still be the most beautiful woman there. Dammit, Rebecca, you're my wife and I want you with me!'

'Well, I'm sorry to disappoint you, but I'm still feeding Toby myself, so I couldn't go even if I wanted to.' And flinging her napkin on to the table, she rose to her feet and swept out of the room.

* * *

She had no idea what time it was, but the room was pitch dark when she was roused from a deep slumber by the sound of Toby crying. She groaned inwardly. She'd tossed in her bed for what seemed like hours before she'd finally gone to sleep, and now her whole body felt so limp she could scarcely move. She snuggled down under the blankets again and listened. Perhaps if she waited a few minutes Toby would go back to sleep. She drifted off again, but when she came to her senses with a start, she could hear her son wailing lustily.

She dragged herself from between the sheets and, fumbling for the matches, lit the oil lamp on the bedside table. She picked it up and crossed the room, but as she went out on to the landing, she was surprised that Toby's cries were louder than she expected and realized that the door to the nursery was open. She sprang forward, and then stopped dead on the threshold.

In the eerie glow of the lamplight, the elongated shadow of a figure holding an infant was cast up against the far wall of the room. The man was jiggling Toby gently on his shoulder, rubbing his little back and crooning softly to him. Not that it was having any effect, for Toby was voicing his distress with gusto, his tiny fists flailing wildly with jerky, uncontrolled movements. Rebecca held her breath in bewilderment. In the dim light the man appeared . . . so dark. No! She must be hallucinating . . . But he was holding the baby with such natural tenderness. Could it possibly be . . . Tom . . . come back to comfort his son? Could it be by some miracle that Tom wasn't dead after all, that it had all been some terrible nightmare? She dared not move, petrified that the vision would dissipate into thin air when she . . . when she wanted it to last for ever, to be real. To be Tom that she could hold and kiss and laugh with . . .

And then she rubbed her eyes and realized that the man was taller and more broad-shouldered than Tom, and that instead of a halo of dark curls, his hair was far lighter and altogether more orderly. Adam!

She felt shot through with anguish, wanting to fight back at the deceitful trick her mind had played on her. She swiftly set down the lamp and as Adam turned to her, she snatched Toby from his arms and clutched the child frenziedly to her chest.

'What on earth do you think you're doing?' she demanded.

Adam stared at her for an instant, his arms hanging limply at his sides. 'What am I doing? More to the point, what the hell are *you* doing! Were you going to let our son cry all night?'

Rebecca's jaw fell open. *His* son? How dare he! It really was too much that this . . . this odious man was trying to take Tom's place! It was as if all the force of her bitter frustrations, the fury of the cruel emptiness, was directed into her free arm as she lashed out in Adam's direction. It was all so sudden, so instinctive, that she was as stunned by her action as Adam was. He had no time to avoid the blow and reeled backwards as her hand stung against his face.

She watched in horror as he touched his cheek and winced. Her mind cried out that she was sorry, that she hadn't meant to do it. She was ready to burst into tears, to beg his forgiveness, and for a fleeting moment, she even craved the comfort of his arms about her small frame. But all she could do was gaze up at him in awe as she expected to bear the full weight of his wrath.

Instead he continued to finger his cheek and grated, 'Hadn't you better see to him, then?'

She gulped hard, suddenly aware once again of Toby's desperate cries. 'Er, yes. I expect 'tis a feed he wants.' She groped her way to the nursing chair and sat waiting for Adam to leave, but several seconds passed and still he made no attempt to move.

'Well, hadn't you better get on with it before he chokes?' he snapped as Toby's yells reached the characteristic point where they seemed to tumble down the scales and end in a hysterical fight for breath.

Rebecca glared back, her lips pressed tightly together, as she undid the buttons of her nightgown and bared her breast. 'You bastard!' she hissed, cringing at the sound of the foul word on her lips as the baby began sucking and immediately all was quiet.

'Then you and I make a good match, don't we?' Adam murmured. 'And I don't know what you've got to be so prudish about. I bet your Tom saw more of you than that, and he wasn't even your husband!'

He had aimed well, his biting words paralyzing her, and before she could think of a suitable reply, he strode out of the room. Rebecca's heart was racing, hatred rasping in her throat. She held the suckling child close, rocking back and forth as tears welled in her eyes. Don't worry, my little love. I'll never let that horrible man touch you ever again!

* * *

'Hetty!' she beamed as she opened the front door a few days later.

Hetty smiled back, reminding Becky painfully of her dead brother. 'Be the captain in?' she asked hesitantly.

Rebecca shook her head brightly. 'No. He left for London yesterday, and then he's sailing from there next week, so you're perfectly safe!' she grinned.

'Oh, I've missed him then.' Hetty's face fell. 'And 'twere him I came to see really. To thank him.'

'Thank him?' Rebecca's eyebrows shot upwards. 'What for?'

'Why, didn't he tell you?'

'No.' Rebecca gave a perplexed frown. 'Perhaps you'd better come in. Toby's asleep and 'tis Mrs Blatchford's day off, so we can have a nice cup of tea. You don't mind coming into the kitchen, do you?'

'Best room in the house,' Hetty assured her, following her friend down the hall.

Rebecca set about making some tea, her heart light with the expectation of a cosy chat with Hetty after the crippling tension of Adam's short stay. She knew she should have apologized to him, and half of her had wanted desperately to do so, but she was still smarting under his bitter words. If he had tried to humour her, as she recognized now he usually did, it might have come more easily to her, but this time she had gone too far, and he was sullen and quite unapproachable.

But Hetty's words had aroused her curiosity. 'Now what's this all about then?' she asked, trying not to sound too eager. 'Thank Adam for what?'

'For giving Robin a job on the *Swallow*.'

'What!'

'Aye. He says the crew were undermanned now they goes across to Europe regular like. So he's took Robin on as cook and for untrained work on board. Not so good pay as a miner, mind, but better than working on a farm. Oh, Becky!' she breathed, her eyes shining. 'Your husband's probably saved Robin's life. He be a good man, the captain!'

Rebecca lowered her eyes. 'So everyone keeps telling me,' she muttered.

'Well, 'tis true.' Hetty dropped her voice, too, then. 'Be things no better between you?' she said quietly.

Rebecca raised her eyes to her friend. 'Thank God I have you to talk to, Hetty,' she croaked. 'I can't tell my family. Not even Sarah. Her least of all! She's so in love with Misha, she thinks I must feel the same about Adam.'

'And you don't.'

'Hardly!' she snorted. 'He treats me like a child.'

'Well, p'rhaps . . . to him . . . you are,' Hetty suggested cautiously. 'And maybe 'tis part of the way he loves you. And look at the way he do provide for you. 'Tis the best house in Morwellham.'

'Money can't buy love, Hetty.'

'But has he ever done anything to harm you?'

Rebecca pulled in her lips. 'No. But he has a sharp tongue.'

'Aye. A tongue used to keeping rough seamen in check! And has he . . . well . . . been to your bed yet?'

Rebecca met her intent gaze and was aware of colour rushing to her cheeks. 'No,' she faltered. 'But Toby woke the other night wanting a feed, and Adam wouldn't go away until . . . well, till he'd seen me.'

'But you be his wife, Becky. And men have needs. You . . . you wouldn't want to drive him into another woman's arms, would you?'

Rebecca stared at her, eyes wide, for the thought had never entered her head. But it aroused in her a strange sensation. 'Well . . . no. I suppose not. But he works so hard, I don't imagine he'd have the time,' she added a little doubtfully.

'Aye, he do work hard. And all for you, Becky. Do you . . . do you not feel anything for him?'

'Oh, yes!' she scoffed. 'Loathing!'

'I doesn't understand you.' Hetty wagged her head. 'He be good and kind, and though you can't but feel respect for him, he don't put on graces like others do. And he be a very attractive man.'

'That makes it even worse!'

Hetty's forehead creased. 'You does find him handsome, then? Well . . .' She hesitated and bit on her lip. 'Could it be that you resents that? That you feels you shouldn't, not so soon after our dear Tom's death?'

For a moment, Rebecca froze rigid, and then she swung her head torturedly from side to side. No! She despised Adam. Hetty's suggestion was ludicrous. And yet . . .

'Tom were my brother,' Hetty went on, her voice quivering. 'And God knows no one misses him more than I does! But he be gone, Becky, and your life must go on. You doesn't realize how lucky you be! You have a good husband, if only you'd give him a chance. Most men would've forced theirselves on you by now. And you did play one terrible trick on him. 'Twould take any man some time to get over that.'

Rebecca pressed her hand over her mouth. She wanted to cry out against it, but she knew that much of what Hetty was saying was true. 'I . . . I could never love Adam,' she whispered. 'Not after some of the things he's said.'

'But you could try and be nice to him. 'Twould make life easier. And would be far better for Toby.'

Rebecca felt her heart wrench. 'Yes. Yes, you're right,' she admitted hoarsely. 'But I think 'tis too late. I did something dreadful the other night. I . . . I hit him,' she mumbled guiltily.

'You did what!'

'Oh, I know 'twere a shameful thing to do! 'Tweren't his fault. And I hit him mortal hard!'

'Aye! Robin said he had a bruise on his face. Thought he'd been in a fight or summat.'

'He had. With me. Not that he retaliated at all. But . . .' She wrung her hands miserably. 'I wanted to apologize, but I couldn't find the right moment. And now 'tis too late. God knows when I'll see him again.'

'Then write.'

'Write?' She shook her head. 'And where to? If I sent a letter tomorrow, 'twouldn't get to London before he leaves.'

'Then give it to him when he do come home. Sometimes 'tis easier to write something down than to say it face to face.'

Hetty's dark eyes bore into her. Tom's eyes. As if he were telling her what to do. But what could she say in a letter to Adam? That she was sorry she'd deceived him? Sorry that she could never love him? Like him, even? That she had never meant to hurt him, and could he forgive her? No! It was impossible!

CHAPTER THIRTEEN

'Happy birthday, Toby!'

'Yes, happy birthday!' Isaac laughed, bouncing his little grandson on his knee as the child reached up to investigate the strange fluffy stuff on the older man's face, far more interesting than any of the toys he'd been presented with. 'One year old today!'

'Who's a lovely boy then?' Sarah cooed. 'Oh, you're so lucky, Becky! I hope Misha and I have children so soon after we're wed!'

Rebecca smiled contentedly at her family all gathered in the homely kitchen of Copper Ore Cottage to celebrate the occasion, her parents, Sarah and Mrs Payne. Just as it used to be. As if nothing had ever happened, except for the joyous addition of her son. As if the clock had been put back, and . . . and Tom were still alive.

''Tis strange what dark skin Toby has,' Isaac mused as he took the little boy's fist and kissed it like a playful bear.

Rebecca caught her breath, and she glanced frantically across at her mother. Anne was helping Mrs Payne to arrange cakes and biscuits on a tray, and she looked up, quite unperturbed.

'Oh, I daresay our next grandchild'll be different,' she smiled naturally. 'Mind you, if that husband of yours doesn't come home, we'll never have one.'

'Oh, he . . . er . . . he really is very busy,' Rebecca stammered, her cheeks crimson.

'Taken on far too much for one man,' Isaac agreed. 'If he insists on mastering that ship of his himself, he should employ an agent to run the rest of his business.'

'Oh, but he loves the *Emily*!' Rebecca exclaimed, her depth of feeling astounding herself. 'And most of the London business is run by his manager and clerks anyway. Adam only has to keep them on their toes and make the major policy decisions.'

'Well, he should make a policy decision not to neglect his wife so much,' Isaac declared.

'Why don't you all go through to the parlour,' Anne cut in swiftly. 'And Becky can help me make the tea.'

Rebecca concealed a grateful sigh, and the next minute she was alone with her mother in the kitchen. But she wasn't expecting Anne's forthright question.

'Is your husband ever coming home again?'

Rebecca glanced up sharply. 'I imagine so.'

''Tis seven months he's been away. And we know from Misha he's been in Plymouth at least twice without coming to see you.'

Rebecca fingered the teapot nervously. 'I'm sure he'll come back soon. To check everything's running smoothly here.'

'But not to see you. Or Toby. Whom I imagine he realizes by now is not his son.'

Rebecca nodded, too choked to speak, the afternoon's happiness ruined. 'Oh, he realized from the start,' she admitted in a whisper. 'All we ever do is row. 'Tis no marriage. 'Tis why he keeps away. But I . . . I wish he would come soon.' She shook her head, unable to express her feelings to herself, let alone to her mother. She'd thought long and hard on what Hetty had said all those months ago. She'd never written the letter, but she longed to see Adam again. She dreaded coming face to face with him, but she wanted to apologize. To promise at least to be civil to him in future.

'Father knows, doesn't he?' she heard herself ask in a small voice.

Anne didn't attempt to soften her answer. 'He's guessed, yes. He said he ought to beat you black and blue, and he certainly wouldn't have asked the captain to marry you if he'd known the truth. But you being married now, 'tis of little consequence, and besides, he thinks you've suffered enough. And if anyone looks down on us because of what you did, then 'tis their privilege. But he's seen no sign of it, and everyone knows how things were between you and Tom. That neither of you were bad . . .'

'Oh, I should hate Father to think poorly of Tom! 'Twas my fault. I led him on.'

'You still miss him so much, don't you?' Anne's words were quiet. Compassionate.

Rebecca felt the familiar constriction tighten her throat. 'There's not one day goes by I don't think of him. How he should be here. To see Toby.'

'I know. But life goes on. You must see the good in what you have left. We buried two sons, remember. Two lovely little boys. But we had you and Sarah. And now, because of you, we have Toby.'

Rebecca nodded and gave a watery smile. Her mother was so right. She should count her blessings.

The sharp rap on the front door made her jump. 'I'll get it,' she offered, thankful for the diversion, and was able to give a bright greeting to the man at the door. 'Oh, good day to you, Mr Samuels. What can I do for you?'

'Oh, er, good day, Miss Rebecca,' he answered guardedly. 'Or . . . Mrs Bradley, should I say. I . . . 'twas your father I wanted to see.'

'I'll fetch him for you,' she smiled. And so saying, she opened the door to the parlour, and telling Isaac he was needed, she rejoined the birthday celebration. Toby was crawling along the floor in pursuit of a vividly coloured wooden train Sarah had given him, his sturdy rump in the air and his legs moving so much faster than his arms that he fell forward on his nose, but was instantly sitting up and laughing. Rebecca dropped on to her knees with her sister to join in the game, the sheer ecstasy of playing with her son blotting all other thoughts from her mind. She looked up with a grin, her eyes sparkling, as Isaac came back into the room, but the consternation on his face extinguished her laughter.

'Father?'

She heard Sarah's giggles cease beside her. Saw her mother come up behind Isaac, her eyes wary.

'I'm afraid 'tis bad news,' Isaac announced gravely, his steady gaze scrutinizing her reaction. 'One of your husband's ships has been lost.'

Rebecca's body was totally stilled. She felt cold. And yet strangely calm, as if the terrible news was unreal. One of his ships. But which one? Was Isaac trying to break it to her gently? And then she caught Sarah's white face beside her. The *Swallow*. Oh, dear God. Misha. And Robin. Oh, sweet Jesus! This wasn't happening! Sarah! And dear Hetty! Oh, no! They mustn't suffer what she had been through. Was still going through. No! It mustn't be the *Swallow*! But whichever ship it was, there would be wives, mothers. Children. Or . . . or . . . what if her father was trying to tell her it was the *Emily*? What if . . . Adam . . . What if Adam had been drowned without her having the chance to tell him she was sorry? And . . . and . . . she couldn't understand the curious sense of loss. Guilt. Panic.

'Whi . . . whi . . . ?' her voice trembled.

'The *Swift*. The gales we had the other day. They were much worse in other parts. She were driven on to rocks on the south Wales coast. She weren't the only one apparently. But all the crew were saved. Other ships weren't so lucky.'

Rebecca felt searing emotion drain through her limbs, but at the whimper of relief beside her, she reached out and squeezed Sarah's hand. 'Oh, those poor men,' she breathed, her mind ravaged by a horrendous vision of powerful waves crashing over half-submerged rocks, the ominous crack of ships' timbers splitting apart, the thunderous clamour, men . . . men screaming, cold, fear . . .

'Aye. 'Tis a miracle the *Swift*'s crew survived,' Isaac nodded grimly.

'That's the most important thing.' Rebecca forced a smile in Sarah's direction and saw the colour returning to her sister's cheeks.

'But your husband has lost a ship,' Isaac reminded her. 'And a full cargo. But I suppose 'tis not such a disaster. Except if the insurance cover isn't enough for a suitable replacement. But then, he may not wish to replace her.'

'Oh, I'm sure Adam will have very definite ideas about what he wants to do,' Rebecca told him. 'He does about most things.'

'Have you any idea where he is? It could be weeks before the news even reaches him.'

She shook her head, trying to push away the unexpected horror that had gripped her at the thought of losing Adam. 'He wrote me a short letter from London before he sailed last. 'Twas some time ago, so he should be back soon.'

'Well, I can put a message through to London, and to Plymouth in case he calls at Sutton Harbour on the way.'

'He often does.' And then she gave a little gasp and her chest swelled with maternal pride. Little Toby was standing up, supporting himself on the seat of one of the easy chairs, and at that moment, he turned and took his first stumbling steps across the room. He fell into his mother's arms, and she hugged the child closely, all other thoughts obliterated from her mind.

* * *

'Now this is a small ketch,' she told Toby as she stood on the quayside of Canal Dock ten days later. 'You can tell by the masts. She has a main and a mizzen mast, so that means the one nearer the bow is taller and carries the mainsail. And you can tell which that is just by looking at it.'

But it was debatable whether or not Toby would have been interested in what she was saying even if he had been able to understand her. What was quite apparent was that now he'd discovered the world of upright mobility, he wanted to explore it at every available moment, and being held securely in his mother's arms was simply not acceptable! He was wriggling fiendishly, reaching out as far as he could until Rebecca's arms were aching with fatigue.

'Becky!'

She turned and smiled broadly as Sarah skipped up to her side.

'The ferry's just come across and someone said the *Swallow* sailed past Calstock about midday!' the younger girl declared with a face-splitting grin. 'The tide's nearly up, so she'll be here soon and she'll be able to dock straight away!'

'So she will!' Rebecca beamed, falling into step beside her sister as she hurried towards the river's edge. 'Oh, I must send a message up to the House to tell Hetty. She might be able to change her afternoon off so as she can see Robin for a few hours.'

'Oh, I wonder how long they'll stay?' Sarah half moaned, at the same time jumping up and down with excitement. 'Oh, look . . . I think . . . Yes, 'tis the top of a mast I can see!' she cried, stretching up on tiptoe. 'Yes, and another! 'Tis a schooner, isn't it, Becky?'

But Rebecca had no need to answer as the clean lines of the ship's bow slowly came into view around the almost complete loop that the river made about the parish of Calstock on the opposite bank. The *Swallow* was under the lightest of sail, and Rebecca couldn't help but feel elated by her stately progress, the shrouds of her rigging silhouetted against the bright spring sky. It vaguely crossed Rebecca's mind that it was unusual for the *Swallow* not to be towed, for she didn't come up to Morwellham often and her captain would not be so skilled in navigating the Tamar's difficult waters. But perhaps she had taken on a pilot, for the last of the sail was now taken in, and two small boats rowed out to bring in the ropes from the ship's bow and stern so that she could be hauled into berth against the wharf during those ten precious minutes of slack water at high tide. Rebecca waited patiently, holding Toby tightly and finding Sarah's excitement beside her quite infectious. She glanced upriver, watching another schooner preparing to be warped across the river and into the Devon Great Consols dock the moment another loaded vessel had similarly been manoeuvred into the flow to sail quickly downstream on the gathering ebb. When she looked back towards the *Swallow*, her heart missed a beat. For watching intently over the bulwarks was not only the ship's captain, but Adam, too.

He didn't appear to notice her at first, and she was grateful that they were obliged to step back out of the way as the ropes were looped around the bollards and the quay labourers began to haul the schooner in. Rebecca's pulse was racing, her mind spinning in confusion. All the things she'd wanted to say to Adam were jumbled up in her brain until they made nothing but nonsense. The *Swallow* came to rest against the wharf with a gentle bump, and instead of waiting for the gangway to be put in place, Adam swung himself over on to the ship's channels and vaulted across the gap on to dry land. And when he strode purposefully towards her, she felt every muscle tighten.

'You shouldn't do that. 'Tis dangerous.'

Her own words startled her, for she'd said them without conscious thought, and didn't they convey that she had some care for him? But if he had caught their meaning, he made no sign of it.

'Rebecca, we must talk,' he told her grimly, and grasping her elbow so tightly that she nearly squealed, he hurriedly directed her away from the river.

She wasn't quite sure how her numbed limbs managed to move, and it was several moments before her tongue was able to complain that he was hurting her.

'Oh, I'm sorry,' he mumbled, releasing his grip, his voice somehow distracted, and Rebecca realized that she had never seen him look so worried. Anxious herself now, she did her utmost to keep up with his long, hasty stride, but Toby seemed heavier by the second.

'Take Toby, would you?'

The request came so naturally, and for a moment, Adam stopped in his tracks and blinked at her. The barb tore at his heart, for hadn't he received a sharp slap in the face for trying to comfort the child once before? But as he took Toby from her without a word, surprise got the better of him.

'He is getting heavy, isn't he?'

Rebecca smiled faintly. Perhaps it was an opening, an easing of the tension between them. And somehow there wasn't room for the usual antagonism just now. She noticed Adam's expression tighten again as they set off up the hill, and in a few minutes they were inside the cottage. Toby was deposited into Mrs Blatchford's arms and Adam led Rebecca into the parlour, shutting the door behind them.

'Adam, what is it?' Rebecca questioned him at once, his obvious sense of urgency arousing her own apprehension. But it suddenly seemed that he didn't have the words to tell her whatever it was, as he stared at her and bit down hard on his lip. For the first time ever, she recognized that she actually felt some sympathy for him. 'Is it to do with the *Swift*?' she prompted.

He lowered his eyes then and nodded, and Rebecca's anxiety deepened as he still appeared unable to speak. 'But there's no problem, is there?' she pressed him. 'The crew were saved and you can buy a new ship with the insurance money, Father says.'

But Adam half turned away, his face twisted excruciatingly as he muttered something under his breath. Rebecca wasn't sure she had heard right, but she caught her breath sharply. 'What did you say?'

He looked at her full in the face now and she saw him swallow hard. 'She wasn't insured,' he croaked.

'What!' Her eyes opened like two full moons. 'But . . .'

'Rebecca, you must know as well as I do that half the merchantmen afloat aren't insured.' He suddenly found his tongue, but he was wringing his hands as he spoke. 'There's no law that makes it compulsory. In fact, it's a point of pride with many ship owners that they don't insure their vessels because it looks as if they doubt the safety of the ship or the seamanship of the masters they employ. And we all know about coffin ships.'

'But . . .' Rebecca stammered, hardly believing her ears. 'All the good lines insure their ships nowadays. I should have thought you . . . I suppose the *Emily*'s insured?'

She hadn't meant it to sound sarcastic, but Adam hung his head like a reprimanded child. 'Yes. And I know I should have insured the others, but I'm always so busy, I never got round to it.' He raised his eyes to her, a wry grimace on his lips. 'My business affairs aren't all as I had expected them to be. A bit like our marriage.'

Rebecca's mouth tightened. Her life wasn't exactly as she had planned it, either. But she understood that the loss of the *Swift* must have been a considerable shock to him, especially so after the trouble he had been to in order to prolong her contract. 'And what will it mean, in real terms?' she enquired timidly.

Adam sank down into one of the chairs and spread his hands. 'Well, the loss of the steady income from her, for a start. And the ship herself, of course, although I bought her outright so at least I've no loan to repay. The cargo itself was insured, thank God, but in the contract there was a hefty penalty clause for non-delivery.' He glanced up, his expression begging her not to recriminate him for accepting such an agreement. 'I'll have to find the money for that. And I've sent out a certain amount to the crew to tide them over until they can sign on with someone else. They've all three shown as much loyalty to me as they did to old Farthingay, so they deserve it. The seaman will probably find a ship in a day or two, but the master won't find it so easy to be taken on in his rightful position, and the mate broke his leg. So I've sent both of them a more substantial sum.'

'There's no law says you have to do that,' Rebecca said quietly, 'even if they were stranded in Australia.'

Adam nodded gravely. 'I know. But I felt I ought to.'

'And I'm glad you did.' She couldn't prevent the hint of a smile as a strange sense of pride swelled inside her. She reached out and squeezed his hand. He looked up at her again, his rich brown eyes searching her face, and she was struck, not for the first time, by their beauty. 'Will . . . will we have to leave here?' she asked solemnly.

'Good Lord, no! Things aren't that bad!' he assured her with a nervous laugh. 'I do keep a certain reserve of capital in the bank which will more than cover my losses. We have a small but steady income from the barge, especially with the arsenic contract, and the *Swallow*'s doing well now, too. I only wish I owned all of her sixty-four shares and not just forty.' He paused, and released a heavy, rueful sigh. 'If only everything I make on the *Emily* didn't have to go on paying back the original loan to the company. I sometimes feel as if I'm working myself to death for nothing.'

His voice rang with defeatism. It was so unlike him that Rebecca's forehead puckered into a frown. 'But you *are* fifty-one per cent of the company,' she reminded him.

'Yes, of course.' He clearly forced a smile. 'So perhaps the situation isn't so bad. I can still afford to provide a decent home for my wife, at least.'

It was true enough, but the loss of the *Swift* had been far more serious than Rebecca had realized, and she hadn't wanted to make matters worse when . . . when she had forced Toby and herself upon him. 'I wouldn't mind if we had to live somewhere else,' she said levelly. ''Tis true what I said once before, that 'twas for respectability, not money, that I wanted to marry you. And I never spend half the allowance you give me. Most of it's still sitting there in the bank.'

'Then leave it there. You might need it one day. And,' he hesitated slightly, 'this may mean I have to spend even more time away, to try and recoup our losses.' He caught his lip and one of his eyebrows lifted enigmatically as he stared into her eyes. 'Thank you. For being on my side for once.'

She had to tear herself away from him. Be on his side? How could she be? But she was! The great businessman Adam Bradley had made a mistake. An oversight. But a costly one. And inexplicably, it pleased her. Not because she was gloating, but because . . . because it made him more human. Vulnerable, even. And his first concern had been for his men. Hetty was right in that, at least. And . . . her stomach clenched fiercely at the realization . . . it was making her feel that she respected him. Liked him for it, even. She glanced furtively over her shoulder as he let out a strained breath and rested back in the chair, his eyes closed wearily. He looked exhausted, pale somehow beneath his permanent tan, his handsome face . . . Her hand clapped over her mouth to stifle the gasp . . . His handsome face that she recognized now was proud, yes, but not sharp with arrogance as she had always imagined. And she suddenly found herself having to admit that the face she had once scorned for its good looks was . . . was even more attractive than . . . than her darling Tom's had been . . .

CHAPTER FOURTEEN

'Hold my hand, Toby.'

The sturdy toddler looked up at his mother, and an angelic grin brightened his little face. His legs had become so strong during the long summer, and now his coal-black eyes blinked wide in expectation of the outing. His dark curls bounced as he turned his head to watch the farm cart slither past on its precarious descent to the port. Laden with late produce destined for Plymouth's markets, its driver had to keep the brakes applied constantly, and the horse was straining between the shafts to hold back the weight.

'When I was a child, 'twere a common sight to see heavy ore waggons struggling to get down this hill in one piece,' she told Toby as she voiced her thoughts aloud. 'But now 'tis only the local farms as use the road. And the canal and inclined plane railway see hardly any mining trade either.'

She sighed ruefully, but glancing down at Toby's radiant face as they followed the cart down to the village brought the happiness back to her heart. He was the cornerstone of her life, holding everything together. Now that he was steady on his feet he wanted to run everywhere, in his child's way so desirous of new experiences. But he was an obedient soul, anxious to please and with a sensible head on his shoulders. Just like his father.

Ah, Tom! Had the pain eased? She still thought about him every day, talked to him as if he were standing next to her. But he wasn't. She missed his physical presence so much, the longing for the comfort of his embrace so unbearable that she would sometimes bang her fists on the wall in a frenzy. Her family supported her undauntingly, but it wasn't the same. As for Hetty, she had done so well in the two years she'd been at Endsleigh that she was now assistant laundry keeper, and was so involved with her job that her visits were rare, leaving Rebecca feeling so alone. There was no one she could lean on when the emptiness was too much. No one she *wanted* to lean on. She sometimes even wished Adam would come home more often. She'd resigned herself to the fact that she would never be in a position to find true love with another man. At long last she'd decided to make the best of what she had. At least she and Adam didn't fight much nowadays. And having Toby made it all worthwhile.

'Boat!' he announced proudly, pointing across at the one small vessel in Canal Dock.

A loving smile broke out on Rebecca's lips as she crouched down beside him. ''Tis a barge, my sweet. It has just one mast, you see, and when the sail's hoisted, 'tis like a triangle. Boats are much smaller, remember, and ships are, well, bigger, like . . . like your papa sails.'

Toby considered her for a moment, not understanding a word, and then pulled her forward. She skipped along the cobbles, relishing in the excuse of her little boy to throw restraint to the wind. For a few minutes her heart was totally immersed in the joy of her son, all else forgotten until she turned the corner of the Ship Inn and her fingers tightened their grip on Toby's hand. Several groups of labourers and their wives had gathered together, talking urgently or shaking their heads, and two quay workers were engaged in a volatile argument. One woman turned her head and glared at Rebecca as if she were responsible for some grave mishap, and Rebecca blinked back, not knowing what to make of it all.

'Come on, Toby. Let's go and see Miss Martin.'

She went up the steps and into the shop, glad to shut the door behind her. Jane Martin smiled at her from behind the counter, and Toby broke loose from Rebecca's hold and ran forward.

'Sweeties?' he asked expectantly and turned to gaze up questioningly at his mother.

'Sweeties, please,' she corrected him.

'Pease,' he repeated obediently.

'He's a lovely lad, Rebecca,' Jane Martin congratulated her cheerfully.

'Yes, I consider myself blessed.' She ruffled Toby's hair affectionately. 'Just a candy stick to suck on, please, so as he doesn't choke, and a quarter of tea.'

'Twinings best?'

'No. It had better be the cheaper one, please.' But her attention was fixed on looking out of the window as Miss Martin weighed out the tea. 'Do you know what's going on out there?'

'Oh, don't say as you're the only person in Morwellham as hasn't heard?'

'Heard? Heard what?'

'It were announced this morning. Gill and Company are giving up their lease of the port at the end of the year. Shall I put this on your account?'

'Oh, yes,' Rebecca murmured, taken aback by the news. 'Are you sure 'tis not just a rumour?'

'Oh, no. 'Twas an official announcement. And can you wonder at it with trade declining so rapidly, and after the mine closed down last year? There can't be much profit to be made. And 'twon't do me much good, either.'

Rebecca looked at her blankly, but her head was buzzing with the likely consequences of the devastating news. 'Come along, Toby. We're going to see Granny, remember? Thank you for the tea, Miss Martin.'

She took Toby firmly by the hand once again and left the shop, a frown creasing her forehead. Jane Martin's business would suffer, but the astute woman had made a pretty penny over the years through thrift and diligence. Rumour had it that, no longer in the flush of youth, she was sweet on Captain Henry Allport, master of a schooner that called at Morwellham on occasion, and that her affections were returned. No. As usual, it was the workers whose lives would be decimated by such a turn of events. As Rebecca hurried her small son towards her parents' cottage, she noticed that some of the groups were disbanding, while others stayed on to despair at what, for many, would mean disaster.

She was surprised to find Isaac at home taking a cup of tea with her mother.

'Good morning!' she greeted them and went to give each a kiss on the cheek. 'I didn't expect to find you here, Father.'

'I came back to discuss the news with your mother,' Isaac answered solemnly. 'You've heard yourself, I suppose?'

'Yes, just now. 'Tis true, then? Oh, Toby, keep away from there.'

'I'll take him into the kitchen for a biscuit,' Anne beamed, scooping her grandson into her arms. 'You two have some peace, and we shall have some fun, won't we, Toby?' And as she carried him away, the child shrieked gleefully as she tickled him under the chin.

'Aye, 'tis true,' Isaac confirmed when the door was shut. ''Twill mean changes for everyone. Pour yourself some tea, maid, and come and sit down. Aye! 'Tis a sorry day for all of us. When Gill's quays stop work, I don't see as there'll be any ore coming through the port at all, so Canal Dock will virtually be the only area operational.' He blew out through his nostrils, his heavy grey eyebrows reaching up to his receding hairline. 'Used to be tons of ore rattling through those chutes. And then there were bricks, tiles, stone from the quarries on the moor, farm and mining machinery . . .' He sighed again, and Rebecca bit her lip, for her bright, vivacious father suddenly seemed his true age. ''Twill just be Devon Great Consols and the manganese mill, and whatever domestic and farming trade be left,' he went on with a lugubrious shake of his head. 'They'll hardly be needing an assaying officer, or even a full-time harbour master for that matter.'

'But you'll be all right, Father, surely?' Rebecca asked in alarm.

'Oh, I can't say as a less busy day won't be welcome, and I expect I'll be able to keep the cottage. But I can see myself having to take a drop in my wages. Still,' he puffed out his cheeks wistfully, 'I've seen it coming over the last few years, and your mother being of a thrifty nature, well, we've been canny with our money, so we'll not go short. 'Tis all the quay labourers and canal workers I feel sorry for. And so soon after the mine closing.'

'Yes. People will move away, won't they? 'Tis a terrible thing for them.' Rebecca averted her eyes from his morose gaze. 'Morwellham's really changing.'

'Aye. The best days are gone. Even Devon Great Consols are bringing out so little ore nowadays. But the arsenic, well, that's expanding by the day. Orders are coming in from all over the world wherever 'tis needed. Your husband did well to get into that from the outset. Just as well. He'll be relying on that almost entirely for his barge now.'

'What do you mean?'

'The limekilns, my dear. They're part of the lease. I can't see old James Wilton being able to come up with enough to take on the lease himself, so I expect he'll retire. So unless someone else comes along, which I very much doubt, there'll be no more lime burning in Morwellham after December.'

Rebecca wet her lips thoughtfully as she understood what her father was saying. 'So there'll be no more limestone to bring upriver. But Adam still has the contract to take arsenic down to Plymouth, and there'll be other things to come inland, to Calstock if not as far as here.'

'Aye. But not like there used to be. And especially not if folk move away, as they will. And all the other barges put out of work will want to be carrying whatever there is, too. And how long does your arsenic contract last, do you know?'

'Adam extended it to October, and then 'tis to be renewed annually.' Rebecca lowered her eyes as she began to grasp the reality of the situation.

'Well, he'll be forced to drop the freight charge. There'll be undercutting right, left and centre, and more than one'll go under, mark my words.' Isaac hesitated only momentarily. 'Your husband should know as soon as possible. Do you know where he is?'

She groaned. 'Not off hand. All I can do is contact his London office, but if he's just sailed, it could be weeks before he receives any message. You know I don't see a great deal of him with his business keeping him away so much.'

''Tis not the only thing that keeps him away.'

Rebecca caught her breath as a sheen of perspiration moistened her forehead. 'I . . . I don't know what you mean.'

'Oh, come now, Becky, I think you do. You married Captain Bradley because of Toby, and no other reason. I should've seen it for myself. It were quite obvious you disliked the poor man, but it never occurred to me that a daughter of mine would get into trouble like you did. And now you've driven your husband away with that sharp tongue of yours!'

'Oh, Adam's quite capable of answering back, I can assure you!' Her eyes sparked with rancour as she met her father's gaze, but then she shrugged evasively. 'We have been getting on better of late, mind.' But she didn't tell Isaac what had happened when Adam had come home for a few days during the summer. He'd arranged a meeting with the Devon Great Consols' arsenic agent early one morning to extend the contract. But she could see he was exhausted, and when she found him still dead to the world in his bed, she hadn't had the heart to wake him, and instead had sent word that he would be delayed. When he finally woke up, he'd shouted at her for letting him sleep on. She had answered back, and Adam had stormed out of the house demanding to know what excuse she might suggest he make to the agent.

'Well, you are his wife, Rebecca. You must make a life out of what you have. And his business affairs affect your security.'

'Yes, I know. And he lost a lot of money over the *Swift*, you know.'

'Aye.' Isaac leaned forward confidentially now. 'And I've heard things about your husband you may not know. He's trying to make up that loss, and driving himself into the ground in the process. He may run the *Swallow* with a full complement, but he's two men down on the *Emily*. And much of the extra work he does himself, on the deck, up aloft even. Doing makeshift repairs. And he's running the ship dangerously close to the wind, so to speak, to get a fast passage. If he's not careful, the *Swift*'ll not be his only loss.'

But Rebecca straightened her spine defensively. 'Adam's not a fool, Father. He loves the *Emily*. He'd not push her beyond her limits.'

'I wouldn't be so sure, Becky. A man under pressure makes mistakes. And if the *Emily* went down, well, you wouldn't want to be widowed twice, as it were, would you?'

Rebecca turned her head away. Her father was right. She had been as good as wed to Tom, and although she might not love Adam, she had grown to respect certain aspects of his character, and she certainly didn't like to think of losing him.

'I'll send a message to London straight away,' she muttered. 'And as soon as I see Adam, I'll speak to him. Try and tell him to take more care. But I know he'll only accuse me of telling him how to run his own business!'

She drew in a deep lungful of air as she gazed apprehensively into Isaac's earnest face, and she was grateful when the door opened and Toby trotted back into the room and climbed on to her lap. She hugged him tightly, her only solace. Little over two years before, her life had seemed so perfect. And now Tom was dead, she was trapped in a loveless marriage, and even the security she'd sacrificed her own happiness for was tainted with uncertainty.

She smiled wanly as Isaac offered her another cup of tea.

CHAPTER FIFTEEN

'Now you give that a good stir, Toby. Oh, no! Not like that! Oh, Toby!'

The child lifted his eyes to her with such innocence that she couldn't help but laugh uproariously at the cake mixture that was splashed all over the table, the floor, Toby himself and her apron. It was even in her hair which she'd carelessly tied back with a ribbon that had since come loose, allowing her long tresses to hang forward over her shoulder.

But her mirth was rudely interrupted by a loud knock on the front door. She met Mrs Blatchford's horrified gaze. They were each just as much a sight as the other, Rebecca perhaps worse as she'd unfastened the top buttons of her plain blouse because of the heat in the kitchen. The situation was so ludicrous that in an instant both women were creased with laughter, and tears were running down the housekeeper's cheeks.

'I'll go,' Rebecca gasped. ''Twill only be Adam. Forgotten his key, I expect.'

'Well, I hope he's come back in a better humour than he went out in.'

'Oh, he's very concerned about the contract. I just hope the meeting went well.'

'Just as long as he don't bite my head off again.'

'He won't. And if he does, he won't mean it.'

Rebecca skipped out of the door, still chuckling, and hurried down the hallway, wiping her hands on her apron. It crossed her mind that it felt strange to find herself defending Adam. She appreciated how worried he must be, but it was certainly true that his temper had been on a short fuse ever since he'd come home three days earlier.

She opened the front door wide and had to look twice at the man standing there. For a moment, she thought it was indeed her husband, for the stranger was tall and had Adam's breadth of shoulder. She was immediately alert with curiosity.

'Can I help you, sir?'

'Indeed you can.' He smiled affably, and she noticed at once his cultured London accent. 'Is your master in?'

'My . . . my master?' she stammered, taken aback.

'Yes. I was told this is where Captain Bradley lives.'

'Oh! Why, yes!' She felt herself flush crimson and she dared not glance down at her dirty apron. 'My husband is at a meeting at the mine offices, but I'm sure he won't be long if you'd care to wait.'

'You?' The man's mouth gaped open in astonishment. 'You're Adam's wife? Well, I never! He's a dark horse, and no mistake!'

Rebecca's brow furrowed. She wasn't quite sure how to take this fellow. 'I'm afraid you have the advantage, sir.'

'Oh, I'm sorry, Mrs Bradley. I am . . .' and he chuckled deep in his throat, 'Alfred Bradley. Fred. Adam's cousin.'

'Oh, I see.' She understood now why she'd thought for a second that it had been Adam standing there. The resemblance between them was quite striking, except that there was something cunning about Fred Bradley's eyes, and his face was fuller and florid compared with the more haggard look Adam had about him recently. And although she judged that this cousin was probably younger than Adam, he was showing definite signs of a stomach paunch. 'Adam always said he had no other family,' she frowned.

'Well, he would, wouldn't he?' Fred smiled undeterred. 'And it would seem that's not the only thing he's kept secret, hiding his beautiful young wife in such a remote place.'

'Remote? I'd hardly call Morwellham remote, not by ship leastways. And I'm not hiding. I've lived here most of my life. My father's the harbour master.' She had kept her voice level, not sure if she was chastising the stranger for his forwardness or merely instructing him.

But Fred was still smiling. 'I stand corrected. But all the same, I can understand why dear Adam would want to keep you to himself.'

Before she knew it, he had reached out and thumbed away a smudge of the cake mixture she hadn't realized was on her cheek. She was astounded, and stepped backwards. 'I . . . I was doing some baking with my son,' she explained hastily.

'A son! Well, I never!' Fred grinned, and with a lift of his eyebrows, sucked on his thumb. 'And I should say you are an excellent cook, too.'

'I believe I do most things well,' she told him, lifting her chin. 'Including assaying copper ore,' she threw in for good measure.

'I'm impressed. But perhaps if I could wait for Adam? We haven't seen each other for years. It will be such a surprise for him.'

'If you'd like to come this way, I'll arrange for the house-keeper to bring some tea.'

She demurely showed him into the parlour and then rushed back to the kitchen, wrenching off the apron as she went. 'Mrs Blatchford, will you serve tea in the parlour? On the best china!' she commanded breathlessly. 'And some of the biscuits we made yesterday. And can you keep Toby with you?'

'Why, yes, mistress, but . . . ?'

''Tis Adam's cousin!'

'Cousin? But the captain don't have no family.'

'Apparently he has!'

'Are you sure, mistress? I mean, he could be anyone!'

149

'No, I'm sure of it. He looks so like Adam. And just look at me!'

She raced upstairs to throw on some more suitable attire, rubbed her face clean in the mirror, and expertly twisted her long hair around her head and secured it with three pins. It would have to do. And when she reached the parlour door again, she stopped to smooth her bodice before turning the handle.

Fred Bradley was on his feet in an instant. 'Oh, Mrs Bradley, there was no need to change on my account. You looked perfectly charming before.'

Rebecca dipped her head to acknowledge his compliment. ''Twould be discourteous of me not to receive my husband's cousin in a fitting manner. My housekeeper will serve tea in just a moment.'

'That is most kind.'

'I expect you have travelled a long way.'

'Only from Plymouth. On a paddle steamer.' Fred gave his dazzling smile again. 'And I shall return the same way after I have seen Adam.'

'I do hope he is not too long then, for the steamer leaves at half past three. Ah, here is the tea. Come in, Mrs Blatchford.' She waited, quite restrained, as the older woman put down the tray, not leaping up to help her as she normally would. She didn't know what sort of person this cousin was but, if nothing else, she did feel some loyalty to Adam and didn't want to let him down. She poured the tea, and politely handed Fred a cup.

'So tell me, what brings you to these parts when I have never heard of your existence before?' she enquired, offering him a biscuit.

'Ah, well, it is a long story,' Fred began in an easy manner. 'I spent some years in America and, shall we say, lost touch with my family. Communication isn't always easy in such a vast continent, you see. I made a tidy sum in one way or another and eventually came home to England. But I went north, to invest my interests in industry. I did write to my dear cousin a couple of times, but he never replied.'

Rebecca raised her eyebrows. It didn't sound like Adam to ignore such correspondence. 'I expect he didn't receive your letters,' she suggested.

'Perhaps,' Fred replied. 'Anyway, my investments have been most successful, and I now find myself in possession of a modest fortune. I decided to come to London to seek out my family for a happy reunion, but found that my uncle had died three years ago and that Adam had made his home in the west country; it was quite a shock!'

'I can hardly say that Adam has made his home here,' Rebecca informed him. 'Most of his time is spent either at sea or directing the London office. You are most fortunate to have caught him on one of his rare visits.'

'Then I think my cousin does not realize how blessed he is, neglecting such a pretty wife so.'

Rebecca knew that she blushed. It was a long time since Adam had paid her a compliment, and recently their conversations had consisted solely of his business worries. But to be spoken to in such a manner by this not unattractive stranger was most pleasant. It made her feel like a lady, something Adam had never managed to achieve.

She smiled. 'You flatter me, sir. But 'tis not Adam's fault his work keeps him away, and he does work very hard.'

'Yes, I know. And I believe he has had some bad luck of late?'

'The loss of the *Swift*?' she said in some surprise. 'I suppose you read of it in *Lloyd's List*?'

'Indeed I did. And I understand there are changes here at Morwellham which are about to affect my cousin's fortunes. So my visit comes, perhaps, at a most opportune moment.' He leaned forward confidentially, and Rebecca noticed that, unlike Adam's honest, chestnut eyes, Fred's irises were flecked with exciting green flashes. 'I have a considerable sum to invest at a time when Adam may be very glad of it.'

Rebecca brought her lips together and slowly lowered her eyes. 'You must be aware that Adam is a very proud and independent man. If he needed a loan, I am sure he would apply to the bank for one. Besides, the London business is doing quite well, and Adam was well able to stand the loss.'

'But he can have little capital in reserve now, and Bradley's Merchants might still be making a modest profit, but nothing like it was when my poor uncle was still alive. Its dividends have dropped considerably, and its shares would be worth a lot less. Not Adam's fault, of course. He cannot do two jobs, try as he may. And his father was a remarkable businessman, and not even Adam can take his place. So you see, Mrs Bradley, Adam may well be glad of my help. I know he is an honest and industrious worker. I cannot fault him on that. But I am more of, shall we say, a business opportunist than he is, although I certainly do not share his expertise in finding a wife who is both intelligent and beautiful.'

'I don't believe Adam was looking for a wife when we met,' she answered in an effort to hide her embarrassment.

'No. I don't suppose he was.' Fred sat back languidly in the chair. 'His first marriage was not a very fruitful one, and I don't imagine he was anxious to repeat the experience.'

'He . . . he says very little of his first wife.'

'There isn't much to say. She was a very noble, charitable woman, but cold, for all that. She cared no more for Adam than one of her destitute urchins. He respected her, but he never loved her. She was too strong for him.'

'Too strong for him?' Rebecca's eyes widened with astonishment.

Fred stared at her and then bellowed with laughter. 'Oh, don't get me wrong! Adam has a will of steel when he wants to. But underneath, he's as soft as blancmange.'

Rebecca swallowed. She wasn't sure she liked the analogy. 'He is very caring,' she said guardedly.

'Particularly to yourself, I'm sure.'

She concealed the wry grimace well. If only he knew how their relationship stood. But she was saved having to search for a suitable reply by the sound of the front door opening and then being closed none too gently.

'Ah, 'twill be Adam now,' she smiled broadly. 'If you'll excuse me.'

She crossed the room and went out into the hall. Adam was hanging his coat on the stand, his face set.

'How did the meeting go?'

He looked at her from under dark eyebrows and sucked in his hollow cheeks. 'Don't ask,' he muttered in frustration. 'You'd think with all the arsenic they're bringing out now, they could renew the contract without forcing me to reduce the freight charges. After all, I was their original carrier. The trouble is, they know they've got me over a barrel, so to speak. They know I'll be losing the limestone soon, and that I'll be desperate for a regular cargo.'

'Oh, I'm sorry, Adam.' She put her hand on his arm. 'But never mind. I've got something to cheer you up. A visitor. I gather you'll be surprised.'

Adam looked bemused but followed her into the parlour. Fred Bradley at once got to his feet and came forward with a grin, and Rebecca glanced over her shoulder to watch Adam's delight.

But Adam's jaw had clamped tightly, and his normally tanned face had turned white. Rebecca was so startled by the hatred in his expression that her heart stood still, and her eyes darted nervously towards Fred and back to her husband.

'What the blazes are you doing here?' Adam grated through clenched teeth.

'What! Not pleased to see me, cousin?' Fred continued to smile. 'After all these years?'

'How dare you!' Adam's usually soft voice was like gravel, his eyes narrowed with hostility. 'How dare you worm your way into my home! Who the hell let you in?'

Rebecca was so numbed that she didn't think to protect herself. 'I . . . I did,' she mumbled.

'And giving him tea, I see!' The colour had returned to Adam's cheeks, and his face was now livid with fury.

'I . . . was only offering hospitality to a guest.'

'Huh! You don't offer hospitality to the devil. Now, get out of my house!'

'Oh, come, come, Adam! After I've travelled all this way to see you. And such behaviour in front of your charming lady wife!'

'Whom you have no doubt beguiled with your fancy words! Now get out of my house before I throw you out!'

'But I hear things aren't going so well for you at present, and I may be able to help,' Fred crooned unperturbed.

'I wouldn't come to you for help if you were the last person on earth! Now I'm warning you . . .'

'At least hear what I have to say,' Fred persisted.

Rebecca's pulse began to thunder as Adam suddenly bolted across the room and grasped Fred by the scruff of the neck. The two men were well matched in size, but Fred surrendered at once to Adam's muscular power and offered little resistance as Adam frogmarched him down the hallway and thrust him outside.

'And don't you *ever* darken my doorstep again!' Rebecca heard Adam yell and the cottage shook as he slammed the front door.

Rebecca stood transfixed, not sure whether she hadn't imagined the whole affair, until Adam strode back into the parlour, his face flushed with rage.

'What the devil did you think you were doing, inviting a stranger into our home?' he rounded on her.

Her eyes opened wide and she raised her chin defiantly. 'There's no need to vent your anger on me! He said he were your cousin, and I had no reason to doubt him. And he looks so like you . . .'

'We ceased to be cousins years ago!'

'And how was I supposed to know that . . . that you . . .' she stammered, part way between her own anger and a desire to burst into tears at the injustice of his accusations.

Adam drew in a gulping breath and then raised his hand in the air as if forcing back his maddened temper. 'All right,' he breathed. 'Perhaps I was wrong never to have told you about my dear cousin, but I never thought . . .' She saw him swallow hard and grip the back of the sofa so that his knuckles turned white. 'Let me explain. Our fathers were brothers. They had built up the business between them. Equal partners, although my father was the real brains behind it. Fred would have inherited half the company, but my uncle disowned him, and when he died, oh, about eight or nine years ago I suppose, we learned that he'd left his half of the partnership to my father. Fred tried to contest the will, dragged us through the courts until he finally lost the case. My father, out of the goodness of his heart, gave Fred five hundred pounds and a first-class ticket to America. I thought I'd seen the last of him until I received a couple of letters from him from up north. I ignored them, but I made discreet enquiries and found he'd invested his ill-gotten gains in industry, exploiting the poor factory workers, no doubt. And I can guess why he's decided to seek me out now.'

'He said he wanted to help you financially with the business,' Rebecca ventured.

'That's what he told you, I suppose!' Adam shook his head with an ironic laugh. 'There's only one reason why Fred's turned up like this out of the blue. Through my father I've inherited what Fred considers to be his inheritance, too, and now he wants his share without lifting a finger to earn it. When I think of the years of bloody hard work I've put in! Well, I'll be damned if I'll give away a penny to that bastard!'

'There's no need to use that sort of language.'

'Well, that's what he is!' Adam's voice was rising again. 'Do you want to know why he was disinherited? Because he's a liar and a philanderer and makes his living cheating other people out of their money. He didn't come here on a social visit, you know, but to swindle your son out of his inheritance!'

Rebecca stared at him and pursed her lips as she thought of the polite stranger he had just thrown out of the house. 'I don't believe you. You're just saying that because he's more of a gentleman than you are.'

'Well, he's certainly worked his charms on you!'

Rebecca flared her nostrils like a cornered beast. She felt trapped, and the only way to save herself was to lash out with her tongue. 'You're just jealous because he knows how to treat a lady, and you don't! He showed me nothing but respect and courtesy!'

'And flattery, no doubt. But that's his forte. How he works. Charms his way into people's lives, notably into the beds of wealthy wives and widows, and then into their fortunes, and when he's milked them dry, he drops them like a stone and moves on to his next prey. Well, you'd better watch out that he doesn't find his way into your bed, madam, for I'll not support another one of your bastards!'

Rebecca felt herself gasp for air, suffocating as bile rose from her stomach and burned in her throat. 'How dare you speak to me like that!' she shrieked. 'I don't believe a word you're saying!'

But Adam was glaring at her more calmly now. 'I might not be the boy you loved so much, but you know I'm not a liar,' he said levelly. 'Everything I tell you about my cousin is true, I swear it. Why do you think I've never mentioned him before? Well, I'll tell you. Because I'm ashamed to be related to him!'

But his earlier words had cut too deep, and she was still smarting under the degradation. 'No! You're saying these things because you're afraid I might find him more pleasing than you!'

Adam released the back of the sofa with such a jerk that Rebecca recoiled from him. He spun round, paced the room twice, his hands clenched as the simmering frustrations suddenly boiled over and he finally lost control. Rebecca couldn't move a muscle as he stepped up to her and seized her wrists in a grip of iron.

'And do I mean so little to you?' He could scarcely wring the words from his throat, his face twisted with despair. 'Didn't I respect your grief? Haven't I cared for you and your son without asking a thing in return? And what have I had out of our marriage, tell me that? Nothing! Not even a tender word, let alone my conjugal rights. All I get is people talking behind my back, laughing at me for marrying a slut who was pregnant with another man's child. Oh, there's no need to look so shocked! Don't think the whole of Morwellham doesn't know. How are you and I supposed to have produced a child as dark as ebony, eh? If it weren't for the fact that you're Isaac Westbrook's daughter and that I was fool enough to marry you, you'd be branded a whore!'

She stared at him, totally immobile, even her chest stilled so that the room began to sway as her lungs fought for air. But then Adam pushed her away from him with such vehemence that she sank on to the floor. But she wouldn't be beaten! She raised her head boldly, though her defiant eyes were glistening.

Adam was gazing down at her, his breath audibly trembling. He rubbed his hand over his mouth, the taut muscles of his face slackening. 'I'm sorry, Rebecca,' he croaked, his voice quieter now. 'But that's the truth of it. You've ruined your own life, and you've ruined mine as well. And if all you can do is to play up to the flatteries of that lying, cheating trickster, then heaven help you.'

And then he was gone, and she heard the reverberations as he stormed up the stairs.

She remained on the floor, utterly drained. Even the need to weep had vanished. Had Adam really said those cruel things to her? She couldn't believe that he had spoken to her like that! Physically hurt her, for her wrists still stung. Not that she imagined he had known what he was doing. He had been . . . incensed . . . crazed . . . like a man possessed. Like a man . . . who had been pushed over the edge. And she caught her breath with a little cry. For . . . for who had done the pushing . . . ?

* * *

The hall clock struck three, and still sleep had not come. She'd lain awake, the brutal scene that had taken place in the parlour tumbling over and over in her head. Adam had petrified her, his usual self-control flung to the four winds as he had lashed out at her with unfettered wrath. How dare he shout at her as if she were some trollop and Toby some brat she had spawned along the way! Well, she wouldn't let him get away with it! In the morning, she would confront him, demand an apology. No. More than that! She would make him suffer the same pain and humiliation he had heaped upon her. Make him grovel at her feet for forgiveness. Which she, of course, would refuse . . .

The thought brought her some sort of satisfaction and eventually allowed her to drift off to sleep. When she awoke, the room was bright and she knew it must be late. Her eyes were still heavy, but the events of the previous day instantly leaped into her mind and she was out of bed in a trice and pulling on her dressing gown. She must challenge Adam before her nerve failed her. She went straight to his room, her lips bunched with furious determination. But her heart sank as she stood in the open doorway. The room was empty, the bed all in a muddle as if its occupant, too, hadn't been able to sleep.

She raced downstairs, prepared to do battle. In the kitchen, Mrs Blatchford was giving Toby his breakfast in his highchair.

'Where's the captain?' Rebecca demanded.

'Why, ma'am, he be gone.'

'Gone?' she repeated inanely. 'What do you mean, gone?'

'Sailed with his barge first thing this morning, back to Plymouth. Left you a letter, mind. 'Tis there on the table. Why don't you take it back to bed with you, with a nice cup of tea? I'll look after Toby.'

'Oh. Er . . . yes,' Rebecca stammered, her heart bursting with frustrated anger as if Adam had deliberately thwarted her planned retaliation. 'Thank you, Mrs Blatchford,' she added absently.

She mounted the stairs slowly so as not to spill the tea, the letter trembling slightly in her hand. Adam had left, and doubtless wouldn't be showing his face again for some time. Well, good riddance! But if he thought she would forgive and forget in his absence, he was mistaken. She climbed back into bed and almost immediately tore open the envelope with piqued frustration. Adam's handwriting was usually so neat, but this letter had obviously been written in some haste. She started reading, her heart beating hard.

Rebecca, I cannot begin to say how sorry I am. I had absolutely no right to say such things to you. I don't know what was in my mind. It is no excuse to say that I was worried about my business affairs, but the idea of my cousin getting his hands on you and destroying that innocence was so abhorrent to me that I lost my reason. Yes, innocence. For I know that Toby was born out of an innocent love, and I know that fate, and not yourself, is to blame for all that has happened since. So, in a way, you were right that I was jealous. For despite all that stands between us, I still love you. I know that you cannot possibly forgive me, and as my presence must be intolerable to you, I will keep away as much as possible and only return to Morwellham when business demands it. But please believe me that my cousin is a dangerous man. I hope we will not see him again, but the reason I have left so quickly is to go to London to check he has caused no trouble there. Besides, the Emily will have been idle for several days, and I cannot afford that. The Sure will have to carry what cargo she can after the limekilns close. For her to break even is about the best we can hope for in the future. I must concentrate on Bradley's Merchants now, and so I shall trouble you very little. Please take care of yourself and little Toby. Adam.

She was staring at the letter, her other hand pressed against her mouth. She had her apology, but it didn't inspire her with the sense of victory she had expected. She reached out for the teacup, and as she sipped pensively at the steaming liquid, her eyes travelled over the words a second time, carefully analyzing their meaning and what Adam was trying to say to her. It wasn't just an apology, but an explanation. He was sick with worry over his business affairs, she knew that well enough, and he was already working himself into the ground. So perhaps it was the last straw when he came home to find her entertaining his hated cousin, and she shouldn't have been surprised at him losing his temper when his loathing for Fred had been so instantly apparent. And what did she really know of Fred? An attractive stranger who had flattered her. But when she thought about it, there had been something disturbing about him she had disliked. No. Adam had not lied to her about his cousin, of that she was convinced. And she was sure of something else as well. That when Adam said he loved her, it was true.

She let the letter slip from her fingers and fall on to the bedspread. Adam loved her. He had married her in good faith, shown her nothing but kindness, and what had she given him in return? She hated to admit it, but she had lied and cheated and hurt him so deeply until yesterday he had finally snapped. It wasn't her fault that she couldn't love him, but it wasn't his either, and she had treated him so badly, driving him away until she had broken him.

She bit on her lip. Oh, Adam! She owed him so much, and yet all she had ever shown him was hostility. Their marriage could not be as it should, but surely there could be some respect, some understanding between them. If only he hadn't rushed away like that, they could have sat down like two rational human beings and come to some sort of mutually acceptable agreement.

But now, God alone knew when she might see him again.

CHAPTER SIXTEEN

Late March had ushered in some wild and filthy weather, and the *Swallow* was overdue. The *Emily* was undergoing some minor repairs, and as the captain of the *Swallow* was unwell, Adam was mastering her on her present voyage. The schooner was scheduled to call at Morwellham with wine and French brandy for the Ship Inn, and also for a merchant in Tavistock, a contract Rebecca had proudly negotiated with her father's help in an effort to show Adam her support. She hadn't seen him for six months, not since that dreadful incident in October. She had written to him, not begging him to come home, but suggesting she would welcome his presence and promising she would treat his cousin as an enemy if he turned up on the doorstep again. Fred, however, had disappeared into thin air, it would seem, although Adam remained concerned. His letters were quite amicable, as if he, too, was trying to make amends, but his work had made a visit impossible. But now, at long last, Rebecca was expecting his arrival.

She had thought long and hard about what she would say to him. She couldn't tell him that she realized what a fool she had been and that she felt she might love him after all, because it simply wasn't true, and there had been enough lies in their relationship already. But she could express her gratitude for all he had done for her together with her remorse for the deep hurt she'd caused him. Her grief over Tom had blinded her, but she recognized now that Adam was a worthy man. She respected him, had even grown fond of him in a strange sort of way, and hoped that they could live peaceably together from now on.

But although the *Swallow* was nearly a week late, she hadn't been sighted. Not that every vessel on the Tamar was reported before its arrival in its intended port, and there were a hundred and one reasons why a ship could be delayed. But there had been severe gales in the Channel, and Rebecca had to admit that she was actually worried over Adam's safety. And of course, Misha and Robin were also aboard, so Rebecca was not the only person to be increasingly anxious.

The blustering wind and lashing rain had rattled at the windowpanes all day, and Rebecca had recently drawn the curtains against the gathering darkness, grateful that the cottage was warm and cosy inside. Mrs Blatchford was upstairs in the nursery with Toby while Rebecca was preparing the evening meal, something she liked to do at least twice a week, and it gave her a rest from the toddler's ceaseless demands. She was humming softly and comforting herself with the thought that despite the present foul weather, spring would soon be blossoming and the local daffodil trade in full swing.

When she heard the front door open and shut, she caught her breath with a little gasp. Adam. For no one else had a key. The relief that he was safe washed through her, followed by a crippling rush of apprehension. The kitchen door opened, and he stood in the doorway. Rebecca had turned to stone, her hand holding a ladle in mid-air, and they faced each other across the room in silence. Rebecca watched, heart vibrating savagely, as Adam dropped his kitbag on the floor and tossing his captain's hat on the table, pulled out a chair and sank on to it with his head in his hands.

Rebecca's lungs tightened. This was hardly what she'd expected, and for a moment she was quite taken aback. 'Adam?' she whispered at last, her feet rooted to the spot.

And when he made no reply, she said again, 'Adam, whatever's the matter?'

She heard the wrenching sigh that trembled from his throat. 'That must be the worst voyage I've ever had,' he muttered without lifting his head. Rebecca knew at once that something appalling must have happened and was afraid to hear what he had to say. 'The entire crew became ill,' he went on, but had to pause to cough harshly. 'Misha and I had to sail her between us, and then we hit a bloody storm. We had to heave to for three days. I had to get the men out of their hammocks, but . . . but . . .' He broke off again, his voice strange and guttural. 'I lost a man overboard.'

Rebecca felt as if there were lead deep in the pit of her stomach. She slowly put down the ladle, and then stood immobile with shock.

'It . . . it was my fault,' Adam rasped so quietly she could hardly hear him, his words sounding unreal. 'They were too ill. Too weak. The fool had forgotten to fasten a lifeline. I'd just ordered him to go back and fix one on, but it was too late. The wave hit and . . .' He stopped again, ran his hand through his hair. 'I tried. God knows, I tried to find him! But . . . He was from Plymouth. Married with three small children. Oh, God, why wasn't it me!' his cracked voice suddenly rose hysterically. 'He had a family. A wife who loved him.'

Rebecca stared at him, motionless, her heart torn with compassion for this man whom she once thought she despised. She came forward soundlessly, as if in a dream, and knelt down in front of him.

'Adam, don't say that,' she croaked. 'These things happen . . .'

She put out her hand and squeezed his arm, and realized her fingers had met with cold, wet wool. She turned her head and saw that his coat was a deeper shade of navy to within a few inches of the hem. Her hand moved to his shoulder and tightened on the sodden material.

'Good God, you're soaking! What happened to your waterproof?'

'It got washed overboard,' he murmured, looking up at her sheepishly. She saw his face then, rain dripping from his chin, which was dark with several days' stubble, and deep shadows under his sunken, bloodshot eyes.

'Why didn't you change, then?' she half accused him.

'I didn't have the chance.' His head drooped forward as if he were having difficulty staying upright in the chair, and he rubbed his hand over his eyes and forehead in a gesture of pure exhaustion. 'Christ, I'm so tired. I don't think I've had more than a couple of hours sleep in days.'

Looking at him, Rebecca could well believe it. 'And when did you eat last?' she asked with a concerned frown.

'Eat?' He sounded surprised. 'Oh, God knows. I can't remember. Robin was cook, remember, and he was ill, too, but he's on the mend now.'

'And Misha?'

'He and I were the only ones who weren't ill. I tell you, I don't know what I'd have done without him.'

He coughed again, dry and painfully, and Rebecca instinctively lay her palm across his forehead. 'Well, I think you're sick now. You're burning like a furnace!'

But he shook his head. 'I can't be. I feel so cold,' he groaned.

''Tis a fever you've got then,' she told him. 'Now take those wet clothes off and we'll get you into bed.'

'No, I can't. I've got to go back and see to the ship.'

'You're not going anywhere. I'm sure Misha can manage. He's not getting sick, too, is he?'

'Not that I know of. But—'

'No buts, Adam. Father will have turned up on the quayside by now, and he'll help. Now you get those clothes off. And drink this.' She turned to the range and dished out a mug of the soup she was heating for Toby's tea. She put it on the table beside Adam as he struggled out of his coat, and then she filled two stone bottles with hot water from the range boiler. 'I'll go and light the fire in your room, and bring down a nightshirt.'

She hurried upstairs and put a match to the ready-laid fire, so thankful that she'd kept the room and the bed well aired in anticipation of his return. She called into the nursery while she waited for the kindling to catch and told Mrs Blatchford what was happening. As soon as the fire was blazing, she went back down to the kitchen. Adam was fast asleep slumped across the table, the soup untouched, only his coat on the other chair and the rest of his sodden clothing still plastered to his back.

'Adam!' she called softly, but when she received no response, she repeated quite loudly, 'Adam!' But still she had to shake him hard to wake him, and he blinked at her, his eyes struggling to focus. The relief of sleep had started him shivering violently, and suddenly, quite unexpectedly, Rebecca recognized in herself the fear she had known once before. In the untidy, fetid malthouse tenement. She shied away from it, forcing the fear aside, and instead thrust her energies into stripping off Adam's clothes as he seemed incapable of doing so for himself. He was wet to the skin, and she used a rough towel to dry him and rub some warmth into his flesh. It was as she worked that it occurred to her she'd never seen his bare torso before. He was so broad and strong, and yet there wasn't an ounce of fat to him, and his muscled stomach was quite hollow. But if he hadn't eaten for days . . .

She pulled the clean nightshirt on over his head and left him to remove his lower clothing while she dished out some more soup as the first mug had gone cold. But he was shaking so much he was in danger of spilling it, and she had to steady his hand as he drank the thick, scalding liquid. And then she made him take some laudanum before helping him up the stairs and into bed. He caught her hand, but his grip was weak as he murmured his thanks. She stayed with him for a few minutes, but he was almost instantly asleep again, and as she watched him, the occasional shudder still jerking his body, she wondered if she didn't feel more for him than she cared to admit.

* * *

'Influenza,' Dr Seaton pronounced the next morning as he put away his stethoscope. 'Lucky it hasn't gone to pneumonia after half drowning yourself in the sea.'

Adam glanced up sharply. 'What! Who told you that?' he grated through his burning throat.

'You can't risk your life to try and save someone else's and expect the crew to keep quiet about it,' Rebecca answered. ''Tis all over Morwellham.'

'It was a damned stupid thing to do,' the doctor reprimanded him. 'Survival in water that cold is only a matter of minutes.'

'I know that,' Adam spluttered as he failed to subdue the hacking cough. 'But all I did was put a rope ladder over the side and climb down to try and find the poor devil. I had two lifelines, so there wasn't any risk.'

'But you were doused in icy water several times, which hasn't exactly helped,' Dr Seaton frowned at him. 'Your lungs are clear at the moment, but I want to keep an eye on that cough. Influenza has a nasty habit of attacking the chest in the later stages, and you're running a very high temperature. Now, I want you to have two or three steam inhalations a day, and keep the room warm and well ventilated, but with no draughts, Mrs Bradley. Plenty of fluids, and a little laudanum to help the aches and pains. And may I suggest you send your little boy to his grandparents? Influenza passes from one person to another very easily, and small children are particularly vulnerable to complications.'

Rebecca nodded. 'Yes, 'twould seem sensible.'

'Well, then, I see no reason why you shouldn't be up and about within a week, Captain Bradley, although you'll need to take life easy for a while. Don't worry. I'll see myself out.'

'Thank you, Doctor.'

He closed the door quietly behind him, and Rebecca turned back to the bed to see Adam sink back wearily against the pillows. 'How am I supposed to take things easy?' he rasped. 'The *Emily*'s repairs will be finished in a day or two, the *Swallow* doesn't have a master at all, the *Sure*'s captain is already complaining about how difficult it is to find an inward cargo . . .'

'Adam, will you stop worrying!' Rebecca commanded as she perched on the bed next to him. 'You'll get better much quicker if you rest properly and stop fretting about the business. Now, can I get you anything?'

'Some more laudanum?' he suggested, looking at her through streaming eyes. 'My head's splitting, and I've got muscles aching where I didn't know I had them. And my throat's on fire,' he added, rubbing his hand over his gullet with a groan.

'Stop talking then!' she chided, but then her lips parted in a sympathetic smile. 'You really do look awful.'

'Thank you. Just what I needed to hear.'

She winced as he coughed painfully and fell back again with an exhausted sigh. A lock of his hair had fallen forward, and she gently pushed it back from his sweating brow. His red-rimmed eyes gazed at her out of dark sockets, and the stubble on his jaw was almost a beard, but the handsome looks she had once scorned now tugged at her heart.

'I'll get you that laudanum,' she said softly. 'And some steam. And then you should try and get some sleep. And would you like another hot-water bottle? That one must have gone cold.'

'Mmm. Please,' he croaked.

But she contemplated him for a moment longer. 'Dr Seaton was right,' she muttered in a low voice. 'It might make me proud to think that my husband was so courageous, but don't you ever do anything like that again. I . . . I couldn't bear to lose you, you know.'

The words all but stuck in her throat, and she hurried out of the room before Adam had a chance to react to them.

* * *

'You look a little better today,' she remarked chirpily as she set down the jug of steaming water. 'I thought a good wash might freshen you up, if you feel up to it, that is.'

'Not really, but I can tell I'm getting unpleasant.'

She chuckled at him as she took a clean nightshirt from the drawer and hung it in front of the fire to warm. She had been quite worried about him for several days, but at last he seemed to be over the worst, although the illness had drained him of energy. She poured the hot water into the wash bowl and gathering up what she needed, placed everything on the bedside cabinet.

'Nightshirt off, then,' she ordered.

She noticed him hesitate slightly, then pull the bed-clothes well over his waist before wriggling out of his night-shirt. She soaped the flannel and handed it to him, averting her eyes modestly while he washed himself, and then she wrung it out again so that he could rinse off the lather and dry himself on the towel. And all the time she was endeav-ouring to be very matter-of-fact about it, when she knew that her eyes were being drawn towards his strong, hard body. And all at once, she recognized the tightness low down in her stomach that she had not known for a long time . . . since the darkness of a wood . . .

She deliberately turned away to reach for the clean nightshirt so that he wouldn't see the confusion on her face. She'd fought against Adam for so long that it didn't seem possible . . . it didn't seem right that she should . . . She helped him to don the garment and then watched as he set-tled back thankfully against the pillows.

'God, I don't think I've ever felt so ill,' he murmured.

For a moment, shame clawed at Rebecca's throat as if she'd taken advantage of his weakened state. 'Well, what do you expect if you try to drown yourself?' She wasn't quite sure herself what she meant, her feelings entangling them-selves wildly in her breast.

'I know someone who really did try to drown herself once.'

His words were unexpected, his voice low, and she flushed as she felt his gaze on her. The day she had almost stepped over the edge of the wharf in a demented trance had been buried in the past, a lifetime ago. 'I . . . I didn't know what I was doing, though. But you did.' She was glad to be able to turn the conversation around. 'You knew the risk you were taking.'

'There wasn't any risk. Well, very little anyway. But I had to try.' He spoke with such vehemence that it made him cough again. 'It was my fault, after all. I got them out of their hammocks when they were feeling as rough as I do now.'

But Rebecca shook her head. 'They were none of them as sick as you've been, from what I've heard. And if you hadn't called for all hands, the ship could've gone down and not just one man but all of you might've drowned.'

She heard him draw in a deep, anguished breath and then he rubbed his hand over his forehead. 'I've been master of a ship for over six years, and I've never lost a crew member before.'

'These things happen sometimes, Adam. You know that. 'Tis a risk every sailor takes. 'Tweren't your fault.'

But he turned his head away, his eyes tightly shut. Rebecca felt her own heart would break. To learn of any man's demise at sea always filled her with an angry sorrow, but this time the pain of it cut deeper than ever. And she knew it was because of the grief and the unfounded guilt Adam was suffering.

It seemed the most natural thing in the world to stroke the back of his hand. 'You must put it behind you,' she choked. 'In fact, I think there's a good deal we should put behind us.'

And she wasn't surprised when, turning back to face her, he fixed his wide, expressive eyes on her, and his fingers closed lightly around hers.

* * *

'Are you sure you feel up to walking all the way to Newquay?'

'But 'tis only a mile down the river.' He mimicked her accent, his face straight.

She pushed his arm playfully as they wandered along the riverbank. Adam had made a rapid recovery and looked better now, she thought, than he had for a long time. And was that because they'd taken increasing pleasure from each other's company? But for her it was far more than that. For with Toby still enjoying his stay with his doting grandparents, she found she wanted to spend every waking minute with the husband she had come . . . it hardly seemed possible, but yes . . . to love.

She slipped her hand into his. His eyes travelled up to her face and she couldn't help but return his surprised smile. She was so brimming with happiness that she could almost have skipped along by his side like a child. The path along the riverbank was still well used, although the grass was already beginning to grow over the tracks to the mine in the time since the George and Charlotte had closed. Where once a hundred women and children had worked the clamorous dressing floor, and men had changed shifts, now there was silence. A barge was sailing past on its slow journey down the winding ribbon of the river. The warm spring sunshine reflected off the water in a dazzling sheen, and Adam squinted thoughtfully into its spangling brilliance. Rebecca knew what he was thinking, and her heart ached that in a few days he would be following in the barge's wake. And she had to tell him before he left.

They stopped for a moment. All so peaceful. But her pulse was racing, her nerves on edge. What would he say? Would he doubt her now, after all she had said and done in the past?

'Adam?' Her voice was small. Trembling. And she had to force herself to go on. 'The man who drowned,' she barely whispered. 'You said his wife loved him. Well, he . . . he wasn't the only one.'

Adam turned to her and scrutinized her face for what seemed an eternity. He said nothing and it made her feel awkward. Unnerved. His silence unsettling her as much as his quick remarks had on the faraway evening when they had met.

But it was Adam who looked away first, his jaw set rigid as he stared after the disappearing barge. She saw him swallow, his forehead creasing into a frown. 'What are you saying, Rebecca?' he grated, his eyes glued on the river. 'You've looked after me. Shown me some sympathy, when not so long ago, you couldn't have cared less. But there's no need to go on with it. I'll be leaving in a day or two, so . . .'

'And that's precisely why I must talk to you. Adam, please listen to me!' The force of her own feelings, her desperation, astounded her as it quivered in her voice. She took a deep breath, struggling with the crippling need to convince him of how she truly felt. 'Adam, I've treated you so unfairly,' she faltered. 'You've been so good to me, and . . . and all I've ever done is to turn you away. When . . . when Tom died, I thought my own life had come to an end. I . . . I didn't believe I could ever be happy again. I didn't *want* to be happy again. So all the kind things you did, I twisted them round in my head to make them into bad things. But I was blind, Adam, and now I know that I can love again. If . . . if only you'll forgive . . .'

She paused, craving his reaction, but he merely lowered his eyes to study his foot as he ground the heel of his shoe into the earth. 'Yes,' he finally croaked. 'I know what grief can do. So, yes. I forgive you. But please,' and he lifted his hand as if to defend himself, 'don't torment me further by saying something that isn't true just because you feel guilty. I forgive you, so let's leave it at that. You can't hate me one minute and confess undying love the next.'

'No, Adam!' The rush of horror made her spring round in front of him, shaking his arms until he was forced to look into her face. 'I've never hated you. And my feelings haven't just changed overnight. They've been . . . growing for a long time. And this last time you've been away, six whole months, I've thought of nothing else but you. Wanting to talk to you. Even found myself missing you. But 'tis only since you've been back that I've recognized it for what it is. I really do, truly, love you, Adam. And I want to be a proper wife to you. In every way.'

Her eyes glistened as they bore earnestly into his, watching his face work painfully. She lifted her hand to his cheek, softly stroking the closely shaven skin, and then her palm trailed downwards to rest on his chest right over where his heart beat with sudden excitement. She felt his ribcage expand beneath her touch, and as he shook his head, the breath shuddered from his lungs.

'Do you really mean it?' he muttered in a hoarse whisper, and as she nodded, her mouth stretched into a grin of relief. Of joy. And then she thought her heart would break as Adam closed his eyes. 'Oh, you'll never know how I've prayed for this moment,' he choked. 'Yearned for it. Oh, my darling, you'll never know . . .' He bent his head, and his mouth brushed against hers almost imperceptibly. And then again, and this time she could feel the warm moistness, and the tidal wave flushed down to her loins. His arms closed about her, encompassing her small frame in a circle of steel. She could feel his hands on her back, pressing her towards him. Her head was spinning, breathless, drowning. And when she opened her eyes, he was smiling down at her. So adoring. So desirous.

'To hell with Newquay,' he murmured thickly.

He grasped her hand and she found herself running back along the path, her heart soaring like a bird. With her full skirt she could hardly keep up with Adam's long stride, and he turned and grinned at her as his strong grip stopped her from falling. They were both laughing now, and when they neared Morwellham again, she found it so hard to suppress the joyous smile that lit her face.

They hurried up the steep incline to the cottage, and when a surprised Mrs Blatchford came out into the hall to see what the stifled giggling was about, Rebecca pulled herself up short and felt colour flush into her cheeks. But Adam faced the housekeeper quite unperturbed.

'We don't wish to be disturbed, Mrs Blatchford,' he said boldly.

And with that, he gripped Rebecca's hand again and made for the stairs. Rebecca could only imagine the older woman's shocked expression, and then she was bounding up the stairs with Adam, her head whirling. In a moment, they were in the bedroom. Unable to check her haste, Rebecca found herself over by the bed, and when she looked back, still laughing, Adam was turning the key in the lock.

They faced each other across the room. Adam's expression was quite still now, and the laughter was extinguished in Rebecca's throat. In its place, she could almost hear her pulse thundering, feel her very breath quivering. She couldn't move, and watched as Adam threw off his coat and waistcoat, and then came slowly towards her, his eyes, dark and smouldering, fixed on her face.

She swallowed hard. Adam continued to hold her gaze, and she felt her stomach clenching even tighter. At last he lifted his hands and cupped her face in them so delicately she could hardly feel his touch. He kissed her just once, their lips clinging softly, and then his fingers carefully began to unfasten her jacket. She stood quite still and allowed him to undress her, too afraid, too yearning, and in a moment all that remained to clad her slender figure were her camisole and drawers. He stopped then, ran his hands lingeringly down her bare arms, bent to kiss her neck, her shoulders. And slowly he began to unlace the front of her camisole.

She stood there, rigid, suddenly terrified. Never, never, had Tom undressed her, and the sensation of her skin naked to the air set her heart hammering and made her want to flee the room. And yet . . . there was a longing inside her, a deep need. And when Adam smiled down at her, his eyes questioning, seeking her trust, she found herself smiling back. This man, who had won first her respect and then her love against all odds, and whose own strong, muscled body had awakened a fire within her. Yes, she wanted to yield to him. Her camisole joined the rest of her clothes on the floor, and she snatched in her trembling breath as he traced the outline of her breasts, his fingertips as light as gossamer. And when she felt him loosening the waistband of her drawers, she felt she might swoon as they dropped to the floor.

He lay her on the bed, and when she dared to look up, he was stripping off the last of his own clothes. He stood quite close to her for a few moments, stark naked, his eyes travelling slowly over her body, before sitting down on the edge of the bed.

'My God, you're beautiful, you know,' he whispered.

And then he was stroking her, caressing her, exploring her body and inciting every fibre of her being to a feverish desire. Her hands reached out to his broad shoulders, his powerful chest. She knew she was lost, drowning in the burning glory of her passion. It was a force she had never known before, not even with Tom, and then . . . she pulled back as Adam finally moved over her, and the ecstasy was gone as she waited for the discomfort to come, the time when the man's virulence erupted and she had to endure . . . But Adam was so gentle, so slow, almost leisurely, that the yearning returned at once and she felt herself responding unrestrained to the growing urgency until Adam suddenly cried out and her own back arched and her loins exploded with an intensity she never knew was in her. She clung on to him, her fingers digging into his flesh, waiting while the exquisite tension gradually relaxed and Adam was kissing her again, her hair, her forehead, her nose, and at last carefully eased himself back on to the bed beside her. He put his arm around her, drawing her close so that she snuggled up to him, her head resting on his shoulder and her body pressed against the lean length of his torso.

'You're shaking,' he suddenly croaked, and lifted his head in concern. 'I . . . I didn't hurt you . . . ? I . . .'

'No! No, not at all!' She realized with astonishment that she was laughing at the pleasure her body had taken from his. ''Tis just . . . I didn't know I . . . could feel like that.' She was aware of the warm skin of his flank against her own flesh, and it seemed so natural. So right. She was even beginning to enjoy her nakedness, to feel proud that she had matched up to the physical demands of this man she had once found so awesome. 'Your . . . your first wife,' she ventured in a near whisper, 'she was very lucky. If you made her feel like that.'

Adam pushed his head back into the pillow with a snort and she saw him swallow hard. 'We were married four years,' he said, staring at the ceiling. 'In all that time, we made love on no more than a dozen occasions. She would lie there like a block of ice . . . I gave up in the end. But with you . . .' He propped himself up on his elbow and gazed down at her, his eyes so melting and full of love. 'I knew from the moment I met you there was . . . a passion inside you, if only I had the chance to . . . I've imagined it so often, you know, thinking . . . how it should be between us. And you . . . you did like it, didn't you?'

Strange tears were welling in her eyes, making them glisten like dew. She reached up and brushed his cheek, and then quite absently trailed her hand over his chest and downwards over his ribcage. He caught her wrist and bringing it back up to his mouth, lasciviously drew the tip of his tongue over her palm.

'You do things like that, Mrs Bradley, and I might not be so gentle next time.'

And very soon her flesh began to purr as he drew her body on to the heights of euphoria once more.

* * *

She stood on the quayside long after the barge had disappeared around the bend in the river, long after the bare tip of its mast had shown above the trees on the loop of land on the opposite bank. A few months ago, a few weeks even, she could never have imagined that she would be choking on her sadness, her eyes stinging with tears, because Adam Bradley had sailed away down the Tamar. Her body and her soul had sung out with joy every night and morning since she and Adam had found each other, but now there was an emptiness inside her, second only to the void she had known once before. The difference was that Adam would be coming back, and perhaps the separation would make his return even sweeter. But the sea was a devil with a hunger for human life, as his last voyage had proved. She'd made him promise, *promise* not to take risks as she knew he had been before, but he'd grinned at her and defied anyone to stop him coming home to his lustful little wife.

And now she was already missing him, and she waited on the quayside, willing the barge to return upstream and for Adam to leap across on to dry land. But it was a vain hope, she knew. And she wasn't sure when she would see him again. She turned away at length, a desolate figure dragging herself up through the port to the cottage which would seem so lifeless without him.

CHAPTER SEVENTEEN

The fir tree looked so pretty in its pot in the corner of the parlour. Rebecca had spent all afternoon decorating it with tiny, brightly coloured boxes containing a bonbon or some sultanas, and tying on the iced shortbread and ginger biscuits they had baked especially with a hole in the centre for the ribbon to pass through. Her mother had found some silvery thread hidden at the bottom of her sewing box, and Rebecca had woven it in and out of the sharp green needles. Now she had just finished securing the miniature candles which, because of the fire hazard, would be lit and carefully guarded for just one hour on the evening of the following day. Christmas Day. She'd stood on a chair to reach the top of the tree and wondered if her father would need to do the same when he performed the ceremony. A taller man . . . Adam . . . could have lit the highest candle with no difficulty.

She tossed her head, rearing away from the tearing ache in her throat. Adam wouldn't be home in time for Christmas. A year ago she hadn't cared, but since the tragedy of the lost seaman which had brought them together back in the spring, Adam was scarcely out of her thoughts. She yearned for his physical presence, to be able to laugh with him, play up to his constant teasing. Most of all, she missed that intimate closeness when she nestled against him in the darkness of the night, safe in the comforting strength of his arms. Her heart was so empty when he was away, that now she was able to admit it: the void that Tom's death had gouged out of her soul had been more than filled.

She stepped back from the tree to admire her handiwork, and turning down the two oil lamps, watched as the silvery thread caught the flickering light from the fire. The effect was quite enchanting for it was nearly dark, and when the candles were lit, they would dance like tiny, magical spirits. Toby would be enthralled, the first Christmas when he really would have some idea of what it was all about. If only . . . But neither his real father nor the man who was beginning to have some place in his life would be there to witness it.

Rebecca lowered her eyes. On the floor beneath the tree were a dozen small packages, her presents to her family and friends. She had bought frugally this year, for they couldn't afford to be extravagant. Adam had decided to send Misha to naval college for three months to gain his official master's certificate, since John Littleworth's health was deteriorating quickly and the *Swallow* would soon be in need of a new captain. In return Misha had agreed a contract to work for Adam for a minimum of five years at a fixed wage, but in the meantime, the college fees had taken most of Adam's sorely depleted capital. The barge was scarcely breaking even, with the limestone trade gone and the freight charges for the arsenic cut, so they were living on Adam's share of the *Swallow* which was fortunately making a reasonable profit. The *Emily*, of course, continued to bring in a high return through Adam's own diligence and physical hard work, but every penny he made went on repaying the loan from the London company. Bradley's Merchants was turning over nicely, but not as it had been in the days of Adam's father. The dividends were much reduced, and Adam was ploughing as much of his personal profits as he could afford directly back into the business. But there would always be good food on their table, clothes on their backs and fuel in the grate, and their home would always be safe, and for that Rebecca was thankful. Her eyes swept contentedly about the room, part of the cottage she had come to love. For it was no longer just a building, but a proper home.

Her heart jolted to a painful stop. Silhouetted in the open doorway was the outline of a tall man standing perfectly still as he watched her in silence. She caught her breath with a little gasp, felt the tremor bristle down her spine. And then she heard the familiar soft chuckle and he came slowly towards her.

She leaped across to him, her heart taking wing as joy exploded within her. He swept her up in his strong arms and swung her around so that her head whirled. When he set her on her feet, she swayed precariously and had to cling on to him, she felt so giddy.

'Oh, Adam!' she cried with elation. 'I thought you couldn't make it home for Christmas!'

'I didn't think I could!' He grinned at her, his eyes moving delightedly over her jubilant face. 'But we had a favourable wind all the way up the Channel . . .'

'Of which you no doubt took full advantage and set every sail!' she accused him.

'Naturally!' He feigned a guilty grimace.

'But you promised . . .'

'There was no danger in it.' He took her by the shoulders and looked deep into her eyes. 'We reefed sail whenever it was necessary, and we didn't have to waste too much time wearing across the wind. And when we reached the Thames Estuary, the wind most obligingly changed direction, so we made reasonable speed up to London, too. I was even paid a bonus for delivering some Portuguese oranges early. So when I realized there was still time, I caught the first train I could, and here I am!'

'Oh, I'm so glad!' The excitement was bubbling up inside her like champagne, making her dance on her toes. A thrill shot through her as, without moving his rich, smouldering eyes from her face, he lifted her hands to his lips and kissed them reverently.

'Oh, God, I missed you!' he whispered thickly.

'And I missed you! But you're here now and it'll be the best Christmas ever!'

He nodded, shutting his eyes with contentment as he smiled, and she cupped his lean cheek in her soft hand.

'You look tired.'

He turned his head and kissed her caressing palm. 'Exhausted, if you must know. And I'm starving. I haven't eaten today. And what I'd really like is a long, hot bath.'

She raised her eyebrows coquettishly. 'Well, we'd better get the water on the go, then. You'll have to put up with Mrs Blatchford in the kitchen, mind, but I've heard she's very good at scrubbing backs!'

'What!'

She exploded in a glorious roar of laughter as his face fell. 'Well, she's really busy with the Christmas preparations. Everyone's coming here tomorrow!'

'Oh, damn!' Adam let out a heartfelt sigh.

'You could bathe up in the bedroom,' she suggested. 'Or even in here if you promise not to make any mess.'

He nodded, and then caught his bottom lip between his teeth in that little habit he had, his eyes dancing mischievously. 'As long as you promise to scrub my back and not Mrs Blatchford!'

He took her in his arms again, brushed his lips over the tip of her nose, her ears, and then down over her throat. She dropped back her head, giggling, and then playfully pushed him away.

'I thought you said you were hungry,' she said lightly.

'But I didn't say what for,' he murmured.

* * *

Rebecca stamped her feet against the penetrating cold and wriggled her fingers inside her thick gloves, and yet there was a fire inside her that burned like a flaring beacon. It seemed that half the inhabitants of Morwellham had gathered in the darkness outside the Ship Inn, each little group carrying a storm lamp. Not a sigh of breeze stirred, the frost so deep it stung the nostrils and set eyes watering. Every head was wreathed in a halo of white, billowing breath as voices were raised in song to celebrate the coming of the infant Jesus. All the people Rebecca loved, or who were woven into the tapestry of her life, had been brought together for the traditional occasion. Her father, somehow retaining, as always, his air of authority despite his beaming countenance, her dear mother and her impish, innocent sister. Jane Martin and Captain Allport — her regular gentleman now — the widow from Morwellham's small dairy, the blacksmith, farrier, the brothers who worked the manganese mill, farmworkers, quay labourers and miners. Ann Richards from the inn accompanied the carols on her violoncello, and her two grown-up daughters, renowned for their voices, led the singing and played the lute and triangle, respectively. So many people, and yet when each tune was ended, the silence of the little riverport echoed back from the steep ridge of rock that all but separated Morwellham from the rest of the world. A small community where one individual depended on another for survival, now more than ever. And in which Rebecca felt lulled in friendship and security.

She caught Ned Gimlett's eye through the crowd. He smiled at her, and his expression said it all. He was delighted that the vivacious young woman, who had touched his paternal heart since she'd been a wilful, strong-minded child, had at last found contentment after the tragic death of the boy she had loved so deeply.

Yes. She was happy now. With a joy she had never before realized could exist inside her. Her eyes lifted to Adam's face, radiant as he sang out with the good tenor voice she'd only recently discovered he possessed. Toby had become irritable and she'd picked him up. When her arms had begun to tire, Adam had taken him from her and now the child was fast asleep, his head resting peacefully on the shoulder of the man he trusted and loved as his natural father. Adam felt

Rebecca's gaze upon him and turned to smile down at her, that wonderful, handsome smile that warmed every part of her being. She wondered now how she could have resisted him for so long. Perhaps because, deep down, she'd felt something for him the instant they'd met but had resented her own attraction to anyone who wasn't Tom. But that was all in the past. Her soul now ran over with love for this good, worthy man whom she felt so proud to be with. Tom was gone. Never forgotten. But gone. And at long last, his ghost was truly at rest.

Rebecca tucked her hand through Adam's elbow, pressed herself up close to his side and leaned her cheek against his sleeve. Their eyes met, and they didn't need to say a word.

Later, with Toby fast asleep in his cot, Rebecca went into the bedroom to change into her nightdress, still glorying in Adam's unexpected return. He followed her a few minutes later, a well-charged brandy glass in each hand. Poking the fire into a roaring blaze, he took off his waistcoat, loosened his collar and sank back in the chair to enjoy the nightcap. Rebecca sat down on the floor by his feet, her head resting on his knee. She sipped at the smooth, burning liquid that oozed its relaxing warmth into every pore of her body. She stretched her back, almost purring like a cat, and quite inadvertently trailed her limp hand along Adam's thigh. He grunted pleasurably, and then she felt him softly stroking her long, thick hair that hung loose about her shoulders in a glimmering curtain. The next thing she knew, he was prizing the near empty glass from her fingers and he turned her towards him, raising her upwards so that she was kneeling between his spread knees. He leaned forward in the chair, and his mouth found hers, warm and moist. Then his lips moved downwards, kissing her neck, her collar bone, and the shock wave darted down to her loins as his hand cupped the gentle swelling of her breast through the flimsy material of her nightgown. Her arms entwined about his neck, holding him close until he disentangled himself reluctantly from her embrace to pull off his shirt. The corners of her mouth lifted appreciatively as her eyes travelled unashamed over his muscular torso, his skin glistening in the flickering firelight. A shiver tumbled down her spine as he drew her against him and his fingers slid sensuously over her flanks. And then, slowly and carefully, he lowered her on to the hearth rug.

* * *

She sighed delectably as her mind slipped into wakefulness, and the knowledge that she wasn't alone in the bed sent a tingle of elation sparkling down to her toes. Adam was still heavily asleep, his head turned towards her and the whisper of his steady breath fanning her cheek as she contemplated his slumbering face. He looked tired, but he always did when he first came home from a long voyage, his long brown eyelashes lying in a crescent on the shadowy circle beneath his eyes. She imagined them opening and smiling at her, deep, honest pools of shining chestnut. Oh, she was so lucky to have his love! To have found someone to relight the fire in her heart after the snuffed-out flame left by Tom's death was more than she deserved, especially after the way she had treated Adam for so long. Perhaps one day she would have the chance to make it up to him, prove the passionate love she had for him now. And as she studied his familiar features, she wanted to touch his powerful shoulder as he slept with one bare arm lying outside the bedcovers. But she didn't want to wake him, and so she bit on her lip and let her eyes wander rapturously over his still figure.

She suddenly gave a little shiver and reached out for her nightgown that still lay in a crumpled heap at the bottom of the bed. She slipped it on over her head and carefully slid out of bed so as not to disturb Adam's much-needed sleep. Christmas Day! And for the first time in several years, she would thoroughly enjoy it!

She put on her dressing gown and slippers and, childlike herself, peeped into her son's bedroom. Toby was still asleep, his dark curls tousled on the pillow. Rebecca smiled to herself and then tiptoed downstairs, but as usual Mrs Blatchford was already contentedly at work for her young mistress and the master who had astounded her in the past months by proving himself not sullen and formidable as she'd originally imagined, but a bantering, mischievous rogue. Her sharp features broke into a grin.

'Good morning, ma'am, and a merry Christmas!'

'Thank you!' Rebecca's voice was like a chirping bird. 'And a happy Christmas to you! Have you made the tea yet?'

'Just this minute. Shall I be pouring you a cup?'

'No, no, you look so busy already. I'll take some upstairs. Adam's still asleep, but I expect he'll be awake soon.'

When she crept back into the room, he was indeed already stirring. When he saw her armed with the tray, he stretched languidly and beamed up at her with a merry glint in his eyes.

'Good morning, Mrs Bradley,' he greeted her.

'Good morning, Mr Bradley.'

'Captain Bradley, if you please! Show me some respect, woman!' he teased, and grasping her around the waist, pulled her on to the bed beside him.

''Tis a good job I'd put down the tray!' she rebuked him, and then gazed at him with loving eyes. 'Sleep well?'

'Mmm, thanks.' He caught his bottom lip and stole a sly glance at her. 'Well, I had a good nightcap, didn't I?'

'Adam Bradley!' she scolded with mock disgust. 'Now sit up and drink your tea before I smack you!'

'Promises, promises!'

'Oh, you're incorrigible!' she giggled, climbing in between the sheets. 'And I love you.'

He grunted appreciatively as he dropped a kiss on her forehead and then took the cup from her. 'Hmm, I'm not used to room service.' He lowered his voice and muttered thickly, 'or bed service for that matter.'

'I should hope not, too!' she grinned, snuggling up to his bare shoulder, her cheek against his warm skin. The sensation made her shudder with delight. 'Mmm, still a little tanned from the summer,' she mused lazily. 'You must be the only captain in Christendom to strip off in front of his crew.'

'Probably,' he agreed. 'But you know I don't see them as crew. I've had the same men sign on for virtually every voyage for the past four or five years. We're friends rather than master and crew. We trust each other. They accept that I sail the *Emily* undermanned, but they also know I do more than my fair share of the extra work. And if that means stripping off under the blazing Mediterranean sun to do a heavy repair job, well, so be it. Besides . . .' He looked at her sideways, his mouth twisted with not a little embarrassment. 'I do actually like the feel of the sun on my back, and I enjoy physical work. I don't want to end up fat and portly with a florid face and gout!'

Rebecca chuckled with a shake of her head. 'I can't imagine that!'

'And talking of ships,' he went on, his tone serious now, 'when Misha gets his ticket, I think I'll sail with him on his first voyage as master. Make sure he knows all the agents. I could put the *Emily* in for repair while I'm gone. I know she had some minor repairs in the spring, but now she needs some more major ones, and I can't put it off much longer.'

Rebecca lifted her eyes to his face. 'Can you afford it?'

'No. But I can't afford for her to sink.'

'What!'

But he laughed aloud. 'Only joking, but among many other things, she does need recaulking beneath the waterline in places, so it's got to be done. I'm not quite sure where I'm going to find the money from, mind.' He glanced at her with an amused smile. 'Of course, I could stop paying the rent on that Bedford cottage, and withdraw the apprenticeship premium.'

Rebecca was sure her heart stopped. 'How long have you known?' she gulped.

But Adam only shrugged. 'The rent? Oh, a couple of years, I suppose. But I don't mind. Or the premium. After all, Matthew Mason is Toby's uncle, and a cooper is a respectable enough trade. Besides, no domestic economies are going to come anywhere near the cost of the repairs. But don't worry. We're not destitute yet.'

'But . . . things aren't good,' she stated sombrely.

'No.' He placed the empty cup on the bedside table with a profound sigh. 'If only the *Swift* hadn't gone down. Or at least if I'd had her properly insured . . . God, I've managed to make a remarkable mess of everything.'

'No you haven't! You've had some bad luck, 'tis all. And when I'm with you, 'tis the richest woman on earth I am!'

She stroked her fingers across his ribcage with a feather-light touch and then lifted her head to brush a kiss against his chest, her lips and tongue leaving a moist trail on his flesh.

'You do that, and we'll never be ready to receive our guests,' he grated.

'So?'

She smiled excitedly and felt the longing plunge deep into her stomach as he turned to gaze down on her with those richly coloured eyes that suddenly burned with urgency. She found herself drowning in them, helpless to resist the all-consuming love she had for him now.

'You will be gentle with me,' she murmured, her hands fluttering about his muscled shoulders.

He lifted an eyebrow. 'Aren't I always?' he whispered.

'Mmm, of course,' she moaned as he began kissing her creamy throat. ''Tis just that I'm with child.'

'What!'

She felt his body become rigid and he sat bolt upright in the bed so that she could only see his back. The glorious intimate moment was gone, and in its place, a cold hostility chilled her bones, her own joy over the child totally shattered.

'It . . . 'twas bound to happen,' she stammered brokenly. 'I . . . I thought you'd be pleased. Don't you want a child of your own?'

'Yes! No!' he cried, his voice cracked. 'But . . .' He turned back to her, his anxious brow deeply furrowed. 'Dear God, Rebecca, you nearly died when you had Toby!' He gave a desperate groan, and then rubbed his hand hard across his jaw. 'Oh, God, this is all my fault!'

'What, for making love to your own wife?'

'Well . . . yes . . .' he faltered in reply. 'I should have done something to stop . . . I've heard they're making . . . something . . . now . . .'

His voice trailed off as Rebecca's chin quivered with emotion, her eyes filling with tears. 'But I want to have your child,' she choked. 'And I thought you'd want it, too.'

'Of course, I do!' Adam took her small hands in his. 'It's just that . . . with Toby . . . Well, it worries me . . .'

'But 'tis not as bad as when I found out you'd gone to France when they were in the middle of their war with Prussia, just so as you could secure your precious champagne.'

Adam blinked at her in surprise. 'The fighting was more or less over,' he said defensively, 'and I steered clear of any trouble areas. I'm not stupid, you know.'

'I know you're not, but you can never tell where there's going to be trouble in a war like that.'

'Perhaps,' he admitted, and his face paled. 'I certainly saw some terrible things . . .' He lowered his eyes at the recent memories and then shook his head vigorously. 'But I was careful. And now I have a warehouse full of champagne and more on the way when other merchants don't have any at all. And customers are willing to pay high prices for luxuries that are in short supply, you know.'

'But anything could have happened to you! I was insane with worry.'

'You weren't supposed to know where I'd gone.'

''Tis not the point!' she rounded on him. 'You risked your life for profit!'

'To protect our livelihood, which right now needs some protection!' He was glaring at her, his firm jaw set, but then his expression softened and his handsome mouth lifted as he recognized on her face that same obstinate will, her eyes challenging him, that had set his heart pounding all that time ago. 'Oh, come here,' he said, drawing her close so that her face lay against his broad chest. 'This is hardly something we should be arguing about. I'm delighted, but you must promise to take the greatest care of yourself. And I want you to see Dr Seaton straight away.'

'I already have.' She felt warm and comforted again, nestling in the circle of his arms. 'He says that what happened last time would've been no problem if he'd been there from the start, and there's no reason why it should be a breech birth again. And I'm going to have chloroform right the way through. Just like the queen did.'

'Oh, well, I suppose if it was good enough for Her Majesty, it should be good enough for my wife.' Adam smiled at last, and a tingle of joyous contentment slithered down Rebecca's spine as he mumbled into her hair. 'But I suppose we shouldn't . . . I mean . . . last night . . .'

'Dr Seaton said 'tis perfectly safe to . . . carry on our marital relationship is how he put it.' She giggled, pulling away slightly and flashing her brilliant eyes at him. She ran the tip of her tongue lasciviously over her top lip and saw the desire flood into Adam's face. But then he sighed with resignation and turned his head. Rebecca followed the direction of his gaze and there was Toby standing expectantly in the doorway, an ecstatic grin on his little face and his Christmas stocking clutched jealously to his chest.

CHAPTER EIGHTEEN

'Surely, you'll not take the child out in this weather, ma'am!' Mrs Blatchford expostulated. ''Tis cold enough to freeze your nose off! I've never known anything like it! The river be froze over for five days now!'

'Yes, I know,' Rebecca replied, firmly tying the ends of the thick scarf she had wound around Toby's neck. 'And five days Toby and I have been cooped up indoors like chickens in a pen, haven't we, angel?' She grinned at the beaming child and then pressed her finger playfully on his little button nose. 'Besides,' her smile faded as she straightened up, 'I feel . . . I don't know . . . restless, and I think a breath of fresh air will do me good.' She didn't add that a dull ache in the small of her back and low down in her stomach had been worrying her all day and that she thought a walk might settle it.

'Well, I'm sure the captain wouldn't approve, and he told me to look after you. You could both catch your death of cold.'

'But the captain's not here, is he? And he wouldn't want me to suffocate. We're well wrapped up and 'tis a lovely afternoon. The wind's dropped now and the sun's out. Perhaps a thaw will set in soon.'

'Well, it don't feel like it to me! But if you must go, don't be too long.'

'We won't, will we, Toby?'

She finished tying on her warm velvet bonnet, donned her gloves and, taking her son's hand, went through the hallway and out of the front door. The biting air at once nipped at their faces, making their cheeks tingle and their eyes water. Toby looked up at her, his dark features bewildered.

''Tis colder than I've ever known it,' she told him with a shiver. 'We'll just go for a short walk, enough to blow the cobwebs away.'

Together they walked up the garden path and then down the steep incline towards the port. The road was frozen solid, but because it hadn't rained for some time it was perfectly dry underfoot and made for good walking. They didn't pass another soul until they came down to the inn. Everyone who could was huddled at home before a blazing fire, and only those who had some necessary business had dared brave the intense cold. That end of the port was quiet enough at the best of times now that the limekilns had closed and nothing at all passed through the quays that Gill and Company had once leased, but today the entire place was deserted.

They crossed over to Canal Dock where the constant deep puddles had turned to patches of slippery ice and Rebecca had to take care where she placed her feet. A small barge was stuck fast in the frozen water, unable to move an inch. She glanced across the higher copper quays to the Devon Great Consols dock and counted the masts of two more vessels equally marooned. For although the larger basin was less affected, the river itself was impassable. The whole port was at a standstill, the trade that remained temporarily suspended, and Rebecca knew it could destroy some businesses for good. Adam's barge, the *Sure*, was stranded somewhere downriver with a hold full of coal for Morwellham's hungry grates, the first decent inward cargo she had secured since the New Year, but now this would only add to the losses she was starting to incur. Thankfully, the *Swallow* was already at sea, having left London for Portugal a few days earlier, but planning to call at Plymouth and Morwellham on her return. Misha was mastering her, having successfully obtained his ticket, but it was his first voyage and, as planned, Adam had gone with him while the *Emily* was in dock. The repairs were estimated to cost even more than Adam had thought, and a ship out of action made no money. He had been forced to take out a short-term loan to be repaid partly out of his dividends from Bradley's Merchants, and partly from his profits from the *Swallow*, meaning their personal income was going to be reduced for some time. Adam had told her not to worry, but she knew that he was deeply troubled. And now he was at sea again, ensuring Misha could act for him as well as Captain Littleworth had done, but not gaining any profit from his own valuable time. They would be away well over a month, and Rebecca shivered, her own bones chilled, as she imagined how inhospitable the Atlantic could be in February.

'Come along, Toby, let's go and look at the river,' she suggested brightly, waggling the little boy's hand.

Toby looked up at her, his face radiant with enthusiasm, the image of his father. Rebecca was used to the strange sensation it evoked in her, the sorrow of Tom's loss always with her but accepted now, and the overwhelming joy that she had his son to love and cherish.

The unexpected sharp explosion jerked up her head, and with her heart thumping with terror, she instinctively drew the child against her and tried to cover his body with her own. Then it came again and the panic slowly subsided as she realized it had the wrong echo about it for gunfire. But the sudden fear had tightened the ache in her stomach to a cramp, and for several seconds she was unable to move until Toby tugged at her sleeve.

'You said we could go to the river,' he reminded her, his eyebrows raised in two expectant arches.

She forced a smile, but as she stepped forward, the pain lessened and was forgotten in her curiosity to discover the source of the unusual sound. As they neared the river, it became louder and more frequent, almost like a fusillade of shots let off at random intervals. She held Toby's hand firmly as she always did when they were at the water's edge, even though he was a sensible child and understood the dangers, but today her grip was even tighter because of her uneasiness. And then she gasped aloud as they reached the end of the quay and looked down on the river.

'Oh, Toby, look!' she breathed as she gazed in wonderment.

The Tamar's surface was a dark, glistening, solid sheet, but the tide was obviously going out and as the water below dropped away, the ice was cracking loudly and large, uneven blocks of it were collapsing and falling into the flow.

''Twill all float back upriver like little icebergs when the tide comes in again and pile up against what were left. 'Tis a sight I've only seen a few times in all my days.'

Rebecca jumped with fright at the sudden voice beside her, but now she smiled at the familiar face of the old man. He was one of only a few hobblers remaining, retired quay labourers or sometimes sailors who haunted the wharves in the off chance of joining the task of towing a ship from one berth to another in exchange for 'baccy and beer', as was the custom. It required extreme strength, Rebecca always thought, being roped like a barge horse, and totally unsuitable for elderly men. They seemed to her so forlorn, as if trying to prove their usefulness to the last.

'Yes, 'tis quite phenomenal,' she agreed. 'But 'twill not do trade any good.'

'No, 'twill not,' the old fellow said with a heartrending sigh. 'Thirty year I've lived at Morwellham, seen it grow and thrive, with so many ships 'twere chaos on the river. Couldn't hear yourself think for the noise on the quayside. And now look at it. Quiet as a grave.'

'Oh, but once the thaw comes . . .'

'Morwellham's slowly dying, take my word for it, cheel. And 'tis taking that husband of yourn down with it. You must tell him to get out of here while he still can. And I'm saying this because . . . well, everyone do think fondly of you, Miss Rebecca, and with all you've been through . . .'

Rebecca blinked at him in horrified surprise, and then lowered her eyes. Yes, she supposed everyone in Morwellham knew her business. As Adam had told her in a maddened rage at the time of his cousin's unwelcome visit, Toby was so like his real father that it would hardly take a genius to work out the whole of their private lives!

'My . . . my husband's business is mainly in London anyway,' she stammered with embarrassment. 'But I wish 'tweren't. I miss him so much when he's away.' She smiled again, but this time through a misted grimace, and she saw the old man nod knowingly. 'Come along, Toby. 'Tis perishing standing here.'

The child obediently turned. He wanted to go home now anyway. He was cold, and the river might look different, but it was no fun without any ships on it, and the hobbler's gnarled and wrinkled face had frightened him a little. He tried to pull ahead and Rebecca had to check him. He slowed down reluctantly, but then the thought of the shop and the sweets his mother sometimes bought for him there got the better of him, and suddenly slipping his hand from her grip, he broke free and started forward.

'Toby!' Rebecca screamed after him, her heart stopping as frenzied panic corkscrewed her stomach into a vice. But the boy took no notice and raced onwards over the slithery puddles at the edge of the dockside, and at every second she could see him falling into . . .

She lifted up her skirt and ran, shrieking as she flew over the treacherous surface, her own feet sliding precariously, stumbling, catching herself. And it was as Toby passed the end of the dock and reached safety that her foot went from under her and the ground slapped her in the face. Darkness closed in on her, but the all-engulfing fear for Toby's safety drove her to keep conscious and she frantically muttered his name through a blinding haze.

''Tis all right, see?' the old hobbler's voice rumbled in her ear. 'Jane Martin's got 'en. Can you get up now? Take your time.'

Her body slackened at the knowledge that Toby was safe, and she let herself slip into an insensible stupor. But it passed in seconds, and soon she was pulling herself back to full consciousness as her dazed vision wavered into focus. With the old fellow's help, she began to draw herself upwards, her head still spinning nauseatingly. But she was hardly on her feet when a crippling pain in her stomach all but brought her to her knees again. She doubled up with a gasp, her eyes stinging, and it was several moments before she was able to straighten up.

The hobbler walked her slowly up to where Jane Martin, alarmed at Toby's arrival alone in the shop, had come outside with the child and was anxiously waiting for her. The pain had eased, and Rebecca gave her son a watery smile as she turned to thank the old man and Miss Martin for their trouble.

'You be all right to walk home on your own?'

'Yes, yes really,' she assured them. ''Tis only a few yards.'

But it seemed more like a few miles as they climbed laboriously up the steep hill which suddenly seemed to rise before her like a mountain. The pain resumed, strong and cruel, and she had to fight to take each step as the agony bore deeper into her flesh and seemed to paralyze her legs. She clung on to Toby, fear and pain pressing on her heart like a stone, and by the time they reached the gate, she could feel something warm and wet trickling down the inside of her legs.

* * *

'I'm so sorry, Mrs Bradley. There really was nothing I could do.'

Rebecca pressed her head deep into the pillows, her mouth twisted as she bit back her strangling anguish. She was trying so hard not to cry, but tears were meandering unhalted down her pale cheeks.

'Does . . . does it mean,' she choked, the words coming in short gasps, 'that I'll never have . . . another child?'

She gazed up at the doctor, her face distraught with grief. Ever sensitive to his patients' needs, Dr Seaton sat down ponderously on the edge of the bed. 'I really can't say,' he answered thoughtfully. 'But I think we can be optimistic about it. I found nothing amiss after the difficult birth of your son, but I should like to examine you again in about a month. However, my guess is that this is an isolated incident, although one can never be entirely sure. The fall in itself won't have caused it, you see, just accelerated what was already happening.'

Rebecca tried to nod, but the knot in her throat was unbearable. 'I wanted so much to have Adam's child,' she gulped.

'Well, I'm sure you will. Just not this time.' Dr Seaton patted her hand paternally. It was so easy to feel affection for this pretty young woman who had displayed such strength of character in the way she had nursed Tom Mason all those years ago. He had seen her son as he'd grown. There was no doubting now who his father was, which surely accounted for the strangeness between herself and her husband when the boy was born. But she had obviously come to love the captain deeply, and he was pleased for her. She deserved some happiness after her tragic loss, and she certainly didn't deserve this! 'Has the pain completely gone now?' he asked gently.

'Yes. It just feels sore,' she managed to reply.

'I suggest you take another dose of laudanum in an hour or so, and try to get some sleep. Call me if the cramps come back or the bleeding becomes profuse, otherwise I'll call again in the morning. Your mother's waiting outside. Shall I send her in?'

'Yes, Doctor. And thank you.'

'Now don't worry. I feel sure we'll get Toby a brother or sister yet.'

She forced a wan smile and watched as the kindly physician left the room. Her head rolled to the side, totally devoid of any strength, and for a few minutes she lay perfectly still. But when her mother came back in, it was all too easy to let go and an agonized cry burst from her aching throat. Anne sat on the bed beside her and rocked her to and fro, while her body shook convulsively with each sob.

'I want Adam!' she wailed desperately. 'Oh, Mother . . .' And her tears broke out afresh.

'But he's not here, my lamb,' Anne answered soothingly. 'And there's no point in sending a cable to Portugal or wherever 'tis he's gone. He wouldn't get it till he arrived, and he couldn't get home any faster. 'Twould be no point in having him worried.'

Rebecca nodded as she wept against Anne's shoulder. But all she wanted then, and for weeks afterwards, was to feel Adam's strong, comforting arms around her.

CHAPTER NINETEEN

It was a glorious day for the beginning of April, such an astounding contrast to the almost unprecedented cold that had frozen the river for nearly a week during February. But the spring weather brought no warmth to Rebecca's heart. For Adam had still not returned. He'd sent her a telegraph message from Portugal to say he'd been delayed and had decided to call in at Bordeaux en route. And for over a week now Rebecca had been pacing the quayside awaiting his arrival in vain.

But this morning, Ann Richards met her with a grin. 'Go and look on the board, Rebecca, dear,' she beamed.

Rebecca's heart missed a beat, and grasping Toby's hand even more securely, she hurried to the inn. And the relief as she read the fresh entry on the blackboard, flushed through her veins and triggered an overwhelming urge to burst into tears. The *Swallow* docked in Plymouth three days ago, which surely meant, Rebecca quickly calculated, that she could even arrive at Morwellham on the higher water that afternoon. At last she would have Adam there to lean on, to share the sorrow with. She'd tried to be so brave, but she knew she wouldn't be over the loss of the tiny life that had been growing inside her until she had wept for it in Adam's embrace.

He would be saddened, too, but he always seemed so strong, like a pillar of stone that groaned but never gave way no matter what the weight it had to bear.

She found no appetite for her lunch, and leaving Toby with Mrs Blatchford, she hurried back down to the port. Sarah was already there, her pale eyes vibrant with excitement, and the two sisters embraced expectantly. They linked arms, walking up and down the quay, Sarah chatting on with exuberance as she always did. Rebecca smiled serenely to herself, the younger girl's gleeful banter infecting her own dulled spirit as the anticipation of being with Adam again eased her distress. But the afternoon wore on, and still the *Swallow* hadn't appeared. The waters of the Tamar were at spring tide when the level rose so high and so quickly that it almost seemed as if the river was flowing backwards. It meant a fast passage upriver, some ships even having to drag anchor to control their speed on the difficult stretches. And it also meant that the water would fall away again to its lowest tide level, so that for several hours the shallow reaches became impassable to all but the flat-bottomed barges.

'Oh, they'll be stranded downstream if they don't come soon, won't they, Becky?' Sarah wailed desperately.

'There's time yet.' Rebecca forced a smile. 'And we don't know how long their business will have kept them in Plymouth. It could be tomorrow, or the next day, even.'

She had tried to sound calm, but inside she was as disappointed as Sarah. Her sister's dejected expression deepened her own emptiness, and she turned her eyes away towards the river to blink back her sudden tears. The valley was so beautiful, yet it hid a growing sadness, and she was part of it. She had lost Tom, and now she had lost Adam's baby, and only Adam himself could save her from her depression.

She was about to suggest that they go to the Ship for some refreshment, when something caught her eye. She stared hard and squinted, grasping her sister's arm tightly.

'Look, Sarah! I think . . . above the trees . . . can you see?' She pointed downriver to where the Tamar disappeared around the horseshoe bend that virtually changed its course to the opposite direction. Above the treeline she was sure she could see the tip of a mast . . . with . . . yes, a second lower one behind.

Sarah was jumping up and down with excitement. 'Yes, you're right! 'Tis a two-masted schooner!'

'But it mightn't be the *Swallow*.'

'Oh, Becky!' Sarah clasped her hands, and the two sisters stood together, their eyes trained on the meander of the river. Their patience was at last rewarded as the bowsprit of a ship slowly slid into view.

'Yes, 'tis her,' Rebecca croaked as the figurehead came into sight. She suddenly felt weak at the knees, so alone even as Sarah danced on the spot beside her. She hadn't thought quite how she would break the news to Adam. Would he notice at once that her figure was its normal slender self when she should have been greatly thickened at the waist by now, or would she have to tell him herself? The *Swallow* was fully visible now, her progress painfully slow as all sail had been taken in ready for the skilled manoeuvre of docking, and she was merely using the strength of the tide to propel her forward, even the towline having been let go. But boats were already rowing out to meet the vessel and take on the lines with which to haul her into position at the quayside.

'Well, my pretty maids!' She started as Isaac came up behind them and clapped his daughters on the shoulder. 'My son-in-law and my son-in-law to be both on the same ship. Who'd have imagined that, eh?' he beamed, and then gave Rebecca a special look, for he knew what was in her heart.

She smiled back wistfully, and then turned her attention to the approaching ship. But on the deck, Rebecca could only see one figure in master's attire. It had Adam's height, but lacked his breadth of shoulder. Misha was accomplishing the difficult task of berthing the schooner with absolute perfection, and she could see why Adam had put such faith in him. But where was Adam?

Misha waved fleetingly when he saw Isaac and the two young women waiting on the shore, but returned immediately to watching carefully the ship's movements and shouting orders to the small crew. The fenders were thrown over the side, ropes were tightened around the bollards on the quayside, and shortly the *Swallow* came to rest against the wharf with a gentle bump. But there was still no sign of Adam.

The gangway was secured, and after a moment to assure himself that all was in order, Misha hurried across on to dry land. He was smiling, but somehow his face was serious. Rebecca was frowning, wondering if she should board the vessel to join Adam, as beside her Sarah threw herself into Misha's arms. He held her briefly, but extricated himself almost at once from her unseemly embrace to turn to Rebecca, his expression grim. And Rebecca knew at once that something was wrong.

She felt her heart drum painfully against her ribs. 'W . . . where's Adam?' she faltered.

Misha fixed his gaze on her, his eyebrows knitted. 'I am so sorry,' he said warily.

Rebecca blinked hard at him. She had heard those words before, words that her mind had managed at long last to bury in the mists of the past. To hear them again made her rock on her feet. 'Sorry?' she forced her voice out in a tiny squeal. 'I don't understand.'

Misha's face twisted even further. 'There . . . oh, *bozhe moy*! I do not know how to tell you, but . . . there has been an accident.'

Rebecca felt herself sway and was glad of Isaac's supportive arm around her. 'Accident?' he demanded from beside her.

'Yes, a few days ago,' Misha explained, the anguish clear on his face. 'We unload much wine at Plymouth, but we find there is equipment waiting for the Devon Great Consols mine, so we take it on board, rope, sawn timber, boxes of nails, and also explosive. When we sail, the current is very strong in the Sound because we are nearly at the spring tide, and the wind is also very strong. Because of the explosive, the captain, he decides to check the cargo. I hear him shout to me from the hold, but as I get to the hatch, the ship, she suddenly roll and there is a crash. I saw the wine casks fall, and . . . and I heard the captain cry out, and . . . and . . .'

'Oh, dear God.' Rebecca wasn't sure who muttered the oath, herself or her father. Her mind was reeling under a threatening faintness, and as Misha attempted to tell them what had happened, his voice reached her as if through a dense fog.

'I think he is dead, but when I get to him, thank God, he is, how do you say, unconscious, because he hit his head as he fell. But he is trapped beneath the barrels, and it takes us some time to free him. He is alive, but . . . he is much hurt, the chest, and . . . and very much the hand . . . I am about to turn the ship back to Plymouth to find a doctor, but he wake up then and insist to come to Morwellham. I am so sorry. I do not understand how it happens. I inspect the ropes myself when we unload the other wine. I do not know how they can be frayed like this!'

'I'm sure 'tweren't your fault.' Isaac tried to calm Misha's growing agitation. 'Where's the captain now?'

'They help him from the cabin. He . . . he is not good. It is difficult for him to climb the ladder. Ah, yes, look. Here they are coming.'

Rebecca turned her distraught eyes towards the ship, her breath shaking. Two seamen were walking slowly across the deck with Adam between them, but the gangway was too narrow and only one of them could accompany him across to the quayside. He was coming towards her, but she was too shocked to do more than stare at him in horror. Pain was etched deep in his ashen face, a dark, jagged gash across a blue swelling on his forehead and blood matted into the hair around it. He was walking as if each step cost a tremendous effort, his left hand swathed in bandages and held tightly across his chest. The ghost of a smile flickered over his features as he neared her, but then his body slackened and his knees buckled beneath him.

'Adam!' she shrieked hysterically, and sprang forward, but the sailor had caught him and Isaac was already at his other side.

'Sarah, run to the inn and send for the doctor!' he ordered his younger daughter. 'And you there! Bring your cart over here and be quick about it!'

Rebecca tried to swallow, but her mouth was so dry, she nearly vomited instead.

* * *

She stood back from the bed, her brow aching from its frenzied frown. It had taken so long to get Adam up the hill to the cottage, every movement causing him agony, that they hadn't long got him into bed before the doctor arrived from Tavistock on his foaming steed. He immediately set about examining the injury to Adam's forehead and checking for the ill effects of concussion, but now he sat back with a nod of his balding head.

'Well, other than an almighty headache for a few more days, I don't think there's anything to worry about there,' he announced pleasantly. 'I'll need to close the wound with a few stitches, but I'd like to look at your other injuries first.'

'I were just about to cut his shirt away when you arrived,' Rebecca told him shakily.

'Perhaps I should do it now I'm here,' Dr Seaton said, calmly taking the scissors from her trembling hands. 'The casks lodged on some crates as they fell, you say?'

''Tis what saved him. But . . .' Her voice dropped to a tremulous whisper. 'Some of the crates came down and 'twas one of them that crushed his hand.'

The doctor didn't reply, but she noticed he paused for a moment before continuing his work with the scissors. She tried to smile reassuringly at Adam even though she wept inside, but his face was contorted, his eyes drowned in two days and nights of excruciating torment. Dr Seaton finally drew the material back from his chest, and Rebecca couldn't suppress the horrified gasp that escaped her lips at the bruising that spread over his body like livid wine stains. She turned away, closing her ears to Adam's stifled groans as the doctor carefully examined him.

'Believe it or not, you're a very lucky man, Captain Bradley,' he declared at last. 'Your lungs are clear and I can find no sign of any internal injury. It's difficult to say if any of your ribs are actually broken or just badly bruised, but I can't feel any displacements. The best I can do is to strap you up for support and leave the rest to mother nature. So, that just leaves your hand.' He hesitated, and Rebecca's stomach knotted even tighter. 'Whoever bandaged it up made a first-rate job.'

'It was Misha,' Adam managed to grate, and Rebecca saw him clench his jaw as Dr Seaton began to unravel the strips of linen. He tried to conceal the pain, but the fight had gone out of him and he was wincing almost continuously, his breath short and trembling. Rebecca took his other hand, stroking his arm encouragingly, but when he turned to her, she could see the fear in his eyes. The bandages were becoming increasingly bloodied, and as the last piece came away, Adam's sudden cry of agony tore Rebecca's heart from her chest. He was struggling to catch his breath, tears finally collecting in his eyes, and Rebecca just felt so helpless . . .

'Good God,' she heard the doctor mumble to himself.

Her gaze moved in his direction and her eyes fell on the broken, mangled hand. She gasped in horror and looked away, unable to bear the appalling sight, but she was aware of the physician peering closely at the mutilated flesh before covering it deftly with a fresh piece of linen.

'I . . . I know . . . what you're going to say,' Adam choked between snatched breaths. 'But I'd rather . . . take my chances.'

Dr Seaton's chest expanded to capacity. 'You have no choice, I'm afraid, Captain Bradley.'

'It's my life . . .'

'I don't think you understand,' the doctor sighed sympathetically. 'Your hand is damaged beyond healing. Very soon, gangrene will set in. It's an agonizing death. If I don't amputate—'

'*No!*' Adam's shoulders lifted from the bed, but he at once fell back with a tortured grimace. Rebecca watched him, her fingers pressed over her mouth as she tried to control her own horror. Oh, dear God! After all they'd been through, to have their peace shattered like this . . .

'I'll give you something for the pain and then perhaps you'll be able to think more clearly.' Dr Seaton unwrapped a package from his bag, revealing a syringe and a small glass phial, and then took out a band which he tightened around Adam's right arm. 'Now, if you can make a fist for me, we should bring up a good vein. It's morphine,' he explained with a confident smile. 'Quite safe if you know what you're doing, and extremely effective. There.'

Rebecca saw Adam flinch as the needle pierced into his good hand. Almost instantly, his face relaxed. He gave out a long, sighing moan, his eyelids drooped, and although he was clearly trying to fight the effects of the drug, he drifted asleep in a matter of minutes.

'Good.' Dr Seaton puffed out his cheeks. 'It doesn't always have such a dramatic effect, but the poor fellow must be exhausted from two days in that degree of pain. Now listen to me, Mrs Bradley,' he went on, drawing Rebecca aside. 'I believe your husband is in no fit state to make such a decision, so you must make it for him.'

Rebecca caught her breath and turned her eyes back to the bed, choking on the torment that clawed at her gullet. Adam seemed so peaceful now, propped up against the pillows and with his injured hand covered again and lying comfortably across his chest. That gentle, sensitive hand that had caressed her body, stroked her so tenderly, to be severed from its strong limb and . . . and thrown on a fire to be . . . disposed . . .

She gazed up at the doctor, blinded by ravaging tears. 'How . . . how can I go against his wishes?' she spluttered almost inaudibly.

Dr Seaton placed his hand on her shoulder. 'Your husband's hand has been crushed,' he said quietly. 'It is of no use to him anymore. And believe me, if we don't amputate, he will die. And it isn't as bad as you think. It's done with care and precision nowadays. The veins and arteries are ligatured to minimize blood loss, we take every precaution we can against infection and, of course, it's all done under full anaesthetic. If I act now, I can make a clean cut just above the wrist, and that will allow for sufficient skin to close the wound nice and neatly. The muscles of the lower arm are basically controlled from the elbow, and although the two bones twist over each other,' and here he paused to hold out his own arm to demonstrate, 'they're held together by very strong membranes. So your husband will retain virtually full use of his arm. Whereas,' he drew in a ponderous breath, 'if we delay and gangrene sets in, he could lose the entire limb. If not his life.'

Rebecca's mouth twisted in a terrible grimace and she bit down painfully hard on her lower lip. She could scarcely see Adam for her tears, but she knew . . . she couldn't bear . . . She tried to speak, but her voice was strangled. And so . . . slowly . . . she nodded her head.

'Thank you.' Dr Seaton's words were low and compassionate. 'You must understand, though, that I cannot promise he'll pull through. We'll be preventing gangrene, but however careful we are, there's still the danger of infection, or even clinical shock. But your husband is fit and strong, and he stands an excellent chance. Now perhaps you'd like to sit with him for a while? I wish to send for my colleague Dr Ratcliffe to assist, and in the meantime, I need to make some preparations. May I speak with your housekeeper?'

Rebecca nodded again. 'Mrs Blatchford. In the kitchen,' she croaked in a voice that wasn't hers.

And then she was alone with Adam. Listening to his shallow breathing. She reached out and stroked his shadowy jaw with the back of her hand. 'I'm sorry, my love,' was all her paralyzed mind could whisper.

* * *

'You can come and see him now, Mrs Bradley. He's awake from the chloroform, but he's still very drowsy.'

Dr Seaton ushered her into the bedroom with a kindly smile. Adam was lying much as she had left him, propped up with pillows and apparently asleep. But as she crossed to the bed, her heart thudding erratically, she realized that his eyes were screwed shut and his face set like stone. The gash on the discoloured swelling at the side of his forehead had been cleaned and stitched, his powerful chest was encased in bandages, and when Rebecca looked down, she sucked in her lips in an attempt to keep back her tears. For elevated on another pillow, his left arm ended in a thick white dressing. This was no horrific nightmare. It was real. Adam's hand was gone.

It took some effort for her not to sink on to her knees, and she was grateful for the chair Dr Seaton pushed behind her. She sat down mechanically, the constriction in her gullet ever tighter.

'Adam?' she forced out a tiny whisper. 'How . . . how is it?' she asked lamely.

He half opened his eyes, but the slight movement destroyed his concentration and, for a moment, he lost control. He drew in a sharp, wincing breath, his lips curled back from his gritted teeth. 'Hurts like hell,' he grated through his clenched jaw. And then suddenly his forbearance snapped. His chest jerked painfully and he almost choked as he tried in vain to swallow down a gagging sob. 'How could you?' he groaned. 'You let them cut off my hand!'

His voice had risen to a shriek, and Rebecca's cry as she catapulted to her feet, knocking the chair to the floor, turned both the doctors' heads. Dear God! What had she done!

'Perhaps you'd better wait outside a moment,' Dr Seaton suggested gently.

She fled the room, groping her way through the torrent of tears that tore at her aching throat. Was there no end to it, to the misery that seemed to assail her life? She stumbled blindly into the bedroom that used to be Adam's before they had discovered their love, and flung herself on to the bed. She wept freely, her wretched moans echoing against the bare walls. She wanted to lash out, to punish whatever it was that seemed so intent on devastating her existence. But whatever it was, it was not tangible, and there was nothing she could do to fight it. Was this her penance for conceiving her son out of wedlock? But why make Adam suffer like this? He had done nothing wrong! Where was the justice in that? And she pummelled her fists into the bedspread.

She hardly heard the light tap on the door. 'May I come in?'

She sat up, wiping her sodden cheeks with the back of her hands. Dr Seaton perched on the bed beside her, his hands joined between his knees.

'Please. Don't be upset, Mrs Bradley,' he began gravely. 'Your husband is in terrible pain. We took the greatest care, but he still lost a lot of blood and he's very weak. I'm sure he has no idea what he's saying. He's going to need a great deal of understanding over the next weeks and months, and a great deal of careful nursing. He's not out of the woods yet. But I can see he's a fighter. But . . .' He paused to choose his words with care. 'That strength could make things difficult for you. He won't blame you, not once he's thinking straight again. But it's human nature to direct one's hurt . . . one's anger . . . against the person one loves the most. But remember, I'm here to help. And if you need me urgently and I'm unavailable, Dr Ratcliffe has my full confidence. He's young, but he's an excellent physician.'

Rebecca nodded as she sniffed hard. The doctor's calm words had soothed her, and her tears had finally stopped.

'Now, will you come back in? I've given him a little more morphine to ease the pain, but not enough to put him out cold this time. It can cause nausea, and I don't want him retching with those ribs. He should be able to talk to you, but he will be very sleepy.'

He stood up again and patiently beckoned to her. She took a deep breath and slowly got to her feet, following the doctor back to the bedroom. She felt half afraid, just as she had when she and Adam were first married, but now there was nothing to fight back with, just a tragic sense of loss. Almost as if he were a stranger again.

She stood looking down on him for several moments. His face was more relaxed this time, his eyes closed, but he must have sensed her presence, for he opened them for a few seconds and held her gaze. The agonizing exhaustion she saw in those deep brown spheres pierced her heart, but then his eyelids drooped shut again.

'You . . . you should have let me die, Rebecca,' he murmured wearily. 'I'm of no use to you now. Whereas you . . .' He swallowed, and his dry lips slowly dragged apart. 'You're still so young. So beautiful. You'd soon find someone to look after you properly.'

The pain that raked Rebecca's gullet returned with a vengeance. She compressed her mouth into a tight line, but her chin still quivered and she had no control over the sob that escaped her lips.

'I . . . I lost Tom,' she wept brokenly, her head hung in surrender to the gnawing despair, 'and while you were away, I . . . I lost the baby. I couldn't . . .' She paused, gulping for air. 'I couldn't stand by and watch you die, too.'

It was too much. She turned her head away, her hands over her face. For a few moments she didn't respond to the pressure on her elbow, but when she did look down, Adam had reached out with his right arm and his fingers were holding her with the last vestige of strength he possessed.

* * *

'Oh, thank God you're here!'

Rebecca glanced up, her eyes alight with agitation. She'd been furiously bathing Adam's face and neck, but it seemed to have little effect on the sweat that was steadily trickling down on to his chest. He was breathing in rapid, shallow pants, his head rolled back lifelessly against the pillows. His mouth was parched, despite the water that Rebecca was giving to him every few minutes, and he was trying to gather enough saliva to swallow.

'When did this start?' Dr Seaton asked without preamble as he felt for the pulse at Adam's wrist. 'He was fine when I called yesterday afternoon.'

''Twas last evening,' Rebecca answered, failing to conceal the panic in her voice. 'It came on so quickly. I hoped it would've passed by this morning, but 'tis getting worse. I hope you didn't mind me sending for you at the crack of dawn.'

'Occupational hazard. And none too soon, by the looks of things.' He placed his palm across Adam's sweat bedewed brow. 'That's a good fever you have, Captain. I'll take your temperature accurately in a minute, but how's the hand? Throbbing, I imagine.'

'Bloody agony,' Adam muttered, seemingly without moving his lips.

'Well, let's have a look, shall we?' the doctor said kindly as he rolled up his sleeves and washed his hands and forearms in the basin of water to which he had added some liquid from a bottle in his bag.

Rebecca held Adam's other hand and forced a reassuring smile to her lips, but his face was contorted with a gasping wince as the bandages were removed. 'You're . . . you're going to have to cut my arm off, aren't you?' he choked, terror glinting in his sunken eyes.

Dr Seaton grunted pensively. 'No, I'm not,' he replied through pursed lips. 'It isn't gangrene, and I'd like to avoid a further operation if at all possible. But the wound is inflamed and suppurating, and we must avoid blood poisoning at all costs.'

Rebecca's heart sank even further, but she was too exhausted to take much heed. She hadn't been to bed since

Adam's return, preferring to doze in the chair beside him until night and day had become one indistinguishable haze. Blood poisoning. She knew what that meant. And so did Adam.

'I want you to watch me very carefully, Mrs Bradley,' Dr Seaton went on. 'My coming to change the dressings twice a day obviously isn't enough. It's a long way to come and I do have other patients, so you'll have to do it for him, four times a day I suggest, and we'll see how it progresses. Later on, I'll bring you a most effective unguent which will help with the healing. It was recommended to me by a colleague who often works with a young wise woman over near Peter Tavy. She effects some marvellous cures with herbs and suchlike. But for now, we need something stronger, so I'll show you how to prepare a phenol dressing. It must be done exactly as I tell you. Too strong and it can have a corrosive effect. That was Lister's initial error, but I believe we've perfected the method now. First of all, we must clean up the wound, then I want it left uncovered for a short while to allow the air to dry it up, but do make sure there are no flies in the room. I do subscribe to the theory that they carry disease and infection. In the meantime, strip off all the bedclothes except perhaps the sheet, and keep on with the sponging. We must bring that fever down. And plenty to drink. Lemonade's a good thirst quencher. And I can remove the strapping from your ribs, Captain, if you think it might be more comfortable. Now then, you can manage all that, can't you, Mrs Bradley?'

Rebecca gulped hard as she broke into a cold sweat. The thought of touching Adam's severed wrist, increasing the agony he was already suffering, made her feel sick. 'I . . . I don't know,' her voice trembled.

'I'm sure you can,' the doctor smiled confidently. 'And put the laudanum back to half a drachm every four hours while it's more painful again. In fact, it would be a good idea to give it to him about ten minutes before you change the dressings. All right?' He saw her hesitation and his eyebrows arched. 'I've noticed neither of you have actually looked at the stump,' he said with firm understanding. 'You'll have to get used to it, and the sooner the better. And stump is a word you'll need to get used to as well.'

Rebecca pulled in her lips. Adam's beseeching eyes were riveted on her, as if he were seeking her strength to support him. But she had none left to give. Too drained. Too empty. She swallowed, and without exchanging a word, they slowly turned in unison to look down on his handless arm. And her own stifled whimper of horror was drowned by Adam's cry of despair.

CHAPTER TWENTY

The afternoon sun shone down brightly with the freshness of early June. Rebecca paused to wipe the sheen of perspiration from her forehead with the back of her hand, leaving a streak of mud across her face. Her sleeves were rolled up to her elbows, she had unfastened the top buttons of her day dress, and her hair, tied back hastily in a ribbon, was coming loose with strands billowing irritatingly about her eyes. But someone had to tidy the garden which had become so overgrown since she'd dismissed the boy she used to pay to keep the rampant vegetation under control. A small economy perhaps, but one of many she had made. She'd rendered the front garden quite presentable the previous week, and now she was clearing the grounds to the rear of the cottage.

She glanced furtively across at Adam. She had hoped that the sight of her fighting to dig up the dead rose tree might have prompted him to come and help her. Even though he only had one hand to steady the garden fork, his weight on it alone would easily lever up the roots she was battling to dislodge from the earth. The accident had happened two months ago now, but the feverish infection that had dangled his life on a thread for well over a fortnight had severely debilitated him. She thanked God that he'd recovered and that there'd been no sign of it recurring, but it had left him a weakened and different man.

He was struggling now to light his pipe which he'd picked up for the first time since he'd come home on that fateful day. He'd managed to pack in the tobacco and was attempting to strike a match, holding the box between his knees, but each time one burst into life, without his other hand to protect the tiny flame, it was extinguished before he could get it anywhere near the pipe. Rebecca watched him out of the corner of her eye, her heart ripped asunder. She yearned to go and help him, for she longed for anything that might bring him consolation, but she'd learned that her assistance would be angrily rejected. If he needed her help, he would ask for it, he'd snapped at her on more than one occasion. She'd bitten her lip, forcing back her tears of despair. Not for herself. But for him.

He finally threw the pipe and the matchbox on the table in frustration, and sank back in the garden chair, his eyes shut. Rebecca turned back to her work, pretending she hadn't seen, her vision misted with sadness. She sniffed hard and rammed the fork into the ground for the umpteenth time. Oh, God! It was so unfair! Adam had always worked so hard, not just for himself, but for her and Toby, and for all the people who relied on him for employment, and also for the pride he possessed in his father's company and the *Emily*. But now that shattered pride had broken him and he wanted none of the business, or even . . . even of her. He was slipping away from her, little by little. And just as when Tom had died and the nights had tortured her with dreams of him, so vivid and alive, now she kept seeing herself with a needle and thread in her dextrous fingers, laughing with Adam as she sewed back on his severed hand, only to wake to the sound of him pacing up and down in the bedroom he'd gone back to sleeping in alone.

Her head whipped round at the sudden, stifled gasp and she quickly thrust the fork into the earth for safety. This time there was no restraining her, for she realized at once that

Adam was suffering one of the unpredictable attacks of pain as the nerves at his wrist suddenly bucked and plunged in confusion at finding no hand to direct. She covered the few yards to his side in seconds. He was bent double in the chair, his left arm cradled in his lap and his face like granite. And all she could do was to put her arms about him and stroke his dull, lifeless hair.

'Shall I get some laudanum?'

But he shook his bowed head with a trembling sigh. 'No. It'll pass in a minute. And I can't keep taking that bloody stuff and walking round in a daze all the time.'

Rebecca drew in her lips. She felt so useless. If only there was something she could do to help him. If only she could take on some of the pain for him.

She felt him move then and he slowly relaxed back in the chair, his face grey and his eyes closed wearily again.

'Has it gone?' she dared to ask.

He barely nodded. 'Almost. Oh, God, when are these spasms going to stop?' he groaned. 'I wouldn't mind so much if . . . if I still had . . .'

He glanced up at her, his liquid eyes glistening in their sunken sockets, pleading, tearing at her own heart. He looked so thin and haggard, his cheeks hollow and the scar on his forehead turning white as it healed fully.

'I know,' she croaked, and squeezed his good arm, about the only way she had of communicating her sympathy. 'They'll stop eventually. You just need to be patient. Dr Seaton said—'

'Oh, to hell with Dr Seaton!'

'Adam! He saved your life!'

'And what for?' His eyes flashed with angry despondency, but then he breathed in hard through his nostrils and she saw him swallow. 'I'm sorry. It's just that . . . sometimes . . .'

He broke off and turned his head away, leaving Rebecca at a total loss. She remained silently by his side for a few moments, unable to think of any words which might bring him comfort. For she knew there were none.

'I'm going to Mother and Father's later on,' she said at length. 'Sarah wants to discuss the wedding. Why don't you come? 'Twould do you good. You've not been out of the house since . . .'

'And have everyone stare at me as I walk through the port?' he growled bitterly.

Rebecca caught her breath. Yes. Of course she understood how he felt, but . . . 'People are very concerned about you. I'm always being asked how you are. And if they stare, well, 'tis out of sympathy. Besides, you . . . you have to face it some time.'

'I know,' he grated through tight lips. 'But not yet. I'm not ready.'

'Mother will put on a fine spread.'

'You know I've no appetite.'

That was certainly true enough. No matter what she put in front of him, he only picked at it. The flesh had fallen from him, and it perhaps worried her more than anything. 'As you wish,' she said, not wanting to press him. 'But you don't mind if I go?'

'Of course not.' And she thought she detected the shadow of a smile.

She went back to the rose tree, grateful for something to vent her frustrations on. Oh, Adam! Where was the strong, forthright man she loved, despised once, for his assertiveness? The loss of his hand was a devastating tragedy, and she felt for him as if the limb had been her own. But he was . . . refusing to accept it for what it was. Not even beginning to try to come to terms with it. And she didn't know how to cope with him.

'Where can I put these, Papa?'

Her eyes darted sideways across the garden. Toby was standing squarely in front of Adam's chair, a box of bedraggled seedlings held between his little hands. Adam contemplated him for a moment, and then got up out of the chair.

'Well, let me see,' Rebecca heard him reply. 'I don't really know much about plants, but over here looks like a good place.'

Rebecca felt a grateful sense of relief as Adam knelt down on the edge of the grass with Toby and actually started to dig a small hole in the flower bed with the garden trowel. It seemed that it was only when he was with his stepson that he became his normal self again. Oh, if only she hadn't lost the baby! She was sure that a child of his own would have provided the spur he needed. But he'd never spoken one word about her miscarriage, and she'd been left to grieve alone until sometimes she felt she would drown in her sorrow.

'What the hell are you doing here?'

Adam's voice, so unexpectedly vibrant with rage, shook her from her melancholy. She looked round, and dread chilled her bones as she saw standing there the figure she knew Adam never wanted to clap eyes on again.

Fred Bradley had put on weight, particularly in his face, robbing him of most of his resemblance to his cousin. Rebecca wondered how on earth she could have thought him attractive, for his expression radiated nothing but treachery and deceit. He came forward, a lopsided smirk on his lips. Adam got to his feet, stretching up to his full height and instinctively thrusting Toby behind him with his right hand.

'Well, that's a fine way to treat a visitor, cousin!' Fred leered, and placing his hat on the table beside the abandoned pipe and matches, slouched back in the chair Adam had just vacated. 'There was no answer at the front door, so I thought I'd come round the back. It's a very pretty garden. And won't your equally pretty little wife serve me some tea?'

Rebecca felt herself shudder as his eyes seemed to feast on her bare arms, and her hand went to draw together the unfastened buttons at her neck. But Adam's voice, clear and uncompromising, turned Fred's head again.

'No, she won't. And if you have anything to say, I suggest you stand up to say it, and then leave before I break your neck.'

'Huh! And how do you propose to do that, eh?' Fred sprang up, his face twisted with a livid sneer. 'I'd heard you'd had a slight accident, and I came to offer my sympathies, that's all. I see it's true, then.' He nodded towards the empty cuff at Adam's left wrist. 'Still painful, is it? My, my, you're in a sorry state, cousin. And look at you, in the garden in your shirt sleeves. What happened to your tie and that smart captain's blazer of yours, eh? And your other sleeve rolled up to the elbow! Couldn't have done that for yourself, now, could you?'

Bile burned in Rebecca's gullet and she had an overwhelming desire to fly at Fred's throat. Her eyes swivelled across to where Adam stood unflinching, but she could see the muscles of his lean jaw working furiously to control his temper. Behind him, Toby was gazing upwards in confusion, sensing that something unpleasant was happening, but not understanding. Rebecca beckoned to him, and was thankful that Toby trotted over to her without questioning.

Fred at once grinned sarcastically. 'Nice little family you have, Adam. And a very pleasing home. Sort of place I'd have liked myself, but could never afford, thanks to you. And I have to say, I admire your choice of spouse. From common stock originally, I believe, her father a vulgar miner before he came up in the world, so I'm told. But you always did have some affinity with the peasant classes, didn't you, Adam? But she certainly has a great deal of rustic charm. You'll need someone like her to look after you now, won't you, with only one hand? Cater to your every whim. Obedient, is she?'

Rebecca's pulse was beating faster with every vile word that spewed from Fred's foul mouth. She didn't care what he said about her, but it was the way he was using her to torment Adam that enraged her.

But Adam was standing his ground valiantly. 'Not exactly,' he grated, and Rebecca's heart bled as she realized he was defending her.

'Oh, so she's a spirited little thing, is she? Well, I wouldn't mind trying her out myself, then! Not like Felicity, eh? Cold as ice, that one. Or was it that you never managed to rise to the occasion? Perhaps it's the same with this one, too? The boy's not yours, after all. So that makes two women you've obviously never managed to get pregnant, doesn't it?'

Rebecca froze, the agony of her lost child lacerating her fragile hold on her emotions. Fred's cruelty cut even deeper than he realized himself as he stood there, taunting Adam and making such spiteful remarks. Rebecca saw Adam's eyes dart across at her, and an almost imperceptible flick of his eyebrows told her to get herself and Toby into the cottage. But Fred was barring her way, and besides, she wouldn't leave Adam to face this barbaric monster alone.

'How dare you speak about my wife like that!' Adam warned in a low but controlled tone.

But Fred remained unaffected. 'I shall speak about your wife however I like,' he replied nonchalantly. 'You're in no position to make threats now, cousin. Everything has always gone your way. And now it's my turn. It's always been the same, you see, Rebecca.' He turned his face towards her with a malicious grin. 'You don't mind me calling you Rebecca, do you? Adam and I were both sent to the same school, you see, and it was always, why can't you do as well as your cousin, he's so bright. And I remember when I was forced to attend the ceremony when he received his first mate's certificate. Everyone was fussing over him because he was the youngest person ever to do so at the naval college he went to. Oh, yes, I remember it well. For it was then that my father told me he wished Adam was his son instead of me!'

'It was your own fault, Fred. While I was busy studying and working so damned hard, you were running up your debts on gambling and women!'

'Learning to be a man.' Fred's lips curled back from his teeth. 'Which you evidently never have! But no matter. My day will come. And it's coming fast. Your little wife here had to sell some of your shares in Bradley's Merchants, didn't she, to pay your doctor's bill? And wouldn't you like to know who bought those shares, eh? Well, let's say it seemed appropriate to keep them in the family. And I understand old Harvey has stepped into the breach as the *Emily*'s master for the time being. But he sails her like a bathtub, and you'll be the one to be in debt soon unless you get back to sea pretty sharpish!

And by the look of you, that doesn't seem very likely, does it? And you always said you never asked your crew to do anything you wouldn't do yourself. Always so magnanimous, your dear husband, Rebecca. But you couldn't do that now, could you? I mean, you couldn't climb the rigging or hoist a sail very easily, not with only one hand. You could scarcely take the helm even in a calm sea, not with a ship the size of your beloved *Emily*.'

Rebecca's stomach screwed so tightly she could hardly breathe. Adam's chin had been raised courageously under the abuse, his right hand clenched into a fist. But Fred had twisted the knife deep into the wound, and Adam turned his head away, unable to take any more. But to see his spirit being so wilfully crushed only served to fire Rebecca with incensed rebellion.

'Only a coward kicks a man when he's down,' she snarled like a wild cat, her voice lashing through the air like a whip. For a moment, Fred's expression reflected his surprised shock. But then he cocked one sardonic eyebrow.

'Coward I may be, but I've waited for this for years. I'm going to bring you down, cousin, destroy you. I'm going to take back everything that was rightly mine. And everything else you've worked for, too. And what's more, before I'm through, I shall have that pretty wife of yours as well.'

Rebecca audibly gasped. She felt sick. Dear God, Adam had been right when he'd told her how despicable Fred was! How could anyone stoop to such low, sadistic behaviour?

'You bloody bastard.' Adam's white lips barely moved as his cracked voice ground out the words.

'Language, Adam, language! But I mean every word, believe me!' Fred's eyes were glinting, the green flecks making them glow like demonic emeralds. 'Your darling little wife here only married you because she had some other man's flyblow growing in her belly! Oh, yes, it's surprising what you can find out when you have a little silver in your pocket. She's never loved you, only ever made a pretence of it for the sake of that gipsy brat of hers. So she's hardly going to love you now, is she, a spineless cripple with one hand missing? When you're out on the streets and I'm the one with the Bradley money, she'll be happy enough to turn to me. After all, just look at her! Hardly a lady, is she? She's nothing but a common whore! A pretty one, I grant you . . .'

'Adam, *no!*'

The shriek somehow wheezed from her lungs as Adam sprang towards his cousin and struck him such a blow across the jaw that he reeled backwards and toppled on to the grass. Adam stood over him, shaking his stinging knuckles, his eyes narrowed with revulsion.

'Get out,' he croaked contemptuously.

Fred blinked up at him before the sneer returned to his lips. 'Resort to violence now, would you?' And as Adam stepped back to let him get to his feet, Fred hurled himself at Adam's waist, bringing them both to the ground. Rebecca heard the sickening thud as Adam landed on his back with Fred's weight on top of him, and her hand went over her mouth in horror. She could see Adam was stunned by the fall on to his scarcely healed ribs, his head thrown back in anguish, but Fred was already scrambling upwards, and grinning like a demented gargoyle, he stamped on Adam's left wrist.

The piercing scream rent the warm summer air and ripped Rebecca's heart from her chest. Her pulse was flying, thundering, reverberating inside her skull. Adam was writhing in agony on the grass, his feet drumming into the earth, as Fred drove a vicious kick into his groin.

'Huh! Thought you could throw me out, did you!' he spat. 'Not anymore, cousin!'

'No, but I can!'

Her fingers closed about the garden fork. Her feet flew across the grass. And before Fred had a chance to turn to her in astonishment, she cracked the implement across his shins. He instantly collapsed on to the ground with a cry, his body squirming as the pain burned through his legs. He looked up at her, and she rejoiced at the fear in his eyes as her wrath bore into his flesh. She thrust the prongs of the fork at him, and he squirmed backwards, raising one arm to ward off any further blows.

'For what 'tis worth, I love Adam with my heart and soul!' she exploded, her eyes gleaming like a tigress. 'And I'd sooner kill myself than succumb to a piece of filth like you! You're an animal! Adam might have lost his hand, but he's a hundred times more of a man than you could ever be in a million years! Now get out!' She jabbed the fork at him again, and this time it poked hard against his chest. 'And if you ever try to touch Adam again, so help me God, *I'll kill you!*'

She allowed him to drag himself to his feet, but she didn't slacken her guard for an instant. He reached out to the table for his hat, and hobbled backwards as she continued to wield the fork at him, but he paused as she followed him round the cottage and up the front path.

'Don't worry, I'll not come near Adam again,' he told her, the bravado gradually returning. 'But I'll be there. In the background. You'll come grovelling to me, mark my words.' And with a groan of pain, he limped away down the hill.

The second she was sure he had gone, she raced back around the cottage, every nerve in her body ready to snap. Adam had struggled up on to his knees, his left arm clutched across his chest, and when he saw her, his other hand reached out to her with the desperation of pure agony. She threw the fork aside and found herself on her knees, wrapping him in her embrace, tears flowing freely down her cheeks as the terror of the last ten minutes drained through her limbs. And then Toby was there, his ebony eyes shining in bewilderment, and he entered the circle of his mother's protection as she held them both so tightly.

'Thank God you're all right,' Adam murmured breathlessly. 'I didn't see . . . Where . . . ?'

'He's gone. And I reckon as he'll think twice before he comes near me again. I think I might've cracked his shin bone.'

'What!'

'With the garden fork,' she told him simply.

He pulled away from her and for an instant, his face lengthened in disbelief, but then his eyes narrowed with a shudder and his lips drew back from his gritted teeth. He was visibly trembling, and when Rebecca looked down at his left arm, a streak of scarlet was seeping through the brilliant white of his shirt cuff. She met his gaze, and heard him suck his breath in sharply through his teeth as she carefully rolled the material back over the tender stump. One of the joins in the skin flap had been split open by Fred's vicious boot.

'Oh, dear God!' she muttered. ''Twill need stitching again. I'd better send for Dr Seaton.'

'What, and sell some more shares to my dear cousin to pay for it?' His tone was half accusing, half bitter, but then he shook his head torturedly. 'I'm sorry, Rebecca. You don't deserve this. All those damnable things he said about you . . .'

'Words can't hurt me, Adam. But I could happily murder him for doing this to you!'

'Well, much as I appreciate your standing up for me, I think that's possibly taking matters a little too far. Besides, I'd rather have that pleasure myself.' He attempted a smile, but his mouth moved into a thin, contorted line, and Rebecca shivered as she helped him to his feet again. For despite what she had said, she knew in the chill of her bones that they hadn't seen the last of Alfred Bradley. Not by a long chalk.

CHAPTER TWENTY-ONE

'There, Toby,' she smiled proudly as she smoothed the miniature bow tie into place. 'You look splendid.'

She held him at arm's length, her chest swelling with emotion. So smart in the blue serge jacket she'd sewn herself from a blazer of Adam's that was wearing through at the elbows. And yet . . . Some wistful sense of inevitability tugged at her forlorn heart. Toby looked so grown up. No longer a baby. But at three-and-a-quarter years old, a real little boy. And so much the image of his real father that it took her breath away.

'Damn it!'

Adam's voice reached her faintly from the bedroom where he was endeavouring to get himself properly attired. Rebecca lifted her eyes and met Mrs Blatchford's knowing gaze as she folded Toby's everyday clothes on the bed.

'Rebecca!'

Adam's demanding tone brought a sigh from Rebecca's lungs, but she could never be cross with him, however much his moods wore her down. For intrinsically mingled with the command was a helpless cry of despair.

'You go down to the parlour with Mrs Blatchford,' she beamed lovingly at Toby. 'And please don't spoil your clothes.'

'Why, we'll read your favourite storybook,' the house-keeper suggested kindly as the child took her hand.

Rebecca straightened up. She'd been looking forward to this, Sarah and Misha's wedding day, for so long. It had been like a star shining out in the darkness since Adam's accident, and she was determined that nothing would mar her enjoyment of her sister's happiness. But at the back of her mind, she knew that she would be thinking about Adam and what he was going through at every single moment.

With reluctant step, she took herself into his bedroom. He was standing at the washstand, stripped to the waist, and Rebecca's heart reared sickeningly at the sight of his hand-less wrist so openly exposed. It was some time since she'd seen him undressed, and her eyes travelled longingly over his broad shoulders. But his powerful muscles were disappearing through lack of use and he'd become so thin that when he leaned forward to have a closer look in the mirror, she could see quite clearly the ridge of every rib across his back. When he turned to her, she saw there was a little crimson trickle meandering down from his jaw where he had nicked himself deeply with the razor.

'It won't stop,' he told her irritably.

'Oh, Adam, you should've let me do it, today of all days.'

The merest hint of a reprimand tinged the sympathy in her words, but it was enough to spark Adam's temper. 'I'm not a bloody child, you know!' he rounded on her.

She bit her lip hard. Adam was becoming more diffi-cult with every passing day, it seemed, and she didn't have the strength to do anything but humour him. So she said nothing, and instead took out a worn but clean handkerchief from the drawer, dampened it in the washbowl and pressed it firmly over the cut.

'Hold that on it while I finish off,' she ordered sternly, steeling herself against the hurt in his eyes. He held his chin up for her, but stiffly. As if he resented every deft movement she made with the sharp blade. 'Now if it's stopped bleeding, get your shirt on and I'll put the studs in for you.'

She deliberately avoided looking at him, knowing the torment in his face would tear at her own breaking heart. He could don the garment easily enough, but it was his best dress shirt, and rather than buttons, it had holes for elaborate shirt studs which he couldn't possibly fasten for himself. So he stood rigid while she performed the task for him, sensing the tension in his body as her fingers inevitably brushed against his skin.

'I feel so bloody useless,' he muttered almost to himself, his head turned away as if he couldn't bear to hear his own strangled words.

This time she felt compelled to say something to ease his anguish. 'You mustn't think like that, Adam.'

'But I do.'

His voice was unsteady, and she saw his face set into the now familiar hard mask, as if he were putting up a shield to protect himself. For a few devastating seconds, she was unsure, not knowing how to handle this man, her husband, who not so long ago had been so strong and vibrant in his love for her. She stifled a sigh and consciously restrained her hand as it instinctively went to help him into his waist-coat and jacket. For surely by assisting him with items he could manage by himself, she would increase his humiliation tenfold.

'You'd better hurry up and finish dressing,' she said at last in the matter-of-fact tone she'd decided fitted the moment best. 'The groom and best man are supposed to arrive before the bride, you know.' She turned her back and busied herself clearing up the washstand and tidying away the clothes he'd been wearing earlier. She heard him moving about behind her for a minute or so, but then her own hands became still as she realized that although Adam hadn't left the room, there wasn't the slightest sound of any movement. She waited, the silence tangible and oppressive.

'I . . . I can't do this, Rebecca.'

His words, when they finally came, were no more than a croaked whisper. She held her breath and turned round slowly. Adam was staring at the ring-box that he held in the palm of his right hand as he tried unsuccessfully to open the lid with his forefinger and thumb.

'We've been through this before,' she smiled encouragingly. ''Tis all arranged. You just give the box to the reverend, and he'll take the ring out himself.'

'That's not what I meant.' She stared as Adam rolled his head as if he couldn't break free from the torture that bound him. He shut his eyes tightly and swallowed hard. 'All those people,' he choked. 'All those prying eyes. And I've got to stand up in front of them all at the church. And then I've got to make that damned speech.'

'Adam.' She fingered the lapels of his jacket, searching to relieve the pain in her own throat. She could tell him that it was his own fault for not setting foot outside the cottage and its back garden since the accident. That he should have listened to her and gradually built up his confidence with short trips to the Ship Inn, perhaps, at first. But it wouldn't help to say such things now. And what could she say that would lessen his anxieties? Her tongue stuck to the roof of her mouth, but surely she could find some words of comfort to offer him? 'Adam . . . There may be prying eyes. But everyone is on your side, you know. And you can't let Misha down now.'

She heard a quivering breath vibrate from his lungs and he nodded slowly and deliberately as if he were trying to take control of himself. 'Yes, I know,' he whispered, but he was shaking like the sails of a ship as it comes into the wind.

Rebecca gazed up at his drawn face and looked deep into his eyes. 'I'll be there,' she told him emphatically, but her voice was as thick and ravaged as his had been. ''Twill be all right.'

She raised herself on tiptoe to plant a quick kiss on his cheek, but as he had done recently at any show of affection she offered, he sharply turned his head and shied away.

* * *

It was already dusk as she climbed the steep hill towards Lavender Cottage, the muffled calls of noisy farewells from outside the hall at the rear of the inn growing fainter behind her. Unlike her own subdued, almost mournful wedding, Sarah and Misha's marriage had been a lively affair with most of Morwellham's inhabitants calling in at some point to join in the frivolities following the nuptial breakfast earlier in the day. During the formal proceedings, Adam had delivered the briefest best man's speech imaginable. The self-assured sea captain who could once have commanded a wilful crew or addressed a difficult board meeting with ease, was scarcely able to express the usual thanks and other expected duties. Everyone was relieved by Isaac's banter which, by contrast, was considered to be far more amusing than it actually was, and Misha's shining praise for his bride whom he obviously adored, all beautifully embellished by his broken English and faltering accent, had all the guests smiling.

Later on, Rebecca had witnessed the torment on Adam's face as people had come to shake his remaining hand. Some made no allusion to the amputation, their eyes nevertheless sliding surreptitiously to his empty left cuff, but many had expressed their sympathy at his 'misfortune' and hoped that he would soon be back at sea, feeling fully recovered. After all, you read a chart and navigate a ship with your eyes and your brain, one of the arsenic agents had proclaimed with inept joviality as he slapped Captain Bradley heartily on the shoulder. Rebecca had seen the muscles of Adam's lean jaw stiffen more and more tightly as she stood next to him. She tried not to leave his side, but inevitably they were drawn apart and shortly afterwards, she'd spied him slipping out of the door. Across the hall, she saw Misha's fair head lift up sharply, and he glanced towards her, his brow corrugated with consternation. She raised her spread palm in the air and gave a small shake of her head, and Misha nodded in reply. If Adam had wanted company, he would have asked for it. He simply needed to escape. And Rebecca soon knew how he felt. For so many well-meaning people came to tell her how poorly the captain looked and to pass on their good wishes to him, that she could have screamed. But then the little band of players had struck up, and there were jigs and reels, and plenty of partners, and for a few hours she was caught up in the merriment of the occasion. And there was Robin, no longer coughing, but whirling Hetty up and down the dance floor with the other revellers. Rebecca was reminded of another time, centuries ago now, it seemed, when she had skipped and twirled in Tom's hold, her delight interrupted only by the brief appearance of the arrogant sea captain from London. And shortly afterwards, Tom had left her, and now Adam was steadily slipping away from her like sand trickling through an hourglass.

Toby had fallen asleep on his grandfather's lap, and rather than disturb him, Isaac said he would carry the child home with him to Copper Ore Cottage. And so it was that Rebecca was making her way to her own home with Mrs Blatchford accompanying her.

''Twere a good celebration,' the older woman was saying a little breathlessly. ''Tis years since I danced so much.'

'Yes. I think they'll be very happy,' Rebecca smiled absently. But the festivities already seemed an age ago as they laboured up the hill. How had Adam fared, alone in the house all those hours, with nothing but his deepening depression for company? But what good would her presence have done? It seemed lately that she had nothing to offer him, and all the while they were rapidly losing money and Adam simply didn't care.

'Mrs Blatchford,' she began nervously, her palms suddenly sweating. 'I've been waiting to have a moment to speak to you alone. I've been putting it off, but the thing is . . . I can't afford to employ you any longer.'

She blurted out the words in a rush, embarrassed to have to say them. Mrs Blatchford instantly halted, and Rebecca felt so ashamed she wanted the ground to open up and swallow her. ''Tis not your work at all, 'tis simply the money,' she went on awkwardly, and began to walk up the hill again with the housekeeper falling into step beside her without uttering a word. 'You know what bad luck we had, and then there was Misha's training and the *Emily*'s overhaul. 'Twere bad enough before Adam's accident, but now . . . There's no capital left, and such repayments to meet, I don't know which way to turn.'

Her voice betrayed the despair she truly felt, and as they reached the garden gate, her hands clutched at it for support. Mrs Blatchford remained silent, deepening Rebecca's guilt even further. 'I . . . I know it might not seem this way to you,' she felt she had to continue, 'but all our money is tied up in the ships and the business. If I sell anything to pay off our debts, then we lose that source of income for the future, and with Adam . . .' she nearly said not working, but changed it to, 'as he is, I don't want to do that if I can help it. We did sell some shares to pay the medical bills, but . . . there is a reason why I mustn't sell any more.'

She broke off, shuddering violently at the memory of that horrifying afternoon when Fred Bradley had mercilessly assaulted Adam in their own home. They'd decided to keep quiet about it, for there were no other witnesses and it seemed better not to stir up any further trouble with Fred if possible. But Dr Seaton had raised a disbelieving eyebrow when he'd been summoned to repair the damage and was told that Adam had tripped over in the garden and instinctively put out his hands to save himself, but had injured the tender stump instead. She shook her head, as if emerging from a thought too appalling to contemplate. 'I have to keep everything together until Adam is well enough to take over again,' she concluded. 'And if that means making domestic sacrifices, then I'm afraid 'twill have to be. I really am sorry. But I'm sure you'll find another position quite easily. In Tavistock, perhaps. I'll give you a glowing character—'

'No!' The small woman lifted her chin obstinately. 'I'll not leave you. Not while the captain be in this state. You need me as much as he needs you.'

'But we can't afford . . .'

'You doesn't need to. The captain first employed me —
on your own mother's suggestion, remember — to look after
the place just while he were in port, and I lived in my little
room in the tenements. And then soon after you was wed,
I came to live in. And right glad I were of it, too, me being
a widow and my Charlie living away with his own wife and
family now. So all this time, I've had no rent to pay, and
you've been more than generous. And now you've fallen on
hard times, 'tis my turn to help you. Just the roof over my
head 'tis all I ask. No wages. And we'll get a pig and some
hens. My Charlie'll be able to fetch some good ones from
the farm he do run now. And we can grow a lot of our own
vegetables. This garden be big enough!' Her mouth widened
into an enthusiastic grin. 'You've learned thrift from your
mother, but I reckon I can teach you a thing or two. I knows
all the tricks. 'Twill be hard work, mind, but there's fun to
be had in that, too.'

Rebecca blinked at her, suddenly swamped with emotion and ready to sink into the comfort she could no longer
seek from Adam. 'Oh, Mrs Blatchford! What can I say!'

'We must all pull together when times be hard. And I
knows you be as proud as the captain, poor devil, and you
doesn't want to be going to your father for help, and he'll be
short himself after today. We'll work together, you and me,
but you've a child and a sick husband to care for, and they
must come first.'

Rebecca tipped her head with a frown. 'Adam's not sick.
His arm's more or less healed now.'

'He's sick in his mind, though, ma'am, if you doesn't
mind me saying so. And 'tis the hardest thing to cure.'

Rebecca drew in a deep breath as she gazed down the
garden path towards the cottage. 'Yes, I know. And he's getting worse instead of better.'

'Give him time, ma'am. You know the good doctor said
many men would've died of physical shock at the operation
itself, but the captain were too strong for that. So I reckon
as he's suffering from a kind of mental shock now instead.'

Rebecca nodded with a strange sense of relief at knowing there was someone else who really seemed to understand. 'Yes. Oh, you're wiser than any wise woman, you know.'

They smiled together, and then Rebecca opened the gate and reluctantly walked down the path. The cottage was in total darkness and as silent as the grave. Rebecca's heartbeat instantly accelerated. Oh, God, what if . . . She ran frantically from the deserted parlour into the equally empty kitchen, calling his name, and stumbled over Mrs Blatchford in the hallway again.

'Adam!' She flung open the door to the study, untouched for months now, and was about to make for the stairs in case he had retired to bed, despite the relatively early hour, when she noticed his long legs stretched out from the enormous, winged chair. She suddenly felt weak, telling herself how stupid she had been to imagine . . .

'Adam,' she whispered, coming forward on unsteady legs.

He glanced up, his eyes glazed as if he'd been dozing. But then she noticed the half empty bottle of rum on the floor beside the chair, and the glass with an inch of the rich, dark liquid still in it. She bent and picked them up, knowing the bottle had been virtually full before they'd left for the church, but Adam reached out and snatched the glass from her.

She stood for a moment, hesitating at the fierceness of his action. 'You're drinking too much,' she dared to murmur.

He fixed her as well as he could with his wandering gaze. 'You know it helps me to sleep,' he grated, and tossed the remaining spirit down his throat.

It was true enough. The nights brought him no rest, despite his increasing exhaustion, and a stiff drink seemed to be the only way his mind would relax enough to allow him a few hours to escape the agony of his waking life.

'But 'tisn't good for you, not this much.' She voiced her concerns uneasily. 'You might at least have had a couple of glasses of wine rather than half a bottle of rum.'

Adam was on his feet in an instant, almost tripping over the chair leg. 'I haven't exactly mastered the art of using a corkscrew with only one hand yet!' he barked. 'Ironic, isn't it? A wine merchant who can't open a bloody bottle!'

Rebecca's mouth fell open in dismay. Oh, how stupid of her! How could she not have considered what twisted into his soul at every moment, gnawing away at him like some rampaging disease? She was instantly choked by her own anger at herself. It must have shown in her eyes for Adam thought it was directed at him and his gaze, clear now with hateful frustration, clashed furiously with hers.

'Give me the damned bottle!' he demanded, his eyes wild and his lips curled back from his clenched teeth. And since his right hand already held the now empty glass, he instinctively went to swipe the bottle out of her grasp with his left. He stopped with his arm in mid-air as he realized what he'd done. His face turned a thunderous black and a howl like that of a mortally wounded beast growled in his throat. Oh, sweet Jesus! How she wanted to hold him, rock him in her arms. But his inbred, stubborn pride, she knew, would not allow it. And so, slowly, calmly, she took the glass from his hand and replaced it with the bottle.

He almost smiled then. At least, she thought the twitching grimace was perhaps a flicker of appreciation that she understood his pain. He tipped the bottle to his lips, his eyes, stormy and brooding, not leaving her face. And then he walked past her, lurching ever so slightly, and climbed the stairs one at a time, rather than taking them in three easy bounds as he always used to.

Rebecca stared after him, long after he'd slammed the bedroom door behind him, her eyes brimming with moisture. And then her arm was being squeezed by a bony, workworn hand not much bigger than her own.

'Oh, Mrs Blatchford,' she moaned. 'When will he face up to it? When will he find some peace inside himself? I love him so much, and yet I can do nothing . . .'

She gagged on the wrenching sob that tore at her lungs, knowing she must not give in. She had to be strong. Far stronger than when Tom had died. For Adam's was a living grief, and she not only had to mourn for her own sorrow over his disability, but bear him up and do her best to support all the other people who used to rely on him for employment.

'You bests get some sleep, ma'am,' the housekeeper, who seemed more like an old friend now, suggested persuasively. ''Twill be easier to cope if you're not tired yourself.'

She nodded, knowing the good sense of the older woman's words. 'Yes. But I think a cup of hot, sweet chocolate would go down well first.' But before she turned to the kitchen, her eyes darted apprehensively up the stairs to the closed door of Adam's room.

* * *

She had been thrashing about in the bed in a fitful sleep for some time when she slipped back into full consciousness. Tension slowly gripped her chest, making her heart pound, as she became aware of the all too familiar sound of Adam pacing up and down his bedroom like a caged lion. She imagined he must have fallen asleep in a drunken stupor for a few hours, for all had been quiet when she had come to bed herself. But his tortured mind must have broken through his vivid dreams as it did almost nightly, causing him to step frenetically from one side of the small room to the other.

Rebecca lay there listening to him, biting her nails in torment. Should she go to him, as she yearned to, or would he snap viciously at her helpless show of affection? Her lips tightened into a thin, trembling line and her wide eyes moved sharply about the room, seeing nothing, but somehow helping her ears to concentrate on every sound from the room across the landing. And when some ten minutes later the pacing ceased, she breathed a sigh of relief and snuggled back down in the lonely bed.

But what was that? The bottom stair creaked and, only an instant later, she heard the bolts on the front door being shot back. She lifted her head, senses alert, as the door was quietly opened and equally silently clicked shut and locked. Rebecca catapulted from between the sheets and reached the window in time to see Adam turn out of the gate.

Panic closed her chest in a vice. Oh, dear Christ! Adam was so stubborn, so demented in his depression, that . . . But surely he . . . She thrust her bare feet into the serviceable boots she wore every day, laced them up to her ankles with skilled fingers and, hurtling down the stairs, swept her coat from the hall stand and pulled it on over her nightdress as she raced up the path. She hesitated at the gate. Adam had turned down the hill to the port. He would already have rounded the stables at the rear of the Ship and be out of sight. She scurried down the steep incline but came to a halt at the corner of the inn, silent now after the jollities of the wedding celebration. Which way would he have gone? Past the idle limekilns and up into the woods by the defunct George and Charlotte copper mine, or down to the port? Either way, he was nowhere to be seen, and the quays were deserted but for a small barge moored in Canal Dock and the *Swallow* tied up at the river wharf while her young Russian master enjoyed his wedding night in the best room the Ship Inn had to offer.

But Rebecca scarcely gave her sister a second thought. Misha was kind and gentle, and although it was wrong of her to consider other people's intimate moments, she was sure he would be likewise in his lovemaking in the same way as Adam . . . Oh, how she missed that closeness. Those precious moments when their souls as well as their bodies became one, and they could glory in the pleasures of the flesh so deeply only because their love was so fathomless, and each wanted to give as much excitement to the other. But now . . .

Oh, God, where was he? In desperation, she hitched up the hem of her nightgown and hurried across to where the schooner rode gently in the rapidly moving waters of the Tamar. The tide was running out fast and — coupled with the downward flow of the river, the sleek ripples glinting in the moonlight — belied the power of the current beneath that tugged at the ship's fine hull and made her strain at the ropes that held her fast against the wharf. The gangway remained in place, and Rebecca hesitated only momentarily as she gazed upwards at the black skeleton of the towering masts silhouetted against the silver-edged clouds in the sky. Masts, and their web of rigging, that Adam would never be able to scramble up again.

'Who be there?'

Her already churning stomach clenched even more ferociously, causing her to gasp aloud, but then she wondered who was more alarmed. In the dim light she could see the *Swallow*'s mate gazing at her in open amazement. He was there to guard the ship and her contents against possible evil-doers, but to come face to face with the lovely young wife of poor Captain Bradley in the small hours of the morning, dressed in what could only be her nightdress beneath a thin summer coat, well, it was a shock indeed! He had a comely wife and a growing handful of children himself at home in Plymouth, but he wasn't too old to be affected by the apparition of this ethereal, wispy spirit of the night.

'Have you seen Captain Bradley?' She spoke so clearly, her voice racked with worry, that the fellow was jolted from what he thought must be a vision.

'Well, no, ma'am. Not for months. Not since . . . well . . .'

Rebecca ran her hand through her hair, oblivious to the way it cascaded appealingly down over her shoulders in the wavy, shimmering curtain that Adam had once found so sensuous when it brushed over his naked chest as they lay in bed together. But at this moment it only seemed to enhance the image of her distraction. The mate was one of those who had helped drag Adam from beneath the pile of fallen casks and, like everyone else, he'd heard the rumour that the captain hadn't been himself since the accident that had left him maimed.

'But if I sees him, I'll make sure he . . . well, he be all right, ma'am. And you oughtn't to be running about like this in the middle of the night. 'Tis not safe.'

Rebecca compressed her lips together. Of course, he was right. Adam could be anywhere and it was fruitless to search for him. Nevertheless, in the vain hope of glimpsing Adam's familiar form, her eyes were everywhere as she took herself reluctantly back across the open quay. She dared not even contemplate the idea of looking in the black waters of the Tamar. And Adam was apparently a strong swimmer, and even with one hand and perhaps . . . wanting to . . . Surely instinct would force one to fight against . . . She arrived back at Lavender Cottage in just as much consternation as she had left it — her stomach screwed into a suffocating knot. She sat up, cross-legged, on the bed, unable to rest as her eyes pricked with fatigue. Eventually, she stretched the slender length of her body across the bedspread, but although she tossed and turned, her thumping heart wouldn't allow her to sleep.

The intense darkness of the night was beginning to lessen, and the birds outside were chirping the overture to their dawn chorus, when she heard the front door opening. She sat bolt upright, her nerves tingling and on edge, listening as the door was quietly clicked shut, and then a moment later, the sound of someone creeping up the stairs and disappearing into one of the other bedrooms. Adam. Overwhelming relief swept through Rebecca's body and her shoulders slumped. The terror that had sickened her stomach all night ebbed away, leaving a draining exhaustion in its place. But her brain refused to be still as she lay down again in a vain search for sleep. What thoughts had been running through Adam's tortured mind as he'd wandered alone in the darkness for all those hours? Had he considered the ultimate action that had choked her with fear, for how was either of them to cope with this nightmare that had come at them from nowhere?

She buried her head in the pillow, and let the tears of despair slip down her cheeks.

CHAPTER TWENTY-TWO

'How delightful to see you, Mrs Bradley,' the arsenic agent purred pleasurably as she stepped into his office. 'I must say, I were quite surprised at your request for an appointment. I take it the captain is still not up to seeing to his business affairs in person, though he seemed well enough to me on the splendid occasion of your sister's marriage.'

Rebecca's spine stiffened. What did this rumbustious fellow, who'd made such thoughtless remarks to Adam at the wedding reception, know of her husband's anguish?

'My husband is not yet fully recovered from his accident,' she said coolly, taking a seat before she was offered one and arranging her skirts with supreme confidence. 'I know 'tis nigh on five months now, but folk forget he sustained injuries other than . . . than the one that's so apparent, and his general health has suffered considerably.'

Mr Mawling felt suitably reprimanded by her disdainful attitude. Isaac Westbrook's daughter had always been a spirited maid, despite the conventional way she had been raised. Lively, and an endearing joy to all who knew her winsome ways. But by Jove, the whole of Morwellham had rocked when it had become clear that her little son could only be Tom Mason's boy, and not the child of the smart captain from London who must have been bewitched by her to take on what he had. But the accomplished young woman who sat so assertively in the chair before him was a totally different kettle of fish. Enchanting still, but with an air of authority which she had perhaps learned from her cultured husband.

'I'm sorry to hear that,' the man smiled apologetically. 'I had not realized.'

''Tis not obvious,' she answered crisply. 'But I didn't come here to discuss my husband's health. 'Tis the arsenic contract I wish to talk about.'

'The contract?' Mr Mawling's eyebrows disappeared into his hairline. 'Why, 'tis all signed and sealed. The captain doesn't want to change anything now, does he?'

'Change?' Rebecca's own brow deepened into a bemused frown. 'What do you mean?'

'Well, I suppose if they were only minor changes, we could both get back to our solicitors. I must say I were surprised by it all in the first place.'

'Solicitors?' She leaned forward now, her composure, her desire to assume the male role of businessman — since Adam had simply shrugged distantly when she'd reminded him the contract renewal date was fast approaching — draining away with the sudden flood of ice into her veins. 'I don't understand. There must be some mistake.'

'I hardly think so. Though as I were saying, we were most surprised by his proposals.'

Rebecca's heart began to drum painfully with some grave sense of foreboding. 'But . . . but Adam's not been in contact with his solicitors,' she faltered, forgetting in her anxiety that she should be referring to him as either the captain or her husband. 'He told me that I could take care of the renewal as I wished.'

Mr Mawling straightened his lips into a thin line, not sure he wanted to discuss the matter with a mere woman, even if she was Isaac Westbrook's daughter and was known to have almost as much interest in the goings-on of the port as the harbour master himself. 'Well, I'm sure I be as confused as you are, Mrs Bradley,' he had to admit. 'But it were all negotiated a week or so ago by his London solicitors, though, of course, 'twere all your husband's idea. He drew up a legal agreement whereby he provides all the barges we need to take the arsenic down to Plymouth to be trans-shipped, and they will return with coal for our engines. He sent us a list of all the barges he's chartered so far, which I must say consists of all our regulars — apart from the *Sure* for some reason — and another list of others he is in negotiation with. In return, we have agreed not to use any other carrier for the arsenic, although we can for the coal as we need so much. But if we have a surplus of powder, we will just have to store it, because the agreement works both ways. If for any reason production slows down, we don't have to pay a penalty for not having a cargo ready and waiting, as we always have in the past with all our former individual contracts. The freight rate is to be raised, but as we virtually have the monopoly of the world market, we can pass that on to our customers easily enough. But the rate is to be fixed for three years, which safeguards us against any general rise in prices, and it means our river transport is arranged for that period without us having to keep negotiating umpteen single contracts which in itself is a waste of time and money.' He sat back and joined his hands over his rotund stomach as if pleased with his summary of the agreement. 'Well, we could hardly refuse, could we, Mrs Bradley, especially as most of our regular barges had already been leased and their services could have been withheld if we hadn't agreed. It were a wily move by your husband to set up a monopoly like that, even if it cost him a pretty penny to start with. As you know, most barges are owned by groups of shareholders with neither the money nor the insight to plan something like this.'

'And the *Sure* isn't included?' Rebecca stammered, her mouth gaping open quite rudely in her horrified bewilderment.

'Well, no.' Mr Mawling half sighed with irritation, for surely she must have been aware of the situation. 'We assumed that with her present contract shortly due to expire, there were other plans for her.'

Rebecca shook her head from side to side, almost sick with disbelief. 'This can't be true.' Her throat felt as dry as sandpaper. 'Adam's scarcely had a thought for his business concerns since his accident. Besides which, he doesn't have that sort of money.'

'No? Well, I can assure you 'tis all correct and legal. I have the documents here if you wish to peruse them.'

Rebecca sat motionless, her face like wet clay, as he rummaged in the drawers of the great desk before handing her a sheaf of papers. 'You will see 'tis all in order, with your husband's signature on the last page.'

Her eyes moved rapidly over the lines of writing, her hands trembling. There was something terribly wrong. All of this was none of Adam's doing, she knew, and her stomach churned savagely. She raised her wide, brilliant eyes to Mr Mawling's complacent smile. 'But . . . this . . . 'Tis not my husband's solicitors.' And jabbing her finger at the final page, she protested, 'And 'tis not his signature!'

'What!' Mr Mawling's florid cheeks blanched and he stood up instantly to consider the document across the width of the desk. 'But . . . yes.' It was his turn to stutter now. 'A. Bradley.'

'No! Adam is Adam James, and he always signs A. J. Bradley,' she insisted distraughtly. 'And besides, 'tis not his writing! Get out the old contract and compare them if you don't believe me!'

The agent's face was a total flustering grimace as he fumbled in a filing cabinet behind him, and in a few seconds the two differing signatures lay side by side on the desk. His eyes met hers, two horrified globes in his drained countenance.

'Then . . . who?' he mouthed, dumbstruck with guilt.

Rebecca swayed on the chair as perspiration oozed from every pore in her body. Oh, dear God, it was beginning. Fred Bradley. Not short for Frederick, as might have been expected. But Alfred. A. Bradley.

* * *

Adam's face was inscrutable for all of thirty seconds when she told him, and then he threw back his head with a harsh, bitter laugh. Rebecca was stunned, frustrated, appalled as she watched him. The situation hardly seemed amusing to her, and it frightened her that he could find such humour in the matter.

'He's a damned bloody idiot!' Adam spluttered at length, his laughter subsiding to a grimacing smile as he gave an ironic shake of his head. 'God knows what it must have cost him to persuade the first few barges to come over to his side. And even if the others were anxious to join when they realized what was happening, they'd have wanted a good deal. Huh!' he snorted sardonically. 'It's a bloody expensive way of trying to put one small barge out of business! He'd have done better to have scuttled her!'

Rebecca's eyes flashed at him, her frustration and despair turning to anger. 'But then he might've been caught, or you might've been able to claim on the insurance, assuming you have her insured now?'

Adam glared at her dangerously, and she realized she'd overstepped the mark without meaning to. 'Anyway,' she neatly sidestepped his threatening look, 'I don't see what you find so funny! It means the *Sure*'s lost her regular downriver trade now as well as the limestone.'

'So?' Adam's face was straight now. 'She's been running at a loss for several months now anyway, so it's hardly going to make much difference. Willis will just have to do what he's paid for and find his own bloody cargo.'

'And what if he can't?'

'Oh, for God's sake, there are scores of barges on the river scraping a living in one way or another. Sand, bricks, gravel, timber, and just because the limekilns here have closed, others haven't. And there are other mines than just Devon Great Consols needing supplies, and the manganese has to be—'

'And most of it already under contract,' she rounded on him. 'And what isn't, everyone is fighting over! And no matter where you go along the river, Newquay, Calstock, Gawton, Bere Ferrers, 'tis just the same. 'Tis really difficult if you don't have a regular trade, and the *Sure*'s lost hers!'

'Difficult, perhaps, but not impossible, despite what Fred might think. I do know what it's like trying to find a cargo against competition, you know, or had you forgotten?' His eyes snapped at her, but their fierceness mellowed almost at once. 'William Willis knows the trade along the river better than any of us. He'll keep the *Sure* going. It's his livelihood, after all. Mind you,' he went on, his voice tinged with annoyance, 'I'm surprised your father hadn't heard about what was going on and warned us.'

'He did know.' Rebecca nodded her head ruefully. 'I met him on the way back and I was so angry I told him. He hadn't said anything because, like everyone else, he thought 'twas you, and he doesn't believe in monopolies. And I know you wanted to keep it to ourselves, but I'm afraid I told him all about your cousin. In confidence, mind. He was appalled. Oh, Adam, we should have told him before, and then we could have stopped this before it all got too far!' She sighed heavily, suddenly feeling lifeless. ''Tis what comes of hiding yourself away like a hermit.'

She caught her breath, her heart battering against her ribs as Adam held her gaze steadily for some seconds before slowly casting down his eyes. Rebecca's teeth clamped over her bottom lip, remorse clawing at her throat. Why was it that her tongue still had the better of her at times, when her very soul bled for him? But then perhaps that was why, because she loved him so deeply and wanted so desperately for him to be his normal self again.

'Oh, Adam, I didn't mean . . .'

But he shook his head dismissively and rubbed his hand hard across his jaw. 'No. You're absolutely right. But I'm . . .' He paused to push his fingers up over his broad forehead. 'I'm just so weary of everything. So sick of finding a hundred times a day that I can't do something a two-year-old can do! I just want . . . for five minutes . . . to be able to forget it. But I can't.'

He lifted his gaze to her, his eyes glittering with unshed tears. Oh, if only he would cry openly, it might ease his pain. But, to her knowledge, he never had, and she could imagine that even when he was alone, his male pride wouldn't allow him to break down, his own strength and determination effectively tearing him apart. And so, once again, she saw him swallow back his anguish.

'So,' he managed to shrug, the effort the casual pretence caused him not as hidden from her as he thought, 'if my damned cousin wants to play silly games, I really don't care. It does puzzle me, though, where he got the money from. I mean, I know he made himself a packet in America, though God knows how — lying and cheating again, no doubt — and then he invested it in industry when he came back and presumably that's how he could afford to buy those shares we sold. But to throw away money like this! It must have cost a small fortune, and it'll take him some time to recoup it. And I doubt it'll put the *Sure* out of business. Huh! But then Fred always was a fool!'

A fool! Well, it seemed to Rebecca he was anything but, for the mine had signed a legal agreement, and she, for one, wasn't convinced the *Sure* could survive without a regular trade.

* * *

'Well, there you have it.'

Adam jerked his head towards her, his eyebrows arched enigmatically, as he strode into the kitchen a few days later. Both Rebecca and Mrs Blatchford looked up, for it was unusual for Adam to do anything with such purpose these days. Even Toby's large, dark eyes stretched with interest over the brim of the mixing bowl he was licking out with relish, having abandoned the spoon his mother had provided for him. With cake mixture smeared over his face and in his hair, the sight of him might have brought a rare smile to his stepfather's lips, but Adam was too preoccupied with the struggle to fold the flapping sheets of the newspaper, using his left elbow and his teeth to assist, until he finally dropped it on to the table in frustration, sending a cloud of flour into the air, and pointing vigorously to a small article among the obituaries.

Rebecca followed the outstretched index finger of his right hand. '"The death of Lady Elizabeth Hennessy after a long struggle against cancer nevertheless came as a devastating shock to all who knew her,"' she read aloud, glancing up at Adam quizzically, since she'd never heard of the deceased woman, and was sure Adam had never mentioned her either.

He saw her hesitation. 'Go on, read it,' he urged irritably.

She frowned and brought her eyes back down to the print. '"The disease had been diagnosed several years ago, but Lady Hennessy's health did not seriously deteriorate until a few months ago. She was well known for her charitable works, especially after she was widowed in 1854, when she inherited her husband's wealth, there being no other living male relative. Lady Hennessy, who was forty-seven, has left certain sums to various organizations, but the remainder of her estate, factories, properties and businesses have been bequeathed to her constant friend and companion over the past few years, a young gentleman who had recently returned from America, by the name of . . ."' Rebecca's voice plummeted as a strangling noose closed about her neck, '"Alfred Bradley."'

She wanted to swallow, but it seemed as if a stone had lodged in her throat. Instead her eyes travelled mindlessly up to Adam's face, but his expression only added to the confusion of her own numbed shock. She'd expected to find his features dark with the same thunderous fury that blackened her own heart, but to her surprise, he merely shrugged.

'Flattering bastard,' he muttered under his breath. 'Forty-seven, and he only, well, younger than me, thirty-two, I think. Now you can see how I wasn't lying to you about the way he works. A rich woman who was dying. I bet he latched on to her like a leech.'

His voice hummed with bitter amusement and Rebecca detected none of the rage, or the fear, that had shaken her to the core. 'Adam,' she croaked, his strange demeanour now filling her with deeper dread than any evil plans his cousin might have hatched. She quickly drew him away from the table and out into the hallway, as she didn't feel it was something they should be discussing under Mrs Blatchford's nose. 'Adam,' she repeated in a flurry of agitation, unconsciously gripping his arm even tighter and trying desperately to pierce the impenetrable shield he seemed to be drawing about himself lately. 'That's how he could afford to charter all those barges, isn't it? He's going to use that money to ruin you!'

Adam's eyebrows dipped questioningly, his head cocked to one side. 'Ruin?' he mumbled.

'Yes!' Her eyes opened wide with exasperation. Adam appeared to be gradually retreating into another world, a prison that would admit nothing but his own personal pain, and certainly not the possibility that they could lose everything and end up facing bankruptcy. She was consumed with sympathy for him, but somehow she must shake him back into reality. 'Yes! Adam, listen to me! Morwellham is declining. The limekilns are closed, the George and Charlotte is closed, almost nothing goes along the canal anymore, no slate and stone from the quarries, no copper, little coal, nothing to or from the Tavistock foundry. The whole port has closed down but for local domestic trade. 'Tis virtually only the arsenic and supplies for the mine as keep the place alive! The *Sure* can pick up other trade along the river, but 'twill go on making even more of a loss than ever, and we simply can't afford it. So as far as your cousin's concerned, he's really only put the last nail in the coffin here, but you know he's got his eyes on your London business, maybe even the *Emily*! Oh, Adam, you've got to fight back, or you really will be facing ruin!'

'And . . . and you don't consider my life isn't ruined already?' he said, so quietly she only just caught his words.

The breath quivered at the back of her throat, nearly choking her. Of course she understood how having such a devastating disability thrust on him so cruelly had wrecked his morale, his masculine independence. Dear God, didn't she live with it every minute of the day, just as he did? But he was far from being an invalid. He had a business to run, men whose families depended on him for their livelihood.

'Adam, you can't go on like this,' she told him firmly. 'You've got to come to terms with what's happened.'

He lowered his eyes then, unable to hold her gaze. He was standing with his back to the staircase and slowly sank down to sit on the second step, his head bowed and his elbows resting on his spread knees with his forearms dangling limply between them. 'Don't you think I've been trying?' he muttered brokenly. 'But it's there. All the time. Glaring at me. Mocking me. As if . . .'

His voice trailed away, leaving a silence that screeched in Rebecca's ears. She stood looking down on him, at a total loss as to what to say or do next. But then, without lifting his head, Adam began to speak again, his words strained and faltering.

'You know . . . sometimes I think . . . if I stare at it for long enough, it'll grow back. I can . . . see it. Dammit, I can *feel* it! I can feel my fingers moving. And . . . somehow I just can't understand why . . . how it isn't there.'

His voice had risen to a demented cry, his breath ragged and gasping. Rebecca wetted her lips. This wasn't the time to press him. If she didn't tread carefully, she could push him over the edge. Better to be patient. Even if the very worst happened and they lost the business to Fred's grasping schemes, surely they could salvage enough to survive? And they would still have each other.

Her hand reached out and her fingers squeezed around his shoulder.

CHAPTER TWENTY-THREE

Rebecca closed the curtains against the pitch-black evening. It was early November and cold in the dining room, but she couldn't afford to waste fuel by lighting a fire to heat the room just while they ate their meal. Perhaps she'd suggest to Adam that they should eat in the warm, cosy kitchen in the company of Amy Blatchford who'd done more than ever for them over the past few months. But then, Adam seemed oblivious to the cold, despite the flesh that had fallen from his bones. In fact Rebecca was beginning to wonder if he was aware of anything very much at all, the way he sat immobile most of the time, staring into the fire or out of the window, seemingly lost in some other existence. It was only at night that he showed any sign of being alive. Often when he couldn't sleep, he would slip out of the cottage and wander off God alone knew where. Rebecca always heard him and lay awake, sick with worry, until he returned. In his weakened state, she imagined him falling in the darkness and lying injured all night until he was found in the morning. And with winter well on its way, that could be too late.

She faced back into the room and, seated at the table, Adam did actually look up at her, his eyes, once a rich chestnut but now the dull hue of mud, staring at her out of sunken sockets. His skin no longer glowed with a permanent tan from his trips to warmer climes throughout the year, but was pale and taut, and without the sun to bleach it, his hair had reverted to its natural darker brown. It matched the stubble on his jaw, for shaving was a perilous task that reminded him only too painfully of his disability and so was no longer performed daily. It saddened Rebecca dreadfully as he'd always been so meticulous about his appearance, but now he seemed to care as little about himself as he did everything else.

She smiled faintly at him as she stepped back to the table, but her smile wasn't returned. The dinner was served in separate dishes, for it cost nothing to keep up such standards, and tonight there was spare rib of pork; the farmer at Morwellham Farm had begun to kill his pigs for the winter and had some joints to sell cheaply. Adam hadn't seemed to notice the economies she'd been making, or if he had, he hadn't made any comment. And as he only ever picked at his food nowadays, it hardly seemed to matter.

She placed his plate before him and then set about serving herself. Oh, the worry of it all was wearing her down! For there was not only Adam himself and the home to cope with, together with the chickens they now kept and the winter vegetables she and Mrs Blatchford — with dubious assistance from Toby — had planted in the garden. But Rebecca also made it her business to keep her ear to the ground to learn of any cargo for the *Sure*, and to watch that every penny that was due to them from the *Swallow*'s profits reached their bank account. As for Bradley's Merchants and the *Emily*, she had to rely on the monthly reports sent to her by Adam's trusted manager. The most recent one had arrived that very day and she hadn't yet had time to study it in detail, but she gathered that nothing had altered the downward slide of their fortunes. Adam's personal dividends were still being drained to make up the shortfall in the repayments on the *Emily* and the loan for her repairs. Without the driving force behind the business, those dividends, and therefore the value of the shares themselves, were dropping. Adam still held forty-eight per cent of the company, but what Rebecca had to keep from him was that, as well as the few shares she'd sold to pay for his medical care, cousin Fred had persuaded several shareholders to sell out to him and he now owned over twelve per cent.

Cousin Fred. Oh, the squall of rage that seethed and boiled inside her whenever she thought of that vicious attack he'd made on Adam in their own back garden! Not only lashing into Adam's mental anguish but opening up his physical wounds again. Even now the stump was still tender to anything more than the lightest touch. So often he'd reach instinctively to perform some task with his left hand and knock the severed wrist instead. He concealed it well, but she winced every time she heard him catch his breath in pain.

'Dammit, Rebecca!'

His angry words snapped her from her thoughts. 'Yes?' she answered absently, and then shuddered as he used his eyes to indicate his plate. She inhaled slowly and then rose with dignified calm to her feet. She'd forgotten to cut up the meat for him. Whenever their meal consisted of food he couldn't manage with a fork alone, she cut it up before she gave it to him so as to save him the humiliation of having it done in front of him like a child. Now she came up beside him, bringing a knife with her, and began to do what was necessary with as much natural ease as she could muster. But Adam turned his head away with wretched despondency, unable to watch the simple procedure he couldn't accomplish for himself.

'There,' she said softly, and bent to kiss the top of his hair that had grown long and unruly because he couldn't bear to contemplate a visit to the barber's. She herself had taken the scissors to it with reasonable success once before, but it was about time she did it again, unless she could persuade him . . .

'Don't forget again!' he barked gruffly.

Rebecca's chin quivered. She was doing her best to ease his distress, but he couldn't expect . . . 'I'm sorry, Adam, but 'tis not my fault,' she murmured defensively.

She saw him raise his eyebrows at her, but then he swallowed, and a shame-faced expression twisted his features. His lips parted as if he wanted to say something but couldn't, and Rebecca wondered if he'd ever release the tearing grief inside him, or whether he'd keep it bottled up for ever.

The knock on the door came as a welcome relief, and Mrs Blatchford poked her head into the room. 'Excuse me, sir, ma'am, but 'tis Captain Kastr— Miss Sarah's husband,' she surrendered, still unable to wrap her tongue around the Russian surname. 'Shall I ask him to wait in the parlour?'

'No, no! Show him in!' Rebecca cried excitedly. Her heart lifted at the unexpected diversion, and as the young man stepped smiling into the dining room, she was ready to embrace him affectionately. 'Oh, Misha, 'tis lovely to see you!'

'What the hell are you doing here?' she heard Adam growl from the other end of the table.

She saw the shock in Misha's bright blue eyes, and then he strode confidently across to stand in front of Adam. '*Da, Kapitan*. I know that I am not supposed to be here. I am sailing the *Swallow* to London, but we dock in Plymouth to unload some wine, and I think I will come here because I think you should know at once.'

'Know?' Adam frowned irritably. 'Know what?'

Misha's gentle eyes shifted uneasily in Rebecca's direction for a fleeting moment, and she felt apprehension grip her stomach as he said hesitantly, 'The cargo that was supposed to be waiting for us in Bordeaux, it was not there. So I travel to the vineyard of Monsieur de Vauclos, and I find that the wine has already been taken away.'

'Taken away?' Adam's words echoed Rebecca's own bewilderment. 'What do you mean?'

'It has been taken away on the ship of your cousin.'

'What! What ship?' Adam demanded impatiently.

'It seems that your cousin has chartered a ship. Monsieur de Vauclos knows, of course, of your accident, and believed him when he said you had sent him in your place. He said

250

he is your cousin and, what do you say, he has some of your appearance, Captain, so Monsieur de Vauclos, he thinks everything is good. So he sells him the wine, and he is pleased because it is at a slightly higher price than you had agreed. And he even sign a contract to sell him all the wine he produce in the next three years.'

Rebecca held her breath, sweat moistening her palms, as her gaze moved from Misha's tense face to where Adam was still sitting at the table. He rubbed his hand over his eyes and kept it there for some moments while he drew in an enormous breath and then released it in a long, steady stream before dragging his fingers down to his jaw.

'Damn,' he muttered so vehemently that Rebecca almost rejoiced, for perhaps this latest piece of bad news would shake him out of his apathy. She knew that Monsieur de Vauclos was one of Adam's most trusted suppliers in the Bordeaux region. The wine he produced was of a high quality, but they always agreed on a very reasonable price, and by purchasing direct, Adam made a substantial profit. Monsieur de Vauclos had been a friend of old Mr Bradley since Adam was a child. If Adam was ever in Bordeaux more than a few days, he would always visit the vineyard and find a warm welcome. He'd often spoken of Monsieur de Vauclos and his wife as fine, homely people, and Rebecca was as shocked as he was.

'Did you not have a contract with him?' she dared to ask.

'No, damn you, I didn't!' His voice, for once, sparked with life. 'I have contracts with most of my suppliers, but not Henri. It didn't seem necessary. It was all based on trust. And then that bastard comes along . . .'

'I do not think you can blame Monsieur de Vauclos,' Misha put in bravely. 'He is very upset when he knows the truth.'

'No, I don't blame him,' Adam sighed. 'But.' His tone changed as he looked sharply up at Misha again. 'I assume you didn't come back in ballast?'

'*Nyet!*' The young Russian's eyes flashed with offence. 'Of course not! There is plenty of other wine. I buy instead some Médoc, a château that is good value for money and that I have seen you buy yourself, and also some good St-Émilion and a little sauvignon. But this I buy from a merchant and so there is only small profit. The ship is still not full, so I carry wine for another merchant also, and some French silks. But it is difficult, and the voyage, I think, makes much less money than it should. And because there is no contract, I cannot claim demurrage from Monsieur de Vauclos.' He took a step forward and, placing the palm of his right hand flat on the table as if to emphasize his words, said with quiet firmness, 'We need you, Captain. We need you out there to arrange the cargoes, to show your face to the merchants and the owners of the vineyards. I can sail the *Swallow* for you, but I am a sea captain, not a businessman! You are both these things, and everything is falling down without you. And you must return to be master of the *Emily* again. Captain Harvey, he is too old! He helps you for when you are sick, but this . . . it goes on too long. No one knows the *Emily* as you do, Captain! No one else can have the speed from her! She loses time and money . . .'

'For God's sake, stop calling me "Captain", will you?' Adam scowled. 'You're my brother-in-law now, remember? And I'm . . . I'm no longer master of the *Emily*, or any other ship for that matter!'

His tone was so final, so heavy with defeatism, that Rebecca's heart lurched with sadness, and she was taken unawares by Misha's sudden passionate outburst in his native tongue.

'*Shto ty! Konyeshno ty yeshcho kapitan!*'

Across the room, Rebecca started and could see the astonishment on Adam's drawn face. It seemed to take a few moments for it to register with Misha that they hadn't understood him, but then he wagged his head with uncharacteristic defiance. 'Of course you are captain!' he repeated in English. 'I know you like to be as one of the crew, to do the physical things on the ship, and that is not always possible now. But a crew cannot work without a good captain. You alone are the one who charts the course, judges the wind, gives the orders! Any idiot can pull on a rope when he is told, but only you can—'

'Any idiot, eh?' Adam's sharp cry cut through the brittle air. 'Well, this is one idiot who can't!'

Rebecca stifled a horrified gasp, but Misha was quick to reply. Rebecca saw in that instant how the normally quiet and serious young man could so easily step into the position of authority that he commanded. 'Perhaps not anymore, but you are a perfect navigator!' he insisted. 'When I sail with you as first mate on the *Swallow*, I am amazed. You judge the ship as if she is part of yourself, even when it is not your usual vessel. I watch you and I try to learn. To me, you are the best captain I have ever worked with!'

'Huh!' Adam snorted. 'Even when I lost a man overboard?'

A deathly hush fell over the room. Rebecca was numbed. In all those long hours of silence, had Adam been dwelling morosely on that horrific incident, his tortured mind blaming himself so brutally for something that was an act of fate? She knew he'd been racked with guilt over the drowned seaman, but she hadn't realized how much the terrible memory haunted him still.

'That was not your fault.' She was grateful when Misha answered in a low, resonant tone. 'I was there, remember. I know what happened.'

'But . . . can you imagine what it was like for him?' Adam's voice trembled with emotion. 'The fear. The panic as he struggled to stay alive? And I was the master of the ship. It was my responsibility.'

'You are an excellent sea captain, but even you cannot control the sea.' Misha drew himself up to his full height as if to give more weight to his words. 'But what you can control are your business affairs.'

'Tell me how to run those, too, now, would you?' Adam grated accusingly.

'That is precisely the point. You are *not* running them!'

Adam stared at him, his face expressionless for some seconds. 'Get out,' he finally commanded.

'*Da*. I will go. But first I must say this. It is because of you alone that I can marry Sarah. That I can leave my own country and start a new life. I owe you so much, and so now I help you by saying what you do not see for yourself. Your business, we, your men, we need you. We need you back at the helm, as I think you say. But more than this, I think that you need to do this for yourself. You are my employer, a man I admire—'

'Oh, that's a good one.'

'Yes! Admire and respect! But, Adam,' Misha said, the Christian name coming awkwardly to his tongue, 'you are also, as you say, my brother-in-law, and the greatest friend I ever have. I think I can understand a little of how you feel. If it is me . . .' He lifted his hand and contemplated it grimly for a moment or two, turning it over and stretching and clenching the fingers. But then he fixed Adam with a steady gaze. 'But it is your hand you have lost. Do not lose your self-respect also.' And with that, he clicked his heels together, gave that jerky bow of his head, and strode from the room.

Rebecca stood stock-still, not quite knowing what to think or say, let alone what Adam's reaction might be. He was staring at the door, and thankfully Rebecca's inborn sense of etiquette came to her rescue and she followed Misha out into the hall.

'I'm so sorry, Misha,' she apologized. 'He's still not himself.'

But Misha shrugged his eyebrows. 'There is no need to be sorry. You are not to blame, and nor is the captain. He is very sad. No, that is not the word . . .'

'Depressed?'

'*Da*. Depressed. And he is become so thin, and he looks ill.'

Rebecca nodded, and as she exhaled, the breath trembled from her lungs. 'I know.' She relaxed now, grateful that Misha seemed to understand, and ready to pour her heart out. 'Oh, Misha, I'm so worried about him. 'Twas bad enough before we lost the arsenic contract, but since then . . . Most of the time he just sits and stares into space. If I speak to him, he doesn't seem to hear, and if I do manage to catch his attention, his mind seems to wander off again. 'Tis as if he's living in another world. Almost as if he's looking for ways of punishing himself. You saw how he was just now. I had no idea the death of Mr Elliman — that was his name, wasn't it? — were still playing on his mind.'

'And do you speak to the doctor about this?'

'Oh, yes,' she answered with a rueful sigh. 'He says there's little he can do. He says 'tis reaction to the shock of it all. He gave me some sort of sleeping draught for him, but he won't take it. Says he prefers a glass of wine. Provided someone's opened it for him, of course. But . . .' She lowered her eyes, almost ashamed to admit it. ''Tis more like a bottle, and then a glass or two of rum or brandy. Insists on the best, even though we can't afford it. Says a wine merchant can't drink cheap wine. Strange thing is, you'd think he'd be four sheets to the wind half the time, but he's not. And 'tis not as if it helps him sleep much either, just makes him even more disconsolate than ever.'

She could feel the moisture collecting in her eyes and tried to hide her distress by turning her head, but she felt the pressure of Misha's hand on hers. 'And you, Rebecca, how is it for you?' he asked softly.

'Me?' She blinked up at him and shrugged her slim shoulders with a wry grimace. 'Oh, I try to do what I can so that he doesn't have to ask for help all the time. Just little things. And I absorb his outbursts of temper, but they don't happen often, thank God. I have tried talking to him. Tried to make him face up to . . . Like you just did. But you saw for yourself, he just won't listen.' She broke off, knowing her chin was starting to shake, and took a deep breath. 'I'm at my wits' end. 'Tis like living with a stranger. He doesn't seem to understand that it hurts me, too, seeing him like this. So, I struggle to make ends meet . . .'

'The money is so difficult? Then I must take less wages.'

'No! Adam wouldn't hear of it, and neither would I.' She lifted her head and smiled courageously. 'You work so hard for us, Misha. Without the income from the *Swallow* we'd have nothing to actually live on at all. And with what you've just told us, things aren't looking too good for the merchants either. And we have to pay Captain Harvey, of course, which we wouldn't if Adam were sailing the *Emily* himself, and there's the pension Adam set up for Mr Elliman's widow.'

'And, I am afraid to tell you this also, but the *Swallow* is in need of some repairs.'

Rebecca groaned aloud as if a leaden weight had dropped down inside her stomach. 'Is there much that needs doing?'

'I regret this, but yes. Many sails need repair, and some must be replaced. Some of the rope in the rigging is worn, and so is the leather on the old pump. There is a boom split and I am not sure it can be mended, so perhaps it will mean a new one. And some blocks are being repaired now while she is in Plymouth. But more important, there are some timbers, vital parts of the ship, which begin to rot.' He lowered his eyes awkwardly as he saw her despair. 'We protect always with paint and tar, but in the end, the salt water will always win. I am sorry . . .'

'No, no, 'tis not your fault.' She unconsciously brought her hand up to her mouth and chewed on her fingernail. 'Can you make it last through the winter? Then at least we'll have finished paying off the repairs on the *Emily*.'

'Yes, I think we can do this. And I will do all I can so that the *Swallow* will make money for you.'

''Tis very good of you, Misha. I know you'll do your best.'

'*Konyeshno*. I have much to be grateful to the captain. But now I must go to see my wife, I think.'

His expression changed from deep concern to boyish excitement, and Rebecca dipped her eyes enviously. She was seven years his junior, and yet at that moment he made her feel like a withered old woman. 'Yes, of course,' she smiled with forced brightness. 'We shouldn't have kept you so long. You'll be leaving first thing in the morning?'

'*Da*. I must join the *Swallow* again so that we can set sail on the evening tide.'

'Of course. But I should be grateful if you'd say nothing about how Adam is to anyone. Not even Sarah.'

'Of course. It is between us only.'

'Well, take care, Misha. And thank you.'

'*Nye za shto*. It is nothing.'

And then he was gone, and Rebecca slumped back against the wall. It just seemed to be one thing after another, with no obvious way out. And the worst thing of all was knowing that Adam would normally have been able to cope with all these problems. As it was, it seemed to her he was becoming more depressed and withdrawn with each day that passed.

She took a deep, steadying breath and braced herself to walk back into the dining room, where she sat down stiffly at the table. 'Did you have to be so rude to Misha?' she dared to mumble.

'What!' Adam snapped at her. 'You heard the way he spoke to me! He is only my employee, you know!'

'He is your brother-in-law. And he put himself at risk to get you out from under that cargo,' she reminded him fiercely. 'If it had shifted further, he could have been hurt himself, and you'd have been killed. He saved your life, you know!'

'How could I forget?'

Rebecca shuddered under his sarcasm, and she watched as he angrily drew the wine bottle towards him. The cork had been replaced and he tried to push it out with his forefinger and thumb, while holding the neck of the bottle between his remaining fingers and the palm of his hand, but it was in too tightly.

'Damn the bloody thing,' he swore under his breath, and pulling the cork out with his teeth instead, filled his glass to the brim. But before he put it to his lips, he gazed at her levelly across the table. 'Saving my life doesn't give him the right to speak to me like that, and anyway, sometimes I wish he hadn't bothered.'

Rebecca felt a hot wave of nausea sweep through her stomach at his words. Yes, she was sure there were times when Adam genuinely wished himself dead, when the pain of his loss became too much to endure and there seemed to be no end to it. She'd been there herself over Tom and over her lost child, but she'd managed to claw her way back and must help Adam to do the same. She watched him swallowing down the wine as if it was the only way he could control his temper, his eyes riveted on her face as he drank, as if defying her to contradict him. But she was ready for the challenge.

'You don't mean that,' she began slowly. 'And as for Misha, well, maybe 'tis time someone made you see sense.'

They stared at each other, eyes locked, each as obstinate as the other. Adam's lean jaw was clamped rigid, the muscles flexing furiously, and he put down the glass deliberately as if he were about to retaliate. But then, to her surprise and relief, the ferocity in his expression faded and he turned his head away.

It was all Rebecca needed. 'You know he's right,' she said firmly, gaining courage when Adam didn't retort. 'You can't just give up like this. You're thirty-four years old, Adam, a young man! 'Tis almost a whole lifetime you have in front of you. You can't let your cousin take away everything you've worked so hard for. You've got to fight back!'

She watched, her pulse racing, as Adam's chin drooped forward, his face contorted, and he tried to bury his head in his hands. But only the empty cuff rested against his left cheek and he had to spread the fingers of his right hand wide to cover his eyes. Rebecca waited. Held her breath. Afraid of what she'd said. Yet still hoping . . . yearning . . .

She was sure she heard him gasp back a sob, his breath trembling and unsteady. Would he break down now, at last, after all these months, and give release to the sorrow that was mangling his soul and changing him into a different man from the one she loved?

'Fight back?' His voice was scarcely audible, and yet it startled her. But though his eyes were glistening, he shouted at her as if to conceal the fact that he was on the verge of tears, 'Fight back with what? This?'

He waved his left forearm at her, and standing up abruptly, strode across to stare down at the empty grate, shoulders hunched and his one fist clenched into a tight ball. Watching him, Rebecca felt . . . oh, she didn't know what she felt, but there was certainly some bottomless chasm inside her that was getting deeper by the day.

She got to her feet and stepped silently across the room. He hardly moved as she came up beside him and placed both her hands on his arm. 'Adam, I know how you must feel . . .'

He shrugged her off, turning to glare at her with maddened eyes. 'Oh, you do, do you?' he snarled. 'Well, I can tell you, you don't have a clue how I feel!' He spun on his heel, took two storming paces, but when he turned back, the savagery in his eyes had melted and he bowed his head sheepishly. 'I feel . . . like only half a man,' he scarcely managed to articulate in a broken whisper. 'As if everything's been swept away from underneath me. And, yes, I feel . . . ashamed . . . that I can't cope with it.'

Rebecca's furrowed brow tightened even further. 'Don't be so hard on yourself, Adam,' she croaked. 'You're such a good, fine man. 'Tis why I love you so much.'

And then she felt the knife twist brutally in her ribs as he shook his head with a bitter laugh. 'Love? Huh! Well, perhaps my dear cousin was right in that as well.'

'What?' she frowned, her bewildered mind turning frantic circles.

'Fred is slowly destroying me, isn't he?' Adam replied with almost calm resignation. 'Just as he said he would. So maybe he was right in the other things he said as well. That you never really loved me at all. We both know you only married me because of Toby, and if you did come to feel something for me, how do I know it was real? How do I know it wasn't some great pretence? How can—'

'*No!*' Appalled frustration foamed up inside her and burst forth in a horrified cry. 'How could you think I would let you make love to me like that if I didn't love you from the bottom of my heart! Let you touch me . . .'

'But how can I be sure? And even if you thought you loved me then, how can you love me now? With this? When it fills even *me* with revulsion!'

They held each other's gaze. In silence. Adam breathing heavily from his tearing outburst and Rebecca scarcely daring to breathe at all. The blood was pulsing in her head as if her skull would explode, and her hand reached out as for a moment she thought from his crumpled face that he might . . . But then he looked down at his left wrist, his jaw clenched tightly.

'But perhaps this is just part of it,' he murmured.

Rebecca drew in a little breath at last and tipped her head on one side. 'I don't . . . What do you mean?'

'Everything . . . everybody I come in contact with,' he answered, each word pronounced with slow deliberation, 'I bring disaster on. My mother . . . And then Felicity . . . If I'd been a better husband to her, she might not have felt the need to go doing her charitable works in the slums, and she wouldn't have caught—'

''Tis not the way I understood it.'

'And my father. If I'd been there more to take the pressure . . .'

'It strikes me you did everything in your power to help him.'

'But it wasn't enough. And so I came down here, and what happens? I lose a ship. My loss mainly, but the crew and a good captain are put out of work through my negligence. And then I lose a man overboard because I didn't check everyone was wearing a lifeline as they came on deck.' He was looking straight at her now, wrenching despair etched deep in his ashen face. 'And what about you, Rebecca? All I've ever brought you is misery and unhappiness. I've let you down so badly. I've got you involved with my cousin, you lost the baby . . .'

Rebecca heard her own sharp intake of breath, and she knew from Adam's expression that he, too, had recognized it for what it was. He had never once mentioned their lost child, as if it had never happened, but she realized now it was because he knew it would be too painful for either of them. His mouth twisted as if he was mortified at having reopened the wound, but it seemed his need for self-recrimination was not yet spent as he choked, 'And sometimes I wonder if Tom only died so that I could have you. Because I wanted you so much.'

Horror stabbed at Rebecca's heart. Dear God! Had Adam been turning these gruesome thoughts over and over in his mind all these months, blaming himself, his depression so intense he was digging a deeper and deeper grave to bury himself in? Deliberately searching out new ways to torture himself? Rebecca's teeth were gritted as she tried to focus her shocked mind, to find the right words to soothe the agony on Adam's distraught, desperate face. Her eyebrows lifted and she stared steadily into his forlorn, liquid eyes.

'Tom died because of an infected water supply,' she breathed thickly. 'He meant the world to me then, but I never blamed anyone. 'Twas no one's fault. Just like everything else. You have to believe that, Adam.'

But he lowered his eyes with a heaving sigh, his face grey and drained. 'I don't know what to believe anymore,' he finally muttered, and walked past her out of the room.

CHAPTER TWENTY-FOUR

'So.' Sarah's bright curls bounced as she bent her head to sip the tea. 'What did you want to see me about, Becky?'

Rebecca contemplated her sister's expectant expression. Apart from Misha's long absences, life was still a happy game for her. Rebecca was pleased it was so, but she wasn't sure Sarah was the right person she needed for the task ahead. However, there was no alternative, as her father couldn't desert his post, and her mother wouldn't leave him, even if only for a few days. So Sarah it would have to be.

Even as she spoke, she was still hesitating. 'How long would it take you to pack for a short trip to London?' she asked cautiously.

'London?' Sarah frowned, and Rebecca was relieved to see her sister appear perplexed rather than excited, as it was to be a critical business trip and not some jolly excursion. 'I don't understand.'

Rebecca straightened her shoulders. 'I need to go to London, and I can't travel alone,' she said simply. ''Tis not really seemly for two young women either, but 'twill have to do.'

'But why? I mean, of course I'll come. The furthest I've ever been from here is Plymouth. Oh, 'twill be wonderful!'

''Tis not a holiday I'm planning,' Rebecca answered gravely. 'I've been studying the latest report, and 'tis not good. If Bradley's Merchants goes down, then 'twill take the *Emily* and the *Swallow* down with it, so 'tis your concern as well.'

'But then . . . surely 'tis the captain who should be going?'

Rebecca drew in a deep breath. She'd tried to conceal her problems as far as possible, especially from Sarah. She knew that her sister had always held Adam in awe, even during the short period of their happiness which fate had so cruelly ended. But it was time her family knew the whole truth, and she may as well begin with Sarah.

'There's something I must tell you,' she said warily. 'Adam . . . well, he still hasn't come to terms with his disability. If anything, he's just getting more and more depressed. He can scarcely drag himself through from one day to the next, let alone sort out a business concern that's rapidly going downhill.'

The exuberance on Sarah's face was quickly extinguished. 'We've all realized there's something wrong, Becky. That he's not gotten over the accident yet. I mean . . . we'd have expected him to be back at sea long ago. Misha . . . well, he knows more about it than he'd let on when he were home last.'

'That was good of him.' Rebecca nodded her appreciation. 'They had a dreadful argument, you see. At least, Adam lost his temper, which can be mighty short at times these days. But Misha was wonderful. He kept so calm. He tried to make Adam see sense, but 'twas no good. He's so dispirited, it seems there's nothing anyone can do or say to lift him out of himself. He has no interest in the business at all. 'Tis almost as if he welcomes the way 'tis declining. As if 'tis just punishment for some crime. For not being a whole person anymore, as if 'twere his own fault.'

Sarah put down her cup thoughtfully. 'Perhaps he shouldn't have been in the hold in a swell. Isn't there some sort of rule about it?'

'I'm not sure. But 'twas only a swell in the Sound, not a gale out to sea. He was just worried about the explosives they had on board.'

'Well then, he can hardly blame himself.'

'You try telling him that. He's been blaming himself for just about anything and everything you can think of.' Her voice rose despairingly, her deep blue eyes searching Sarah's grey ones, but then she shook her head in bewilderment. 'And he's been behaving even more strangely of late. A few days after the row with Misha, he started going out during the day instead of at night-time. Well, at first I was pleased, but then I realized he was disappearing up into the woods. So as he's unlikely to meet anyone, I suppose. And doubtless avoiding the canal and the Consols railway.'

'Yes, 'tis what I've heard,' Sarah told her gently. 'People have noticed it, you know. Hands in his pockets . . . or . . . well . . . to hide . . . Collar turned up and hat rammed down on his forehead so as folk mightn't see who 'tis, and if anyone dare speak to him, he just ignores them and hurries on.'

Rebecca sighed softly and lowered her eyes. 'Yes, I know. But 'tis not rudeness. 'Tis shame and . . . and fear of people's sympathy. He really is afraid, you know, of people seeing him. I thought that this losing himself in the woods, or wherever else 'tis he goes, was perhaps the beginning of his . . . I don't know . . . regaining his confidence, but he shuns company as much as ever. He's out hours, all day sometimes. And the strange thing is . . .' She leaned forward confidentially. 'You won't repeat this to anyone? I mean, 'tis only Amy and I as know.'

'What?' Sarah's eyes widened with curiosity.

'Well,' she began mysteriously, 'when he comes back in, he demands a pitcher of hot water which he takes upstairs. He has a wash and changes into a clean shirt. But the dirty one really is dirty. I mean, sweat-stained, and with green marks on it, like if you lean against a green tree trunk and it comes off on your clothes.'

'Oh, Becky!' Sarah snorted and rolled her eyes heavenwards. 'You know how easily that happens if you go in the woods. Mother was always chiding us for doing just that when we were children, remember?'

'Yes, but 'tis on his shirt. Under the armpits and down the inside of the sleeves mostly, so 'tis mighty queer. He obviously takes his coat off, and 'tis the beginning of December and he rarely wears an undershirt. He'll catch his death.'

'Oh, you worry too much, Becky. These seafaring fellows get hardened to the cold. Misha's just the same.'

A faint smile crept over Rebecca's face. 'Yes, I'm sure you're right. He does look better for some fresh air, and his appetite's improving at last.'

'There you are, then.' Sarah stood up purposefully. 'I know he's gone as thin as a rake, but I'm sure your Mrs Blatchford will fatten him up over Christmas. Well, if I'm coming to London with you, I'd better go home to pack. When do you want to go? Tomorrow?'

Rebecca had to laugh at her enthusiasm. 'The day after would be better. I need to organize things for Toby.'

'Of course.' Sarah linked her arm through Rebecca's as she walked down the hallway. 'Oh, 'twill be quite an adventure. And we can do some Christmas shopping in all those smart stores.'

'If you think you can afford it,' Rebecca said grimly. 'I certainly can't. I can hardly afford the train fare. 'Twon't be first class, that's for sure.'

Sarah smiled back, and then bent down as Toby came out of the kitchen and ran up to her. 'And how's my lovely nephew then?' she crooned, hugging the boy to her chest and glancing ruefully at Rebecca over his head. 'I've not fallen yet, you know. But 'tis early days. And with Misha away so much . . . I don't doubt you'll fall again before I do.'

Rebecca shuddered. Sarah's visit had cheered her spirits, but the moment had been shattered. For how could she tell her that Adam had rejected all physical contact with her since his accident other than what was necessary in their day-to-day lives. That he slept in his own room and refused her the slightest show of affection. And that the glorious, heady days and nights of their passionate love had been banished from her life?

* * *

''Twere as bad as you feared then?' Isaac's bushy grey eyebrows arched with concern.

Rebecca took off her bonnet and sat down at the dining table in the parlour of Copper Ore Cottage, where her mother had left them alone to talk. She nodded gravely.

'I went through all the figures for the last nine months,' she told her father wearily, 'and Mr Gibbs showed me all the documentation. 'Tis not his fault what's happening. He can't leave the London office and go abroad himself. He's needed to see to the demands of the clients here, and many of them have become so disillusioned at not being able to buy all their usual merchandise at Bradley's that they've gone elsewhere. He's had to dismiss two junior clerks because of the reduction in paperwork, but he's even busier himself trying to attract new custom, or at least keep the regulars they still have. He's doing his best, but all he can do is send new contracts out by package to the suppliers as they fall due, and hope they'll be happy to renew them.' She raised her eyes to Isaac in desperate supplication. ''Twas Adam who arranged all the contracts abroad in person, negotiated prices, tried and bought new wines, all that sort of thing. The business simply can't go on without him. I never realized how hard he worked, I mean over and above being captain of the *Emily*. Mr Gibbs is doing all he can, but 'tis impossible, and . . .' She paused, running her finger around her collar. 'You know how Adam's cousin set up the monopoly with the barges, leading everyone to believe 'twas Adam himself?'

'Aye, I do, the scoundrel! Ought to be hung, drawn and quartered, if you ask me.'

'Well, 'tis not all he's done. He's one step ahead of Bradley's all the time. Recently he stole one of Adam's best suppliers near Bordeaux by pretending to be acting on

266

Adam's behalf while he was still recovering from the accident, and signed him up with a legal contract for three years!'

'What! Oh, the contemptible blackguard!'

'But it didn't stop there. When I was in London I discovered he's been doing it again since. A couple of other contracts were coming to the end of their term, and they found cousin Fred had been there first, offering higher bids and saying he was helping Adam out while he's still convalescing. It's happened two or three times! And he knows the particular wines Adam likes to buy that aren't on contract and buys shiploads of them so that when the *Emily* or the *Swallow* arrives at the port, there's no cargo and their captains have to search for one or await instructions, wasting time and money.'

Isaac contemplated his daughter as her deep blue eyes snapped dangerously. She had always shown a keen wit about the goings-on of Morwellham's port, but he'd never envisaged seeing her involved in a London company such as Bradley's that dealt with several European countries. And she was taking it as a personal attack, which indeed it was, at least upon her husband.

'He must have a fortune to spare if he's going about outbidding you all the time, this cousin,' Isaac commented pensively. 'I can't understand why he should want your husband's wealth as well.'

'Wealth? 'Tis not that any longer. Rather 'tis debts and a failing income. And as for his motives, 'tis not about the inheritance anymore. 'Tis hatred and pure jealousy.' She shook her head vigorously. 'Oh, you'd understand if you'd met him. 'Tis sly as a fox, he is. You know, Mr Gibbs reckons he must have found someone who used to work at Bradley's and is paying them for inside information. If I could find out who 'twas . . .'

The fury that suffused her face reminded Isaac of the wilful, pouting child that this beautiful, accomplished young woman had once been. But this was no longer a situation where she could be sent to her room to calm down. Isaac ran his hand over his hairy chin and lowered his eyes hesitantly.

'You know there have been rumours about the *Swallow*?' he said, his voice dark. 'The extent of the repairs she needs has been vastly exaggerated, so 'tis said there'll be no profit for the shareholders for some time.'

Rebecca's brow creased into a deep furrow. 'Yes, I know. But Misha says the repairs can be delayed until the spring, and then I might take out a separate loan to cover them.'

Isaac puffed out his cheeks. ''Tis a mighty big step. And it should be the captain's decision, not yours.'

'Oh, Adam never decides anything nowadays. But you see, come the end of February, the loan for the repairs on the *Emily* will have been repaid. 'Tis hard it's been, but we've scraped through, and the new loan won't be nearly as much.'

Isaac hunched his shoulders. 'Well, 'tis not what's rumoured. And while you've been away, I've learned that several of the other shareholders in the *Swallow* have sold out because of it, and at a good price while they still could. And,' he faltered briefly, 'you can guess who 'twas as offered them that chance.'

He watched as a thin, white line formed about Rebecca's compressed lips. His graceful, teasing, buoyant daughter turned into a seething, almost unrecognizable effigy. ''Tis the same thing he's trying to do with Bradley's Merchants,' she groaned passionately. 'Reduce the profits so much that the shareholders are happy to sell to him at a moderate price. You see, when Adam originally sold nearly half the business, 'twas doing very well. But most of the people he sold to were business acquaintances of his father's and his uncle's. People Fred has also known most of his life, so 'tis easy for him to work out who to approach. They trusted Adam to bring in a high return, and now that's no longer the case, well, you can't blame them for accepting Fred's offer to buy back the shares. He's playing on the accident, telling them the future is uncertain, and that, as Adam's cousin, he feels a responsibility, and as he's come into some money . . . Oh, yes,' she snarled bitterly. 'He's twisted everything round to suit himself, and they've fallen for it! The truth about Fred was always kept secret for the family's sake, so 'tis not exactly easy to warn them about him, and we can't stop them selling to him if they want to. So he'll go on until he owns almost as much of the company as Adam does, seeing as I had to sell some shares to pay the doctor's bills. I just gave instructions to sell, you see, not who to sell to, and Fred found out and jumped at the chance to buy them. And when he has sufficient influence, he'll make sure the company runs into ruin until either Adam goes bankrupt or he's forced to sell his shares to Fred for next to nothing. And then all Fred has to do is transfer back all the trade he's stolen, and Bradley's will thrive again, and Fred will own it lock, stock and barrel, while Adam will have lost everything!'

Her sapphire eyes blazed darkly out of a face that was pale with anger but for a bright-red spot on each white cheek. Isaac observed her fierce expression, beautiful and glorious in its rage. But he was afraid for her. In more ways than one. For he knew that her spirit was not to be argued with.

'And what is to be done about it?'

Rebecca pursed her lips. 'A written promise to the remaining shareholders of the *Swallow* that the repairs won't come out of the profits. They should, of course, but if 'twill stop them selling out . . . And Jane Martin, or Mrs Allport I should say, bought some shares a while back when the *Swallow* was beginning to do so well, and she won't let us down. He won't be expecting that!' she said triumphantly.

'And what of the merchants?' Isaac prompted quietly.

'Well, I'm writing to everyone begging them not to sell until Adam's well enough to take over the running of Bradley's again, whenever that might be. And in the meantime, I've got to stop business from getting any worse. I've a list of the main suppliers, so I shall write to them all explaining that Alfred Bradley is nothing to do with us, and would they kindly continue to supply us in the normal way. I've only the French I learned at school and I've forgotten half of that, but 'twill have to do. Of course,' and her eyes shifted downwards with a mixture of nervousness and resignation,

'Adam should be writing if he's not up to going in person. His French is fluent. But . . . I've tried persuading him, but he just laughs at me and says 'twon't do any good.'

'He could be right,' Isaac answered hesitantly.

'I shall also tell Misha to make personal visits to all the vineyards and merchants he can,' she went on determinedly. 'He speaks good French. And in Lisbon, they communicate in pidgin English and sign language. Even Adam doesn't really speak any Portuguese.'

'Well, at least you haven't hatched some hare-brained scheme to go yourself. 'Twere bad enough you gallivanting up to London, and dragging your sister up there, too. Two pretty young ladies on their own! Anything could have happened to you, and God knows what people thought.'

'Mr Gibbs was somewhat surprised,' Rebecca admitted with a grimace. 'I don't think he believed at first that I was Adam's wife.'

'No doubt he were shocked to find you unaccompanied. He would have expected to see the captain himself, I'm sure.' Isaac leaned back in the chair and deliberately sought her gaze. 'You know, that husband of yours really ought to face up to his responsibilities instead of allowing his business affairs to fall into ruin. He has a wife and child to support. And . . . and it were very nearly two children.'

She knew he didn't mean it as such, but the knife cut agonizingly into Rebecca's grieving heart. 'Yes, I know.' She forced out the whisper. 'And I think 'tis all part of it. Adam wanted the child as much as I did. He's only ever spoken of it once, 'tis so painful for him. But . . . 'tis in his nature to hold things inside. I've learned that over the years. 'Tis like the seaman who drowned. Adam still blames himself, though 'twas not his fault.'

'Then he must stop blaming himself and pull himself together, for your sake if not his own. When I first wanted you to marry Captain Bradley, 'twas for security. And I could see he were a kind, honest man, and a handsome one, too. I were sure he would make you happy. But I never would have believed he would let his life disintegrate like this. After all, I hate to say it, but he has only lost a hand. I've seen worse in my time. Men who didn't have the captain's intellect or his knowledge of business, and they got on with their lives straight away. Doing whatever they could to make ends meet.'

Isaac's brow had wrinkled in earnest. Rebecca knew he was only expressing his anxiety, but her inborn defiance rushed through her body like a bore tide. Defiance, and the raging, suffocating despair that she was trying at every moment of her life to swallow down into the pit of her rebellious stomach.

'Even you don't understand, do you?' she accused her father, her throat choking on the words that had been aching to come to her lips for months. ''Tis precisely because of what he was that he's taken it so hard. He was always so strong, so sure of himself. As if he could achieve anything he wanted through his own hard work. Not just giving orders, but doing things himself, joining in the physical tasks with his crew. But now . . . Well, he can't do that anymore, and . . . and he feels as if that strength has been swept away from underneath him. And not just if he were to be on board ship again, but in every aspect of his life. As if he's only half the man he was.' She spread her fingers over her face to quell the torturing cascade of her thoughts, but the torment of it was too great and the shattering words tumbled from her lips unchecked. 'Have you any idea what it's meant to him? Really thought about the hell he's going through? Every day there are dozens of things he can't do for himself anymore. He can't cut up his food, fasten his boots, do up his collar studs. He can't shave without cutting himself to shreds! At first, when the stump was too sore to use in any way at all, he couldn't even do up his trouser buttons after using the privy, and if I wasn't there, he had to get Mrs Blatchford to do it for him. Can you possibly imagine how humiliating that was for him? If he'd lost a leg, he could have had a false one, or . . . or a crutch to get around with. By God, he could hop if he had to. But with a hand . . . Can you wonder that he feels so low? And it makes it even worse because he knows he's got to come to terms with it, but he just can't. I've spoken to Dr Seaton again recently, and he says 'tis a type of illness in itself. Dwelling on the past, irrational feelings of guilt. He says only time can heal him, and we just have to be patient.'

She was gazing at Isaac more calmly now, her frustration spent. Isaac studied the grief-ravaged beauty of her face for a moment, and the sorrow of it overwhelmed him.

'You really have come to love him, haven't you?' he almost whispered.

She nodded, unable to speak as she tried to subdue the trembling of her narrow shoulders, and suddenly she found herself held in her father's arms, the smell of him, of his cigars, so familiar that she surrendered to the misery that swirled inside her. 'He's . . . such a good man,' she sobbed wretchedly. 'He's helped so many other people, and now . . . now it seems that no one, not even I can help him. I . . . I just don't know what to do!'

Isaac patted her back, just as he used to when she was a child when there was no answer to her broken heart. 'I'm sure that just by being there, 'tis helping him. And, however it might seem just now, he loves you. I'm sure something will happen to change things. Perhaps . . . I know you're not a great one for church, Becky, but a few prayers might help. God can come to our assistance in strange ways sometimes, you know. And 'tis nearly Christmas. Perhaps that'll help to lift the captain's spirits a little.'

Rebecca drew back from him, nodding in agreement, but inside her throbbing head, she thought nothing of the sort. Last Christmas, she had been ecstatic. As if the world lay at her feet. She had at last been carrying Adam's child, Adam had come home unexpectedly, and she had been cradled in the glory of his love. But now she felt as if there was nothing left at all.

CHAPTER TWENTY-FIVE

Rebecca jerked up her head at the sharp, urgent rap on the front door, and her pulse began to race. Adam had been out all morning, disappearing to wherever it was he went in the woods or beyond to spend such long hours in grim contemplation, and the nature of the knocking brought a terrible dread to the pit of her stomach. She got to her feet at once, dropping on to the floor the mending she'd been performing, since it was patch and darn and patch again nowadays. Without waiting for Amy Blatchford to do the honours as was proper, she ran frantically into the hallway herself.

A chilling gust of blustering, mid-February wind quite took her breath away as she opened the door, but she relaxed when she saw who was there. But the relief of finding Mrs Mason on the threshold was tempered with surprise and not a little curiosity. Though she'd often been invited, Tom's mother had never set foot inside Lavender Cottage. A friendly smile nevertheless broadened Rebecca's lips, although at the same time, her eyes rested on the carpet bag on the ground by Mrs Mason's feet. As she lifted her gaze again, she spied Matthew, the image of Tom as he approached manhood, and his two younger siblings, all standing impatiently by the gate, each with a bundle in his arms.

'I be come to say goodbye,' the woman announced, her voice and her expression hard, but with sadness deep in her eyes.

Rebecca's brow puckered. 'Goodbye? I don't understand.'

Mrs Mason's thin mouth twitched. 'We be leaving Morwellham,' she answered flatly. 'There be not too much here for us no more, what with my husband and Tom passed on, and Hetty with a new life for herself up at the House and maybe to wed Robin afore the year's out. There be a position as general labourer coming up at Endsleigh, and if he gets it, there be a tied cottage to go with it. He be good with his hands, Robin, and a good practical brain in his head, him being a miner. Oh, I mean, 'tis not that he do not be grateful for what the captain did for en. But what with the rumours that the *Swallow*'s being sold out . . .'

Rebecca felt the hairs prickle at the back of her neck. 'Well, 'tis not true,' she assured the woman a little tersely, but then her mouth softened. 'Of course they'll want to be together if they can. Robin's not really a seaman, and even if he were, he'd be under no obligation. Officially, the crew only sign on for one voyage at a time.'

'Aye, I knows. But . . . you do not be upset at hearing it from me?'

'No, of course not!' Rebecca shook her head. 'Hetty's my best friend. I'd be only too pleased for her. I'm sure she'd have told me herself, only I see her so rarely nowadays. 'Tis just these rumours about the *Swallow* . . . But 'tis not your worry.'

'Aye, everything about Morwellham be falling apart unless you be part of the arsenic trade, and then you be well set-up. But we're not, so 'tis time to leave.'

Rebecca pursed her lips at the bitter taste left in her mouth by the mention of the arsenic trade whose transport arrangements Adam had helped establish in order to guarantee a safe and regular cargo for the *Sure*. So many others had benefited from his example, taking confidence from the

274

work he'd done with Ned Gimlett to design leak-proof casks for the deadly powder, and now he'd been forced out of the trade entirely.

'But what about Matthew's apprenticeship?' Rebecca asked, reminded of the cooperage where . . . where she had virtually grown up with Tom.

'Ned Gimlett's arranged for en to go on with it with someone he do know in Falmouth. 'Tis to Falmouth we be going, see. To my brother's. He be recently widowed with little uns to be took care of, so we'll be doing each other a favour. I hopes you doesn't mind, seeing as you paid the premium. Passed it on, has Ned. And well, with trade so bad and Devon Great Consols having its own cooperage now, he don't really need an apprentice.'

Rebecca nodded sadly. Yes. Everything Mrs Mason had said was undeniably true. Morwellham's future lay only in a trade she had no more connections with.

'This be my brother's address.' The woman's abrupt tone made her emerge from her thoughts as she pushed a grubby scrap of paper into Rebecca's hand. 'Write to us, maid, about my grandson once in a while, will you? You knows I cas'n read, but my brother do a little. Let me know how he . . . grows up.' The words were suddenly choked. Faltering . . .

Rebecca raised her eyes to the woman's tortured face. So much sorrow. Forced to leave the place where her husband and her eldest son lay at rest. Where her daughter led a separate life. And where her grandson — the child she had never been able to acknowledge, never love as a grandmother should — would grow up a stranger. A savage ache burned in Rebecca's throat, for whose fault was that but hers?

'Did . . . did you want to see him?' she rasped.

'No. No goodbyes. 'Twould make it worse. And 'twould confuse the little mite. Just . . . just love en for me. And for Tom.'

She turned away brusquely, and Rebecca could only stand immobile as her vision misted with emotion. But then

Mrs Mason spun round again and thrust something else into her hand, before dragging herself up the garden path to the gate, her shoulders drooping with the weight of the carpet bag.

One bag. Not much to show for a whole lifetime.

They had gone. The silence returned, for there was no sound now to reach them from the deserted end of the port. And still Rebecca somehow couldn't move from the doorstep, despite the biting wind that swirled viciously about her. Tom's mother and brothers gone. Oh, Tom . . .

Her eyes shifted down to her hand as she uncurled her fingers. In her palm, on top of the paper, was a key. The key to the Bedford cottage Rebecca had rented for Tom's mother for nearly four years. No longer needed. She would have to see to that, too. But perhaps . . . she would keep it on just for now. The rent had gone down to one shilling and sixpence a week. A pittance compared with the cost of Lavender Cottage. And it was only a few short months before the lease was due for renewal. At a price Rebecca wasn't sure they could meet.

* * *

She was so lost in thought as she plied her needle that the second, more temperate knock at the front door didn't register with her for some moments. By the time she'd put down her mending, Mrs Blatchford had already answered it, and a familiar, friendly voice reached her from the hallway. She relaxed the instant she recognized who it was, and the tone of the conversation coming from the other side of the door told her there was no devastating news.

Mrs Blatchford tapped on the parlour door before poking her spritely face around it. 'A visitor for you, ma'am,' she smiled.

'Ah, Mr Willis!' Rebecca came forward with an outstretched hand. She'd known the master of the *Sure* since she was a child, although he hadn't held that position in the early days. But he'd been an acquaintance of her father's, a visitor to Copper Ore Cottage on occasion, who'd winked knowingly at the boisterous little daughter of the respected harbour master. And now she, or at least her husband, was his employer. ''Tis indeed always pleasant to see you!' she greeted him amiably.

'Oh, the pleasure be all mine,' he replied, removing his cap and holding it awkwardly between both hands.

'Won't you sit down?' Rebecca invited, aware that he appeared uncharacteristically ill at ease.

'Thank you, Miss Rebecca, but no,' he said, his eyes shifting apprehensively. ''Twere really the captain I came to see.'

'Oh, well, I'm afraid he's out, and I'm not sure when he'll be back,' she answered truthfully, but wishing for the umpteenth time that she didn't have to be constantly making excuses for Adam. 'Can I help at all?'

'Well, aye, I'm sure you can.' He seemed almost relieved and lifted his bowed head. 'P'raps if you'd tell him . . . Well, thing is, see . . . I'm leaving his employment,' he concluded in a rush.

Rebecca snatched in her breath and held it for a few seconds while she tried to think what to say. It was . . . well, such a shock. She'd thought Mr Willis had come to announce the availability of a cargo for the *Sure*, or not, which was more likely. Or perhaps to tell her the vessel needed some costly repairs, which would have made her heart sink like a rock. The final repayment for the work on the *Emily* was to be met at the end of the month, and then Rebecca would have to think about the overdue repairs to the *Swallow*. So in that way, at least, she was relieved, but for the minute, she couldn't think of what Mr Willis's resignation would mean.

'Er . . . oh,' she stammered. 'Oh, I do hope we've not done anything to offend you,' she went on after a few moments, cringing at the sudden thought that Adam could so easily have affronted the man with his strange, unsociable behaviour. At least, that was what it must seem like to so many; Rebecca alone realized that his habit of snubbing anyone he met, as he scuttled off up into the loneliness of the woods, was actually fear of coming face to face with another human being.

'Good Lord, no.' William Willis was adamant in his denial. ''Tis circumstances that's brought me to this. The captain pays me a modest regular wage, and then a percentage of what he makes on each cargo. Well, you knows that seeing as you be the one as pays me nowadays. But thing is, see . . . with there not being so much cargo to be had, I'm just not making ends meet. I've kept the *Sure* running all this time, but 'tas not been easy. You know how so much be under contract these days. I've picked up whatever cargo I can, and knowing the river so well has always helped. Bits and pieces for individual traders and market gardeners, but very little first-class freight, no coals or bark, for instance, for ages. I've relied mainly on dock-dung, unpleasant though 'tis,' he wrinkled his nose in mock disgust, 'but 'tis only second class, as you know, for all that. But the boy and me, we've been offered regular work on the arsenic barges from Devon Great Consols. I mean, I don't like to seem disloyal to the captain after all these years, and I shall miss the *Sure*, but I have to make a living, and 'twill take out all the worry . . .'

Rebecca had nodded her head in understanding as she'd listened to William Willis's explanation. It had almost come as a relief, for despite his valiant efforts, the *Sure* had until recently been steadily losing money and she'd only been kept running to keep her master and his son in employment. But at the mention of the arsenic barges, Rebecca's heart had contracted with suffocating anger.

'I . . . I believe he be some sort of relation of the captain's, this . . . Mr Bradley,' the man standing before her stammered, seeing her face harden like limestone. 'So, 'twill still be in the family. Sort of thing.'

His brow furrowed excruciatingly and Rebecca forced a smile. 'A distant cousin,' she murmured. 'Nothing to do with us. Certainly not businesswise.'

'Ah.' It was partly an acknowledgement, partly a grunt for want of something to say. Mr Willis wasn't quite sure what young Mrs Bradley meant, but he felt something was wrong and it made him uneasy. Besides . . . 'I've moored her just upriver so as you won't have to pay any dues. She'll be in the mud at low tide, but she'll come to no harm. And . . . here's her logbook and the most recent accounts.'

He fumbled in the inside pocket of his overcoat and brought out the long, narrow book with several folded papers tucked between the cover and the pages. Rebecca took them from him without a word, her face impassive, so that the fellow felt even more apprehensive than before delivering his notice.

'We cleaned out the hold and stowed away the sails. Nice and dry, like, so they'll not rot.' Again, she nodded pensively, but said nothing, her thoughts preoccupied. He wanted to leave, but . . . 'Time were you couldn't move on the river,' he began afresh. 'Ships and barges coming up with coal and sailing back down with copper ore. And Morwellham the busiest port by far. Baths Quay were as busy as 'tis quiet now. Sawn timber in holds, and unsawn logs lashed together like rafts and floated up on the tide. And then there were everything else that came or went along the canal, slate and stone, clay, bricks, you name it! And then everything to do with the local farms, grain, dung and the like.' He paused, seeing Mrs Bradley's eyes still on him, though her expression was blank. He wanted . . . needed some reaction from her in order to . . . 'Of course, the river still be quite busy, but 'tis not like it were. And then there were the iron trade. That were almost as important as the copper, what with bringing coal and limestone as well as the ore to the Tavistock foundries, and then transporting so much of the finished products. Anything from railings and drain covers to kitchen ranges and pots and pans. Most of it were for the mines, though, and all the beam engines around.'

He stopped to catch his breath. He knew he was gabbling, but why was she staring through him like that, as if

. . . as if she knew. But she couldn't. And . . . should he tell her? Could he summon up the courage? He wished his heart would stop leaping about in his chest as he went on, 'I remember once taking the beam of just a small engine on upriver to Gunnislake for one of the mines that way. Can't go any further by barge, of course, 'cause of the old bridge. 'Twere the devil's own job to unload—'

'Mr Willis,' Rebecca suddenly interrupted him so sternly that, after her seemingly interminable silence, he visibly started. She'd been aware of his rambling voice but hadn't been listening to a word he'd been saying. For it had hit her so forcefully that it felt as if she'd been shot between the shoulder blades. Initially she'd received his news with relief, as it meant that the *Sure* would be one less matter to worry about. But it also meant that Fred had won, and the bitterness that burned in her gullet was enough to choke her. He'd finally managed to put the barge out of business. And the kindly man who was now turning his cap nervously in his hands was to bear the brunt of her anger. 'Mr Willis,' she repeated, 'is there something else you wish to tell me? I have the distinct impression that there is.'

William Willis swallowed hard. By God, that was both astute and forthright. But that's what had made her a handful for her father as a child, far too strong-willed and intelligent for a girl! And here she was, a slight wisp of a thing that a breath of air might blow over, running her husband's business — what was left of it — while he was . . . incapacitated. And those lovely, arresting eyes, as blue as the deepest ocean, seemed to penetrate the very core of his thoughts.

He cleared his throat. 'Well, aye, yes. They told me not to say anything to anyone, but I . . . I feel you ought to know.'

'They?' she demanded. 'And who are "they"?'

'I don't rightly know exactly who they be,' he answered, shifting his feet. ''Twere me and the boy, see. Had the barge down in Plymouth overnight and, well, we went ashore for a few jars at an inn among the maze of little streets behind the old harbour, you know. And then on the way back I were sure we was being followed, and suddenly there we was, cornered in a dark alley. Four o' five o' them, there were. Got the boy by the collar and a knife to his throat, and me with my hands pinned behind my back. And . . . and they told us if we ever sailed the *Sure* for Captain Bradley again, they'd do for us both. Well,' his eyes rolled dramatically, 'I told them that this'd be our last cargo, 'cause we'd been offered, well . . . pardon me, ma'am, but better positions elsewhere, and they said we'd better take them, or we'd both be found floating face down in the river. Well, I don't take too kindly to being treated like that, but 'tis the lad, ma'am. He were terrified.'

Rebecca's fists were clenched so tightly the nails were on the point of drawing blood as they dug into her palms. A hot sweat slicked her skin, and yet she felt ice-cold inside. The seething rage and guilt at what Mr Willis and his son had endured on her account made her feel sick, and it flashed across her mind that it was the same torturing shame that Adam was suffering over Mr Elliman.

'I'm sorry, ma'am.' William Willis took an anxious step forward. Mrs Bradley had turned such a strange colour, he thought she might faint. 'I shouldn't have told you. 'Twas not fit for a lady's ears.'

'No, you were quite right.' Rebecca took a deep, calming breath. 'I can only offer you my sincerest apologies. 'Twas quite outrageous. And . . . you've no idea who these men were?'

'None at all. Couldn't see their faces in the dark. They had local accents but could've been anyone in a town the size of Plymouth. But I shouldn't like to meet them again. You . . . you won't tell anyone? I mean . . . the boy . . . Not even the captain?'

'Him least of all,' she came back quickly. 'You know he's still not so well?'

'Aye, so I gathered, poor man.' His shoulders moved uneasily. 'Well, if you don't mind, Mrs Bradley, I should be off. I'll see myself out.'

'Yes,' she answered flatly. 'And I am sorry for what happened. And . . . good luck.'

'Thank you, ma'am,' he said with relief that the interview was over. 'But I think 'tis you that needs the luck.'

She heard him leave, and then sank into her chair, hands clasped in an iron grip in her lap. She'd had no need really to ask Mr Willis if he'd recognized the men who'd waylaid him. She knew who they were, or at least who had hired them. Dear Lord, what lengths would the man go to in order to wreak his jealous vengeance? For that was what it was now. He had wealth enough of his own, and she shuddered as it occurred to her that perhaps after flattering and cajoling Lady Hennessy at first, he might have resorted to threatening the poor, dying woman into leaving her estate to him. So, what would be his next cruel and calculated move? What hideous trick did he have up his sleeve? Her flesh crept with fear and anger. Anger at Fred, but also anger at herself for feeling so helpless.

* * *

'Adam?'

He was lounging in an easy chair in front of the parlour fire, long legs outstretched and looking for all the world totally relaxed. He'd returned from his wanderings as it was getting dark, appearing not exactly pleased with himself, Rebecca had thought, but certainly in a better humour than normal, and demanding his jug of hot water with just a hint of his old banter. Rebecca was convinced his daily excursions were beginning to lift his spirits, whatever it was he found to occupy himself all those hours, although he shut up like a clam if she ever dared to enquire what it was he did all day. His thin body was rapidly regaining its covering of flesh, his appetite had improved enormously, and the colour had returned to his pale, gaunt face. He was still quite capable of drinking himself into oblivion, and Rebecca still felt she was treading on eggshells, but she was grateful that, physically at least, he had made some improvement. It was his mental state that still worried her. He shunned human contact as much as ever, earning himself the reputation of a fearsome recluse, and still showed little interest in his business affairs. And that was why her pulse was racing now, as that was precisely what she needed to discuss with him.

'Mmm?' he answered distantly but turned his head to look up at her with an amiable lift of his eyebrows. He was wearing one of his knitted guernseys since he found them far more comfortable than a jacket, and the dark navy wool contrasted strikingly with the brilliant white of the cotton shirt beneath, just visible around the neck for he'd abandoned the struggle to attach a collar. For once, however, he had shaved, although she could see where he'd nicked himself in several places. His handsome looks made her stomach turn a complete somersault and sent the yearning down to her thighs. Oh, how she needed his physical love, his touch, to soothe and caress, to make her forget what was going on outside, to feel safe, curled up against him in their marital bed. But it was a dream long passed, and she could only remember . . .

She smoothed down the bodice of her day dress with nervous fingers. 'William Willis came to see you today,' she began tentatively.

A dark frown immediately pursed his brow. 'Came to see me?' he growled. 'Came to see *you*, you mean.'

'Well, 'twould not be surprising, seeing as I'm the one who has to deal with everything nowadays.' Oh, God, why had she risen to the bait like that? Aggravating the situation, when she had known what Adam's reaction would be. 'But as it happens, 'twas you he asked for,' she humoured him, 'but as you weren't here . . .'

'And what did he want?'

Rebecca breathed in deeply, bracing herself for his tirade of anger. 'He came to say he and his son will no longer be working for us.'

'Really.' Adam's glacial sarcasm startled her. She'd been expecting some furious outburst. 'Well, that's gratitude for you when I've kept that barge running at a loss for months just so that he wouldn't be out of a job.'

'No, Adam, that's not quite true,' she ventured. 'Mr Willis has kept her going for *you* since we lost the arsenic contract, and through his efforts alone, trade was just beginning to pick up a little.'

'So why has he left, then?'

Rebecca caught her breath. She couldn't possibly tell him about the threats to William Willis and his son. It would only add to his devastating feelings of guilt to know that the bargemaster and the young boy had suffered such fear because of his feud with his cousin. She thanked God they had no idea where Fred could be found, for in his volatile state she could imagine Adam seeking him out in a maddened rage and heaven only knew what might happen then. But on the other hand, he might accept it with a wry grimace, for really, she never knew from one minute to the next what mood he might be in.

'He and his son have been offered more stable employment,' she answered evasively, hoping he didn't see the tremble in her hands.

'Oh. And let me guess where. Not on one of Fred's arsenic barges, by any chance?'

Rebecca lowered her eyes, but she caught Adam's despairing toss of his head as he swore vehemently under his breath. His earlier calm was totally shattered, and Rebecca herself cursed Fred Bradley for forcing her to need to raise the matter just as Adam was showing signs of regaining his mental equilibrium.

'I've . . . been thinking about it all day,' she stammered. 'And I've decided to sell the barge.'

Adam was on his feet in an instant, his hostile eyes glaring at her. 'Oh, you have, have you?' he snapped. '*You* have decided to sell *my* barge!'

'Oh, Adam, you know 'tis not like that!' She stepped forward, her hands earnestly grasping both his upper arms, and started in surprise when he instantly drew away with a stifled wince. She frowned up at him as he half turned his face from her. 'Adam, what's the matter?' she questioned him.

'Oh, I've been having phantom pains down my arm again, that's all,' he murmured.

'Oh, no!' she groaned compassionately. ''Tis ages since you've had that.'

'I know. It's probably my own fault, though.'

'What do you mean?'

'Oh, nothing,' he mumbled mysteriously. 'So, you've decided to sell the barge?'

'Well, you know it makes sense,' she went on with more confidence as he sounded more rational now. 'Mr Willis was just beginning to make her pay again with all his years of experience and knowledge of the river. But who else would we find to do that for us, to build up her trade again with things the way they are? And we could use the money to pay for the repairs on the *Swallow*.' She raised an eyebrow at him as a strange expression came over his face. 'You . . . you can't be thinking of sailing her yourself?' she stuttered incredulously.

He drew in a long, slow breath through pursed lips. 'A year ago I damned well would have done, but now I think I'd find it a trifle difficult to sail her literally single-handed,' he laughed bitterly. 'So tell me, my dear little business woman, who do you think will buy our splendid barge?'

Rebecca's frown deepened. 'She is a good barge, isn't she?'

'The best,' he nodded mockingly.

'Then we shall advertise her as such.' She blinked up at him, not sure how to take his remark. 'You do agree to it, then?'

He shrugged dismissively. 'To be quite honest, Rebecca, I don't really care what you do with the bloody thing.'

But she somehow had the feeling that, deep down, he was beginning to care very much indeed.

CHAPTER TWENTY-SIX

'There! I told you no one would want to buy the barge. Mr Griffin's withdrawn his offer.'

Rebecca took the letter from Adam's hand and her eyes travelled swiftly over the brief message. It was six weeks since William Willis had given his notice, and a fortnight since the one and only reply to the advertisement which, to her surprise and delight, Adam had actually drafted for her. He had even come close to showing Mr Griffin over the vessel himself, seeing as the gentleman was a stranger and his attention would be concentrated on the item for sale, rather than on the fact that the vendor seemed to have his left hand glued into his pocket. But Adam's courage had failed him at the last minute, and Isaac had stepped into the breach instead. His knowledge of the barge was limited in comparison with Adam's, of course, but Mr Griffin had known exactly what he was looking for and had quite quickly come up with a reasonable offer. But now it had been withdrawn, and Rebecca had a shrewd idea why. She couldn't tell Adam of her suspicions, of course, but she was convinced Fred had something to do with it. And if she was right, it meant he must have someone watching the barge in order to have discovered the identity of the prospective buyer. The thought made her shudder.

'Never mind,' she answered, trying to hide the tremble in her voice. 'I'll just have to put the advertisement out again.'

'Ha!' Adam grunted sardonically. 'Much good it'll do.'

'Well, if you've no better suggestion . . .'

'Oh, I'm entirely in your hands, my dear. I'm sure you know what you're doing.' He wriggled into his jacket and quickly fastened the buttons with the dexterity that had come to him with practice. 'Well, I'm off. I'll see you later.'

He was out of the door before Rebecca had a chance to reply, leaving her unsettled and ill at ease. If only she could tell him. If only she could tell *someone*! But she had to keep the fear to herself. After all, she couldn't make any allegations. It would do no good, and would only reveal that Mr Willis had told her of the threats he'd received, which could even make matters worse. And now that she suspected Mr Griffin had bowed out to similar pressure, she must think of him also. But it was such a deplorable sensation that there was someone out there, working against them in such an unscrupulous, underhand manner. Perhaps Fred even had someone watching the cottage, waiting for some way to . . . She leaped forward and flew up the garden path.

'Adam!'

He stopped with his hand on the gate, waiting for her with one eyebrow raised questioningly. She looked up into those glorious rich brown eyes, so much brighter now, and her pulse quickened, swamping her with dread. Adam took himself off to the loneliest places, and for a second, the vision flashed before her of . . . It was with a supreme effort that she forced herself to think rationally. Fred worked in a cold and calculating fashion. Any — oh, dear God, dare she even think of it — attack would lead to an investigation, and he wouldn't want that. But something that was made to look like an accident . . .

'Adam, be careful,' she muttered, nervously fingering the lapels of his jacket.

'What?' An amused smile played on his lips. 'Aren't I always?'

'Yes, but . . .'

'Well, don't worry, then.' And with his left wrist thrust deeply into his pocket in his habitual manner, he strode up the steep hill away from Morwellham.

Rebecca watched him for a few moments before dragging herself back to the cottage on leaden feet. Adam had definitely been more his old self the last few weeks, but she was afraid that some quite trivial event might plunge him headlong back to the damning despair that had choked him for so long. Anything Fred did now might completely rob him of his returning confidence, and it made her even more determined to beat the blackguard at his own game.

And she would start by selling the barge.

The corners of her mouth lifted in a satisfied smile as the plan began to formulate in her mind. But it must be done carefully in order to fool cousin Fred and not have anyone else involved.

She put her head around the dining-room door. Toby was at Amy Blatchford's side, duster in hand, helping her to polish the vast expanse of the tabletop.

'I'm going out for a short while, Amy. Keep an eye on Toby for me, would you?'

'Can't I come with you, Mama?'

The child skipped towards her, black curls bouncing around his jubilant, cajoling face. Rebecca smiled wistfully, but for once it wasn't appropriate for him to accompany her.

'No, sweetheart, not this time.' She knelt down and wrapped her arms about him. 'And when I come back, we'll do your lessons and then if you're good, you can do some painting.'

'Oh, yes! But do I have to do my lessons first?'

'Yes, you do!' she laughed. 'You want to grow up clever like Papa, don't you?'

'He doesn't do lessons!' Toby pouted. 'He doesn't do anything!'

'Well, that's because he hasn't been very well for a long time, but he is beginning to get better.'

'Good, because I want him to teach me how to sail a ship!'

'Oh, I don't know about that,' Rebecca answered her son truthfully. 'It takes years of learning and experience. And I'm not sure if Papa will sail again. But when you're big enough, you can sail across to France with Uncle Misha.'

'Promise?' His ebony eyes gleamed.

'Promise!' she smiled, straightening up. 'But there's something I must do now. I shouldn't be very long. You be good for Amy now!'

She planted a kiss on Toby's forehead and then going back out to the hallway, she donned her paletot and her hat, and let herself out of the cottage. The sun shone radiantly from a clear late March sky, but a keen wind whipped about her full skirt and tossed the heads of the daffodils at the side of the lane. Spring had definitely arrived, and the crop of early blooms that were cultivated on the sheltered slopes of the region were being whisked up to the London markets nightly by train, ready for the morning trade. It was a business that had been able to expand massively with the coming of the railways, but some flowers were still transported by river to the Plymouth markets as in earlier years. Had the *Sure* still been sailing, she would doubtless have carried some among her cargo. But now she was moored all alone just upriver from the port, riding the lapping water, or resting in the muddy shallows at low tide.

Rebecca paused as she turned the corner of the Ship Inn. This was Morwellham Quay, the place she loved, her home. The friendly little port that nestled between the steep ridge of Morwell Down and the meandering ribbon of the Tamar, a cradle of contentment where she had always felt safe and secure. And to think that there must be someone out there, watching. But it was her territory. Her father's port. And there was no way she would be cowed by some despicable, twisted scoundrel from faraway London!

She strode out purposefully, head high, fine chin set with total confidence. Jane Allport waved to her from the shop window. Her husband, captain and owner of a fine schooner and with shares in many a nautical pie, would be on a standing with Adam. God willing, they might become friends and colleagues if Adam ever . . . No! *When* Adam was fully recovered. For today she was determined that everything would go the way she wanted it, and nothing would stop her!

She passed the squalid malthouse tenements where Tom had died, scarcely turning her head. But she remembered. And in some small way, she felt that what she was doing was for Tom. For she would rid Morwellham of the manipulating evil that had come among its population, and return the port to the haven of honesty and companionship that it had always been when Tom was still alive.

Past the manganese mill she walked, the slow, rhythmical clunk of its great wheel still turning majestically to grind the sought-after powder. The farriers, the blacksmith serving the needs of the ships that still called, the cooperage that was kept busy enough by the arsenic and manganese trades, her father's assaying office, her parents' cottage. But where she was headed was the marshy land on the far side of the extensive Devon Great Consols dock, the bank where the *Sure* was moored, to search among the tall reeds and find whoever was . . .

'Good day, Rebecca.'

She had crossed the dock now, and a glacial thrill of horror trickled down her spine as she stopped dead in her tracks. Those three words were enough for her to recognize the voice of the man she loathed and despised more than anyone else on earth. When he stepped into her line of vision, her throat dried like desert sand.

'What? No return of greeting when you are hailed by a gentleman?' Fred Bradley chided mockingly, one eyebrow cocked in derision. 'Tut, tut, where are your manners, Rebecca?'

'My manners are reserved for gentlefolk, and I see none here.'

She started at the sound of her own voice, for surely her mind was senseless with shock. But the hatred inside her was spurring her tongue to its razor edge. She saw the slight twitch of his eyebrows at her sharp rebuff, and the supercilious smile slid from his face. It was all she needed to regain her wits, and though her heart beat furiously, a composed defiance strengthened her resolve.

'Come, come, my dear cousin,' Fred purred in an oily voice. 'What have I said to offend you?'

'You are no cousin of mine!' She twisted her arm free from the hold Fred had attempted to take on her elbow. 'And you have no need to say anything at all. Your presence is offence enough in itself.'

'Well, I'm sure you're the only person in this contemptible rathole to think so. After all, I have secured the employment of scores of bargemen for several years,' he grinned complacently.

'By creating a monopoly they were too frightened not to join! 'Tis you that's contemptible, not Morwellham!'

'My, my, Adam was right to infer you had a will of your own. I do admire spirit in a woman. It makes things more of a challenge.' He paused to run the tip of his furred tongue over his top lip, and Rebecca shuddered with revulsion. 'And how is poor Adam nowadays? Not quite his usual self and not yet back at sea, so I believe?'

His mocking sneer made Rebecca feel sick. How could anyone be so cruel? The man was inhuman, his twisted mind consumed with jealousy. 'Adam is well enough,' she answered tersely. 'And now if you'll excuse me . . .'

She turned on her heel, the familiar sights and sounds of the busy dock but yards away bringing her reassurance. But Fred would not let her escape and sprang round in front of her.

'You have a barge for sale,' he said with cunning indifference.

Rebecca tilted her chin, her eyes narrowed warily. 'As if you didn't know,' she scowled.

'Hmm.' Fred glanced down at his white, trimmed fingernails, hurred on them, and then polished them languidly on his lapel before looking back at her. 'I understand no one will buy her, so, as your cousin, I think it behoves me to help you out. I'll give you ninety pounds for her.'

'What?' The colour deepened in Rebecca's cheeks. 'She's worth three times that, at least!'

'Oh, well, in your opinion, perhaps,' he shrugged casually. 'But she is only an inside barge, as I believe you call it, only able to work inside Plymouth break-water. And trade along the river is declining—'

'Not that much, it isn't,' Rebecca snapped back. 'Besides, I'd never sell to you! I'd as soon apply to the workhouse!'

'The way things are going, you may have to, my dear, you and your precious husband. So I suggest you think on it, pretty lady. Consider my offer well before you turn it down.' His mouth moved into a sly smirk, just like a fox, Rebecca thought. 'It's the only one you'll ever get.'

'And you'll see to that, no doubt.' Rebecca's eyebrows arched scornfully. 'But there'll be no bargain struck between you and me, come what may.'

'I wouldn't be so sure about that. You'll come begging to me once I've ruined you for good. I congratulate you on that clever little move you made with the *Swallow*, persuading all your pox-ridden friends to hold on to their shares by promising to pay for the repairs yourself,' he nodded with sarcastic approval. 'Although I don't know how you expect to do so. But . . .' his eyes hardened like steel, 'there's more than one way to kill a cat. You must admit I was destroying Bradley's with some dexterity until you managed to hold on to the loyalty of some of your suppliers with your begging letters. What quaint French you write, *ma belle cousine*! But it's not enough, you know. And as for trying to slander me to the other shareholders in Bradley's, well, some of them feel so sorry for Adam, especially now they know he's married to a conniving little bitch who's trying to squeeze every penny out of him while he's indisposed, they're happy to sell to me so that I can take care of my poor cousin and defend him from *you*! Really, Rebecca, I was never one for work, but I do find I am quite enjoying myself,' he chortled triumphantly. 'I never realized business could be such fun!'

'You call that business? Treachery and deceit I call it!'

'Oh, well, I suppose we all have a different way of looking at things. Personally, I believe I've been rather successful, unlike poor Adam whose business affairs seem to be declining with alarming celerity, it has to be said. But unlike him, I have no moral scruples to restrain me. I can manipulate people however I need to without any conscience. And it does make life so interesting!' He paused to grin malevolently. 'So you see, sweet Rebecca, I shall regain my true inheritance in the end, and I shall also have my revenge.'

Rebecca stared at him, struggling against the scorching desire to fly at him, to rake her fingernails down his face, gouge out the bloated flesh from his florid cheeks. But, with supreme dignity, she held back. Of course, he would easily restrain her, his height and weight too much for her slight frame, and he would laugh down at her, delighting in his ridicule. That was not the way to fight Fred Bradley. But to stand her ground and outmanoeuvre him was. If only to gain time to allow Adam to recover his physical and mental strength which at long last he was showing signs of doing.

'Are you so inhuman that you have no pity or shame?' Her voice was steady, but so laced with disdain that she saw the hint of provoked annoyance flash in Fred's eyes. 'You have fortune enough of your own now. And what has Adam himself ever done to harm you? Can't you leave him be? Hasn't fate made him suffer enough already?'

Fred thrust forward his chin as if in surprise, and then his head fell back in a full-throated bellow of laughter. Rebecca glared at him, her forehead creased in a bewildered, angry frown.

'Fate?' Fred finally spluttered, and his gaze locked with hers, his eyes pitiless. His voice dropped to a snarling whisper, his lips curled back viciously from his teeth. 'You don't think fate caused that rope to fray, do you? Or that your meticulous Ruskie brother-in-law would have been so careless as to allow a worn lashing to be used? Oh, no, my dear Rebecca! He checked everything as it was being stowed, as a good captain should. But it's amazing what a penniless docker will do for a few guineas. The plan was actually to lay a slow-burning fuse to the explosives Adam was fool enough to be carrying, so that some time as she cruised upriver, the *Swallow* would be blown sky-high, and Adam with it. What satisfaction that would have given me! But no matter. It worked out so much better in the end. Adam was clucking over the explosives like a mother hen and my man couldn't get anywhere near. So he did the next best thing he could think of. When Adam's back was turned, he hacked through those ropes after they'd been checked, so that at least some of the other cargo stood a good chance of being ruined, or even cause the ship to list dangerously when it fell. As it happened, all you lost were a few crates of wine, but to have Adam go past just at the moment it all broke loose and be crushed beneath it, well, it was more than I could have wished for. To see my dear cousin brought down from his high horse and have the wind taken out of his sails — ha! If you'll excuse the pun, seeing as he doesn't seem to be of a mind to go back to sea. To watch his humiliation. See him destroyed. And to know that it's all my own doing!'

Rebecca was transfixed as she stared at his gloating, merciless face, her blood turning to water as she digested the full gall of every heinous word that had spewed from Fred's evil lips. It hadn't been an accident! Not an accident! Her brain seemed to rattle in her skull as the godless revelation tumbled relentlessly inside her head. Adam had nearly died, had suffered months of physical agony and now the mental anguish that was tearing him apart, and all because of Fred. Her knees were near to buckling, her lips trembling, but she wasn't ready to give in and her heart rose in rebellion.

'You damned bloody bastard,' she croaked in a whisper so taut and hoarse it was scarcely audible.

'Oh, language, Rebecca, dear!' Fred's sarcasm snapped back at her with a taunting laugh.

Spit, claw, strangle, stab. *Kill!* The hate inside her was something she had never known before. She wanted to see that detestable, demonic face run with blood. And yet in it was still some resemblance to that kind, honest, handsome man she loved so passionately, and the thought made her despise it even more, the hatred giving her an unsurpassable strength.

'Language?' she grated, her narrowed eyes blazing. 'The language has yet to be invented to describe something as despicable as you! Oh, you can sneer, Fred Bradley, but I shouldn't like to be in your shoes. To know what 'tis like to be lower than something disgusting you might tread in in the street, for that's what you are! You're not a man! You're an animal! No, not even that! For even a dog wouldn't turn on its own kith and kin the way you've turned on Adam.'

'All I want is my inheritance. Half of all that Adam has is rightfully mine, you know that, Rebecca.'

'No,' she rounded on him furiously. 'Even if you hadn't been disowned, you'd only have been entitled to your father's share of the business as it was at the time. Adam and his father worked like slaves for years after that to build it into what 'tis now, or at least what 'twas before you dug your greedy paws into it! And now you're trying to take everything. No! You're just riddled with jealousy because you know you're nothing compared with Adam. Oh, yes, the truth hurts, doesn't it!' she hissed as she saw from the expression that flickered over his face that she had touched on a very raw nerve. 'You're so eaten up by your own inadequacy—'

'Oh, you wouldn't have a clue, would you!' Fred grasped her wrist with such a swift movement that she had no time to avoid his vice-like grip. She could have squealed with the pain of it, but somehow all her attention was riveted on his livid face. 'How could you possibly have any idea what it's like to be rejected by your own family?' he went on, his eyes enflamed with wild savagery. 'To be abandoned when you're still only a child? You have a loving home, a father who dotes on you as if you were a son and a daughter rolled into one, from what I've heard. The minute my mother died — the only person who ever came close to loving me — I was packed off to boarding school because my father couldn't stand to have me at home. And not to any school, oh, no! It had to be the same school as Adam, didn't it? Where he was already looked on as one of the brightest pupils they'd ever had. He was thirteen, and I was just eleven, and for the next four or five years I was forced to live constantly in his shadow, always being compared to him, and never, *never* being able to live up to his standards no matter how hard I tried. Always being looked down on as inferior. How can *you* ever imagine what that was like? I was never even allowed to go into the family business, to show that I had some worth, however small. My father even denied me that chance. Oh, I don't suppose Adam ever knew that, did he? So what was I supposed to do, eh? I was given a small allowance and told to get on with my life. Well, if the cap fits, wear it. And so I did, until my father told me he wished Adam was his son instead of me and that I was to be disinherited in Adam's favour. So don't talk to me about inadequacy when I've had my own inadequacy rammed down my throat from the cradle!'

For a fleeting moment, Rebecca's heart found room for a glimmer of pity. She herself had felt somewhat in awe of Adam when she'd first met him, his tall, broad-shouldered figure, his self-assurance that she'd misinterpreted as arrogance. How long had it taken her to discover the kindness and sensitivity beneath his formidable exterior, the strength with which he'd borne her own deceit with patient forgiveness until his personal tragedy had finally shattered his spirit? So, yes, she could understand how a lesser, weaker man could feel intimidated by Adam's natural bearing, which even in his present state could be quite unnerving. But it was no excuse for what he had done to Adam, for leaving him maimed for life. But perhaps she'd discovered the chink in Fred's armour which she could use to fight for Adam now. She glanced down at her arm with caustic disapproval and Fred at once released his hold.

Relief loosened her tongue. 'Then why don't you take this opportunity to redeem yourself?' she said earnestly, not quite knowing how her brain was finding the desperate words that came to her lips. 'Prove to yourself that you can be a better man than others think you are. You can never give back what you've taken from Adam. You can never give him back his hand, and by God, I can never forgive you for what you've done to him! But you don't need to ruin him as well. All you have to do is go away and leave Adam to pick up the threads of his life as best he can in peace. God knows he's finding it hard enough to do as 'tis, without you hounding him at every turn. You've had your revenge, unjust as 'twas. And now 'tis time to show you can be a man after all.'

Fred stared at her, the bitterness melting from his face as a million thoughts darted about inside his head. She was glorious, this wife of Adam's. So graceful, so ethereal, her wrist so fragile in his grasp just now. Those bewitching sapphire eyes, that abundance of shining hair escaping from beneath her hat, the stubborn tilt of her jaw. And she had seen inside him. Just for a few moments, she had seemed to understand. There was a compassion in her . . . He'd always had women in his life, but none of them had ever really loved him. Not in the way he'd craved. Not even Lady Elizabeth Hennessy. And now he was in possession of her not inconsiderable fortune, and was proving he could be good at something, even if it was only destroying his cousin! But it was a lonely life. If only he had someone gentle and caring to love him, he would give it up tomorrow. If only he had someone like Rebecca. He'd gathered she had conceived a child out of wedlock and that, had Adam not married her, the boy would have been born a bastard, but no one had ever called her a slut. Rather she was respected, pitied, because the lad whose child it was had been as good and kind as she was. They were betrothed, deeply in love, and she had apparently been broken by his untimely death, until she'd grown to love Adam in his place. And she did love Adam, Fred had no doubt of that. It radiated from her like the rays of the sun! By God, he was a lucky sod,

Adam! He always had everything! And now he had this passionate, spirited, beautiful young woman as his wife. Well, Fred wouldn't let him get away with that as well! He meant to have everything that was Adam's, including her.

'Oh, you think you're so clever, don't you?' he jeered, his face grotesque in its insanity once more. 'Trying to trick me with your fine words. Well, I'll not stop until I've made Adam feel as low as I always have!'

Rebecca had waited, praying for the impossible, but now she threw him such a withering look that he almost recoiled. She had given him that one chance and he'd thrown it back in her face. Not an accident. Well, she was the one seeking vengeance now.

'Oh, Adam feels pretty low about himself just now,' she answered, her voice cold and ruthless. 'Just you try tying your hand behind your back for a day and see how damning it is to your pride. And then imagine how 'twould be to know you have to spend the rest of your life like that. But no matter how degraded he feels, he could never be as worthless as you are. I don't know how you can live with yourself. But I do know this. People like you might have their moment of false glory, but it never lasts. They always get what they deserve in the end. So I should look out if I were you. Because I shall make sure that you are no exception.'

Her dark blue eyes glinted with venom, scorching into Fred's stupefied face. She saw him colour and his chin dropped, but she could endure his hateful company not an instant longer. She spun on her heel, fully expecting Fred to harangue her again, but he didn't. She marched back the way she'd come, still shaking inside, but more determined with each purposeful stride. Not an accident! When she thought of Adam staggering from the ship in a state of collapse, the agony he'd borne with such courage, the infection that had nearly taken his life, and the depression that even now he was only beginning to escape . . . Raging frustration swirled dangerously in her head. How could she bring Fred down? There was no point now in attempting to track down whoever he had paid to watch the barge. But nothing would stop her carrying out the move she had planned earlier.

When she reached the cottage, she went straight to the study and took out paper and pen. Mr Edward Brooming of the shipyard opposite Calstock had built the *Sure* no more than ten years earlier. She was a Tamar barge, he knew every inch of her, had carried out the few repairs she had ever needed. He would know exactly what she was worth without having to look her over. He traded in vessels as well as building and repairing them, and what was more, he was a long-standing and trustworthy friend of her father's. If she could persuade him to purchase the *Sure* on that basis alone, Fred's spy, whoever he was, would have no idea and Fred could do nothing to sabotage the sale until it was too late and the transaction completed. She would have to word the letter carefully. Persuade Mr Brooming of the need for secrecy without revealing the true reason for it. And if she could outwit Fred on this, then maybe it was just the beginning.

She pensively dipped the pen in the inkwell.

CHAPTER TWENTY-SEVEN

''Tis a letter for you, ma'am, delivered by hand. Some scruffy little urchin, not from hereabouts.'

Rebecca frowned curiously as she took the envelope from her housekeeper. 'Thank you, Amy.'

She turned the paper over as she reached the study where Toby was diligently copying some simple words on to a slate. The envelope was quite dog-eared, but the writing was well formed, as if produced by an educated hand. Rebecca tore it open, and her eyes swiftly scanned its contents.

Dear Mrs Bradley, I should be most interested in purchasing the barge Sure from you. I know she is a sound vessel and I am willing to offer you a good price for her. I should be obliged if you would meet me on board at three o'clock this afternoon. If you can bring the registration documents and a bill of sale, I will bring a bank draft and we can complete the transaction immediately.

Your faithful friend.

Rebecca rubbed her hand thoughtfully across her mouth. Her pulse had suddenly quickened and she instinctively hurried out into the hallway, opened the front door and ran up the garden path to the gate. Her eyes searched both up and down the steep lane, but in both directions it was deserted. There was no point in pursuing the boy. He'd be long gone by now, and it didn't really matter anyway. Mr Brooming, the shipwright, had obviously received her letter and had taken her pleas to heart. She'd stressed that although her husband's health was at last improving, she felt he was not yet sufficiently strong for the strain of selling the barge, and that if she could possibly do so without involving him, it would come as both a relief and a pleasant surprise for him. She trusted Mr Brooming implicitly, her being a woman and not up to such matters, and relying on her father's association with him, she would be greatly obliged if he could possibly settle the matter for her with the minimum of contact. And Mr Brooming, being a kindly gentleman, had taken pity on her and fallen in with her plans beautifully.

She strolled more leisurely back down the path. It was the second week in April. Although still chillsome with a keen wind, there was the definite scent of spring in the air, and she felt more hopeful than she had for some months. If she could conclude the sale of the barge that very day, it would perhaps buy sufficient time for Adam to take up the reins of the business again. He was definitely recovering. She was sure of it. His general health had virtually resumed to normal and he looked altogether far less gaunt. He still spent hours alone somewhere up in the woods — he was there now — and continued to avoid the company of anyone outside the immediate family, but his natural good humour was re-emerging from its hidden depths. He was even starting to display a little interest in their business affairs, and Rebecca was convinced it was only a matter of time. But how much of that did they have?

'So 'twas no one you recognized?' she asked Amy as she went back indoors.

'No, ma'am,' the housekeeper called from the kitchen. 'Didn't say a word, neither.'

Rebecca returned to the study, smiling at Toby when he glanced up from his work. He was such a bright little fellow, and she wondered quite how she'd have survived without him. But now her attention was drawn back to the letter. A friend. Why had Mr Brooming signed it like that? It must be his way of acknowledging he understood her desire for secrecy. Not for the true reason, since Rebecca hadn't told a soul, but because she'd imparted to him that she wanted to sell the *Sure* without Adam being involved. She'd have preferred to complete the negotiations without going near the barge, so that whoever Fred had engaged to keep watch would have no notion of an impending sale. But as it was, Mr Brooming was bringing a bank draft and she was to bring the necessary documents so that they could conclude the matter there and then. And once that was done, it would be too late for Fred to do anything about it.

Now, how should she word a bill of sale?

She'd hardly withdrawn a blank sheet of paper from the drawer of the desk when she heard the front door fly open and slam against the wall beside it. Her heart jolted as she sprang towards the hall in time to see Adam shut the door behind him and slump back against it, his head bowed and the fingers of his one hand spread across the right side of his face.

'Adam?'

She stepped anxiously towards him, a glance taking in the smear of mud and the dead leaves that clung to his clothes. As he straightened up, oh, good God, there was partially dried blood where it had trickled between his fingers and down his neck. He came forward, his gait slightly unsteady, and Rebecca flew to his side. Oh, sweet Jesus! Had Fred been up to his heinous tricks again? Anger and fear spewed up into her throat, setting her heart pounding like a drum.

'Adam, what on earth happened?'

They'd reached the kitchen, and Amy Blatchford's eyes grew wide with horror as Rebecca sat Adam down in a chair.

'I was up in the woods and I fell over,' he mumbled his reply.

'Fell over?' Rebecca's eyebrows lifted incredulously. So it had nothing to do with Fred? Well, that was a relief, but

Adam had obviously taken quite a knock. 'Let me look at that.'

He obediently took his hand away from his face, wincing as he did so. A dark split, about an inch long, had opened the skin across his swollen cheekbone. The bleeding had more or less stopped, but the wound was deep and embedded with grit.

'Did you hit it on a stone?' Rebecca frowned gravely.

'More like a bloody rock.'

She ignored his understandably vexed reply and turned to thank Amy who, helpful as ever, had already placed a dish of water and some clean rags on the table beside her. 'You must have fallen heavily to have done this.'

'Well, I was running,' he murmured, and sucked the breath in sharply through his teeth as she began to dab at his cheek.

'Running?'

'Yes, running,' he snapped irritably. 'There's no law against it, is there?'

'No,' she answered cautiously. 'I were just surprised, that's all. I mean . . .' She paused to rinse out the bloodied cloth. 'Is that what you do up in the woods? Run?'

His eyes shifted nervously. 'Sometimes,' he shrugged.

'But . . . why?'

She was aware of him sighing as she concentrated on the delicate task. 'To run off my frustrations, I suppose,' he muttered bitterly. 'You don't need two hands to run. But I'm so bloody useless, I can't even do that!'

He jerked up his head with such vehemence that Rebecca had to draw her hand away quickly. She shut her eyes, giving herself a few seconds' respite. Adam's fall had been a complete accident, but it appeared to have rocked the confidence he was beginning to find in himself again.

'Anyone can trip over, you know,' she told him. 'It just shakes you up more as you get older.'

He gave a wry grunt. 'I certainly feel a little dazed. Ouch!' He pulled away sharply with a pained gasp. 'And

303

if you must subject me to your ministrations, perhaps you could pour me a drink first!'

Rebecca met Amy's concerned eyes across the table. It was weeks since Adam had drowned his sorrows in hard liquor, but for once she considered that a stiff drink might not come amiss. She nodded at Amy who reluctantly did as she was bid, and Rebecca waited for Adam to swallow a good measure before she resumed her task.

'Now do keep still while I clean it,' she ordered. 'You know, I do think Dr Seaton should take a look. 'Tis gaping, and might need a stitch.'

'No, it's perfectly all right!'

'Well, at least let me put a cold compress on it to bring down the swelling, or 'twon't knit together.'

'For God's sake, Rebecca, stop fussing!'

He stood up abruptly and his eyes clashed fiercely with hers. She knew there'd be no persuading him when he was in this mood, and she watched submissively as he picked up the bottle of rum that was still on the table, and took himself off to the parlour.

* * *

She heard the hall clock chime its mellow tones. Half past two. Time for her to leave. She'd made out the bill of sale and had all the necessary documentation stowed away in a drawstring bag so that she could carry it more easily. In her mind, the affair was already completed, but her satisfaction was marred by her deep, nagging worry over Adam. His state of mind was so precarious that it seemed the fall had been quite enough to shatter all the progress he had made. Useless. Couldn't even run a few yards without falling flat on his face. His angry words of self-condemnation echoed in her ears as she gazed down on him. He was sprawled in a chair, sleeping off the rum he'd consumed and the wine with which he'd washed down the little he'd eaten of the midday meal. His mouth was slightly open, his strong even teeth a brilliant white among the dark shadow of his unshaven jaw. She felt the pain as her heart tried to tear itself out of her chest. But for now it was perhaps best he slept. Hopefully, he'd feel calmer when he awoke, and in the meantime, she would take a major step in fighting back against Fred.

'I'm just going out,' she told Amy who'd crept into the room on tiptoe. 'I'll be about an hour or so, I should think. You'll take care of Adam if he wakes up?'

'Yes, of course. But that don't look too likely, do it? 'Tis such a pity when he were doing so well. And a nasty cut he's got there, too.' Her sharp features moved into a sympathetic grimace, but then she smiled as she took the hand of the small child who'd wandered into the room. 'Toby and me'll be in the wash house. I thought I'd get the copper going and wash all they sheets and towels ready to put on the line come morning.'

Rebecca nodded absently, her eyes taking a last glance at Adam before she left. But she mustn't keep Mr Brooming waiting. She went out into the hall and, watching herself in the mirror, pinned her small hat on the top of her head and fastened the buttons of her serviceable paletot. Beneath it, the skirt of her day dress hung loosely since she'd left off all her petticoats. She hardly wanted to be encumbered by them as she rowed out to the *Sure* and climbed aboard.

A cool breeze fanned about her neck as she walked briskly up the garden path. What had been a clear spring sky was rapidly clouding over and she hoped it wasn't coming on to rain. She made her way down the steep hill and, turning the corner of the Ship Inn, strode out towards the far end of the port, her boots clicking on the old rails of the inclined plane railway as she stepped across them. How many hundreds of times had she trod this way? But how different it all was now. She shivered as she recalled the day, little more than a fortnight ago, when she'd been accosted by Fred on her way to the very place she was going now.

Past Copper Ore Cottage and across to the far side of the Great Dock. Her father's little rowing boat was moored in the shallows of the river just at the end of the reinforced wharf, not so far from the *Sure* herself, for which Rebecca was grateful. The tide had turned and was coming in steadily, but it hadn't yet gained its full momentum. Nevertheless, it would give her some assistance in rowing against the fast-flowing stream of the river. She pulled in the painter, drawing the boat close into the bank. Her feet nearly left the ground when a gnarled brown hand reached from behind her and held on to the varnished gunwale rail.

'I'll hold it steady for 'ee, ma'am.'

Rebecca looked into the grizzled face of the old hobbler who'd been so kind when she'd fallen on the ice and lost the child she'd been carrying. 'Thank you,' she said.

'I just did the same for that gentleman,' he winked, nodding towards the barge where, sure enough, another small boat was tied up beside her.

Rebecca felt herself flush. ''Tis a business arrangement,' she told him haughtily, since what else would it be with Mr Brooming a good ten years older than her father?

'Of course, ma'am. My lips be sealed.'

Well, what did it matter what he thought? And she was grateful for his assistance in climbing down into the boat. She used the oars to push off from the bank, and then dropping them into the rowlocks, began to move out into the stream of the river. It was some time since she had rowed. It was hardly seemly for a captain's wife. But as a child, she'd spent hours on the water and knew the Tamar well. At low tide, the *Sure* sat in the soft mud, her virtually flat hull still level, but as the tide rose, she was already riding in a few feet of water, just enough for Rebecca to be able to row. The exertion was warming her body to an uncomfortable moistness, but her bare face and neck remained ice-cold from the increasing wind as the first raindrops began to fall.

By the time she reached the barge, she was beginning to feel the force of the rising tide. Skilfully using it to bring the boat side on against the *Sure* behind the other skiff, she firmly secured the painter. Mr Brooming had left the amidships gangway open for her, and she clambered with extreme care up the rope ladder and on to the deck, shaking out her crumpled skirt. Mr Brooming was not to be seen, but the corner hatchway of the main hold was propped open and she assumed he'd gone down to begin his inspection while he was waiting. After all, if he was to buy the vessel, he'd want to check out her timbers and make sure she was in as good condition as Rebecca claimed.

'Mr Brooming?' she called from the open hatch. The rain was pattering heavily on the deck now, the sky darkened to an ominous grey, and the heavens promising to open at any moment. Rebecca didn't wait for a reply, but climbed backwards down the stepladder into the gloomy darkness of the empty hold. In the faint glimmer from an oil lamp, she could just distinguish the silhouette of a man crouched at the far end. Although she could stand upright in the shallow hold, anyone taller than her would need to stoop awkwardly, and sitting or crouching would be far more comfortable. She came forward eagerly, but stopped dead as the figure half turned its face into the dim light.

'Good afternoon, Rebecca,' a smooth, silken voice greeted her. 'You got my letter, then? I was afraid you wouldn't come. And who the devil is Mr Brooming?'

* * *

Hetty ambled down the Duke's Ride from Endsleigh House with her long, loose-limbed stride lending an almost manly grace to her tall, willowy figure. Her jaunty gait betrayed the bursting joy in her heart. She was on her way to meet Robin off the paddle steamer! The *Swallow* had been taken into dock for her repairs and the crew temporarily laid off except for Misha Kastryulyevich, who was to master the *Emily* while Captain Harvey took a much-needed rest. And so Robin was coming home, hopefully for good. He was to be interviewed the following day. As head of the laundry now, Hetty was on good terms with the housekeeper, who in turn was on an equal footing with the head of maintenance, who'd implied that a skilled miner with a clean character would fit the bill admirably. And even as a married woman, Hetty would be permitted to continue her work until such times as a family came along.

Oh, the happiness of it was enough to make her sing like a lark, as indeed she had for part of the way, in a low, crooning voice that hinted of the gipsy ancestry in her. It was such a pity that the sunny weather, which had matched her mood so perfectly, had deteriorated so quickly, and that heavy rain seemed imminent. She was too early, she knew, but her excitement was such that she couldn't wait around another minute at the House. Her mother was no longer there for her to call in for a quick chat, and she pushed to the back of her mind that pang of sadness. She could make her way up to Lavender Cottage, but if she were honest, she was afraid of coming face to face with Captain Bradley. She had the greatest sympathy for the poor man, but his sullen attitude wasn't exactly welcoming, and she didn't want anything to spoil her present happiness. So to while away the hour or so she had to wait for the steamer, she would wander along the riverbank in the direction of Morwell Rocks, and just be alone to savour every second of her joyous anticipation.

An awkward splashing in the water drew her attention to the river. Someone was rowing against the current, not very well and catching crabs at almost every stroke. She couldn't quite see from where she was, but it looked for a moment a little like Captain Bradley. But it couldn't possibly be him because the fellow was rowing, or attempting to row, with both oars. Hetty watched inquisitively, hidden from view by the tall reeds, as the boat crashed into the side of the moored barge as the stranger failed miserably to turn broadside on. Hetty smiled to herself at his incompetence and then her eyes opened wide in astonishment as he tied up to the *Sure* and proceeded to climb aboard. Well! She knew the barge was up for sale, but surely anyone likely to be inspecting her would have better rowing skills than this chap possessed?

She shrugged and walked on. It was none of her business, after all. Robin would be disembarking at the wharf at about half past four. If he was offered the position tomorrow, as seemed likely, they could go and see the minister, have the banns read and be married before May was out. Oh, what bliss that would be! Seven long years they'd waited, nearly four of them spent in long separations while Robin sailed back and forth to Europe on the *Swallow*. To be with him all the time . . .

Surely that was Rebecca now in her father's boat, rowing expertly up the river. What on earth was she doing? Especially as it was starting to rain. Hetty frowned and, looking up at the darkening sky, turned back towards the port with the intention of taking shelter in the manganese barn. The wind was getting up, too, and it really was very unpleasant indeed, and yet Rebecca was making straight for the barge and several minutes later was standing on board, before quickly disappearing, Hetty assumed, down below deck.

Hetty stopped in her tracks. What in heaven's name was going on? Rebecca, on a secret tryst with a stranger? No! It simply wasn't possible. And yet . . . she and Tom . . . But that was totally different. And although Rebecca's life with Captain Bradley was so difficult at the moment, she *loved* him! Unless everything Rebecca had confessed to her was a lie. But, no! It couldn't be! She trusted Rebecca implicitly! But then . . . And who was this fellow who put her in mind of Captain Bradley? Dear God! Surely it wasn't the cousin who had deceived everyone? After all, few people had actually seen him. But what was Rebecca doing? Surely she wouldn't be . . .

But what if she didn't know?

Something was definitely wrong, Hetty was sure. She paced up and down, wringing her hands in distress. Should she interfere? Was it any of her business? And from where she was, what could she do, anyway? But if Rebecca was in trouble, and she did nothing? What would Tom have thought of her if she allowed . . . when she could have done something? Her mind was made up. She was still some way from the port, and hitching up her skirt, ran as fast as she could through what had turned to lashing rain.

'Be . . . your . . . husband in?' she gasped to an astonished Anne Westbrook as she banged loudly on the door of Copper Ore Cottage.

'No, he's up at the mine offices.' Anne shook her greying head in confusion. 'He'll be back very shortly, mind. Oh, come in, cheel. You're wet through.'

But Hetty's ebony eyes rolled wildly. It could be too late by then. There was only one thing for it. Right to the far end of the port and up the steep hill to Lavender Cottage. And Captain Bradley himself. But how in the name of sweet Jesus could she tell the man that Rebecca was possibly . . . deliberately . . . seeing his hated cousin in secret?

The thought of his reaction terrified her. But she was willing to risk the weight of his wrath for her lifelong friend.

* * *

Rebecca froze, every taut nerve ready to snap and her mind whipped into a terrifying whirlpool of fear and hate. She wanted to move, to flee, but her feet were rooted to the spot, her muscles powerless with shock.

Fred rose to his feet, his bulk a dark, threatening outline against the menacing shadows, his wide shoulders hunched to keep his head down clear of the hatch beams. Rebecca swallowed down her terror, forcing herself to push aside her panic and focus her thoughts clearly again. The letter had been from Fred! She was so convinced she'd foiled his devious tricks that she hadn't even questioned it. What a stupid idiot she'd been! And now she was here, marooned alone with Fred down in the hold of the isolated barge. And no one knew where she was.

'You didn't answer my question, Rebecca. Who is Mr Brooming?'

She couldn't have spoken even if she'd wanted to, her tongue clinging to the roof of her parched mouth. She dared to dart her gaze over her shoulder back towards the open hatch, but the sky had turned so black with the torrential rain that was battering on to the deck above their heads, that the stepladder was scarcely discernible from the surrounding gloom. Besides, if she made a dash for it, Fred would be on her in a trice. What she had to do was humour him, use her wits to defend herself, and hopefully edge nearer her escape route without him noticing.

'Well, I don't suppose it matters. You're here now. And alone. But then I knew you would be, after Adam's mishap this morning. He was hardly likely to accompany you after such a nasty blow to the head.'

Despite herself, Rebecca's voice rasped in her throat. 'How . . . how did you know?'

'Oh, my sweet Rebecca, how naive you are! But of course, it only adds to your charm.' He took a couple of steps forward, keeping his head low, but stopped the instant she instinctively backed away. The lamp glowed dimly from behind him so his face was in shadow and his looming figure was no clearer than a black silhouette in the darkness. And when he spoke, his words seemed to come at her from all directions, echoing back from the unyielding planking of the empty hold. 'It was just another of my little plans that succeeded so admirably. I had the boy set up the tripwire and then sit and wait, knowing that Adam runs the same way every day. It was so perfect with those jagged rocks so well positioned.'

'What!' Rebecca's fury snapped her brain into action again, and her tongue sprang into life. 'So you've been spying on him, have you?'

'Not me personally. But the boy has, and he's told me all about it. I found him poaching on my estate in Herefordshire, and it struck me how useful he might be. Stealthy as a cat. Adam didn't have a clue anyone was watching his antics, although what he hopes to achieve by these . . . these exercises, shall we call them, I've no idea.'

''Tis none of your business anyway!' Rebecca rounded on him, her rage enflamed further by Fred's knowledge of

Adam's clandestine activities when she remained so ignorant of them.

'On the contrary, everything Adam does is my business. And in this case, it was most convenient. The boy judged Adam's height to the inch and set the wire exactly so that he'd likely hit his head on those stones when he fell. And fall he would, because he'd never notice the wire at the speed he was going. Fell quite hard, too, and didn't get up for several minutes. It gave the boy ample time to deliver the note and then tell me it had all worked.'

Rebecca's eyes narrowed venomously. 'You're despicable! Adam might've been badly hurt!'

She heard him puff out his cheeks. Her vision was beginning to adjust to the lack of light, and she could just distinguish the whites of his eyes and the flash of his teeth as he spoke. 'Oh, I do hope not.'

'Huh! You wouldn't have given a damn . . .'

'Oh, but I would, Rebecca! I care very much about my cousin, especially since I realized what he means to you. I . . . well, I did what you suggested.' He took a step nearer, and this time she didn't move. She didn't want him to see how terrified she was, and there was something different . . . humble . . . in his voice that had thrown her into confusion. 'Don't you remember? You told me to tie my hand behind my back and see what it was like. Well, you made me feel so bad about myself that I tried it. And after ten minutes, I was so frustrated that I gave up. Don't you see, Rebecca? You made me realize what I've done, and the guilt of it is destroying me, just as I tried to destroy Adam.'

They were still some fifteen feet apart, but as he poked his head forward in earnest, their noses might have been touching. She shuddered as the still, musty air in the hold stifled her breathing. The tone of his words was so strange, his stance expectant, waiting for her to . . . to do what? Forgive him? But how could she? How could he possibly . . . ? But she could pretend . . . To save herself . . .

'You don't believe me, do you, after this morning? But I had to do it, don't you see? I didn't want to hurt Adam. Not again. But it was the only way. I had to make sure you came alone. You are my saviour, my dear, sweet Rebecca. The only person who can save me from my own sin. You do understand, don't you?'

For a moment her heart stopped beating. She blinked at him, her lips pursed with the effort of forcing herself to think straight. 'Yes, I understand,' she muttered, as realization dawned. His mind, so riddled with jealousy, had turned. Oh, dear God, how ever was she going to . . . She took a deep breath, fighting against the faintness as her heart raced on again. 'So why did you have to . . . speak to me here on the barge?'

'Because what I said in the letter was true. I want to help you. Make amends. I want to buy the *Sure* from you.'

She jerked up her head. It was on the tip of her tongue to retort that she'd told him once before she'd never sell to him. But the situation was different now. She was in danger, but of quite what nature, she wasn't entirely sure. All she knew was that, somehow, she had to get off the barge. If she went along with him, played his game . . . He had sounded genuine just now, desperate.

'She's an excellent vessel. I'll want a reasonable price for her.' Did that sound natural? Calm? Or could he hear the petrified quake in her voice? 'She's only an inside barge, as I think you know, but she's bigger than most. She used to carry over thirty tons of limestone. You could load her to within two inches of freeboard, and she'd still float. And if you wanted to use her for arsenic, I think she carried nearly two hundred and fifty casks. 'Tis less in weight because of the density of the powder, but you'd know all about that, of course.'

She paused. Swallowed hard. Her eyes wide as she waited for some sort of answer. But Fred stood as still as a statue, his bowed head to one side as he stared, contemplated her in silence. A sheen of sweat broke out over her skin under his unnerving gaze and began to trickle down her spine. For God's sake, say something, will you! But her silent plea went unheeded. She must, *must* put more space between them. Move towards the ladder.

'She's . . . of a very high specification,' her voice quavered. Please, please don't let him see how scared I am. 'All her frames are five-inch oak, and . . . her deck beams are oak, too. Her ceiling and planking are all two inches thick, her keel is strong elm and . . . her keelson's teak.' She dropped her eyes to the great square timber that ran the length of the hold, like a rigid spine. And her heart rammed against her ribcage as she saw Fred step over it on to her side, only six feet away. Getting nearer. She must — needed — to break away soon.

'You'll not find a drop of water in the bilges,' she mumbled on. Oh, sweet Jesus, what were all the things Adam had said? Must buy herself time. Oh, Adam . . . think . . . think . . . she could hear his voice telling her . . . telling her . . . 'Her hanging knees are iron, and not a spot of rust. And closer together than on most barges, see? Gives her more strength.'

She felt the mindless smile on her face as she stepped backwards, pointing at each of the enormous metal brackets as she moved . . . towards . . . the open hatch. Could feel the cool air breach the breathless stillness of the hold. 'She has a small forward hold, and a small aft hold with two hammocks. And two sweeps for calm weather. And a strong loading spar with a cleverly geared winch. If you come up on deck, I'll show you.'

'There's no need, Rebecca. I'll give you four hundred pounds for her.'

Four hundred pounds. But . . . She hesitated. And in that instant of confusion, he sidled round her and . . . and came to rest between her and the hatchway.

Oh, dear Jesus Christ! Save me! Her legs were buckling beneath her, her head spinning dizzily. But she must keep her senses . . .

'But . . . but why so . . . ?' she gulped as her throat closed.

Fred frowned quizzically, taking a pace towards her. 'I just told you. I want to make amends. I need to redeem myself. To make up for what I've done. Please, Rebecca, help me do this.'

His face, thrust forward in its agitation, was inches from hers. His heavy breath fanned her cheek. His eyes harsh. Demanding. She stumbled backwards. Into the deep sepulchre of the darkened hold.

'You do want to help me, don't you?' His head swung oddly and a violent shudder rippled through her body. Another step.

'Yes, of course I do. But . . . I believe she cost little more than that new.'

'Yes, I know,' he barked irritably, and she caught her breath. She mustn't anger him.

'Then, 'tis most generous of you.' That's right. Humour him.

'But do you think it's enough? I mean, enough to keep Adam going until he gets back on his feet? And I'll do as you asked. I'll go away. Leave his business alone. Sell back all the shares I've bought. Maybe even *give* them back to Adam as a gift. He'll never hear from me again, I promise. But . . .' She squealed more from fear than pain as he grasped her wrist. 'I need your help to do it.'

'My . . . help?' she gasped.

'Yes! Oh, my dear, sweet, kind Rebecca.' His voice had completely changed. Soft, passionate. Her lungs ceased to move, her senses paralyzed as, releasing his grip on her wrist, he removed her hat and tenderly smoothed back from her face the tendrils of hair that had been tugged loose by the wind and the rain. Every muscle was numbed, only her wide eyes following the movements of his hands. 'Oh, my dearest, dearest love. You've shown me the way to save myself, but I need you to keep me on the path. Oh, please, please say you'll help me!'

She stared at him. Transfixed. The man was . . . demented. The whites of his eyes glinted as he edged her nearer the lamp. A tiny whimper emitted from somewhere inside her as she cast a glance over her shoulder into the black shadows behind her. Further than ever from the hatch.

'You . . . don't need my help,' she croaked. Oh, God, another step backwards. 'You need to do it by yourself for it to work. And you *can* do it on your own. I know you can.'

'But that's where you're wrong.' His tone hardened again. Sardonic. 'I need you to support me. To show me some of that love you give so freely to Adam. And in doing so, you'd be helping him. Just once. It isn't much to ask, is it? And you'd be free of me for ever.'

His hands were on her shoulders, guiding her towards him as he bent his head beneath her chin and kissed her throat, sucking the delicate skin with his lips. She felt her stomach heave, the bile scorching up into her gullet. Somehow . . . from somewhere . . . her weakened limbs found the strength to push him away, his tearing grasp ripping her collar as she fled. Fled. But where to? She stopped dead as she faced the solid wall of the bulwark.

'There's no escape, Rebecca, my love.'

His whisper hissed in her ear. And slowly, slowly, she turned around. Against the inky obscurity of the hold, his face glowed luridly in the eerie, flickering lamplight, the amber shimmer licking about his jaw, his features illuminated grotesquely from below. Above his flared nostrils, his eyes gleamed savagely, a mixture of lust, frenzy and crazed insanity.

She felt her senses slipping away. Nowhere to run. Defenceless. Her eyes closed, wanting it all to be a hideous nightmare. She could feel herself begin to slide towards the floor, but her mind battled to remain conscious. She must not let him win. Not after what he had already done to them. The vision of Adam's severed wrist swam in front of her, spurring her to retaliate.

She was staring into Fred's maddened eyes. He was responsible. He had broken Adam. But he would not break her.

'How dare you speak to me of love after what you've done to Adam!' she snarled at him.

'But I do love you, Rebecca, don't you see? I've never known such love before! Surely you'll not deny me, just this once? And then I'll disappear from your lives for ever, I swear it.'

His voice rang with anguish, his hands lifted in begging supplication. Deranged. Petrifying.

But she had to fight back. 'And do you think Adam could ever rest if that were the only way you'd leave him be!'

'He need never know. It could be our little secret.'

'Of course he'd know! He'd sense it!'

'No, he wouldn't. He's a lost cause, Rebecca. He can't provide for you anymore. Just look at him. A useless, one-handed drunkard. What sort of a life can he give you now? Let me take care of you. Forget Adam. Come away with me! You can have everything you ever wanted. Think of your son. Wouldn't he like a little brother or sister? Adam can't even give you a child. But I can. We'll have—'

'*No!*' Her scream seemed to lift the planking above their heads, shattering the drumming of the teeming rain. ''Tis Adam I love, and as far as I'm concerned, you can rot in hell!'

Her cry vibrated with hatred, and Fred pulled back sharply, shaking his head with slow deliberation. 'You shouldn't have said that, Rebecca.'

Before she could move a muscle, he launched himself at her. She felt herself fall backwards under his weight, heard the dull thud as her head cracked against the great deck beam behind her. Her vision clouded with black stars, numbness spreading through her limbs. She knew she was slithering to the floor, but could do nothing to stop herself.

She couldn't see, couldn't hear, cradled in a black cocoon. But then she was aware of being moved, partly lifted from the bare planking, and something was done to her clothing before she was carelessly dropped back again. The jolt of it shook her senses and made her claw her way back to consciousness, and she forced her heavy eyelids to lift. Her head had rolled to one side, and it took several seconds for her wavering vision to focus on the crumpled heap of her discarded paletot and the small bag containing the papers that had evidently slipped from her fingers. Slowly, she turned her eyes on to the figure that loomed over her. The front of her dress gaped open, the material viciously ripped, and Fred was drooling over her bared flesh as his fingers feverishly wrenched apart the hooks of her stays. Her body was lifeless, leaden, her mind dulled with shock and the throbbing pain at the back of her skull. She couldn't move, was powerless against him.

Then one of his hands reached down and started to move up her leg beneath her skirt . . .

She didn't hear her own piercing shriek as she thrust her hands against his shoulders with strength born of desperation. Her slight frame was no match for his weight, but taken off guard, it was enough for him to lose his balance and roll sideways, and in his moment of surprise, she rammed her knee into his crotch. She didn't wait to witness her triumph, but careered along the hold, fighting against the breathless agony as her heart exploded against her ribs. The rain that poured through the open hatch in stair rods cascaded down on her uplifted face as she sprang on to the ladder, blinding her vision and trickling down her cheeks in rivulets. She clung on to the rungs for dear life, feeling for the precious footholds and screaming at her damnable skirt as she tripped on it. And then, oh, dear God, she could hear Fred's weighty footsteps as he lumbered along the hold behind her.

The squeal lodged in her throat as she redoubled her desperate efforts. Her foot slipped on the wet wood and for a few seconds she hung only from a handhold on the ladder, oblivious to the pain as her shins swung against the rungs. And Fred was there, beneath her, his arms around her legs as he tried to drag her down. No! Oh, Adam, help me! But Adam couldn't help her now. She had to save herself. And with a heaving jerk of her body, she kicked out frantically again and again until one foot finally came free and she felt the heel of her boot crash against something hard.

She was up on deck, gasping to breathe through the lashing rain that beat deafeningly on to the wooden planks. Her feet skidded as she ducked swiftly beneath the boom and hurtled across to the amidships gangway. She faltered momentarily above the rope ladder, pulse thundering at her temples. The water had risen several feet, the tide in full surge now and the two rowing boats swirling hazardously in the turbulent eddies. She would have to climb down to where she'd secured the straining painter and draw her father's boat in before she could make her escape.

She spun round to begin the backwards descent, and her nose brushed against Fred's chest. She gasped as she stared up into his livid face, blood spilling from his lips where she had kicked him in the mouth.

'You little bitch!' And as he spat at her, she could see the gap where his front teeth had been.

His hands were on her shoulders, shaking the life from her and trying to wrestle her to the floor. She forced herself upwards, her feet sliding on the rain-washed deck and, with a desperate effort, managed to reach up and rake her fingernails down his cheek. With a foul oath, one of his hands crushed her wrist and twisted it away, and in that moment, she contorted her body to drive her other elbow sideways into his stomach and crack her boot against his shin.

But the force of it sent her other foot skating across the treacherous surface, and as she tried to right herself, her ankle corkscrewed beneath her. The agony that screamed up her leg drained the last vestige of strength from her exhausted body, and as she lost her balance, she gazed over her shoulder in horror at the gaping chasm of the open gangway. And as she toppled backwards, she tugged violently on Fred's coat. For if she was going to drown, by God, she'd take him with her!

The black waters closed over her head, muffling the incessant clamour of the battering wind and rain and instead filling her ears with a strange, muted babble. She tried to hold her breath, totally disorientated as she was tossed and spun like a plaything. Instinctively, she kicked out, and just when her panicking lungs were about to explode, she some-how broke the surface and gasped a mouthful of air. In the split second before she was dragged back under, her eyes met the ghoulish vision of Fred floundering beside her. As she sank down again, she kicked wildly, and a moment later was spitting out water and spluttering on air as her hair, loos-ened from its pins, floated about her. In the instant before she went under again, she glimpsed Fred's head, and just as the gurgling filled her ears once more, she heard him shout that he was stuck in the mud. The water could not yet be so deep, five feet perhaps, but Fred's cry had alerted her to the hidden danger. A strange calm invaded her terrified mind, and she knew she must keep her feet clear of the soft, marshy riverbed. And then, through the murky water, something massive was looming ominously towards her. Oh, God, one of the boats, or maybe even the barge, was swinging round in the powerful current. She couldn't swim, but she had to get clear.

How she propelled herself, she had no idea, bubbles gushing up above her head, clear, bright spangles in the grey dimness, the slap of a ripple against her face as she was able to snatch a desperate lungful of air. Wheezing, suffo-cating, as she was suddenly swept into the undertow and rolled helplessly in the brutal battle between fast-flowing river and incoming tide. This time, there was no respite, no vital second to refill her lungs. Instead, the air dribbled from her nose and mouth in tiny diamonds, and she felt herself slowly drifting away into oblivion. And she didn't mind. She was so tired of the fight now. The rest came as a relief, welcome. And there was Tom, smiling at her, waiting for her, so serene. Her heart leaped with the joy of seeing him again, so calm, content. It had been so long. He held out his arms to her, took her in his embrace. Oh, Tom. Tom! I never thought . . . But, Tom, no! Don't try to take me with you! 'Tisn't time yet! I have . . . yes, someone else who needs me now! Our son, and . . . Oh, Tom, no! Please, let go of me! Tom, let me *go*!

'For God's sake stop struggling, or . . .' The voice coughed and croaked as they were both dragged under again. 'Or you'll drown us both!'

She couldn't see, blinded by her hair that whipped about her face. Water spurted out of her mouth and she snorted it from her nose, gulping in frantic, sucking breaths of air, choking as her chin was repeatedly submerged. But something was buoying her head above the dark, swirling water. As she managed to clear the hair away from her eyes, hope finally left her as she saw that she'd been washed out into the middle of the river at the mercy of the treacherous undercurrents.

'Get this round you and then hold on to it!'

She'd heard a voice just now, hadn't she, a voice she loved and trusted above all other? And there he was, holding out to her his handless arm with a rope wound about the crooked elbow, while he gripped on to her ferociously with his right hand. She struggled, spluttered, fought the raging water that dashed them about like flotsam, and by some miracle managed to wriggle her head and arms through the loop of rope.

'Ready?' Adam's face was a blur as one or the other of them bobbed beneath the surface. 'Hold on . . . to the rope with both hands in case . . . the knot doesn't hold,' he gasped at her. 'And . . . hold your breath. You'll . . . be pulled under . . .'

She nodded, and as Adam waved his arms above his head in a definite, unmistakable signal to those who were waiting anxiously on the bank, she felt the rope tighten and the next moment was being dragged through the water. The force of it sucked her downwards, the undercurrents tearing angrily at her body, reluctant to relinquish their prey. The rope squeezed about her chest, crushing her lungs, water gushing about her face, up her nose, in her ears, until she couldn't bear the agony of not breathing, wanted to cry out with panic . . . And just when she thought she could take no more, she had the sensation of being lifted upwards, hands carrying her awkwardly, stumbling up the rough bank. She feasted greedily on the air, wheezing, choking, as she was laid on the ground, her head on someone's lap, a crooning voice, fingers that stroked the wet strands of hair from her face.

Adam!

She sat up abruptly, sick with dread, but there he was, crawling up the bank on all fours, as people ran to his aid. For a few frightening moments, he was hidden from her view, but then he was walking towards her, coughing deeply, his shoulders hunched. Relief surged up inside her, and something else, so suddenly it took her completely by surprise, as she vomited up the foul water she had swallowed. A hand, a strong hand, was on her shoulder as she retched violently.

'She be fine, Captain,' a calm, soft voice assured him. 'You see to yerself.'

The vicious spasms slowly subsided, and Rebecca lay back, every fibre of her body exhausted. She was in pain, she knew, but she couldn't work out where it was coming from, and she didn't really care. The sheer bliss of being able to breathe again . . .

'Good God, man, you cas'n go back!'

'I can't just leave him to drown! The water'll be over his head in a minute!'

'Risking your own life to save Becky were one thing, but—'

'Let go of me!'

'For God's sake, help me hold him!'

Rebecca's vision cleared just as Adam broke free. *No!* She sprang to her feet, ignoring the pain that tore through her ankle, launching herself on to his arm.

'Adam, no!'

She stared up at him, willing him . . . unable to find more words. Still breathing heavily, his eyes met hers, wild in their anguish, then darted back towards the barge where Fred's arms were flailing above his half-submerged head.

'But I . . . I . . .' Adam stammered.

'Adam . . . please . . . don't,' the tiny whisper died in her throat.

But in that instant, Fred must have kicked himself free. They watched in horrified fascination as the jubilation on his face turned to terror as he was swept out into midstream and disappeared beneath the swirling waters, not to be seen again until his swollen, putrid body was found by a ferryman a month later.

A macabre hush settled over the small assembly that had gathered at the end of the Great Dock. The driving rain was soaking them to the skin, but no one took any notice. This was a port, where everyone understood the dangers of the river and the open sea. But to witness such a death, even of a virtual stranger, weighed on every heart.

Adam turned to Rebecca, his face ashen. And then his eyes travelled down to where her ripped clothing hung open, revealing the bruised, scratched flesh at the top of her breasts. His head swung from side to side, eyes wide and demented as his lips curled back horribly from his teeth, and his howl of outrage was carried away on the blustering wind.

'No! Oh, no!' The wail subsided to a wrenching sob. 'Not you, Rebecca!'

The horror on his face was almost palpable as he reached out his trembling hand to her, afraid . . . to repulse her . . . It took a few moments for her confused mind to comprehend what he had wrongly assumed, and she shook her head vigorously.

'No, Adam, he . . . he didn't!' she groaned in earnest. 'He tricked me into meeting him on the barge, and . . . and he tried to . . . But he didn't. He were like a madman, deranged. But I swear to you, he didn't.'

She gazed at him. In silence. No more words. His seaman's eyes narrowed keenly, his mouth twitching as if battling the conflicting emotions. His arms finally opened, and she went to step into his embrace. But the moment of release drained her spirit, and as she put her weight on her injured ankle, she couldn't suppress the screaming pain that raked up her leg and through her body to join the dull, suffocating ache in her head. The world turned yellow and then black — her exhausted brain happy to slip away from reality.

Someone caught her as she fell, arms of steel lifting her upwards and holding her, oh, so close . . . so safe . . .

'No, Annie. 'Tis each other they need just now. And Hetty's going with them, see. She'll send for us if need be.'

Voices she knew and loved. Soothed . . . rocked as she felt herself being borne quickly and purposefully through the port, could sense exactly where she was. The pace slower now, the chest she lay against rising and falling more heavily with the increased exertion of carrying its burden up the steep hill. She could hear the strong heartbeat accelerate. Then a pause while she was shifted awkwardly and she heard the gate-latch click. She lost the next few moments, but she was indoors now, could hear the crackling of an open range.

'Dear God in heaven!'

'It be all right, Mrs Blatchford. She nearly drowned, but the captain, he saved her. He were the only one brave enough to go in after her.'

'Probably the only one who can swim,' the wry voice added from somewhere just above her head.

'Oh, dear Lord, save us! Look at the state of you both! I've got the copper going in the wash house, but we could bring the hot water in here in buckets and fill the tub for you instead.'

Rebecca felt herself being deposited in a chair, whimpering as the softness that had cradled her disappeared. She could distinguish noises in the room, something being dragged across the floor, the clanking of metal buckets and kettles, the splash and swish of water. And a gentle, lulling voice, deep for a woman, talking to her. So calm.

'Ran like a deer, he did.' Someone was taking off her boots. 'Ort that were in his way, he clears in a bound. I doesn't think as I've seen anyone run so fast in all my born days.' Tentatively drawing her arms from the clinging bodice of her sodden dress. 'Were all for plunging straight in, he were, till your father makes him wait to take on a line. And swim! My, Becky, the strength of the man.'

The give as the remaining hooks of her stays were unfastened. Oh, God, someone had tried just now . . . The vile horror of the memory suddenly rallied her senses and she opened her eyes with a pitiful moan. But in doing so, her reviving mind became aware of the piercing cold that penetrated to her bones, and the violent, uncontrollable shaking that rattled her teeth in her head. The trembling was so intense that it set every nerve on edge, and she yearned to drift back into blissful nothingness.

But then Adam was kneeling in front of her, his anxious eyes desperately searching her face. 'Mrs Blatchford, Hetty, leave us now,' he ordered. Steady. In total command. 'And let's have the rest of those wet clothes off you,' he told her firmly.

She was happy to obey, like a small child doing as she was told, helping Adam to strip off every stitch of her clothing, oblivious to her nakedness, so glad was she to rid herself of the icy wetness against her skin. Her brain still not functioning, she waited to be told what to do next, still shivering with cold and shock, wordless, as Adam wrapped a thick, warm towel about her quivering body. A moment later, he passed her a mug of the piping hot chocolate Amy had quickly prepared for them and steadied her hand so that she could sip at the thick, sweet liquid without slopping it over the rim. The warmth of it seemed to seep into her blood, she relaxed for a few seconds, and then a few more, and slowly, slowly, the spasms eased, until Adam was able to leave her to fetch his own scalding drink, his deep chestnut eyes scarcely leaving her face.

She finished the chocolate, knowing his gaze was riveted on her, and he took the mug, setting it on the table beside his own half full one. The compassion, the softness in his expression was almost too painful for her, but then he reached out his right hand, tenderly cupping her chin, and the stump of his left wrist, forgotten, resting on her shoulder.

'Dear Christ, I thought I'd lost you,' he choked.

She blinked at him, swallowed. The man she loved with such a passion it was often unbearable. Who had once rescued her from her own suicidal grief, and who had just now risked his own life to pluck her from the clutches of a watery grave.

She turned her head, rubbing her cheek against the seamed folds of his stump. She heard him gasp in dismay, hold his breath, his body rigid. But slowly, deliberately, she brushed her lips over the sensitive skin, kissing away the anguish as she would a bump on little Toby's knee. And just as slowly, she saw the tension ease on his face.

'Oh, Adam,' she croaked in a whisper. And there they remained for several minutes, both shocked by the horrific ordeal they had just survived together, and the awesome realization that they were both still alive. Rebecca's eyes wandered over his beloved face, his strong jaw in need of a shave, his straight nose with the little tilt at the end which gave him that youthful air, the gash on the swelling on his cheekbone, already turning purple, the result of Fred's conniving plan. She would tell him, of course. She could tell him everything now. But this minute, it didn't seem so important. They were alive, and they were together. And as the warmth of the kitchen, the dry towel about her and the hot drink melted the ice in her veins, it dawned on her that the cold was affecting Adam, too. He was shivering as she had done, his hair plastered to his forehead, water from it dripping down his neck, and his drenched shirt moulded to his body like a second skin.

'Good God, Adam, you'll catch your death!'

He straightened up with a faint smile, and she watched him struggle with the sodden shirt as it clung obstinately to his back, refusing to submit to the efforts of his one hand. She instinctively stood up to help him, the towel slipping from her shoulders. And they faced each other as they hadn't done for over a year.

Rebecca drew in a little breath. She hadn't seen him undressed since the morning of Sarah's wedding when he was so thin she could have cried. But now, the muscles rippled beneath the skin of his bare torso and down over his slender waist. He looked, yes, fitter and stronger than ever. A frown flickered over her brow as she recalled, as if in a dream, something Fred had said about exercising, wasn't it? She was still confused, not sure what it all meant. The sight of the body she worshipped, the need she had inside her to obliterate from her soul the terror of what she'd just endured, was unbearable. Yearning plunged down to her taut stomach, her own nakedness deepening the desire in her loins, and making her forget the angry throbbing in her ankle. She lifted her hand, tracing her fingers over the strong contours of Adam's shoulders, and he stood stock-still, allowing her to kiss his chest, delicately drawing her tongue over his skin.

He gently pushed her away. Oh, surely he couldn't deny her what she needed so desperately, had longed and prayed for? What Fred had wanted to take so violently from her, she needed so urgently to give to Adam, to bring her peace. But he was looking at her, his head to one side, his breath quickened. His eyes travelled downwards, feasting . . .

'Oh, God, I'd forgotten how beautiful you are,' he murmured vehemently, and they were in each other's arms, her bare flesh pressed against his, clinging to each other, then hungrily, frenziedly, stroking, caressing, each totally lost.

'No, Rebecca, not now.'

Her heart sank like a lead weight and she wanted to cry out. He couldn't stop, not now.

'We're both filthy,' he told her sternly. 'God knows what's in that river water. And I don't know about you, but I'm freezing and that hot bathtub looks mighty inviting. But,' he turned to her, one eyebrow slightly raised, 'dear Amy very thoughtfully put a couple of hot-water bottles in your bed. And that to me seems a much more welcoming prospect than the flagstones on the kitchen floor.'

And Rebecca couldn't hide the smile that crept across her lips.

* * *

Amy Blatchford glanced up as the captain came back into the kitchen over an hour later, looking quite flushed and his eyes as bright as buttons. His shining hair was clean and dry now, brushed back neatly from his forehead, and although he hadn't shaved, he looked smart and gentlemanly in a fresh set of clothes. My, he was a handsome man, and wasn't her mistress the most lovely creature you could set your eyes on?

'The constable called, sir,' she informed him at once. 'I told him you was neither of you in a fit state to talk to him yet.'

'Thank you, Amy. I'll go and see him straight away. And Rebecca's family will want to know how she is. Doubtless everyone I meet will want to speak to me.' He sighed with a wry grimace. 'And I'll send for Dr Seaton, too. I'm sure Rebecca's ankle is only badly sprained, but I'd like him to take a look just the same.'

'And he can take a look at that cut of yours while he's at it,' Amy said fiercely. 'The mistress were right about that, you know.'

To her surprise, Adam smiled good-naturedly. 'All right, I submit. But while I'm out, can you take Rebecca up something light to eat, some broth from your hotpot, perhaps?'

'Of course, sir, 'twill be a pleasure. And you'll have some yourself when you get back?' she added as she accompanied him through to the front door.

'I shall look forward to it.'

She watched as her master strode confidently up the front path, and something made her follow him to the gate. The sky was still a dirty grey, but the rain had finally eased off, and Amy noticed that as Adam turned down towards the port, he didn't bury his left wrist in his pocket as he usually did, but let it swing easily at his side, his head held high and his shoulders strongly braced as they always used to be. She smiled knowingly to herself as she went back inside. He had been a long time in the mistress's room, and she had a shrewd idea what they had been up to. Well, 'twas queer how shock could take some folk, but 'twas about time those two were lying in the same bed together again.

CHAPTER TWENTY-EIGHT

'Go on, then,' Adam urged.

She smiled up at him, the warmth of his love surging through her veins, and then, leaving his side, she went to kneel by the simple gravestone and place the little posy of flowers on the grassy mound. *Thomas Mason, died 2 September 1867, aged 22.* Five years to the day. It seemed like a lifetime. The pain had gone now, and in its place, a contentment that she had once known such an innocent love, and had a beautiful son to remind her of it. She could visit his resting place without the fear of tears, remembering only the happiness they'd shared together. She could see him lying beneath the soil, not as a rotting corpse as she once had, but in the full glory of his living flesh, his eyes softly closed in his dark, gipsy face as if he were merely asleep.

'You still love him, don't you?' Adam's choked voice came to her as if from a dream. 'More than you love me.'

She felt a shudder ripple through her body as she slowly rose to her feet and turned to face Adam as he came silently up behind her. But then he shut his eyes, his mouth twisted as he seemed to shy away from his own words.

'Oh, God, Rebecca, I'm sorry,' he croaked. 'I shouldn't have said that. Forgive me, please.'

She stared up at him as he met her gaze, his rich, chestnut eyes desperately seeking her reassurance. Dear Adam. Saving her life, despite his disability, when no one else had the courage to risk their own safety, had made him start believing in himself again. But there were still times when he struggled against that damning sense of self-doubt, and Rebecca recognized that this was one of those moments.

'No, 'twas a fair question,' she said quietly, 'and one that must be answered once and for all. Of course I still love Tom,' and she glanced momentarily at the grave. 'I always shall, and there will always be a place for him in my heart. But 'tis entirely separate from what I feel for you. Separate, like my love for Toby is. And,' her eyebrows arched earnestly, ''tis locked away deep inside me, only I haven't thrown away the key. Just sometimes, when I come here, I like to take a little peep. To remember. And then I shut the door till next time.' She put up a hand and brushed his lean cheek, sunbrowned once more from his second voyage abroad as master of the *Emily* from which he had returned the previous day. ''Tis you I love now, Adam, and 'tis such a precious thing to me. God knows, we've come through so much together, and if that isn't love, I don't know what is. Perhaps . . . perhaps Tom and I shouldn't have been so steadfast.'

Adam had been staring at her unblinking, his brow furrowed, and now she could see the moisture collecting in his eyes. But then he swallowed hard as his arms crushed her to him, tucking her head beneath his chin. 'Dear God, I love you so much it hurts, you know,' he mumbled into her hair. A long silence. The hot sun beating down on their shoulders. The peaceful stillness of the churchyard. A bird taking flight from a bush. 'There was a time when I thought the only thing that mattered in my life was the open sea,' he finally went on, his voice thick. 'But I miss you so much when I'm away that . . . I really don't care for it so much anymore.'

She glanced up at him in surprise, and in that instant, felt his body stiffen against hers. He was looking across to the far corner of the churchyard, his jaw rigid, and she followed his gaze to the more recent, unmarked grave. She bit her lip, knowing Adam's feelings for his dead cousin were more complicated than her own.

''Twas not your fault you couldn't save him,' she prompted gently.

'Save him?' Adam snorted wryly. 'I'd only have strangled him if I had, once I'd found out everything he'd done. That is, if I could have managed it with one hand.'

'But you still feel unsettled because one shouldn't feel like that about family.'

He turned to her with a rueful sigh. 'Oh, Rebecca, you understand me better than I do myself sometimes. I just feel so . . . so bitter. And yet it was such a terrible thing to stand on that riverbank and watch him drown.'

'Yes, I know. But 'twould have been worse for him if he'd lived. If you could have seen him. I'm sure his mind were turned. I reckon as he'd have ended up in an asylum. So 'tis best for everyone he's gone.'

'He's certainly left me a rich man,' Adam agreed with an ironic lift of his eyebrows. 'That was his one mistake, forgetting I was his only relative and not making a will. So now I have back everything he stole from me in the first place, plus an estate in Herefordshire I've never even seen, and all Lady Hennessy's other business interests as well. I really haven't time to—'

'You have some excellent managers,' Rebecca broke in, 'so let them do what they're paid for. You're supposed to be on leave, remember?'

'Yes, of course.' He smiled at her, his handsome face relaxing. 'Shall we go back now, or do you want to stay a little longer?'

'No, no. 'Twas good of you to come with me. 'Tis a long trek up the hill in this heat.'

'I agree with you there. Would you mind if I took off my coat?'

'Not at all. I think 'tis one of the hottest days we've had all summer.'

She glanced up at him, the perfect gentleman that she'd first known, so smart in the dark trousers and new serge jacket, perfectly tailored to fit his broad shoulders and slim waist. The light sweat on his forehead had dampened the tips of his hair which had flopped forward in that roguish way it so often did. But although he removed his jacket and swung it by its loop over his right shoulder, he didn't attempt to loosen the starched collar of his shirt or the grey cravat she'd had to tie for him. She linked her hand through his other elbow as they began the long walk back to Morwellham, scarcely aware of the arm that ended abruptly at the cuff. But as they sauntered down the long, straight road, she caught his eyes glancing downwards several times. She said nothing, not sure of what was in his thoughts and not wanting to deepen his anguish by any intrusion. But when he spoke, it took her quite by surprise.

'You know, I think I might go and have a word with Dr Seaton while I'm home,' he began tentatively, and she noticed his teeth clamp down on his lower lip in that habit he had when he was unsure of himself. 'I thought I might discuss with him the possibility of . . . well . . . of having a false hand.'

Rebecca's heart missed a beat and she fought to stifle her delight. She'd never pressed him on the matter, but was hoping he'd come to such a decision on his own, since she felt sure it would provide him with the final confidence he needed. 'I'm sure he'd be very helpful,' she commented tactfully.

'I expect it'll make it quite sore at first,' he went on, his voice low, 'but I think I'm ready for that now. I thought . . .' He paused to study his left forearm as he turned it back and forth. 'Something that really looks like a hand. So that if I wear a glove on it, it won't be so obvious. In a natural position, with the fingers slightly crooked so that it'll be quite useful. Not as useful as a hook, but I couldn't stand that. It would be . . .'

''Twould bring back the nightmares,' she suggested compassionately. 'Oh, Adam, I think 'tis a wonderful idea.'

He smiled down at her, a full, broad smile that filled her with joy. 'I still don't think I could use a sextant on my own, though. I'd still need someone to tighten the screw for me at just the right moment, which isn't always easy when the ship's rolling. But . . . I think I'm learning to live with the idea.'

'But you'll never fully accept it.'

'No. I don't suppose I ever shall. But . . .' He turned to her, his eyes suddenly animated. 'Let me show you something, Rebecca.'

She tipped her head in puzzlement. They'd reached the tiny hamlet at the crossroads, but instead of turning down the steep, twisting lane to Morwellham, he beckoned her to follow him along the path that led into Morwell Woods. She fell into step beside him, perplexed, but not questioning the spring in his stride. The pastureland at last gave way to woodland, and once they'd crossed over the Devon Great Consols railway that cut through the dense trees like a die, he handed her his coat and then broke into a run, his long legs bounding through the undergrowth at breakneck speed. She laughed at his antics, but the merriment inside her faded as he hurtled away from her, faster and faster.

'Adam, *stop!*' she shrieked at his back as her heart vaulted in her chest. ''Tis Morwell Rocks ahead!'

Oh, dear God! You came on them so unexpectedly, he mightn't be able to stop! He'd disappeared from view . . . Suffocating as she hurried after him, imagining . . . If he didn't know what was there . . . Oh no, not after all they'd been through.

Relief surged through her as she found Adam standing well back from the edge of the narrow limestone cliff, his keen eyes gazing down on the meander of the river below.

'It's the most incredible view, isn't it?' he said as she came up beside him.

'Oh, Adam, you frightened me!'

'What? Oh, surely you didn't think . . . ?' He turned to her, raising one rueful eyebrow. 'I can't say the thought didn't cross my mind once or twice. But not seriously. I wouldn't have had the courage. Besides, there was always something holding me back.' He took one of her hands and brought it up to his lips. 'And that was you. I know I distanced myself from you. Hurt you. And that was so wrong of me when I knew all you wanted to do was to help me, and God knows if you hadn't been there . . . But . . . it was something I had to come to terms with, in my own way. In my own time.'

Rebecca felt her lip quiver, her throat choked. 'I . . . I do understand, Adam. But we must get on with our lives now.'

'Yes.' He nodded his head in agreement. 'It's what I want more than anything. But just let me show you this.'

He led her back into the woods, the dark shade welcoming as he suddenly let go her hand and seemed to spring up into an oak tree, his legs dangling in mid-air. She stepped forward in curiosity, craning her neck to peer up into the foliage. To her amazement, Adam was suspended by his upper arms which were straddled over the fork of a strong branch, and he began to pump his bodyweight up and down by the power of his arm and shoulder muscles. Rebecca's jaw hung open in astonishment as he finally dropped to the ground, grinning at her like a young boy.

'I used to do hundreds of those every day!' he announced proudly.

Rebecca was still gaping at him, her eyes wide. 'So that's how you used to get those stains on your shirts!' She laughed now, pointing at the fresh green marks on his clothes. But then her brow tightened into a frown. 'Doesn't it make your skin sore?' she winced.

'Rubbed it raw at first,' he admitted. 'Or if I'd been a little overenthusiastic. You nearly caught me out once. The evening you told me William Willis was giving up the *Sure*. You took hold of my arms when I wasn't expecting it. I told you I was having phantom pains, which was no lie because I was having them as well because I'd overdone it. But it wasn't the whole truth, I'm afraid.'

'Oh, Adam,' she smiled at his sheepish expression.

'And here . . . Yes, no one's taken it down.' She watched as he went to another branch and, holding his left arm straight above his head, used his right hand and his teeth to wind around it a rope that was suspended from the tree. And then as he stood still and slowly pulled the elbow down to his side, a massive stone in a net tied to the other end of the rope lifted from the leafy debris on the ground. He saw Rebecca blink her sapphire eyes, and he laughed aloud as he carefully lowered the stone again. 'Oh, I devised all sorts of things,' he chuckled, breathing heavily as he came towards her.

Her eyes lifted to his face. 'But . . . but why?'

'To prove to myself that I wasn't totally useless. That I still had some physical strength. That I could still achieve something, even if I only had one hand.'

'And did you? Prove it to yourself, I mean?'

'I think so. If I hadn't built my strength up again doing this, I wouldn't have had a hope in hell of getting to you in the river. As it was, a few more minutes and it would have been too late. We have Hetty to thank for that.'

'Yes, I know. 'Tis so good to live among people you can trust.'

'Oh, yes,' he agreed adamantly. 'The people of Morwellham have been wonderful. I shouldn't have cut myself off from them, I realize that now. Just like the crew of the *Emily*. They'd all kept signing on, just waiting for me to return. It was as if I'd never been away. The first thing Mr Thompson said — he's the mate, and a dry old seadog if ever there was one — was that if I expected them to run around after me, I'd better think again. And he said he thought the logline had died of boredom and he was looking forward to some proper sailing.'

'And did you? Sail her properly, I mean?'

'Of course! Kept her as close to the wind as you can with a square-rigger all the way!'

He tossed up his head with exhilaration, his eyes radiant, so happy and handsome again after the long months of looking so gaunt and haggard, that Rebecca's smile stretched broadly, her heart full. 'You see, you *do* still love the sea!' she teased.

His face fell almost at once. 'Yes, I suppose I do,' he shrugged. And then his expression intensified. 'But I miss you so much. In a few days, I'll have to go back to London to sort out various business matters, and then I'm sailing to Italy. I haven't imported Italian wines for some time, but some of them are very good and they tend to be cheaper. And by transporting them myself, I can ensure the price stays low, and so it should attract more clients. But once I've built the business up again, I intend to look for another captain. I'll still sail several times a year, but I won't be away quite so much and I can attend to my new affairs as well. But for now . . .' He grasped her hand and they began to make their way down through the woods to the port. 'Let's not spoil the time we do have together.'

Rebecca sighed softly with an inner contentment. At long last everything was settling down, and the happiness she had known with Adam once before had returned. There would always be that one, dreadful regret, for nothing could restore Adam's hand and they would both have to learn to live with the sight of the ugly stump, but she would not let it mar their future together.

'I know!' Adam stopped in his tracks and turned to her, his face alight. 'Why don't you come with me? The weather would still be good out there. We could drop anchor in a quiet bay, and I could teach you to swim so that next time you fall in the river, I won't need to come in after you!'

He was almost breathless with excitement, and Rebecca's eyes opened so wide her long brown lashes nearly touched her eyebrows. 'But I thought as women were supposed to bring bad luck to a ship?'

'Superstition!' Adam scoffed. 'You'd have to accept some of the crew's . . . er . . . coarser habits, shall we say, but they're decent, God-fearing men all of them. And if we'd . . . well . . . had the cabin door locked,' he murmured, his eyes dancing rakishly, 'there could be some ribald remarks, but

. . . Oh, I can just imagine it! There are some magnificent, deserted coves along the coasts. I could row you ashore in the boat . . . Well, I say I'd row, but you'd have to take one of the oars yourself, or we'd just end up going round in circles!'

Rebecca's heart jolted. He was actually joking about his disability, his mouth wide with amusement showing those straight, white teeth.

'We could find a secluded spot,' he went on, his voice suddenly low and rasping as he bent his head to kiss her neck. 'And then I could . . . very slowly . . . undress you . . . inch by inch . . .' He traced his finger down the front of her dress and tenderly cupped the soft swelling of her breast.

'Adam! Someone might see!' Half a shocked reprimand, half a response as her stomach tightened. She closed her eyes, savouring once more that intense emotion of the previous night and again that morning when she had answered so freely the demands of Adam's tall, strong body, his gentleness that led to those moments of enraptured ecstasy.

'I've always dreamed of making love in the open air,' he muttered as he kissed her again, her nose, her chin . . .

'Oh, Adam, it sounds wonderful,' she scarcely had the breath to reply. 'But I'm not sure 'twould be wise this time. You see . . . I'm with child.'

She felt his body judder and he pulled back. 'What! I mean . . . are you sure?' he stammered, his jaw quivering.

A smile played on her lips at his incredulous expression. 'Oh, yes. About ten weeks. I've missed twice and Dr Seaton confirmed it last week.'

'Oh,' Adam shook his head in disbelief. 'What, so soon?'

'Yes!' she grinned now at his shocked reaction.

'And . . . then what on earth do you think you're doing walking all this way? We could have hired a trap . . .'

''Tis fine I am!' she assured him. 'I feel a bit sick sometimes, 'tis all. And Dr Seaton says 'tis a good sign. It means the baby's making a good, strong home for himself. You . . . you are pleased?'

'Well . . . yes! I'm delighted!' He ran his right hand over his chin. 'I'm just . . . so surprised. So soon. But as long as you're all right. You're all that matters to me, you know.' He held her gaze, his eyes wandering over her face, and then he stretched out his hand and lay his palm on her slender stomach. 'Pleased to meet you,' he said so seriously.

'Oh, Adam!' she chuckled aloud. 'I don't think as baby can hear you!' He met her laughter, still somewhat nonplussed, as she took his hand away. 'Come along. I'd like to tell my parents now.'

'Yes. Yes, of course. I can't believe it, you know.'

They set off yet again, the leaves on the branches above their heads barely whispering in the still afternoon. Not far away, the engine house of the Devon Great Consols railway was hissing and puffing as some trucks, full not of gleaming ore now, but of meticulously packed kilderkins of arsenic, were being carefully lowered down the steep descent through the woods to the quay. All so familiar. Comforting.

'I could come with you to London, though.'

'Oh, yes! I'd like that!'

'I could come and live there if 'twould mean we could be together more.'

'What? Oh, Rebecca, no. I wouldn't do that to you.' He turned to her, tipping his head in the direction of the railway tracks. 'We don't know what the future holds for us. Morwellham relies on the arsenic trade now. But who knows? One day, in ten, twenty years' time, the deposits may become exhausted, just like the copper. And arsenic's so damned poisonous, they might find something less hazardous to do the same job. But . . . this is your home.' He stopped once more and brushed his fingers lovingly over her cheek. 'You're part of it. You belong here. When I'm away and I think of Morwellham, I see you. Here. Waiting for me. Warm. Constant. Something I can always rely on. I couldn't change that. I mean, I can't predict how our lives will turn out in years to come. There's the estate in Herefordshire to consider. And our children. But for now, I want you here, and nowhere else. In this very special place. The place where we met. And where we've found each other again.'

Rebecca's lips twitched as she fought back the moisture in her eyes. Oh, Adam. She loved him so much. And now, pray God, all their troubles were over.

She smiled to herself as she linked her hand through Adam's arm. Yes. No matter where the future took them, if they ever had to move away, Morwellham would remain her spiritual home. But it didn't seem so important anymore. Because there was another place she belonged now. At the side of the man who needed her just as much as she needed him.

And together they walked down towards the port.

THE END

ACKNOWLEDGEMENTS

With grateful thanks to Joffe Books for re-publishing this novel, and to my agent, Broo Doherty, who helped to arrange it. My thanks go also to everyone at the original Morwellham Quay Trust who helped me with information, especially the late Mrs Kathleen Pymm of the Friends of Morwellham, without whose assistance and encouragement this novel would never have come to fruition.

AUTHOR'S NOTE

Morwellham Quay stands twenty miles inland from Plymouth on the Devon bank of the River Tamar, nestling in one of the West Country's most picturesque valleys. By mid-Victorian times, the port had become a bustling and prosperous centre of activity, serving the local mines and quarries of Dartmoor and south Devonshire, as well as the wealthy market town of Tavistock to which it was connected by the famous canal. But times change, as depicted in this novel, and by the turn of the century, the port had been abandoned. Morwellham slept, most of the buildings fell into ruinous decay, the docks and river silted up with mud. But in 1969 the Morwellham and Tamar Valley Trust was founded to restore the port and open it to the public. The majority of the restoration is complete and Morwellham thrives again as a working, living museum, now in private ownership. Within the pages of this novel, you will discover Morwellham brought to life in a different dimension from the recreation you would experience during a visit. You will learn about such places as Copper Ore Cottage now known as Quay Cottage, the cooperage and the inn, as well as what remains of the huge malthouse which later housed the tenements. You will meet such real-life characters as Jane Martin, and Ann Richards, the landlady of the Ship Inn. You may be interested to know that an elderly Mr Brooming was indeed the owner at the time of what became the famous Goss Shipyard at Calstock where Morwellham's ketch, the *Garlandstone*, was originally built. If you have never visited the Quay, I hope this story will inspire you to do so and see everything for yourself. You can even take a journey into the George and Charlotte copper mine or a leisurely stroll up to the remains of the canal. For further details, please visit the website at

www.morwellham-quay.co.uk

ALSO BY TANIA CROSSE

DEVONSHIRE SAGAS
Book 1: THE HARBOUR MASTER'S DAUGHTER
Book 2: THE RIVER GIRL
Book 3: THE GUNPOWDER GIRL
Book 4: THE QUARRY GIRL
Book 5: THE RAILWAY GIRL
Book 6: THE WHEELWRIGHT GIRL
Book 7: THE AMBULANCE GIRL

Thank you for reading this book.

If you enjoyed it, please leave feedback on Amazon or Goodreads, and if there is anything we missed or you have a question about, then please get in touch. We appreciate you choosing our book.

Founded in 2014 in Shoreditch, London, we at Joffe Books pride ourselves on our history of innovative publishing. We were thrilled to be shortlisted for Independent Publisher of the Year at the British Book Awards.

www.joffebooks.com

We're very grateful to eagle-eyed readers who take the time to contact us. Please send any errors you find to corrections@joffebooks.com. We'll get them fixed ASAP.

Printed in Great Britain
by Amazon

65601076R00208